A WHITE DEATH

S. N. SHORT

WICKED INK

PUBLISHING

Copyright © 2025 by S.N. Short

Published by Wicked Ink Publishing Ltd.
www.wickedinkpublishing.com

Cover and book design © 2025 by Wicked Ink Publishing Ltd.
Editors: Raymond Griffiths & Adam Bamford

First Edition: January 2025
Printed in Canada

The National Library of Canada Cataloging -in-Publication Data is available upon request.

ISBN 978-1-998278-09-1 (paperback)
ISBN 978-1-998278-10-7 (ebook)

I would very much like to dedicate this book to my twin sister, Sylvia. Who continues to humour me by reading everything I thrust in front of her. Even being so kind as to lend an ear whenever I feel the need to read a passage or two aloud. I also want to thank her from the bottom of my heart for understanding when I can't come out to play (use your imagination) and for making a mighty fine gin martini.

A WHITE DEATH

**The whitest snow…
holds the darkest secrets.**

1

JOEL

Present Day

Joel couldn't believe his good luck, he only just graduated from university but instead of having to pound the pavement in search of practical experience, his favourite professor had enviably handpicked Joel to accompany him on the expedition of a lifetime, up to the 'Great White North.'

This year's trek comprised a small team of professionals whose sole purpose it was to study the effects of global warming on the northernmost part of the earth's polar bear population. With a Bachelor's degree in Zoology now under his belt, Joel only dreamt that a Master's in Biology would someday follow. Until this very moment, he had been gearing everything towards his goal of becoming a full fledged 'Polar Bear Scientist.' Some might say only pipe dreams, but the little boy who was born and raised in a remote community in Northern Alberta knew better.

He was blessed with a wise and caring *Kokum*, Cree

grandmother, who from a very early age instilled in him a sense of responsibility to protect the environment and its inhabitants. Unfortunately, though the corrupt powers currently governing his beautiful country didn't feel the same, but Joel hoped he might be the one to make at least a minor difference. And despite his degree being nothing more than a piece of paper, it had importance, bestowing his opinions with merit and respect finally.

Greeted by Jack Frost nipping at his nose the moment the heavy doors of the institute closed loudly behind him, Joel couldn't help but have a smile plastered on his face and a spring in his step as he exited the always impressive century old brick buildings and grounds of the university.

He was bursting at the seams with anticipation of sharing the good news with his family, especially the mother of his child. Without a doubt, Geraldine would be just as excited as he was, after all they had given up for him to complete his degree. Case in point, Joel would be forever indebted for the altruistic kindness that Geri's auntie showed by letting her niece and their son live under her roof throughout the duration of his schooling.

However, starting today, his future belonged solely to him…he finally could fulfill his promises and begin supporting his family. Joel raced across the campus in a hurry on his way to the nearest LRT station, hoping to make it to Geri's auntie's home, within the inner-city before she left for her part-time job that evening. Public transit was crowded and slow as always, but taking a cab or Uber was impossible on a limited income.

LATER, AS THE TRANSIT CAR'S DOORS OPENED AT A SLOW pace, Joel wasted no time in getting off and sprinting down the ice-covered streets, on the last leg of his journey across the large city. His only focus was envisioning Geri's expression when he eventually found a moment to reveal the specifics of his good luck. Although there was still one significant factor weighing heavy on his mind, and try as he might, he couldn't find a way to sugarcoat it.

Right as Joel was rounding the corner to the avenue, he swiftly slowed his pace and tried to catch his breath as he joyfully caught sight of his pint-sized ladylove heading up the sidewalk in his direction. It was impossible for him to not grin as he observed her winter attire. Geri was anything but hard to miss in her rather quirky loud ensemble, not to mention her telltale bleached blond ponytail poking out from under her toque.

Maybe because of his exuberance or her very exhalation in such frigid temperatures had caused a thick plume of condensation to form. Joel completely missed the perturbed look on Geri's usually pretty face as he swept her up into a bear hug while attempting to playfully plant a kiss on her full lips. Her almost instantaneous and incomprehensible response to his embrace utterly blindsided him as she fought to be unhanded and then angrily spit out, "You're fucking late again!"

What could have caused such fury? Everything appeared seemingly copacetic when he left for school that morning. Or was her anger displaced? Now, holding her at arm's length, it quickly became apparent that something was terribly wrong between them.

"Geri, please tell me what's happened?" he implored. "Whatever it is, we can fix it!"

She wouldn't even dignify his question with an answer, her only response being a snipe. "Let go of me. I'm gonna be late for work…something you know absolutely nothing about!"

Joel attempted to avoid being goaded into an argument, evidently something caused her to rehash a much earlier bone of contention. "I'm truly sorry for whatever I did to upset you, but I have wonderful news. My prof has offered me a job."

Oddly enough, this did little to satisfy his easily angered girlfriend. Maybe she didn't understand the full ramifications. "Can we at least talk about this tomorrow?" he pleaded.

When she reverted her gaze, her demeanour resembled a petulant child as she visibly stiffened her backbone, giving the distinct impression she couldn't bear to be touched by him one second longer.

"Your son is with my aunt right now and she would appreciate it if you took him home to your father's place," she coldly asserted.

Joel was baffled, seeing as it was only a few hours since they parted…he chose not to wake her at such an early hour, so he left quietly in the dark.

"Didn't you hear me? I've been offered a job. We can finally get a place of our own…"

Despondent, his voice audibly cracked, and he found himself unable to continue with this no-win situation. However, his mind was still going a mile a minute. Why was she not jumping for joy, but trying to pick a fight? Did someone say or do something in the meantime to make her ignore him, and why was Dinnie suddenly a bother? In the end, Joel took a much needed step back, regain his composure, and prevent their discourse from escalating into irreversible words.

At first he assumed by her silence that Geri was of the same mindset, but soon realized his error as she unashamedly saw fit to continue testing the turbulent waters. Using all her petite 5'1" frame, she simply shoved him aside, even though he towered over her…possibly to reaffirm his vulnerabilities. Because she was aware he would never raise a hand to her. Without a backward glance, Geri briskly marched to the nearest bus stop.

Regrettably, Joel continued to stare down the street after her, somewhat dumbstruck right until the moment that a city bus pulled up alongside the mother of his child. Before boarding it, Geri turned back towards Joel, seemingly for one last look and then smiled in a self-satisfied way prior to yelling belligerently in his general direction.

"Go get your son. My aunt is sick of looking after him," and then, like a cold Arctic breeze, she was gone.

Joel didn't know what to do. Should he run after her, but what good would it do to instigate a screaming match on public transit, in front of complete strangers? He just wanted to cry, because today should have been the happiest day of his life. After all, he worked hard to achieve his degree, and he did it all on his own. He truly believed he and Geri resolved everything.

Yes, little Dinnie was a big surprise, but they both agreed he should finish his university education to provide a better standard of living for his young family. Joel even moved in with his elderly father to not put a burden on Geri's auntie and, sure, he slept over from time to time, but he never ate her food or took up space on her couch. Left to contemplate his choices, Joel couldn't ignore the fading light in the sky due to the barren tree branches overhead, as he found himself figuratively kicked to the curb. Thereupon realizing he'd better get a move on since frostbite was a genuine possibility and he didn't need to add that to his list of 'shitty things that happened today'.

❄

WHILE SWIFTLY CLIMBING THE OLD WOODEN STAIRS TO Geri's auntie's strawberry box house, something he had done many times before, Joel hesitated before knocking on the front door. Was she mad at him too or did Geri embellish her story? It didn't take him long to realize the folly of his actions as he stood there in the cold, stomping his feet to stay warm. Banishing all negative thoughts, he finally made his presence known by ringing the doorbell. Within a split second, Joel heard the distinct sound of someone grappling with a sticky door lock, and shortly after, a growing beam of light revealed him on the stoop.

As the door to the little tract home opened further, the look greeting him was one of warmth and compassion as opposed to Auntie Mona's alleged indignation. Not that he would even comprehend what it was supposed to resemble, for Joel never saw the woman without a warm smile on her face and genuine merriment in her heavy hooded eyes.

Earlier trepidations were all but forgotten as Dinnie's sweet freckled face and unruly mop of dark brown hair now struggled to peer around the middle-aged woman's long skirt. The instant the little boy realized his father was the unannounced visitor, his smile quickly spread from ear to ear before throwing himself with abandon into Joel's arms.

The pure spontaneity of his child's actions tugged at Joel's heart strings, causing him to suddenly break into tears, frightening the poor little 5-year-old. Auntie was intuitive enough to read more into Joel's outburst, as she stepped in and took control of the situation. Whatever was going on between her niece and the girl's boyfriend, she was aware her great-nephew was much too young to be privy to the drama of his mother's life.

"Dinnie, honey…please step out of the way and give your father a chance to get inside where it's warm. Quickly now. If I've told you once, I've told you a thousand times, we aren't paying to heat the entire blessed neighbourhood." She laughed, albeit dryly, mostly for the benefit of the child, before attempting to make eye contact with Joel. However, when that plan didn't work out as intended and the boy refused to be separated from his father's side, Auntie Mona felt compelled to adopt a more direct approach.

"Dinnie, would you be a good boy and run along? I have something rather important I would like to discuss with your father." Then, as an afterthought, she added, "Besides, don't you have some new superhero colouring books you've been itching to get started on?"

Her words only made the child more anxious. Being as he knew from experience whenever adults wanted you out of the room, it meant somebody was in deep doo-doo, but who? Had he himself unknowingly incurred their ire? Or was his mother at fault because she had been short with him lately and he didn't understand why? Dinnie had been truly attempting to be a good boy, not talking back to his elders, even if he didn't agree with them, and helping his auntie around the house as much as he could. Although whenever he asked his mother where she had been or why she was always late, she would jump down his throat.

Sensing the boy's hesitation about leaving the room, Auntie Mona was quick to interject. "Dinnie, there is nothing to be concerned about. No one is in trouble. As soon as I've finished talking with your father, he will be free to give you his full and undivided attention."

Once she had the boy settled in his makeshift bedroom and preoccupied, at least for the time being, she rejoined Joel in the living room to discuss his fragile emotional state.

At first, she couldn't get a single word out of the young man as he sat there on the couch, staring at his hands and then, finally, he opened up. "I'm here to pick up Dinnie and take him back to my father's…" But before he could even finish, Geri's auntie became distraught and her voice high-pitched.

"Why on earth would you do such a thing? Isn't he happy here? I know it's not the Ritz, but he has a room of his own."

Right away, Joel could tell by the change in the woman's demeanour she misconstrued his words and her feelings were indeed hurt. He couldn't help but inwardly chide himself for upsetting such a gentle soul and then, somewhat apprehensively, he divulged his earlier conversation with Geri.

"I'm so sorry Auntie, I didn't mean to imply that Dinnie was not happy here…he loves you…I love you. I just ran into Geri on her way to work and she was mad as a hornet. I have been taking advantage of your kindheartedness, and for that, I apologize. She did not mince her words or her feelings. I honestly did not know she was so unhappy with me and our living situation."

"Work…what are you talking about? The girl's been on benefits for months and if she landed a job, then this is the first I'm hearing of it. And as far as that sweet little boy is concerned, he's my family too and I love him. Just leave Dinnie with me for the present. There's no need to uproot the child. We'll sort this out in due time."

Joel was so confused, his head hurt, but foremost, he needed to address his son's living arrangements before heading off to pursue his new career. Unfortunately, he kept the kicker a secret and would be absent for months at a time. Truthfully, when he got up this morning, his thoughts were preoccupied with final exams, submission of term papers and just looking for a job. Geri's subsequent change of heart indeed came as a revelation, but regardless, Dinnie's welfare was paramount. He still had a small window of opportunity to get all his affairs in order before leaving for an 'undisclosed location', somewhere north of Baffin Bay.

JOEL WAS ASSIGNED TO THE EXPEDITION TEAM ALREADY IN place for months and, as luck would have it, several individuals from their group quit. Regrettably, he missed out on the end of polar bear mating season, along with delayed implantation and the subsequent digging of dens by the pregnant mother bears.

So during these coldest months, Joel's directive would be to assist the remaining scientists as they tracked the solitary males and then document births once the mothers and cubs emerged. This should give him plenty of time to become acclimated, as well as familiarize himself with the local Inuit population. Joel was also keen to take part in an ongoing research project involving the mating behaviour of polar bears, specifically the unique placement of scent producing glands on the footpads of the females. Although difficult to study, popular theory dictated that in the spring, females wishing to breed would leave chemical trails on the ice as a signal for the males to follow, but this had yet to be proven beyond any doubt.

Opportunities truly abound for Joel in this new environment. For example, the Inuit, who were descendants of the Thule culture, would be collaboratively working with his team. He was honoured and excited to meet them and absorb whatever wisdom they imparted during his tenure. After all, who knew more about the region's ecosystems than the brave peoples inhabiting it for centuries? Their wealth of knowledge would undoubtedly be far greater than any modern satellite's transmitted, analyzed, and interpreted data.

Joel would find out he was not as prepared as he first thought, since his schooling taught him a rather homogenized version of the Inuit culture. Considering their stories tended to be relayed through the generations by spoken word alone. Fact or fiction, the Indigenous Peoples of the Arctic always had a rather semi-nomadic way of life, benefiting from geographical isolation, but because of climate change and decreased whaling, their independence had in time become endangered.

Catalyzing the banding and migration of regional groupings north, some moving between the islands and bays seasonally to hunt game and keep their independence. While others, sadly, became subject to the widening jurisdiction of the federal government, who sought to exploit their homeland's riches. Zoology had taught Joel about the animal kingdom, but words on a page were merely that. He would need to heed the members of his team, his elders and not neglect the aspects of oneself; mind, body, and spirit. Not to mention, he would need to be ever conscious of his new surroundings, specifically regarding the extreme weather he would now experience and the fact exposed skin could literally freeze in only a matter of minutes.

Suddenly and for no apparent reason, a foreboding 1700s quote came to mind…

"Our Mother feedeth thus our little life, that we may in turn feed her with our death."

Later that night as Joel lay awake in bed, all he thought about was Geri and their son…he desperately needed to talk to her and find out what exactly had precipitated her earlier outburst. Current circumstances aside, they frequently talked at length about his future dream job after completing university, albeit no one could have ever foreseen it coming to fruition so quickly…in fact, Joel was still somewhat in shock.

He always presumed that only after years of applying himself at a zoo or animal shelter, one day he might observe the objects of his fascination in their natural habitat. Everything that he had done since finding out that Geri was carrying their baby was for his family's future and not a 'flight of fancy' as his mother used to say. Although Joel knew whatever happened between them as a couple, Dinnie would be looked after in his absence by people who genuinely cared for his well-being.

Try as he might to remain positive and focus on the fact that tomorrow was a new day, his thoughts kept returning to his son and on how he was going to maintain their connection over the miles that would soon separate them. He truly hoped a video call would suffice and that once he settled into his new job and proved his worth, he could arrange for Dinnie to be flown up north for a brief visit, instead of him coming home. It would be wonderful to get the chance to see everything through his child's eyes. After all, he was getting older…really, how much trouble could he possibly be?

2

JOEL

THE FOLLOWING MORNING, JOEL JOINED HIS ELDERLY father for an early cup of coffee and a much needed heart-to-heart. However, whilst staring across the old arborite table top in their tiny little kitchen, Joel couldn't help but notice just how much his father aged over the last couple of years. Sure, he was no longer a spring chicken, but he always was a very imposing figure and a pillar of strength within their family.

At first, his father seemed not at all surprised by Geri's attitude, it was common knowledge just what he thought of her as trashy. But when Joel explained he never found the time to inform her about his upcoming living arrangements, the older gentleman was there for him to commiserate.

"Dad, I will not ask you what you would do in my shoes since you've never liked Geraldine, but do you think I'm being selfish?"

His father seemed to weigh his answer before speaking. "It's no secret I thought she trapped you by getting pregnant, but that's neither here nor there. You epitomized the pride of our community, kindhearted, smart, athletic and easy on the eye. You took after your old man all right," he laughed uproariously, but, unfortunately, it spun into a loud wet cough.

Alarmed, Joel jumped up from the table and began looking frantically around the room for a box of Kleenex. To which his father responded by nonchalantly removing his faithful old hankie from his pants pocket and wiping the blood-tinged spittle off of his lower lip.

"That scholarship you won most certainly set you up for bigger and better things. Truthfully, I would have been very disappointed if you stayed put and wasted the chance you had been given. Your mother would be so proud… God rest her soul. And about your mother, when are you going to grow your hair back, son…the time for mourning is long over?"

In the end, no one could argue the years of living apart had most certainly been hard on Geraldine because she had been the primary caregiver for their child, but it wasn't like they had never discussed a future together. With his heart in his mouth, Joel concluded he needed to have that face-to-face with Geri as soon as possible. He had a deep understanding that an opportunity of this magnitude would not come around again, despite not wanting to lose his family or his new job.

As the morning hours ticked by, Joel kept glancing at his phone and willing for it to ring, but by lunchtime he had still not heard a word from her, not even a text. She should be up by now, since most night shifts end around 4 or 5 in the morning. That's if she was telling the truth. Finally he reached a point where waiting was no longer possible, so throwing caution to the wind, Joel headed over to Auntie Mona's house, hoping to catch Geri in a better frame of mind to talk.

AS HE AGAIN STOOD ON THE STOOP OF HER AUNTIE'S HOME gathering the nerve to ring her doorbell, all Joel could think about was getting on with his life, which included having a wonderfully fulfilling career and his family all under the same roof. When halfway through his not so pleasant reverie, the front door swung open and there was Geri, looking a tad worse for wear and definitely not her usual coiffed self. Reaching out in a well-meaning attempt to hug her, he couldn't help but notice the pungent smell of alcohol on her as he closed the distance between the two of them. Joel didn't want to start their conversation off with a fight. For all he knew, she might have gone out with a girlfriend after work for a drink to discuss her woes, but sadly, the cold shoulder she presented him with was more than clear.

"Can we talk? I'm so sorry about yesterday, but I have so much to tell you. Everything is happening so fast and I need your input?" Again, he tried to take a step forward, but this time only to gain entrance to the home, and Geri unexpectedly blocked him with her outstretched arm.

Joel would never forget how she nervously looked around, as if she was worried someone might overhear their conversation. With venom in her eyes, she just spit it all out, "We're fucking through! I've found someone else, and he's going to take care of me and Dinnie. I'm moving, so chase your stupid little dreams!"

Joel couldn't believe what he just heard. Where was this coming from? What if anything had changed in the last 36 hours? He was gobsmacked by her total disregard for his feelings. Was their relationship a charade, and she had been leading him on for all these years while waiting for something better to come along? Had she ever even loved him? When had she started sleeping around? Had there been signs, red flags and he had been too stupid to see them or was he so caught up in his "career" and she had only been window dressing for his goal…who was really to blame for this deception?

"How long have you felt this way and why on earth didn't you tell me?" Joel struggled to maintain his equanimity. He was not a violent man, but he could not keep his voice from getting louder and louder.

The cacophony caused Dinnie to become alerted to his father's presence, he ran to the front door to greet him, only to be confronted by his parent's yelling match. The little boy was unaware of how to handle the situation since this was unfamiliar territory for him, as he had never witnessed such anger and hatred directed at another person in his short life. Dinnie's instant response was to break out into great hiccupping sobs. At first he didn't seem to know which parent to turn to for solace, then decided on his mother's embrace.

"Look what you've done! Dinnie will be much better off in a normal home. Chris will make a great father!" and, as those words left her mouth, Joel felt completely gutted.

Geri had been making plans for her future for some time now…how could she share two men's beds and look at herself in the mirror…was Dinnie even his? He so wanted to voice his assumptions right there and then, but not in front of Dinnie. He loved his son and only wanted what was best for him. Turning to go, he looked back at Geri and growled two words before leaving, "Joint custody!"

As the door slammed shut behind him, Joel was positive that he heard Geri's shrill voice saying something about, "Over my dead body!" and she was going to make him pay. Again, left out in the cold to gather his thoughts, the only thing that he could think about was contacting legal aid and, thankfully, he had friends at school that might help.

Upon arrival at the hallowed halls of the university, Joel was quick to make his way to the Faculty of Law and, in no time flat, he was spilling his guts to a childhood friend who was studying at the same school.

He knew Anita since grade one and when they both left the small town they grew up in to further their educations, as luck would have it, they promised to always stay in touch. Joel had also been fortunate that his father had likewise moved to the same city, but sadly, it was because of his ever-deteriorating health. Anita had been a good family friend and spent many a joyous evening around Joel's father's table. So much so his father expressed admiration for the girl and, in his own humble opinion, she would make a mighty fine wife for some lucky man. It didn't hurt either that Anita was downright voluptuous… not scrawny, like Geraldine. However, Joel did not have the heart to tell him that Anita was also two-spirited and definitely not interested in him that way.

Thankfully, after hearing all the sordid details pertaining to Joel's relationship woes, Anita could put his mind at ease. "You have rights, you know? That *scunagoose*, can't just take your kid away!"

She reassured Joel that Geri slipped up big time by mentioning she was going to make him pay. After all, she wouldn't have said that if Dinnie was not his biological son. Unfortunately, time was not on his side. Joel needed to organize his affairs pronto and although Anita's specialty wasn't Family Law, she thankfully knew someone that could help.

With only a couple of weeks before Joel's looming departure date, Anita's friend turned out to be a godsend. Besides treating him like family, she assured Joel a custody agreement could be drafted and, at the very least, filed with the courts. Thus making it damn near impossible for his ex to move away with the child while he was working up north. So with those worries put to rest, Joel could now focus his energies on getting ready for his very first expedition and luckily for him, almost all of his gear would be provided by the university and backing company.

Large conglomerates loved to put their logo on anything that looked planet friendly and fortunately, the one that was funding his research had yet to be discovered doing anything underhanded by the mass media. Plus, it didn't hurt that they were prepared to pay their scientists half upfront before even leaving shore since they would be away for such long periods of time and bills don't pay themselves.

Joel was beyond ecstatic to give his father some money in order to lessen his burden, as well as give Anita's friend a retainer to look after his interests while he was away. As the big day drew nearer, Geri did not contact Joel or even make good on any of her earlier threats. And when he called her auntie to arrange a last visit with Dinnie before leaving the province, Mona was cordial and reiterated her displeasure with her niece's earlier actions.

"I don't know what's wrong with that girl. Frankly, nothing has ever been good enough for her. Mark my words, she'll be sorry if she lets you get away." It was as if she was oblivious to the fact Geri had been making plans to marry someone other than himself.

ON THAT LAST DAY AS JOEL ARRIVED AT GERALDINE'S aunts home, a feeling of melancholy, an almost longing for the happiness he had mistakenly thought to have shared with Geraldine, suddenly overcame him. However, he soon regained his senses and felt relieved she had not been there to cause a scene, allowing him to spend the whole day together with his son.

They ended up going to the big mall to play games, eat junk food and ride rides…not necessarily in that order. Just hearing his son's laughter and ceaseless nonsensical chatter meant so much to Joel, he couldn't help but stare at the child in wonder because he could plainly see himself. With great sadness, he had to say "goodbye" to Dinnie later that evening, promising him he would stay in touch.

"You be a good boy and look after your mother and auntie, and I'll be back when the snow is gone."

Then with tears in his eyes, he kissed the little boy goodbye and presented Mona with a new cell phone and cash laden envelope. And as he slowly walked down her front steps on his way to the darkened street, Joel made the mistake of turning around one last time to wave, there was his little man being restrained by his auntie as he reached for his father with his free arm.

"Please don't leave me too, Daddy…" he sobbed.

3

UKI

November 1919

Nunavut, formerly known as Rupert's Land and the North-Western Territory. Night was falling quickly as Uki huddled between the snow-covered rocks and large windrows of debris on the shoreline, hoping for some reprieve from the ever blowing north winds. It was hours since her so-called brethren left her to freeze to death on an ice floe, and thankfully, they left in such a hurry they had not bothered to collect her discarded clothes after violating her. Not to mention the fact her hands were now almost useless and ached incessantly from the extreme cold. But at least the bleeding stopped from what little remained of the fingers they hurriedly amputated, in some vengeful reenactment of a childhood tale. In this her time of solitude, she reflected on her life to comprehend where it had all gone wrong, all the while pacing back and forth trying to keep warm.

To begin with, Uki experienced a very hard start in life. Story has it she was abandoned on the edge of a small formation of land-fast ice as an infant, left to the mercy of the elements with only a soiled animal hide wrapped around her tiny body.

Call it fate or intervening spirits, when a group of Inuit hunters chanced upon the distraught cries of a forsaken child. Given the practice of adoption had always been an intricate part of their culture, these good men could not ignore the gift of life they had been entrusted with, no matter the parentage.

Being as their charge was a newborn, a connection or bond with its new parents would undoubtedly be easier to secure. By the same token, the child would also hopefully take on the blood memories, which the Inuit have always known to be true, of their adopted family. The selfless tradition aimed to strengthen kinship alliances, but more importantly, it contributed to ensuring the survival of the community.

Under certain circumstances, such as times of famine, infanticide would not have been an unusual occurrence, especially where female children were concerned. However, people thought her discovery was attributable to a cruel act of vengeance upon an unfaithful wife for copulating with a *Qallunaaq*, a white person.

Overall, the child's characteristics resembled those of an Inuk, but her skin and eye colour were tragically too pale to evade scrutiny. Although in due course and with daily exposure to the sun's rays reflecting off an almost never-ending sea of white, she grew to look much like her adopted kin. They named her "*Uki*" for the survivor she was and, in no time at all, she deftly embraced the culture of her new people.

Granted her journey was not without its trials and tribulations, especially for learning the traditional life skills of an Inuk woman. Uki was obstinate, to say the least, and tomboyish in her ways, qualities that gave rise, over time, to the rather standoffish coexistence she shared with the other women in their community.

Whereas, the young men and boys found her to be quite intriguing from the get-go but regrettably, her insatiable hunger for acquiring and mastering new skills proved to be a large contributing factor in alienating her from them as well. Her adopted brothers could not bear losing to or being seen as inferior to 'a female', especially a pretty one.

Thankfully, though, in due course, the community's welfare won out over hurt feelings as Uki developed into an indisputably skilled hunter and was later bestowed the honour of teaching the younger generations her skill-set. The elders revered her status, as they trusted only her to pay proper respect to all of her kills and thus ensure the spirit of the animal would return in another, one that would sacrifice its life again.

The Inuit elders believed this to be a significant matter because they feared that if they didn't perform the ritual correctly, the animal's spirit could come back as a demon and terrorize their people. Uki also excelled in training the community's dogs to sniff out seal air holes in the ice, and many nights, she slept with them as opposed to spending time in the company of eligible kinsmen. This too added to the frequent gossip spewing around the communal campfires, while the other women were preparing meals of the freshly killed meat.

The group flourished in the Arctic on a steady diet of whales, walrus, caribou, seal, polar bears, muskoxen, birds and fish. Uki was happy and slept well knowing that when she passed into the realm of the ancestral shades, it would most likely be with spear in hand.

It wasn't until she was into her early twenties that she first experienced heartbreak following the loss of a true friend, someone much like herself, for Alornerk too danced to the beat of his own drum. He was a respected elder in their community but had never taken a wife and from the moment that he laid eyes on the helpless, abandoned child all those years ago, he had become her mentor, the grandfather she never had.

ON THAT ILL-FATED DAY THEY HAD BEEN OUT WITH A LARGE hunting party and even though their bounty was rich, several of the younger men were just not satisfied and wanted to stay out longer hoping to find a certain polar bear that was rumoured to be of exceptional size and had a taste for sled dogs. Uki heard those same rumours too, but she knew them for what they were and trophy hunting was something that went against her nature.

As the day wore on and darkness was fast approaching, the hunting party set up camp for the night to avoid getting caught out on an ice floe with the sleds after dusk. The younger men had the audacity to consider Uki as their camp cook because she was the only female in the group. However, thankfully, her dear friend Alornerk stepped up and demanded all the hunters contribute.

Later that night, with bellies full of fresh seal meat, an unexpected winter storm descended upon them and the hunting party was forced to secure everything and turn in early. No one took the time to inspect the camp before lights out, in order to make sure nothing had been left out that would attract the unwanted attention of the local wildlife.

As the outside temperature plummeted, the hunters were thankful for the protection of their hide tents and the fact that their cramped sleeping quarters resulted in a rather soporific effect. Tragically, though, the sound of barking dogs and fierce growling interrupted their peaceful slumber, even over the white noise of the never-ending north winds. Uki recognized the sound of a polar bear, but still habitually looked to her mentor, Alornerk, for confirmation.

"You know what to do," was all the old hunter replied and then nodded his head as if handing the reins over to her.

Uki hesitated slightly, before clearing her throat, "Brothers, arm yourselves with bow and spear. Do not shoot until you see your target."

The next sound she heard was the mournful cries of several of her sled dogs in distress. With no thought as to her fellow hunter's awaiting her further instructions, she threw caution to the wind and was out of the tent flap ahead of the rest of her party.

Luckily, the polar night was not upon them just yet as it varied by latitudes, a phenomenon where the sun is below the horizon all day and can last anywhere from 24 hours to 179 days at the poles. But because of the severity of the storm, visibility had become almost nonexistent.

As Uki ran blindly toward the baying dogs, she was tackled from behind. Thankfully, someone thought with his head and not his heart. After all, Alornerk was a seasoned hunter and knew better than to get between a polar bear and its quarry. Almost immediately, their fellow hunters rejoined them in a huddle, but when Uki tried once again to take the lead, her orders fell on deaf ears.

"Forgive me…I wasn't thinking straight. We need to plan our approach, but keep in mind the safety of our sled dogs because, from the sounds of it, they have already whipped that animal up into a frenzy. Whoever is first to get within shooting range, try to stand fast, or at least until someone else can back you up…no one wants to be charged by an angry bear."

Uki wasn't sure if it was the loud howling of the wind or the single-mindedness of the younger hunters because they only seemed interested in being the first to take down the large beast and not at all concerned with the welfare of the group's dogs.

"We're wasting time, woman! Some of those dogs are already dead."

"You heard him. Get a move on!"

"I'm not missing out on a chance to kill that bear all because of you!"

"Who's with me?"

Their angry yelling voices bombarded Uki, and it took all of Alornerk's energy to hold her back as the young hunters charged recklessly toward the life and death confrontation, distinguishable only by the terrifying sound of growls and barking over the wind and now horizontally blowing snow.

"Why did you just let them leave?" she screamed at Alornerk.

Alornerk was a man of few words for as long as she could remember, so it only took a deep frown to crease his weathered brow for the realization to finally set in and common sense to prevail…Uki begrudgingly returned to the tents in search of torches.

Once found, they headed back in the direction the rest of their hunting party had gone. In no time at all the sound of men's raised voices and jubilant shouting, made them cognizant of their party's location. As they soon after surveyed the bloody scene, it was quite clear the hunters had not bothered to ensure their aim was true before throwing their spears or shooting their arrows.

There on the ice amongst the dead and dying bodies of her beloved *qimmiit*, dogs, was the prone body of the biggest polar bear Uki ever laid eyes on. The poor creature's beautiful white fur was now streaked with red. She noticed several spears still protruding from its hide and the bodies of her faithful sled dogs.

Uki didn't know what to do first, she wanted so badly to punish the young men, lash out at them for their blatant contempt for protocol…they knew better! But after seeing the smug looks on their faces and witnessing the general air of celebration, it was more than evident they were oblivious to any wrong doings or they just didn't care. In that moment, she needed to focus her energy on the task at hand and try to block out their childish rhetoric…

"Can you believe the sheer size of that animal?"

"Never saw anything like it before. He just kept on coming, swiping those dogs out of the way with his massive paws."

"I wonder how old it was?"

"Shame about the hide, though."

"Does anyone know who dealt the killing blow?"

"It will make a great story to tell around the campfire."

As Uki stoically endeavoured to hold back her tears, she approached the bodies that lay strewn all over the ice, hoping to find at least a few of her dogs she could save. Even in the reduced visibility of the blowing snow and varying degrees of darkness, her keen eyes caught sight of a large trail of blood coming from the direction of the tents.

On closer inspection by torchlight, she could make out

bits and pieces of the butchered seal they had for supper earlier in the evening. Uki immediately saw red as everything fell into place. She swung around quickly to face her fellow hunters, intending to gain retribution, but the sound of a lone dog whining loudly in pain regrettably waylaid her.

As soon as she located the source of the mournful cry, Uki ran to its aid, paying no heed to the fact it was in very close proximity to the downed polar bear. Then everything happened all at once as the huntress laid down her spear on the ice before kneeling to get a better look at the animal's injuries. The great bear suddenly became re-animated and struggled to gain its footing.

But Alornerk's ever-watchful eyes were the first to witness the inception, understand the events as pure bedlam ensued and took action. Unlike the younger hunters, he had years of experience behind him and reacted accordingly. With spear in hand, Alornerk launched himself at the bear as it strove to stand in an upright position.

An injured animal will not always act as one would think; the immense bear let out an angry bawl and turned around catching Alornerk mid-air, in its deadly embrace.

Startled, Uki fell backwards the moment the animal reared above her and could only watch in abject horror as her friend was being crushed to death in front of her. She was unable to move or speak, but miraculously regained her motor skills in time to grab her spear and throw it with all of her might at the side of the bear's chest.

The point of her weapon connected with the animal's lungs as hoped and downed the bear for good.

Looking back on that evening, Uki wasn't sure if she was responsible for her friend's death, as the other hunters unanimously claimed. It would have been up to them to ensure the animal was, in fact, dead by poking and prodding it with their spears before anyone approached.

She took a chance by aiming so close to the bear's front leg, but the sheer power of its initial embrace was most likely culpable.

4

UKI

Uki would always remember that hunting trip and the terrible task she was obligated to carry out. Her friend did not pass away from his confrontation with the great bear but his injuries were so severe his impending death was certain.

As custom dictated, as a sign of respect, Uki would be obliged to assist him in ending his own life. She'd like to say the whole thing was a blur but she still remembered every little detail, every nuance of that frigid morning as she pushed the bone and animal skin kayak carrying Alornerk's broken body off of the ice floe.

Looking back, it could have been worse, the hunting party had to redistribute the weight of their cargo between all the remaining sleds and discard what was unnecessary due to the heavy loss of sled dogs. Therefore, Uki was not compelled to end her mentor's life with her own blade, but given the option of sending her friend to his death in his own *Qajaq*, watercraft.

Sadly, her beloved dogs did not meet the same fate because nearly a third of them suffered mortal wounds or died during the altercation with the polar bear. She took it upon herself to ensure every one of their bodies was disposed of respectfully, honouring their importance to the community.

Days later, when the hunting party returned to their winter camp, they mentioned little about Alornerk's untimely demise, only acknowledging he died a great hunter and now his shade resided with *Nanook*, Master of Bears.

Lip service, as far as Uki was concerned, because the lack of sincerity in her fellow hunter's words was more than flagrant. She felt devastated her mentor could not receive a proper burial, one befitting his status in the community, after all, Alornerk dedicated his whole life to selflessness.

Uki wanted to inform the elders about the events, but considering her ongoing responsibilities to her people and future trips with the hunters, she realized it was advantageous for her to remain silent. This was reaffirmed soon after, just by stolen looks and chancing upon the occasional conversation that would mysteriously be cut short. Again, she settled into a daily routine of hunting and gathering, but much of the joy disappeared, along with her friend. Luckily, she still had some of her dogs, and as far as she knew, the Inuit way of life would always consider them an important part.

As the seasons changed, so too did her duties. Large bands would separate to follow the game, their snow houses replaced by driftwood and animal skin tents, allowing for more portability. Uki substituted her rather large and cumbersome spear for a bow and arrow as she hunted across the tundra of the Low Arctic, occasionally venturing into the woodland areas farther south. She never saw this as a demotion since she was happiest hunting alone with only her dog for company and protection.

Uki would make a habit of stashing her kill in rock cairns at prearranged locations so that her kin would have the ability to recover her bounty and she would be free to travel. It wasn't until one of the group's hunting parties encountered the Norse of Greenland that everything changed and, from then on, Uki could no longer venture out on her own.

Being an inquisitive girl, she couldn't get enough of hearing the other hunters tell tales around the campfire of their encounters with the giants from the east. They were fair-skinned under all that dirt and had enigmatic horizontal grooves carved into their teeth, making them even more fierce when they growled at you. Uki always laughed when the hunters would pretend to be these so-called giants and chase the children around the camp, gnashing their teeth at them. However, something about their description piqued her curiosity…possibly the fact she too was fair-skinned. After much pestering of the elders and the eventual disappearance of the supposedly barbaric invaders, Uki could once again accompany the men on their hunting trips as opposed to doing women's work. Not that it was beneath her, but Uki had no interest in cooking, sewing, gathering berries, and caring for someone else's home.

WITH ANTICIPATION AND A LITTLE TREPIDATION, SHE AWOKE early each morning to attend the day's hunt, something that was fast becoming all too frequent…what had changed to cause the community's food supply to diminish?

On one such day, the elders assigned her to a small group of young hunters, hoping her excellent character traits would rub off on them. They were tracking a small herd of muskox through the fog since before dawn and all signs pointed to the herd being only moments ahead.

Uki bent down to examine the disturbed dew on several branches of tundra shrubbery, she was feeling her old self again as she instructed the inexperienced hunters what exactly they should look for when pursuing prey. With muskox, dogs would have been highly beneficial today because the male emitted an extremely pungent odour during mating season, but her favourite dog, *Amka*, meaning friendly spirit, was not at her side. This was due in part to the community's quarry being rather ambiguous of late, causing their hunting parties to travel less encumbered. Along with the fact that the young men had a propensity to play with her sled dogs whenever bored, she opted to leave the pack back at camp and keep the men focused.

As they crested a rather rocky incline, Uki immediately hushed the party with a hand signal. There at the bottom was a small harem of half a dozen young oxen with one adult bull in sight. She glanced around as if expecting the rest of the herd to turn up and then, much to her chagrin, her fellow hunters became as antsy as the juvenile animals they had in their sights. Uki again reprimanded them, but this time with a stern look and meaningful silence before motioning for the closest young man to join her, as she assumed the correct stance for shooting her bow.

Again, with hand signals, she instructed him to observe her closely as she withdrew an arrow from her quiver and placed it on her bow. Uki positioned her fingers on the string, making sure not to grip the arrow. After pulling back the string to touch her nose, she took a deep breath and aimed.

Upon relaxing her grip, she released the arrow, which hit its intended target flawlessly, striking the dominant animal's heart. With its tail tucked down, the large muskox made a run for cover, but she did not follow. Uki instructed the young man beside her to aim carefully at another of the beasts and shoot. Unfortunately, he seemed rattled by the entire experience as he clumsily lowered his bow and arrow, shook his head, and then turned away in noticeable embarrassment.

Uki couldn't help but feel angered by his actions, or lack thereof. Their people needed food and this boy's fear caused them to lose out. Maybe if they had the luxury of more time and options, she might have quietly taken him aside, but not today.

Out of nowhere, a random arrow went sailing overhead and struck one of the remaining oxen. Even from their current vantage point, Uki could easily ascertain it was a gut shot and to make matters worse, it took all of her efforts to restrain the young man from not running down the hill in pursuit of his quarry. She didn't want the meat tainted or tough because of the adrenaline that would most likely be coursing through the animal's body when chased.

This was something only a seasoned hunter would know, and these boys had yet to learn control. With all the commotion and distressed animal noises, the now spooked and leaderless herd scattered. Uki instructed the men to follow her after the bull because she knew it was a good shot and the animal would most likely be nearby, whereas the gut shot animal would probably look for a hiding place to hold up in. Thankfully, the young hunters complied, and the party quickly found a blood trail to follow.

In about half an hour, the muskox bled out, giving Uki plenty of time to instruct the young man with the errant arrow on the proper way to remove the entrails from the body cavity of the immense animal.

Glancing overhead, Uki was more than pleased to see there was still plenty of daylight left in the sky, meaning if they got a move on with the field dressing, they might just make it back to camp early. This left her free to retrieve her dog and track down the wounded ox on her own...all before anyone noticed her absence or nightfall arrived.

Deep down she knew there would be a plethora of objections to her plans, but leaving an animal to suffer unjustly was not something she could live with and, after all, Uki was much faster without the encumbrance of inexperienced help. Worst-case scenario would mean she would have to spend the night out on the tundra, but on the bright side, if she manages to salvage the meat for her people then all wouldn't be for naught.

A SUCCESSFUL HUNT WITH AN OVERABUNDANCE OF MEAT marked the party's return to camp. The mood was lighthearted and jubilant, so no one took notice of Uki's departure as she later slipped away with Amka in tow. And as intended she could swiftly cover the distance between her people's current camp and the last known site of the muskox herd, giving her plenty of time to take a breather while she watched her dog as he searched for the wounded animal's scent trail.

Uki couldn't help but keep mulling over the decision she made earlier...asking for approval would have most definitely wasted valuable time. Hopefully, the one person who she confided in would give a good argument in her defense, if need be.

Trustworthy friends were still few and far between for Uki, since Alornerk's death, but there were at least a few elders who genuinely respected her and valued her contributions to their community. Uki knew deep down she differed from her adopted people, and it wasn't just superficial.

However, she was not about to conform to make them happy, either. She always believed in earning their respect by deeds alone and settling for a traditional woman's lot in life would not suffice. She found a kindred spirit in Aama, a female elder who took it upon herself years ago, to be a surrogate "mother" to all, since none of her offspring had lived past infancy.

Word has it she was a beauty in her younger years and a bit of a rebel by Inuit standards. Lots of her fellow kinsmen tried to tame her, but only one had succeeded by breaking her heart. As in most cultures, the men have all the power, so important decisions such as marriage, adoption, migration and so on, were solely at the whim of any given community's elders, who were predominately male. Alas, they might claim women had their utmost respect, but you soon found out you're replaceable if someone else could do your job more to their liking and that applied to everything.

5

UKI

Uᴋɪ ᴀɴᴅ ʜᴇʀ ᴅᴏɢ ǫᴜɪᴄᴋʟʏ ᴘᴜʀsᴜᴇᴅ ᴛʜᴇ ᴡᴏᴜɴᴅᴇᴅ adolescent muskox from the morning's hunt. Just as she suspected, the blood trails were abundant and the presence of green matter confirmed a gut shot. Uki knew the *Omingmak*, bearded one, should be close by, so she only needed to look for a suitable place that would give a little shelter to a frightened animal in need of bedding down.

Lo and behold, her dog's bark changed in pitch as he tore off toward a small stand of trees below a rocky outcrop. Uki followed as fast as she could. She wasn't worried about her dog, she wanted to make sure that the ox's flesh remained salvageable. She crept around the sizeable rock formation where her dog recently disappeared behind because, oddly, she no longer heard his call.

When much to her surprise and disdain, there in front of her was a very imposing light-haired man already in the process of field dressing her ox and alongside him, her traitor of a dog, was enjoying the same spoils. She yelled at both of them to stop what they were doing, "Asu!" But the only one that seemed to understand her was the dog. He quickly returned to her side and cowered.

Uki didn't know what to do, for she had never killed another human being before. She raised her bow and withdrew an arrow from her quiver. The man took her seriously and stopped what he was doing, proceeding to raise both hands in supplication, as if pleading for mercy. Uki approached the kneeling man with her arrow pointed at his heart. She glanced around to see if he was alone and then vigorously motioned for him to back away from the downed animal.

"Uqausiit, that is my property!" she declared.

At first he seemed unaware, but later he smiled at her, shaking his head and gesturing towards himself. The instant she saw the deep grooves cut into his teeth, she uncharacteristically panicked and let an arrow fly. Luckily, it was in haste and only pierced him through the arm. He let out a string of curses, although none that she understood.

While this was all going on, Amka was quick to react to the fact his master might be in danger and attacked the downed and injured man; automatically, he went for the already bloodied arm. Uki, who was normally unflappable, chose this very moment to let her guard down as she dropped her bow and ran to the stranger's aid. Fortunately for him, she trained her dog well and could control Amka with only a few commands before he inflicted further trauma.

Sensing no present danger from the outsider and realizing their language barrier was fast becoming an issue, Uki raised her hands as he had done earlier with palms up. She pointed at the downed muskox and back at herself to show the animal was indeed hers.

He shook his head in disagreement. Apparently, he

believed in 'finders keepers' and began doing the same motions except pointing at himself. Sensing the futility of their charade, Uki took the lead, retrieved her bow, pointed her weapon at him and motioned for the man to move away from the animal and when he didn't respond, she bared her teeth at him and growled. Her actions didn't have the desired effect because the stranger broke out into peals of laughter and fell backwards onto the ground from a kneeling position.

Uki didn't know what to do now. After all, she couldn't kill him for laughing at her, but she was mad as hell, so she bent down and picked up a sizeable rock. He was just in the throes of trying to right himself again when she let fly with the projectile. He never saw it coming as it hit him squarely in the side of the head, dropping the stranger like a sack of potatoes the remaining short distance to the cold earth.

Now what to do and judging by the position of the sun in the sky, she gauged there wasn't enough time to haul the animal's remains back to camp and she couldn't, in all good conscience, leave the man in his current condition?

Uki opted to finish the field dressing of the ox before storing it for the night and then deal with the man as soon as he regained consciousness. Once Uki wrapped and hung the meat in a tree, she went about scattering dirt over as much of the bloodletting area as possible so as not to attract any unwanted scavengers. Because of her general lack of trust, Uki couldn't help but return periodically to check on the Norseman's status. For if he were playing possum and surreptitiously watching her labour all the while, there'd be consequences.

As she stood watching his chest rise and fall rhythmically, her paranoia eased, but did not completely dissipate. This led her to bind his wrists and ankles before continuing with her tasks. In doing so, Uki got a better look at the severity of his injuries, and felt sorry for the man as she dressed his wounds as best she could. Once the make-shift camp was to her liking, she collected kindling and started a fire on top of the ground where the muskox had died…now to wait for the stranger to come to.

Uki hadn't intended on spending the night out in the elements when she had come back for the injured ox, but she found that the animal's hiding spot made an excellent camp since it provided shelter from the wind.

With the night almost upon them, Uki and her faithful dog settled in, both keeping a watchful eye on their sedate "captive" because that's what he now was. This was such a strange predicament she got herself into. Hopefully, after meat in her stomach and a good night's rest, she'd be able to think more clearly. While gazing across the firelight at the Norseman, she couldn't help but find herself drawn to his uniqueness…he differed from her fellow kinsmen.

He was much bigger in stature, with fine facial features and high cheekbones. However, his attributes were somewhat hidden behind his long beard, giving him a more rugged appearance. For the first time in her life, Uki felt 'something' for a man. Previously, they had all been annoyances except for her good friend Alornerk, but he had been like a father figure. She laughed quietly at her own hormone driven musings, uncharted territory to say the least and shortly afterwards, with a smile on her face, she drifted off.

Uki didn't know just how long she had been asleep for when she became conscious of the sound of someone's muffled groaning and it was clearly emanating from across the fire pit…her captive was finally awake.

At first, he seemed disorientated, but everything changed the moment he realized he was tied up. His eyes flashed white, and he fought to release himself. Amka stayed by her side but began incessantly barking as the man continued to flail about. In the end she quieted her dog long enough to get the man's attention and calm him down as well, so he wouldn't injure himself further.

Brandishing her knife, she gestured to cut his leg bindings in order to help him sit up. He appeared to understand, but she wasn't about to take any chances. Uki approached cautiously, keeping enough distance so he couldn't kick her in defense. After cutting the ropes, she continued to maintain eye contact in the hope of coming across as confident, as opposed to aggressive.

Now that she took a closer look at the man, she noticed the rather large lump on the side of his head that her rock had caused and dried blood accumulated in his dirty hair. A part of her felt remorseful for what she had done earlier, but she also knew she couldn't take undue risks when it concerned the safety of her community. If this man's own people were to blame for the current shortage in wild game, then they must face the consequences.

Uki resorted to hand gestures and crude drawings in the dirt to convey her message, as she refused to untie the man's hands. But she quickly grew frustrated because without the benefit of spoken words, there was no commonality of interests to explore.

Never one to give up, Uki decided to feed the outsider so as to keep their lines of communication open and as friendly as possible. Luckily, she had taken the time to cut several sizeable pieces of muskox meat off of her kill earlier, so after a little finessing of the fire, she skewered the meat with a piece of sharpened kindling before placing it over the embers to cook. Making it easier to get his undivided attention since he was obviously hungry, although a little unnerving to have her every move watched.

However, in a fleeting moment of carelessness, she diverted her attention by turning her back ever so slightly, when shearing off a piece of the meat and soon found herself uncomfortably close to the stranger as he scrambled forward. She threw up her hands to block his advance and then instructed him to sit back on his feet before she would proceed.

Once seated at a safer distance, she pretended to eat the meat as a visual cue, before attempting to hand feed her captive. It was the oddest sensation, the act itself a form of intimacy as he steadily chewed the food, all the while staring into her eyes. Unfortunately, though, the sound of Amka's growl interrupted their moment, he was also hungry.

THE NORSEMAN WAS MUCH MORE AGREEABLE WITH HIS current situation after being fed, although he still needed to come up with an escape plan, except he now had to take into consideration his limitations since he only had the use of one good arm.

He crossed great continents alongside his Viking brethren, pillaging village after village and now, when he came to that time in his life when putting down roots was the order of the day, this happened. He couldn't believe it…this woman single-handedly took him down, but was thankful she had not chosen to kill him. Never once he felt threatened in all his thirty-some years until setting foot on this godforsaken frozen tundra…if it hadn't been for the wealth of game this land possessed, he would have never stayed.

The climate displayed its cruelty and unforgiving nature, much like its northernmost people, and when they weren't attempting to harm you, the heathens would snatch your metal possessions. Most of his people already gave up trying to make a go of it, uprooted their settlements and began their long journey back home…that was why he had been hunting alone today. Hungry and rather disheartened, but ever hopeful right until the moment he had miraculously come upon a fallen muskox. The fresh kill served as a promising omen from *Skadi*, Goddess of Winter, and like her, his favourite interest had always been the hunt.

As he now looked across the fire at this enchanting huntress, try as he might, he could barely distinguish her from having any kinship to the warring factions his people had encountered farther north. First, she seemed to be taller in stature than most and only had a slightly rounded face. Her eyes were a beautiful bluish-green with somewhat heavy lids, making her more exotic, and her hair was the colour of a nuummite, which she wore in a solitary braid. She dressed as the Inuit did and upon first perusal, her suntanned and tattooed skin might have helped her blend into the cultural woodwork, but this woman was truly different. The Norseman was mesmerized by her, and as he observed her, he couldn't help but be captivated.

He was suddenly rousted from his wool-gathering by the sound of her very large sled dog's growl. The animal had been keeping a watchful eye on their captive as well, and it most certainly didn't appreciate the amount of attention he had been paying to its master. Caught red-handed, so to speak, but still starving, he motioned for Uki to give the last piece of meat to the dog.

She understood and smiled back at him.

Later, as the icy winds swept across the tundra and their fire burned low, he soon found himself shivering as he tried to get closer to the coals. Whereas mere feet away, the huntress slept soundly, curled up next to her dog for warmth. The Norseman couldn't help but be a little jealous. But what to do?

He was in no position to ask the woman if he could share her bedroll, if she even had one because she was travelling light. So after feigning a rather boisterous coughing fit, he then waited not so patiently for her to take pity on him.

6

UKI

The noise awakened Uki and her dog. One part of her wanted to ignore it, while the other part was concerned his wounds might have become foul.

Across the fire, she watched as he shivered uncontrollably, likely due to a fever. As she surreptitiously inched closer to examine his injured arm, she discovered she would have to cut the remaining ropes in order to do so. With knife in hand, she gripped his shoulder and shook him rather forcefully to see if he was coherent and/or still posed a threat to her. The Norseman, thinking himself quite cunning, remained limp as he mumbled a response as if still asleep and then tried to rollover but the instant his arm contacted the ground, he cried out in pain.

Uki cut the remaining ropes and helped him into an upright position.

He didn't say a word as she unwrapped the bandages from around his arm and, for the second time that evening, examined his injuries. Although he couldn't understand a word, it was still quite clear by the tone of her voice as she mumbled under her breath and the worried look in her eyes, his arm had most likely taken a turn for the worse.

Uki motioned for him to stay put before calling her dog to lie down next to him, presumably for warmth, all conveyed through gestures, and then she disappeared into the darkness.

It seemed like hours before she returned with a hide bag filled to the brim with what looked to be pine cones, old mushrooms and moss. The Norseman sat in absolute wonder as she prepared her heathen remedies by the firelight.

First, she grabbed handfuls of moss and squeezed the water out of them. The very moment she collected enough liquid to fill a crudely shaped cup, she presented it to the Norseman and motioned for him to drink. At first he was reluctant, so she herself took small sips before again, presenting it to him…the taste was bitter but soothing to his parched throat. As he leaned forward to hand the cup back to her, she reached towards him and gently placed her palm onto his fevered forehead.

She cut up and vigorously chewed some of the pine cones and once they reached a rather gummy consistency. She set them aside and repeated the task repeatedly. The Norseman grimaced as he only imagined the horrendous taste of whatever she was concocting. As she did that, Uki rummaged through her bag for the scads of mushrooms she harvested, and in an almost frenzy she shredded the tops only.

The Norseman made many trips to this land but usually farther south, although he was familiar with the extolled virtues of seal fat for healing by the Indigenous

Peoples of the region. However, it was irrelevant since they were miles away from the ocean right now.

His own people relied on potions of leeks and garlic, along with herbs, to treat a plethora of ailments. After getting a closer look at the condition of his wounds by firelight, he realized he was direly in need of a seasoned healer and could only pray to his gods this woman knew what she was doing.

Once she amassed a sizeable amount of mushroom tops and chewed up pine cones, she did the oddest thing… she positioned his arm away from his body and motioned for him to stay still while she dropped her pants and urinated on his wounds.

The moment he saw her undo her crude leggings, he thought she was offering him the warmth of her body, but the instant she squatted over his arm and hot liquid splashed onto his wounds, he was shocked. As he struggled to back away from her, she merely pushed him back down onto the ground. With an exasperated look on her face, she continued on with what she was doing. He tried to remain still as she wiped away the excess urine, as if cleaning the surrounding area.

She packed the various wounds with tree sap and pieces of the shredded mushrooms, followed by a layer of moss and finally strips of animal hide. The Norseman did not know if any of this was going to heal his arm, but he didn't have another alternative at his disposal. When she appeared to be finished seeing to his needs, she dropped to her knees and nestled in behind him, spooning his body with her warmth. Even her dog returned to its earlier position and the three of them slept soundly the rest of the night through.

❄

By the time the sun peeked over the horizon, Uki was wide awake and tending to her morning rituals, but her dog remained nestled up beside the stranger. It was so unusual to see her animal treating this man as if he was a pack member, although she took it as a good sign…animals were always more intuitive than humans.

It wasn't until she relit the campfire and the delicious aroma of cooked meat wafting through the air that her captive finally opened his eyes and looked around. His rather alarming smile again greeted her. One part of her found the grooved teeth startling, but another part of her, the inquisitive part, found them fascinating.

Much like the tattoos her people wore, when Aama first approached her as a young girl offering to permanently mark Uki with chin stripes so that her kinsmen would know she reached puberty, she was terrified.

Then later, when she successfully hunted and killed her first whale, Uki demanded to be adorned with whale-fluke tattoos beside the corners of her mouth to mark the occasion and to act as a future charm. In fact, she herself even wanted to learn the ancient art of skin-stitching *Kakinniit*, Inuit tattoos, for it had all seemed so mystical.

The tradition involved lubricating a thread-like material made of caribou sinew with seal oil and then soaking it in a mixture of lampblack, urine, and dark graphite. After, they would push a bone needle under the skin. They used lampblack as the pigment, believing it, along with graphite, to be highly effective against evil spirits and the sicknesses they brought.

Uki wished she could converse with the stranger and learn more about him and his people. First things first, he needed to stay alive to accomplish that. She came to his assistance once again and helped him into a more erect position because the moment he tried to lift his own body weight with the injured arm, he could not conceal his pain.

After feeding everyone, including her sled dog, Uki carefully unwrapped the Norseman's arm dressings to re-evaluate his wounds. But since her patient was not familiar with her people's healing practices, based on colour alone, he assumed he was going to die, or at the very least lose his arm, and overreacted. Uki took control of the situation before it escalated any further.

She grabbed his face in her hands, forcing him to peer her in the eyes, where he immediately searched for answers. Once she had his undivided attention, Uki smiled in response and nodded her head, as if to say everything would be fine. Again, he faced the humiliation of being peed on as she cleansed his wounds and redressed them, but he had the bonus of seeing her muscular body in the daylight as she dropped her pants and carried out her strange healing practice.

Once Uki tidied up everything and put out their fire, she retrieved the packed meat from where she stored it the evening before and built a travois of sorts to haul it back to her people's camp.

The Norseman watched in amazement as the more than capable woman went about fashioning a rather unusual apparatus with branches and the meager tools she carried…he couldn't help but wonder if she was the property of anyone. When all was said and done, Uki helped her captive to his feet to assess his condition. Finding him to be stable and fit enough for the journey; she went about attaching the travois to his shoulders before motioning him to follow her.

Uki was none too happy when the stranger began hauling her kill in the wrong direction, as if to take it back to his own people, wherever they might be. The moment she started yelling at him, her once again faithful dog joined in and barked at the stranger to corral him in the right direction. They faced a stalemate, as neither one wanted to do the other's bidding.

The Norseman was not about to go blindly into enemy territory. After all, he saw firsthand what atrocities her people were capable of. Though he was in no condition to overpower her or her dog and his people's last settlement was miles away to the south. He was on his own.

As he stood contemplating his limited options, an idea came to him. He turned to Uki and motioned for her to come closer. Once she was within arm's length, he reached for her hand and placed it on his chest. At first she seemed anxious, but he made sure to not hold it too tight.

Then he patted his chest with her hand and repeated his name out loud, "Asbjorn," she was quick to understand and soon followed suit with her own name…they both couldn't help but smile at each other.

7

UKI

It took most of the day for Uki and Asbjorn to cover the tundra's rocky terrain on their arduous journey back to her camp but thankfully his captor took into consideration the fact he was still suffering. Albeit a slight fever from his wounds and chose to not hold him up to her usual pace. She even tried frequently to help him by lightening the load, but he only shook his head in denial… if he was going to meet her people, he would do it with his head held high.

Unfortunately, it did nothing to ease the nagging premonition he sensed in his bones since they departed that morning. A fixation on the genuine possibility he was probably walking to his own death. He only hoped he was wrong and her kin differed from the hostiles his people had encountered previously. The few remaining people were driven back to Greenland and eventually Europe after the hostiles wantonly massacred the Viking settlements. They came to hunt and found a better life, but the Indigenous Peoples saw them as invaders.

Asbjorn heard stories of assimilation, where Norsemen

took Inuit women as wives, but these were quite rare. If luck was on his side and Uki's parentage was as it appeared, maybe her people might indeed welcome him with open arms or, at the very least, not try to kill him on sight.

LATER THAT DAY, WHEN THEY CAME WITHIN EYESHOT OF her people's camp, Uki helped him pull their load the remaining distance and he allowed it. Asbjorn observed the expression on everyone's faces. His presence troubled them and as he passed by her fellow kinsmen. Some even tried to intimidate him with their unfriendly stares or acts of aggression, but his huntress would not abide by their behaviour.

Advancing further into the camp's proper, Uki and Asbjorn were surrounded by her brethren. Even the small children emerged to gaze at the Norseman in awe. He was much as her kinsmen previously described, fair-haired and large in stature, but not frightening at all. Uki wondered what all the fuss was about and why she was not allowed to hunt on her own. After all, it couldn't possibly be because of this man's people.

They came to their journey's end and stopped in front of the elder's oversized communal caribou skin tent. Uki removed the makeshift harness she made for Asbjorn to pull their meat laden travois with, motioning for him to take a seat beside the camp's central fire pit. Several men were currently seated there and didn't seem to want to give up any of their space.

In response, Uki raised her voice and pushed them out of the way.

"He is my captive and I've worked him hard. Can't you

see he is injured? Make room so he might warm himself. I didn't bring him all this way so he could die on me."

Asbjorn did not know what the pecking order was, so he followed her lead and hoped for the best. He watched in silence as his captor ordered her fellow kinsmen about and triumphantly presented the remains of the kill to who he assumed were the elders of the group.

Initial silence, followed by a violent outbreak as Uki and Asbjorn were besieged by an angry mob.

"Kill the Norseman! His people have taken the food right out of our mouths. Let his death be a message to his people. You're bringing disease into our camp. Burn the intruder…" they screamed.

Her people were none too happy about their current visitor, but thankfully, cooler heads prevailed as the elders shouted orders to those in attendance. "Kinsmen and women…hear our huntress out…he is her prisoner, not her guest!"

Whatever the elders said to the large crowd eased their enmity as most took a step backwards, albeit reluctantly.

Asbjorn watched as several young men removed the muskox meat from the makeshift sled and carried it away. Although, still painfully aware of their suspicious eyes never truly leaving him for more than a moment. Sensing a general mood shift or loss of control among the elders, the huntress grabbed his injured arm and forced him to the ground. Asbjorn cried out in pain.

Uki felt horrible for her actions but she must present herself as dominant in order to show her people the Norseman was of no danger to them. She hadn't thought every scenario through, whilst on their long walk back to camp…would they accept him as a future contributor to the well-being of their community, enslaved or free…or merely execute the perceived invader?

Deep down, Uki knew her people possessed great compassion. Her reaching maturity was clear evidence of that. Not all *Qallunaat*, white people, were a threat to the Indigenous Peoples of the far north. Broad strokes more than likely were used to paint a picture of past conflicts and personally she still saw no threat from this man.

Uki waited patiently as the men and women who made up the council of elders filed by Asbjorn, stopping to get a better look at him, including his injured arm.

Aama approached and removed the hide dressing, and only then did he dare to utter a sound or make a gesture, thankfully surrendering rather than defying. The Norseman somehow knew these people would make the final decision as to his future so he tried to not look them in the eyes as they passed. Submissiveness was not in his nature but in his current state, staying alive to fight another day was paramount.

As the old woman inspected his wounds, she ordered Uki about in a commanding tone. She grabbed him by his good arm and motioned for him to stand up. Once he was on his feet and his true height was unmistakable, she almost looked approvingly at the Norseman as she placed Uki's hand in his and gestured for them to leave.

Uki smiled at the woman, stopped, and lovingly kissed the dorsum of both of her hands before escorting Asbjorn away from the circle of elders. Asbjorn couldn't make head nor tail of what was happening, but he knew he was outnumbered in unfriendly territory. Without the help of this woman, her people would most likely slit his throat as opposed to showing him hospitality.

She guided him towards a cookhouse of some sort, as he noticed smoke coming from a hole in the structure's roof. The moment Uki threw back the flap of the makeshift door to the cookhouse, surprising a small group of Inuit women busy preparing meat, crude vegetables and hides within…mayhem ensued.

It was as if a fox entered a henhouse and the obviously terrified women lost their ability to function as they gathered in the far corner of the tent. Uki did not have the time or patience to coddle the women as she briskly ordered them about as to just what supplies she needed. Soon after, they begrudgingly presented her with several large slabs of what looked like fat. Then the women again cowered in silence.

Asbjorn immediately sensed relief as he noticed the bits of telltale seal hide were still attached to the blubber. As an almost afterthought the women also provided a few clean dressings and a small bucket, which they quickly ladled hot water into from one of the large steaming cauldrons. Once they completed their tasks, they wasted no time in escorting Uki back to the door, as if her continued presence was unwelcome.

The sheer animosity on their faces was more than clear, although Asbjorn couldn't be sure who it was directed at more. Uki, now with her hands full, gestured for her charge to follow using her head and chin movements, which he did happily.

The distance was short to her *tupiq*, caribou skin tent, although she seemed to falter before entering and motioned for him to follow her inside. As soon as he stepped over the threshold, he heard the familiar bark of her sled dog, which mysteriously disappeared when they first arrived at camp.

In all the commotion, he had not given it any further thought until now…and there he was looking very comfortable laying on what he assumed was her bedroll. The space was clean, although there was the smell of burnt seal oil in the air, along with Arctic cotton grass and moss used as wicks for their lamps. Once inside, she glanced around as if searching for something and carefully put her supplies down on a small, crudely fashioned table. With hands now free, she pulled him towards the bed and motioned for him to take a seat, scooting Amka off the bed.

The kindly old woman had already removed the prior dressings, so Uki could get down to business.

She deftly cleaned the whole arm with warm water this time and cut skinless strips of seal fat to lie over the wounds. Because of their texture, they readily stuck to the open lacerations and once she was content with her administration, Uki gently pushed him back down onto the bed and gestured for him to stay there. After looking him straight in the eyes, she took a brief pause before carefully enunciating one word, "Sinippoq," meaning rest.

Placing the palms of her hands together in a sort of praying position next to her cheek, she tilted her ear towards her shoulder and closed her eyes…feigning sleep. Assuming he got the gist of it, she stood up and exited the tent in order to find aliment for Asbjorn and herself, seeing as a considerable amount of time passed since they last eaten.

8

UKI

It seemed like hours passed before her return, time spent dwelling on his predicament and all the outcomes out of his control, instead of resting. When she came back, she was bearing gifts of food and water.

Asbjorn exerted all his self-control to wait patiently for the meal to be offered, and when she did, he was relieved. He dove into the food, becoming self-conscious of her ever watchful gaze and of her sled dog's. Only after he satisfied himself did he offer food to the dog. Their coexistence comprised large periods of time spent in silence, but Asbjorn hoped it would change because right now he needed to make water and wasn't sure of how to express himself without offending or scaring Uki.

He peeped around the tent for inspiration and when his eyes fell on the water bucket, he stood and reached for it. Once it was in his hands, he motioned for her to watch. He positioned it in front of his groin and poured some of the water onto the dirt floor slowly…she understood and gestured for him to stop.

Asbjorn sensed her anxiety as she looked nervously

around the tent. He offered his wrists to be bound, but she shook her head back and forth. She grabbed his arm and escorted him out of the tent, leading him a short distance away from the other dwellings but still within view of the rest of the camp.

Dusk arrived, making what he was about to do less of a spectacle. Asbjorn turned away and did his business, although it seemed to go on forever. After completing that, they both returned to her tent where he used the remaining water to clean himself up before bed and have Uki redress his wounds as needed.

Unlike her kinsmen described, Norsemen were usually spotless and took pride in their appearances…the harsh Arctic climate was the only reason for his lapse in grooming. Asbjorn's heart swelled with joy at the sight of Uki already settled comfortably on the bed. But alas, the moment he went to lie down beside her, her sled dog filled the remaining space and growled his displeasure when nudged. With no other suitable space in sight, Asbjorn risked a dog bite to hunker down for the night. He spooned in behind the twosome on the bed and was asleep in no time.

Sunup came much too soon the following morning, but Uki and her dog rose early and left him undisturbed. Left to his own devices, Asbjorn addressed his wounded arm on his own and was pleasantly surprised by the miraculous effects of seal fat.

The only injury which still looked rather grotesque was where the arrow pierced his arm, but it, too, was healing nicely. All the others appeared superficial now.

As he surveyed the tent, it was evident his huntress did not yet trust him as there were no knives or even sharp objects around, so he would have to wait for her return in order to cut the remaining seal fat for fresh dressings. He found it downright maddening to be sequestered inside a tent, but he wasn't about to go for a walk and imperil his life.

Uki didn't leave him to stew for long, as she returned soon thereafter, again carrying sustenance. She seemed happy he was up and about. This time, she joined him for their morning meal, although they didn't share any conversation. However, she smiled and gestured towards certain objects, calling them by their Inuit names. Such as the *aqiggiq,* ptarmigan, a bird species found in tundra areas and quite tasty, along with the *akutaq,* meaning wild berries mixed with fat, that they devoured. Not to mention the *sinittarfik,* meaning bed, and most importantly, *pigiarvik...* home.

THEIR TIME TOGETHER WAS INDEED AWKWARD, BUT considering unusual circumstances brought them together in the first place, they surprised everyone by surpassing their expectations and flourished. They even created their own means of communication, relying on gestures and looks. Something they tended to not display in public, so as not to alienate themselves any further from their fellow kinsmen and women.

Uki knew Asbjorn's conduct would reflect on her, and vice versa. In retrospect, neither would have changed a thing for the world as both found someone to love and, more importantly, worth suffering for.

The Norseman's initial acculturation was exasperating, to say the least, as his daily routine comprised prolonged periods of solitude.

Although the moment his wounds healed, and he regained his strength, everything changed. Without knowing the boundaries set in place and by whom, the community expected him to contribute to their welfare. He persevered, trying wholeheartedly to fit in. Being a larger man, the first opportunities to present themselves, he pursued by helping whenever something heavy needed to be lifted. It took a good long while for mutual trust to be earned between the two different cultures, but when they allowed him to carry a weapon of his own, Asbjorn showed them his true value as a skilled hunter.

His relationship with Uki blossomed, and she became very prideful of his accomplishments. In some ways, this might have been a mistake because his fellow hunters did not like to be one-upped by the outsider. But in due course, Asbjorn peacefully coexisted with his new kinsmen. He learned their language and customs, and shared some of his own with them. Never once did he run across a fellow Norseman in all the subsequent years he spent journeying through the Arctic and subarctic regions of his adopted homeland; *Inuit Nunangat*, meaning the place where Inuit live. This was most likely because the Inuit people moved frequently whenever the weather changed or their food sources declined. They would up and move camp to far northern regions where the hunting was more abundant owing to less competition.

Even the elders grew to appreciate his talents and value his contributions to the community's welfare. Uki and Asbjorn were both respected, but never truly loved. Possibly on account of their light skin colour and the more time they spent together, the more she visibly changed. She dressed as her people did and proudly sported her facial tattoos, but she had modified her teeth as a show of respect for her man's heritage.

Uki always was aware the fabric of her life had made up much of the idle talk around the campfire by both sexes, but she would not abide by any disparaging gossip about the man she chose. She couldn't contain her joy as she found a mate she admired.

However, the couple would never really be married, in the eyes of their community, until she gave birth to their first child. None of this bothered Asbjorn, or at least he never let on that it did. He was content and insisted on not returning to his own people. Life was filled with joy and happiness as he affectionately called her Heima, the Viking word for home. They kept busy and mostly to themselves.

It wasn't until her fellow kinsmen encouraged Asbjorn to go hunting with them, suggesting Uki's time would be better served back at camp, teaching the young…that she worried. Their hunting parties were always successful and Asbjorn appeared to enjoy the camaraderie of spending time with the other men. Uki had a sinking feeling some of their smiles were merely painted on.

As the months turned into years, Uki's suspicions subsided until one evening, when, upon returning from a hunt, Asbjorn brought up the subject of children.

"My dearest Heima. Are you satisfied with our lives together? I don't want to rush you, but wouldn't you like to have children, little ones we can teach to be great hunters? I've seen you with the youth in our community and you would make a wonderful mother," and then he hesitated, looking into Uki's eyes. "I know you were a virgin when we first lay together, but can you think of any reason we have not been able to conceive?" He was not laying blame, only stating the obvious.

Evidently, Uki's fellow kinsmen planted the right seed of dissension because deep down, Uki's heart weighed heavily with guilt as she considered her potential responsibility. The start of their relationship, she abstained for as long as she could and sought contraceptive help from Aama.

Goldenthread was an accessible plant with a wide range and a plethora of well-known antibacterial properties, but it also contained a harmful chemical called berberine. Which had the potential to prevent an unwanted pregnancy or act as an abortifacient, assuming the person dispensing it is knowledgeable. After all, she couldn't take the chance of becoming with child until she knew Asbjorn secured his own position in the community and was safe from her brethren's petty animosities towards the 'white man'.

Uki didn't want to be on the offensive, but she needed to know just where this was all coming from. The members of his hunting party were teasing him incessantly about not knowing how to impregnate his woman and even offering their services. All said, of course, with a laugh and a good-natured pat on the back.

Uki was mad as a wet hen and it took Asbjorn, using almost all of his strength to detain her from marching out of their tent and seeking reprisal. After resolving everything, they agreed Uki should seek help from her friend.

Maybe the elder could enlighten them on the best ways to ensure a fruitful union. So the following morning, after a very public display of affection for the benefit of Asbjorn's "loose-lipped" fellow hunters, Uki sent them off and made her way to Aama's tent in search of wisdom. The old woman knew various successful ways to plant a man's seed. She herself got pregnant on numerous occasions but unfortunately could never carry the children full term or it sadly passed soon after birth.

"Uki, my child…I'm so happy you have finally put your worries aside and let nature take its course. You are not too old to give birth, but a little help wouldn't hurt. Are you familiar with those lovely little yellow-flowered plants we see growing everywhere in the spring…they're called rose root. I can make you a decoction of their flowers in no time."

"Aama, you honour me with your thoughtfulness. I was frightened I destroyed my chances of becoming a mother. Having a child would only strengthen the kinship relations we have established and bring joy to all our lives. Thank you, mother."

Later, after a morning of instructing young hunters on how to follow their dog's lead in looking for air holes in the ice, Uki had the rest of the day to herself and she spent it wisely.

Instead of eating that evening's meal with the rest of the group, she busied herself preparing a meal of local fare intended to promote Asbjorn's sex drive and heighten their chances of conception.

The moment she filled her list of items needed, the camp buzzed with new gossip fodder since most women already knew what these ingredients were used for…Uki smiled to herself as she made her way back to her tent to take care of the final preparations.

9

UKI

As night descended upon the camp, Uki couldn't help but nervously sneak peeks out of her tent's door flap in anticipation of her man's return and the moment Amka barked, she could tell by his tone Asbjorn was indeed near. She didn't know why she was all aflutter.

They made love countless times, but this time she was now armed with age old potions, herbs, charms and the goodwill of the elders. Uki even bathed herself and was anointed with a special oil by Aama. The citrus smell was quite pleasant, which they said increased her chances of fertility. She surveyed the tent to ensure everything was in order, and pondered whether she should lie provocatively across their bed. She hoped when he entered, desire would overwhelm him, and they would engage in intercourse.

They could always eat later and continue throughout the night. She knew her man had stamina, but there was now an urgency because, by Inuit standards, she should have reproduced in her teen years. The tent flap opened and as soon as Asbjorn saw her draped across their bed, a huge smile spread across his face and made small talk in order to bait her.

"Did you have a good day, Heima? I can't wait to tell you about the abundance of game we saw…" He didn't want to make her mad, he just couldn't help himself because he knew this was her interpretation of a seduction and it was adorable coming from his huntress.

When he thought he had gone just far enough with making her wait, he broke out into a hearty laugh and lunged for her. It was like music to his ears to hear Uki giggling as he tore what little she had on off of her beautiful body and began ravaging her with kisses. They spent an amazing evening of carnality and feasting, tried new positions, laughed, and loved throughout.

The next morning, the couple slept in. The elders postponed the usual duties, and when they finally showed up, it was quite clear the entire community knew about their endeavours. Uki couldn't have been happier. These actions showed her just how important they were to their fellow kinsmen and women. She even chided herself for her earlier doubts.

UKI WASN'T SURE IF THE REDUCED TENSION AND ANXIETY IN her life had anything to do with her conceiving so quickly or if Aama's remedies did the job. Barely two weeks passed, and she already noticed physical changes.

She was pregnant and ecstatic. And with every inch her stomach grew, Asbjorn became more overprotective, wanting her to stop hunting during the pregnancy. You'd have thought she was the first woman to have ever given birth by how he treated her with kid gloves. But she would have none of it. Uki couldn't imagine herself stuck back at camp. Exercise was good for her physically and mentally… this baby would be strong like its parents.

As the months crept by, Uki's skills were yet again in demand because wild game became rather sparse in the area, and the community needed all able-bodied hunters to fulfill their dietary needs. Talk resurfaced that the Norsemen had returned, and they were most likely to blame for the shortage.

In order to prove the validity of the gossip, the community even sent out war parties. Of course, this worried both Uki and Asbjorn greatly, especially since he was assigned to accompany the parties and track down whoever plundered their lands. The extra time away meant Uki was by herself a lot. Usually it didn't bother her, but strangely she found several of her fellow kinsmen spending a little too much time hovering.

At first she thought it was sweet, then it became quite unsettling, as if in her pregnant state she became even more desirable. Uki didn't want to think ill of these men since everything had gone their way. Their existence had become harmonious within the community. Even the women became friendlier and more apt to lend a kind word or deed.

One exceptionally cold winter's day, her luck changed. A fierce storm whipped up out of nowhere and descended upon the camp just before dusk. Her brethren were encouraged to join for an early meal in the elder's tent before returning to the safety of their own dwellings for the duration of the night.

The hunting parties hadn't yet returned, but that

wasn't strange because they frequently had to seek shelter whenever freak snow storms hit with a vengeance.

Uki, as usual, was making her rounds later that evening to confirm the camp was indeed secure for the night. She made sure nothing attracted polar bears and similar animals in search of an easy meal. That's when she heard it.

The unmistakable sound of a small child screaming in terror, followed by the distinctive growl of a bear. She dropped what she was doing as her heart sunk into her stomach and ran in the direction she thought the sound came from. The howling winds made it almost impossible to narrow in on the child's exact location. Later, she discovered she wasn't the only one who heard the initial sound. The child's mother was searching for the little girl outside as soon as she realized she wasn't in her bed.

Uki might have tackled a lone polar bear on her own, but in her current condition, she needed to play it safe. She needed to alert her fellow hunters so they could help in the search for the wayward child who was clearly now in harm's way.

Like a phantom, from out of the swirling snow appeared the form of a woman running full bore towards her. Grabbing hold of the stranger's arms as she passed, Uki shook her fellow kinswoman violently in order to get her full attention, cupping the woman's face between her own palms.

The moment the two women made eye contact, it was more than obvious to Uki the frantic young woman must indeed be the child's mother. The sheer terror in her eyes said it all, and rightly so. Children and dogs were targeted by animals higher on the food chain, often by an unhealthy predator seeking weaker and easier prey.

"Look at me!" she screamed. "Listen to what I'm

saying. Go get help! You'll only get yourself killed if you try to save her on your own," she shoved her back toward the tents. "Go now!"

Uki searched for a weapon, preferably a spear, something she could throw from a distance. That's when she heard more screaming. The sound abruptly stopped. The implications nauseated her and it took all her willpower to not run recklessly into the fray without the help of her fellow kinsmen. Uki hated herself for being so ineffective. She screamed at the top of her lungs, hoping to alert someone, anyone, to the tragedy unfolding.

Then she heard another shriek pierce the night air and against her better judgement, once again ran towards the sound, barely stopping long enough to pick up a piece of lit firewood from the camp's communal pit, but she was too late.

Uki froze in awe as she came upon the horrific aftermath of the attack. A large polar bear ripped a poor little girl of undetermined age to pieces. Even in the reduced visibility, Uki witnessed the child's spilt blood and dismembered limbs covering the snow, and she noticed the obviously sick, blood-stained animal dragging the bulk of the body away into the darkness. Uki was now running on instinct and the only sound in her ears was the pounding of her own heart as she stood her ground and let loose with an ear-piercing screech to get the animal's attention.

The bear turned and swung its head menacingly in her direction, affording her a better view of the mutilated corpse. With torch in hand, she approached the animal and started yelling again, hoping it would drop the body and run away. To her surprise, the bear refused to retreat and made chuffing noises. It showed clear agitation, but did not advance.

Its bizarre demeanour perplexed Uki. She couldn't

stop herself from trying to close the distance between them. With the aid of her torch light, it all became crystal clear what originally transpired.

Deep lacerations covered the animal's hide, and its fur was more red than white. Apparently the bear engaged in mortal combat with what could only be another apex predator. It also became clear the reason for its head being cocked at such an odd angle. It was blind in one eye.

She again started waving the torch around and thankfully, the bear dropped the little girl's torso. Then the unexpected happened. Uki had no time to think as the animal charged her. She remained motionless, however, several fellow kinsmen launched a hail of arrows. Lessening the impact of the enormous bear's body as it collided with her own.

WHEN UKI AWOKE HOURS LATER, IT WAS WITH A START. She was not in her own tent, but the elders surrounded her and Asbjorn was there by her side.

As she tried to sit up, intense pain racked her body. Everything hurt. Instinctively, her hands moved to cradle her belly as if to protect the baby within. Or was she too late? She sobbed. Asbjorn sensed what Uki was thinking and immediately tried to soothe her.

"Praise be *Freyja*, Goddess of Fertility, it's her will that our child is still safe within your womb," he gently took one of her hands in his own and placed it on her belly again so they could feel the child's movements together.

Aama came forward and embraced the distraught couple. She, too, confirmed Uki miraculously survived the ordeal with nary a broken bone and only minimal abrasions.

Everything seemed fine regarding the baby's heartbeat. It was strong like its parents, although its positioning in the womb shifted downward slightly, resulting in a sooner delivery date, but only time would tell. The elders filed out of the main tent, leaving Uki and Asbjorn to their privacy.

Or so they thought, because unbeknownst to them, the mother of the slaughtered little girl was eavesdropping in the shadows. The grief-stricken woman had nothing but loathing in her heart as she gazed upon the young couple as they held each other tight and the father-to-be once again caressing his pregnant wife's belly, telling her and their unborn child he loved them and he would always be there to protect them.

10

UKI

Later, Uki begged to go back to the security of their own tent for the rest of the evening. Despite the cozy warm temperature in the community's main tent, thanks to the large fire burning within.

For the first time in her life, the darkness frightened Uki. Most likely because of the vulnerability she was now experiencing, brought on by pain. Asbjorn convinced her to ingest some herbal tea to get some much-needed rest and to help with the healing process. He thanked all the gods that his woman was alive and their baby had not died in the confrontation with the polar bear. He would have to think long and hard about an appropriate name for this child. After all, his own meant 'God of Bears.' Maybe there was a correlation?

The rest of the night was uneventful as the couple slept undisturbed in each other's arms. Asbjorn was only awoken by the occasional kicking of his yet to be born child as it slept suspended in its mother's womb and the infrequent quiet growls of their faithful sled dog as he guarded them.

The following morning, they could hear shouts as their fellow kinsmen and women hurried about, preparing the bear's carcass. First, they skinned the large animal and then they ensured the extraction of the liver before the feast to follow. This they learned from experience as polar bear's have a very high accumulation of vitamin A in their fatty tissue, specifically their liver. Making it toxic to humans and responsible for an array of egregious symptoms, mainly the skin peeling off of your entire body.

Both Uki and Asbjorn returned to their tent so as not to be underfoot while their kin went about planning for the evening's festivities. Traditions needed to be followed and spirits honoured. After all, a child lost its life the night before.

Tapeesa, the young girl's mother, wanted to at least be able to braid her daughter's hair as tradition dictated before placing the body out on the tundra to be stacked with cairns.

However, because of the condition of the corpse, her kinsmen encouraged her to only follow the procession. The distraught woman drew no solace from her husband or the small crowd that gathered.

She placed a customary white rock on the top of the grave. She hoped by doing so, she would protect her daughter from roaming spirits. The absence of her huntress or her man did not surprise Tapeesa.

Only vengeance would appease her now and hopefully let her finally close her eyes in dreamless sleep. The elders had other plans for all involved. Their version of healing would see Tapeesa taking over the midwifery duties for

Uki's impending birth and being given the honourable position of *Sanaji*, name-giver to the child.

The latter being the most important because of naming the baby. They believed the newborn would take the soul or spirit of the deceased family or community member and assume the relationships of their namesake through the name. In this way, Tapeesa's daughter would live on.

Uki accepted the elder's wishes and was more than happy to give the lifelong role to her fellow kinswoman, a position of great esteem. Although it was a little difficult explaining to Asbjorn a relative stranger such as Tapeesa would now be a big part of their child's life.

As the day wore on, Uki kept to herself and rested to prepare for the long night ahead. She wasn't sure if she should approach Tapeesa before the feast, because there was nothing she could do or say to take away the woman's heartache. Although lying around fretting would accomplish nothing, either.

Just as Uki was about to leave her tent in search of Tapeesa, the flap door flew open and there was Asbjorn carrying a large bundle of freshly skinned polar bear hide in his arms. She was taken aback because she could plainly see someone had not cleaned off all the blood from the hide, something which never bothered her until now.

"Asbjorn, what do you think you are doing by bringing that bloody hide in here?" spoken rather abruptly.

"I'm sorry if I startled you, Heima. But the elders thought it only fitting our child should have it as a tribute to the poor little slain girl. Should I have declined their wishes?"

Uki wasn't sure how she felt about this information, but believed it was only right to share the news with her unborn child's new midwife.

"I want you to turn around this instant and go right back out that door. You need to enlist the help of a few of our fellow kinswomen in order to finish washing the hide properly. I want the animal's beautiful white fur to be the only thing our people see when first laying eyes on the massive blanket, and Asbjorn, it must be done posthaste in time for tonight's presentation."

As per usual, he rarely second-guessed his woman, and he could tell by the look in her eyes she was up to something. Asbjorn smiled to himself as he watched Uki waddle down the path leading to the center of the camp. Without being cognitive of his own actions, he wiped an errant tear from his eye…one of happiness.

Tapeesa was quite easy to locate, as her heart-wrenching lamentations could be heard from across the camp. Followed shortly thereafter by the unexpected manifestation of maternal aggression in Uki, urging her to hurry along so she could comfort the young woman in her time of need. Stopping only long enough to turn back the flap entrance to the woman's dimly lit tent, Uki ventured forth, but the reception she received was mystifying, to say the very least. Tapeesa seemed downright angered by Uki's perceived invasion of her privacy. She was all by herself.

Evidently, her husband had more pressing matters to attend to, and where were her friends? Uki didn't want to think ill of the couple, but at moments like this, kinship was the most important resource. She was not about to leave the distraught woman alone. At one time in her life, she might have backed away owing to the estrangement some of her fellow kinswomen subjected her to as early as puberty. But as a young child, Uki was just like every other little girl in need of a cuddle, nose wipe, laugh or stern talking to.

Albeit awkward and probably not the best time to get to know each other, Uki began with, "Words cannot express how sorry I am for your loss. If only help had gotten to her sooner, I blame the weather, I blame myself…"

Before the words had even finished falling from Uki's lips, Tapeesa immediately stopped crying, sat upright and slowly turned towards her with a look of acrimony. Uki didn't know what to do. She had no choice but to lower her eyes and endure the woman's vilification.

"How dare you show your face in my home? My daughter would be alive if you hadn't stopped me and ordered me back to camp?" spit flew from her lips as she screamed at Uki. Grasping at straws, her tirade took another direction… "You didn't have the decency to attend my baby's burial. You're nothing but a stray! You and that outsider are no brethren of mine."

No matter how absurd or misplaced the accusations, Uki held fast, waiting for the woman to finish saying her peace. But the moment she raised her fists in anger, all bets were off because now her child was in danger.

Tapeesa launched herself at Uki as she stood in the doorway. But thankfully the huntress, although very pregnant, was still the more experienced adversary. She quickly stepped to the side and punched the charging woman in the ear, just shy of the jawline. Letting out a howl of pain, the midwife dropped to the ground. Uki was not about to continue the fight. She came here for a reason and Tapeesa needed to hear it.

Tapeesa wailed while holding her ear and acted as if someone attacked her unprovoked. She realized no one was coming to her aid and Uki was still blocking the entrance. She tried to stand, but needed help to make it back to her bed. Once there, she begrudgingly gave Uki the floor and waited to hear what the huntress had come there for.

"Again, I am sorry for your loss. I tried to save her. I even put my unborn child's life in danger to do so. This hostility has got to stop. The elders have spoken, and you are to be my midwife. My child's life will be in honour of your loss. I can give you no more."

How could this be? Tapeesa broke into fresh tears. She was no midwife, and she certainly had no plans of attaching herself to this woman's baby. She must plead her case with the elders. Uki stood patiently as she watched the younger woman's reaction. It was one of internal turmoil and not one of joy.

"How could you expect this of me? After all, my child is hardly cold in her grave. Do you think swapping spirits will bring me comfort?"

Tapeesa wanted to tell the huntress what she thought of her, but her husband returned to their tent the very moment she opened her mouth and silenced her.

Uki sensed a chill in the air from him as well, although she was not sure exactly who he directed it at. Yet he was cordial as she left. Uki didn't know what to do now. She couldn't have an unstable person charged with the care and development of her baby.

It is imperative she speak to the elders and inform them of her trepidations.

Thankfully, it was common knowledge the community as a whole handled the upbringing of a child. Her kinsmen and women would most certainly not stand back and let anything happen to her baby, but doubt was a hard seed to be unsown.

11

UKI

After a long discussion with the elders, they assured Uki and Asbjorn that Tapeesa would pose no danger to their unborn child.

The distraught mother was very young, and she needed the distraction of midwifery to help her with her loss. She would come to see everything happened for a reason and hopefully bear another child. But until that time, they pledged their protection to the forthcoming and tiniest member of their community.

Later that evening, as they made their way back to the main tent, Uki and Asbjorn detected no hostility from the rest of their adopted people. The mood was jovial, considering what happened less than 24 hours earlier. Upon entering the big tent, they saw four seats of honour remained vacant at the front of the meeting space, close to the warmth of the fire and across from the elders.

They waited for a moment, hanging back, to be escorted upfront, and breathed a sigh of relief when Tapeesa and her husband arrived.

Uki was happy to see several women stopped the

mourning mother, in order to show their affection before she and her husband took their places. Now that everyone took their seats, a hush fell over the room, people whispered and looked around, as if expecting something significant to occur.

Aama stood and addressed the assembly, "I want to thank each and everyone of you for the support you have shown during these grievous times. Not to mention, our esteemed hunters showed bravery and skill by putting an end to the animal's miserable life before it harmed or killed anyone else. But out of darkness comes great joy because a new life will join us soon."

As she was speaking, a small group of women quietly entered, carrying the now pristine polar bear blanket and placed it before Tapeesa's feet. The young mother lost all the colour in her cheeks as she stared at the hide as if awaiting the rationale for its presence. Aama came to her aid and asked her to stand.

Both women bent down and lifted the heavy hide. As they did so, Uki noticed they were exchanging words under their breaths. Without further ado, they carried their burden the remaining few feet to where Uki was seated and presented her with the beautiful hide. All she could think about was to thank the spirits that it didn't still have its horribly disfigured head attached.

Uki graciously accepted the gift, hugged Tapeesa and thanked her. Although the moment she touched the younger woman, she sensed this was all a show for the benefit of the elders. She took this moment to recognize the woman's loss and express her sorrow for not being able to save the little girl.

"Tapeesa, sister…I can't imagine what you are going through. I know words will never be enough to ease the pain and suffering you have endured since the death of your beloved daughter. But believe me when I say my heart is breaking for you and I wish I could have only gotten to her sooner."

The crowd easily voiced their opinions, and it seemed unanimous that they all felt the same. No one blamed Uki.

With a somewhat more confident smile painted on her face, Uki slowly turned back towards Tapeesa and grasped the woman's hands. "Thank you for letting us honour the spirit of your daughter by becoming an integral part of our immediate family, both as midwife and teacher to our child."

She reassured all those in attendance she would give Tapeesa the task of naming the child as soon as it was born. If it was a girl, Uki promised she would be more than happy to name her after the fallen child. In response to her words, everyone seemed overjoyed by the news, especially the fact there would be a happy ending

The crowd became louder as more of their kinswomen brought out trays of cooked meat and rudimentary vegetables. Whereas Uki herself couldn't wait for the festivities to be over with and to speak to Asbjorn away from prying ears, but she needed to show a united front before her community.

As they walked back to their tent with Asbjorn carrying the enormous hide, Uki gasped as she experienced her first contraction. Right away, Asbjorn wanted to drop everything and carry her back to the safety of the main tent. It was too soon, and he wasn't prepared to watch the miracle of birth.

Thankfully, Uki could calm his worried mind. "Everything is fine, my love. I'm just tired, that's all. It's been a very long day. For all we know, the brief stab of pain I experienced had more to do with all the rich meat we consumed than the baby. Trust me, I would tell you if there was something truly wrong."

THE FOLLOWING MORNING, ASBJORN DID NOT WANT TO accompany his fellow hunters, especially since they would be away for several days.

As luck would have it, they sighted a large herd of caribou and they needed him. Most of the men knew his trepidations and promised him first choice of the hides, something thick he could make into a *qaat*, mattress, or birthing bed for Uki since late in the season they tended to be rather scraggly.

"Uki, I must trust my gut. I don't know what I would do if anything happened to you or our baby. Surely, the other hunters are able-bodied enough to harvest a herd of caribou on their own? And wasn't there something bothering you about last night's feast you so desperately wanted to discuss with me?"

Sensing Asbjorn's desperation and the certainty he wouldn't leave her side until she divulged what transpired, she opened up.

"First, last night's contractions were only a false alarm. Amka warned me about them months ago. They weren't all that bad. It just took me by surprise. I don't need or want you getting in the way while I ready our home for the new arrival. We should still have plenty of time before I give birth to him or her. If I go by the last full moon and my calculations are right. And regarding what I wanted to talk to you about, it wasn't all that urgent. I too have a little voice in my head and it's telling me to not trust our midwife, Tapeesa. She might be in mourning, but she is looking for someone to blame all of her woes on."

As the community watched the hunting party head out in search of the late caribou, there was a feeling of eagerness in the air. It was always good to have plenty of varied meat because soon they would have to rely primarily on seal.

Disappearing over the horizon, an unexplainable feeling of apprehension washed over Uki and, try as she might, she could not shake it. Was it a premonition or simply the fears of a pregnant woman?

She heard so many stories. Any way you looked at it, it was common knowledge she and her dogs brought in the largest percentage of seal meat. But she was working hard to train the young ones. And once winter fully set in, depending on how the delivery went, she hoped to not be homebound for too long.

She was excited about giving birth to a child that was equal parts herself and Asbjorn, but deep down Uki prayed it would be a boy. That way it would never have to answer to anyone. Although it would probably be born looking like an outsider weighed heavily on her mind.

She had little time to dwell on things that were out of her control while her man was away. Not to mention, she also filled her thoughts with making preparations for her people's final relocation before winter arrived.

The plan was to move camp as soon as the hunters returned, so they would have plenty of time to make the trek safely and be able to settle in with sufficient stores. Usually they would already be on their way, but because of the lack of game, the unexpected windfall of caribou would ensure no one went hungry.

As the days blended into each other, Uki worried something went horribly wrong. However, every time she voiced her concerns, her fellow kinswomen scolded her for her pessimism. After all, the hunting party was quite large and experienced.

Surely, they had abundant kills, so it only seemed reasonable for them to extend their time away in order to ready the carcasses for all intended uses.

Uki had nightmares involving Asbjorn, being injured and trying to crawl his way back to her and their unborn child. Although her visions never made it clear what caused his wounds. She sought the guidance of one of the group's elders, who had a reputation for being gifted with second sight.

To her disappointment, the man would only assure her she would reunite with Asbjorn, providing no details of when and where it would happen. When the days turned into actual weeks, so too did her fellow kinsmen panic.

The waiting was intolerable in her condition, especially since she sensed her baby inside was ready to come out. This was not how she dreamed of her and Asbjorn welcoming their first child into the world and, sadly, Tapeesa never became the rock she needed.

12

UKI

THE SOUND OF YELLING AND DOGS BARKING AWOKE UKI IN the middle of the night. She bolted upright in bed and immediately donned her boots and threw a warm blanket around her shoulders.

The moment she attempted to exit her tent, she was just about bowled over by several kinsmen as they appeared to be rushing about in the dark haphazardly, shouting orders. When she stopped to listen, she realized the hunting party indeed returned, or at least some of them.

She needed to find Asbjorn.

Trudging onward through the camp on her way to the main tent, Uki stopped anyone who made eye contact long enough to acknowledge her inquiries into the whereabouts of her husband.

When asked if they saw Asbjorn among the returning hunters, they all shook their heads in an unequivocal "no". If not for the fact she was heavy with child and emotional, she might have been able to cope with the unsubstantiated bad news.

Fearing the absolute worst, she cried uncontrollably. She needed to know where Asbjorn was this very minute. He promised to be there for her, for them! Excruciating pain coursed through her lower back and she sensed the urge to defecate. Alas, her tears soon evolved into guttural sobs. Taking in great gulps of air as her body writhed in need of oxygen, then the unimaginable happened. Her water suddenly broke as she went into labour.

No one seemed to notice as she fell to her knees disorientated and struggling to figure out just where the closest refuge might be. As she crawled her way towards the main tent, in the reduced visibility of the night, Uki screamed Asbjorn's name until she lost all consciousness.

Poor Uki. She had no idea how long she was unconscious for, but when she came to, Tapeesa's face was hovering above her and the contractions mysteriously stopped. Although the moment she tried to raise her head to get a better look at her surroundings, the midwife pushed a crude cup to her lips and ordered her to drink.

The smell alone was enough to induce vomiting and when she tried to press her lips together to fend off Tapeesa's assault, the woman grabbed a fistful of her hair and forcibly tilted her head back. Uki's mouth opened as she attempted to express her anger. This provided the midwife with the opportunity she sought. The viscid liquid clung to her lips and mouth, tasting as she had first surmised, dreadful and would not go down without a fight. Digging way down deep into whatever reserve she still possessed, Uki struggled to turn over and spit the runny concoction out onto the floor but Tapeesa was quicker, grabbing her by the shoulders and giving her one last forceful shake before pushing her back down onto the bed.

Utterly exhausted and suffering from the onset of

shock, Uki did not know if the midwife was trying to help or poison her. All she knew was she must find Asbjorn.

Uki wailed in utter despair. "You don't understand, Asbjorn promised me he would be back in time for the birth of our child! Something terrible must have happened. We have to find him now!"

"Stop your foolishness, woman! You are in no condition to go running after that man, or give birth, for that matter. If you don't want me to split you open and pull the child out of your belly this instant, then you had better drink up." Tapeesa did not hide the malicious smile that crept across her face as soon as she finished spewing her rhetoric.

Heated words were indeed exchanged, but Tapeesa coerced Uki into drinking the mysterious liquid, maintaining it was for her own good and she must sleep in order to regain her strength, if she intended to give birth in the traditional way. Although before Uki would willingly swallow, she made Tapeesa promise to find Asbjorn and escort or physically help him back to the makeshift birthing tent.

Uki recognized she was in no condition to carry out that feat on her own. Even if she was, tradition dictated all new mothers be subjected to a period of isolation after giving birth, contingent upon the sex of their child. So she was going nowhere.

Again, she hoped the baby would be a boy as the length of time was always shorter for males. Therefore, the community's shaman would be able to baptize the child sooner, usually within 8 days, as was customary, in order to provide it with a protective spirit.

Uki couldn't help but grasp the consequences of postponing their departure. The journey north was likely to become more grueling with each passing day, and transporting a newborn or injured hunters would inevitably endanger the community. Blessed sleep finally took her, but when she awoke hours later, it was to an empty birthing tent. No kinswoman saw fit to keep vigil or provide comfort to their sister.

An unreasoning terror overcame Uki. Just how long had she been asleep? She tried to once again sit upright in bed and instantly perceived a pain so intense it made her feel as if the baby was trying to tear itself free from her womb.

In her panic, she screamed at the top of her lungs, hoping someone would hear and come to her aid. Thankfully, her cries did not go unanswered for long. As soon as the tent flap was thrown back, Aama's kind face came into view, filling Uki with hope. Her warm feelings instantly dashed when she saw her old friend's face filled with abject horror. The elder began yelling for help and that's when she saw it. She was hemorrhaging in her sedated state and the dirt floor beneath her was literally now a mirrored pool of blood.

Uki thought she was going to pass out again, but Aama did not let her. "Girl, you need to roll over onto your knees. Your fellow kinswomen will help you. Let them! Hold onto my hands to steady yourself. Now bear down and scream with all your ferocity. The child must come out now!"

The birthing that followed was far from a traditionally silent one. A blur of activity as women came and went, but the one thing Uki would never forgive or forget was her midwife was nowhere in sight. Did Tapeesa even go to find Asbjorn, and how long was she left to bleed out on the bed?

Later at daybreak, completely spent and still in tremendous pain, Uki clasped her newborn daughter and cried. She cried for her man and their baby girl, as well as their unknown futures. As she looked around, she was relieved to see several of her fellow kinswomen stayed with her throughout the night, but oddly, there was still no sign of Tapeesa.

Uki couldn't help but smile as she gazed upon her baby. It warmed her heart to see she looked so much like her father. Sunlight ripped away the euphoria of her woolgathering as it shone through an opening in the tent. This happened because the flap of the tent was brusquely thrown back.

Tapeesa returned, looking self-assured, and immediately exerted her authority as midwife and sanaji, to anyone within the sound of her grating voice. Shouting orders to the women in attendance and demanding they shift their attention to the needs of the returned and injured hunters, after all, Uki wasn't the first woman to have ever given birth.

Upon hearing this, Uki voiced her concerns, "Tapeesa…has there been any news regarding Asbjorn's whereabouts? Has anyone seen him? Please tell me my husband is still alive! Was he injured on the hunt? What happened? Why won't you answer me?"

At first Tapeesa didn't seem to want to respond to her questions, or even make eye contact for that matter. Uki couldn't tell if she was trying to protect her feelings or being cruel.

"He didn't come back with the others," she finally said in an almost matter-of-factly manner and began busying herself.

Overwrought with emotion and not knowing where to turn, "I must talk to the men immediately. What if he's lying injured somewhere? We have to find him!" she hysterically bawled.

"Your job is to look after this baby and the needs of

our people…you won't be any good to us running after that Norseman!"

Uki couldn't believe her midwife's apathetic attitude, nor the words coming out of her mouth. "Asbjorn is not expendable! He has more than earned his place in our community and his life is as important as the next man!"

Rolling over, she placed her daughter in the middle of the bed, then began inching her bottom to the edge before gradually letting her legs drop to stand. Blackness.

Later, when she regained consciousness, Uki was on the cold dirt floor in a heap and her baby was now in the arms of that terrible woman. Tapeesa seemed fascinated by the child as she cooed and fussed about. Her daughter was safe for now.

Again Uki attempted to stand, this time using the bed as leverage, but found herself right back where she started. Tapeesa, having surreptitiously watched the events unfold from across the room, averted her eyes back to the baby as if she had not witnessed the fall.

Although not one for charades, especially when it came to the huntress's feelings, the midwife no longer held her tongue. Gazing up from the infant, she turned towards Uki, making direct eye contact before muttering, "Stupid woman!"

After the blatantly goading comment but before Uki made another attempt at gaining her footing, several young kinswomen she was unfamiliar with entered the birthing tent in a flurry of chatter. They were all there to see the new baby. Their arrival caught Uki by surprise at first, but she felt relieved, hoping at least a few of them saw her midwife's deplorable behaviour because anything less would be hearsay.

Immediately, silence prevailed as the women came to her aid and helped Uki back onto the bed. The look on their faces was not one of indignation, but one of fright, as their eyes darted about the room. Once she felt relatively comfortable, Uki banished the elephant in the room from her thoughts. What good would it do since she was currently at the mercy of her caregiver?

She addressed the gaggle of young women surrounding her. "Sisters, thank you for your kindness. I would have never made it back onto the bed without your help. Would one of you be so kind as to fetch Aama for me?" Uki tried to maintain a humble posture while speaking because she needed to convey to these women she posed no threat. All the while, struggling to not make eye contact with Tapeesa whatsoever.

The youngest of the group stepped forward and offered to do her bidding, but not before they all shared some sort of secret look. Uki saw the power Tapeesa wielded over these girls. Asking for anything in her presence would most likely depend upon the midwife's whims. Peering straight at her daughter, she motioned with open arms and outstretched hands for the benefit of all in attendance, for the child to be returned to her. No one made a move.

Her baby chose that very moment to make a fuss and Uki was quick to take advantage of the opportunity presenting itself by opening her garment and revealing her swollen breasts. The child's needs trumped that of the midwife's and her baby daughter was placed on her stomach. The natural act of nursing instantly calmed the huntress, as opposed to letting her stew further over what previously transpired.

Uki's entire world indeed became smaller overnight, now centering predominantly on the well-being of the child she cradled lovingly in her arms.

Whilst gazing upon her sleeping infant's face, she soon

lost track of all time and space, unaware of her surroundings until the moment Aama entered the empty birthing tent. At first Uki sensed overjoyed to see her old friend, someone who could support her, since she was in no condition to do so.

"Aama, mother…it warms my heart to see you. Finally, a voice of reason! I need to confirm Asbjorn's whereabouts. Was he injured? And if so, have they brought him in yet, so they can attend to his wounds? Honestly, I feel like I've been trapped inside this birthing tent for days. I have heard nothing about what transpired on the hunting trip. Were they attacked by another group of hunters vying for the same herd? Why am I being kept in the dark?"

"Daughter, no one is keeping anything from you. You know childbirth and care are the most important responsibilities you will ever undertake as a woman. Your midwife was only trying to help, and apparently you have baulked every step of the way. I know you are also our huntress, but please set that aside for the time being and focus your energy on the well-being of your little girl. I do not know where your husband is right now, but I promise you I will get to the bottom of this."

By the end of their talk, Uki's worries were no less allayed, and she was having doubts as to where the elder's loyalties lie, for Tapeesa clearly intercepted her visit.

After many tears were shed, Aama agreed to question several of the hunters herself, reiterating it was still against tradition that Uki have male visitors. She wanted to scream in frustration because the more time they wasted, the worse Asbjorn's chances were of returning to her in one piece. She needed to come up with a plan.

It did not take long for Aama to return with the news. Evidently, the hunting party indeed tracked down a large herd of caribou, but shortly after the cull, a fierce group of Greenlandic Inuit set upon them.

Apparently, theirs was not the only community feeling the effects of the current shortage of game in the region. Then the story became somewhat convoluted with contradicting details being voiced between the surviving men.

Some say Asbjorn fought bravely alongside his adopted people, while others claimed he deserted them at the first signs of a conflict. The only thing they agreed on was no one saw him die. The elders held an impromptu meeting to discuss their next move, and they agreed a small party of their kinsmen would backtrack the hunter's course.

Once they accomplished that, they would need to dispose of their fallen kins' bodies properly in a manner befitting their end and prepare their people for the impending migration north.

Uki could not believe her ears: Asbjorn was no coward. She must accompany their men to the site of the battle… she needed to see it with her own two eyes.

13

UKI

No one wanted her to come along, not even kinsmen she knew as boys and trained as hunters. In the end, she agreed to follow at a distance but, her dog sled was much smaller and nimbler than the others.

She had the ability to surpass them and reach the site earlier. It was quite easy to find since all parties involved had left trails of animal debris for miles, along with the occasional mortally wounded hunter. Not to mention the large flocks of carrion birds were seen circling overhead for quite some distance.

Uki couldn't help but sob as she came upon the bloodied bodies of her fallen brethren. Without considering her current condition, she dragged the corpses towards her sled so she would give them a proper burial. She wasn't about to leave them out in the open for scavengers to continue picking their bones clean. Uki was focused on what she was doing she never heard the sounds of her fellow hunters' arrival, but they saw her and what she was trying to accomplish single-handedly.

No matter the bygone ill feelings regarding her

previous pursuits or choices, they couldn't help but respect her and all she had done for her adopted people.

Everyone knew it was against the rules to communicate with Uki, as she gave birth recently, but they couldn't let her go on as she was. Again, the youngest was the first to approach.

At first he called her name as he slowly advanced, not wanting to startle her. When she didn't seem to hear, he tapped her on the shoulder. The two exchanged knowing glances before he gently took their fallen kinsman's wrists out of her hands and dragged the body towards the pile she already started.

In no time at all, the men loaded their larger sleds with the dead and had unceremoniously departed for open water, leaving Uki surrounded by the inescapable horror of what transpired. As she stood there watching them leave, dissociated from her feelings…numb, a brilliant thought revealed itself. Asbjorn used her sled frequently. Therefore, his scent must be on the blankets in her cargo bed.

She unharnessed Amka and led him back towards the sled. At first, he didn't seem to understand…Uki held her tears back but sensed herself teeter at the sheer frustration of trying to get her point across. Then suddenly, her dog began his usual routine of scenting prey, but this time it would be one of his masters he would be hunting.

The dog seemed to grasp the urgency of the situation as he sniffed around the battle site, making many whimpering noises. Finally, he let out an almost human, grief-stricken howl and tore off in the exact opposite direction her fellow hunters had gone, leaving Uki to scramble with the sled's harnesses and straps.

She removed Amka's tugline from the central gangline and repositioned the dogs so two would now lead. Thankfully, the team still seemed to be of one mind as its remaining members became impatient to narrow the distance between each other. Uki hopped onto the foot boards of her sled to avoid being left behind.

After several false stops and starts, she chanced upon a well-beaten path obscured by large pools of frost encrusted blood. Following her instincts, as well as the dwindling trail of carnage, she was rewarded. For in its wake was the undeniable proof that many a sled indeed passed by on this route.

While stopping to study her vast surroundings, Uki inadvertently caught sight of what appeared to be more tracks or drag marks in the snow, veering away from the main trail. If not for the fortuitous placement of the sun in the sky overhead at that precise moment, casting shadows, she would have missed the indentations altogether.

Although the larger path most certainly substantiated the Greenlander's retreat, who or what was responsible for the smaller less obvious trail?

Upon closer inspection, Uki was able to ascertain traces of blood splatter amongst the depressions in the snow, but she needed to hurry, lest they lose the trail. Making her way through the deepening snow, she became oblivious to her surroundings while straining to look for further clues. Only to berate herself later for wasting valuable time, as her instinctive behaviour resulted in her having to backtrack, to verify she missed nothing of importance on the first go-round.

Where was the body. Could Asbjorn still be alive?

She needed to find him. After all, he would never have given up the search if roles were reversed. With renewed vigour, she urged the dog team onward with shouts of encouragement and raw nerve. Though, dusk was on the horizon and her breasts became painful and swollen with milk, but returning to camp was not an option.

Without closure, there would be no peace. Amka began barking and pouncing repeatedly on something in the distance. To Uki, it resembled a small mound of snow, and then her heart sank as she approached. Jumping off the sled, she cradled her stomach with both hands and ran the remaining short distance to the mound.

She dropped to her knees and started frantically brushing a layer of fresh snow off the concealed form, which turned out to be her beloved.

The cry which escaped her lips caused her sled dogs to join in mournful unison. Uki tried to find a pulse but, Asbjorn's skin was already cold to the touch but not yet discoloured.

She had to act.

Leaning forward over his prone body, she attempted to breathe life back into his mouth, realizing she was too late and any further efforts to resuscitate him would be futile.

Refocusing her energies, she struggled to turn him the rest of the way over to see the extent of his wounds. She needed to know exactly how her Norseman died and to her horror, the arrows protruding from his back told the story. She couldn't help but recognize the workmanship because she herself carried them in her quiver.

Asbjorn died at the hands of their own people. Surely, someone stood to defend him and, more importantly, were they still alive to stand witness to this flagrant betrayal?

Uki knew she couldn't return to camp and start yelling accusations. She would need to be smarter. The guilty must pay.

As she looked down at her beautiful man, the urge to kiss him one last time overcame her. Running the tips of her fingers across his eyelids to close them and block the memory of their milky appearance, she pressed her lips firmly to his and whispered, "Your spirit will always be with me, my love."

Uki quickly reattached her lead dog to the team and summoned up what little remaining strength she had left to maneuver Asbjorn's now rigid body onto her sled and secure it. Once she achieved that, she attempted to stay focused and not allow herself to be overwhelmed, both physically and mentally.

Only the spirits knew what lay ahead. Now choosing another route back to camp became the next order of business, one long enough to afford her some clarity in making the right decisions regarding her future and of her child's. And one which would also allow her sufficient time to commend Asbjorn's body to the sea, but not before removing the arrows as evidence and a lock of his beautiful flaxen hair.

LATER THAT NIGHT, WHEN DARKNESS BLANKETED THE frozen landscape, Uki released what she believed were the last of her tears.

She hurried her team towards the now strangely portentous lights of the camp. They always provided a warm and inviting atmosphere, but everything shifted as her earlier concerns became reality.

As Uki neared the entrance to the camp, she saw her dear friend, Aama, waiting with a torch in hand, accompanied by several fellow kinsmen and women. The others most likely waited with the elder to ensure her safety, but it warmed Uki's heart to know she could still place her trust in at least one person. As she reined in her sled dogs just shy of the small group, Aama rushed to her side and threw her arms around Uki in a flourish of motherly concern and emotional tears.

The elder's uncharacteristic display of affection only worsened the situation. Thus striking pure terror in the huntress, since the two women always shared a respectful relationship with almost no physical contact.

"Where is my daughter? Please tell me she is alive!" Uki sobbed the instant she dared to voice her inner thoughts and fought to untangle herself from the woman's embrace.

"Yes, she is fine," Aama nodded in agreement, but would not let her go.

"Where are the hunters? Surely they made it back to camp before me?" Uki glanced around frantically for any evidence of their return, only to have Aama once again nod her head and pat Uki's arm reassuringly as if her mental state were in question.

Taking a deep breath before continuing, Uki attempted to unburden her soul. "I found him. I found Asbjorn, but I was too late. I paid tribute to his spirit by placing his body into the sea, utilizing the teachings you gave me. I tried to do everything I was supposed to do, even putting a piece of ice into his mouth so he would not be thirsty on his journey…" when she thought she could cry no more, her tears flowed anew and the deluge drowned out her words.

Again, the elder embraced Uki and rocked her slowly back and forth like you would a child. When she showed signs of regaining her composure, only then did Aama divulge the real reason behind her puzzling behaviour.

Tapeesa gave everyone the impression the new mother's emotional well-being was in question and that she showed signs of being self-destructive. To which Uki denied the woman's claims as being preposterous, but she was too exhausted and in no mood to argue the point any further. She would choose the time and place, although right now she wanted time alone with her daughter to mourn.

Not surprisingly, someone informed her that her daughter was under the care of her midwife and she would be found living with the woman's family. It took all her willpower to thank everyone for their unfounded concerns, retrieve her belongings from her sled and walk, not run, to Tapeesa's tent.

While making her way across the camp, she tried to calm herself by taking deep breaths. After all, she didn't want to frighten her child by her more than obvious overwrought state of mind. Once outside the midwife's tent, she called out to announce her arrival before attempting to enter, but someone silenced her because the baby had only just fallen asleep.

Uki felt utterly floored by the anger welling up in Tapeesa's voice, and the look of undisguised abhorrence on her face when she exited the tent. Although she wasn't sure if it was because she awoke the child or she simply returned in one piece.

"You're an unfit mother!" she then blurted out. "How could you have abandoned your daughter so soon after giving birth, to go running after that…man? Children are truly a gift and you are undeserving!"

An awkward pause followed, leaving Uki reeling from the woman's unwarranted outburst. After all, her intentions surely were common knowledge when she set out early that morning. With that said, Tapeesa wasn't through with her just yet.

"I'll have you know I went above and beyond my duties as a midwife to care for her in your absence. I expect…no, demand you pay due respects!"

"Please, I don't want to quarrel with you. I would've

never left my baby if I didn't think she was in more than capable hands. I am indebted to you, but I need to be alone with my daughter right now."

Uki once again struggled to hold back a torrent of tears. "I was too late…Asbjorn is dead. Still, his spirit's journey weighs heavily on my mind. I can only hope his soul has found its way to the warm underworld or he is enjoying a glorious afterlife in Valhalla with his own gods."

Uki was spent, and no longer cared to wait for a reply before entering the woman's tent to collect her sleeping child. The midwife let her pass but continued with her verbal assault at a relatively safe distance, demanding she leave the little girl right where she was.

Sleeping or not, their combined raised voices alerted the infant that something was amiss, prompting her to let loose with an ear-piercing wail. Tapeesa feigned concern and maneuvered her way to the child's bedside, acting as if she needed protection from her mother, of all people.

She wanted to pick a fight, but Uki held back until she knew the real reason behind the woman's antagonism. Letting her have her way tonight might be in Uki's best interest.

Maybe a good night's sleep in her bed would do her a world of good by restoring her strength and sanity. As far as Uki was concerned, there was no need to return to the birthing tent.

She was now a widow.

Uki took her leave, somewhat defeated, and made her way across the camp to her own tent. Only sad reminders of the brief life she and Asbjorn shared met her. A life so promising, but was neither here nor there now. She needed sleep.

As she changed into her sleeping garment, she was alarmed by the amount of blood loss she incurred during her rather strenuous day. Even her faithful dog whimpered at the sight and would not leave her side. There was still a bucket of water in her tent, albeit cold to wash up with and dried meat to sustain her.

Sleep did not come easily, even though she was exhausted. Vivid dreams of Asbjorn's last moments, not to mention the fact her breasts were still swollen and very tender.

THE FOLLOWING MORNING, IT WAS AAMA WHO CAME TO her tent to check in on her.

However, she seemed rather agitated because of Uki's abandonment of protocol by not returning to the isolation of the birthing tent. She also reminded her the shaman had a maximum of eight days to perform his ritual to protect the child's soul. If anything should happen to her now, they would lose her. Uki took this as a warning something might be wrong with her daughter, and glanced around for something to throw on, but unfortunately the closest item at hand was the damn polar bear hide.

After a little digging she found what she was searching for, her caribou *amauti*. A parka with a built-in baby pouch below the hood and hide pants. She might not be ready to take on the world, but certainly this camp.

"Where do you think you're going? Haven't you heard a single word I've said? Your midwife is quite competent in looking after your daughter's needs until you are fit enough to take over your duties, but first you have obligations to her child's spirit."

Aama seemed shocked by Uki's blatant dismissal as she turned her back on the elder mid-sentence and threw open the flap to her tent.

As she greeted the beautiful rays of sunshine, it immediately blinded her, and with a purpose in her stride, she headed off toward Tapeesa's tent. This time she didn't hesitate before entering, and what she saw stopped her in her tracks.

There was her midwife attempting to coerce her daughter into feeding from another woman's breast and Tapeesa's forcefulness distressed the child. Uki didn't say a word. She pushed past the wet nurse and gently as possible, removed her daughter from the midwife's clutches. She placed her into the pouch of her parka and secured the carrying strap to keep her daughter from falling out the bottom.

With the infant now snug against her back, Uki intuitively knew her baby girl sensed their bond because the child calmed down and Uki herself lactated.

14

UKI

Uki hurried back to her tent and, upon entering, was startled to find Aama never left but was waiting her return to continue their earlier conversation.

"I'm truly sorry if I came across as rather patronizing when we spoke earlier. I can only imagine what you are going through right now. When you said you found Asbjorn's body, were your questions answered?"

Once more, Aama was forced to let go of her line of questioning as Uki concentrated on her daughter while trying to reposition the baby inside her parka to breastfeed. Something all new mothers needed to learn and Uki did not have the luxury of time or help.

As with every year, the impending relocation resulted in a general upheaval within the camp, placing added stress on its members as everyone hurried to accomplish their own tasks before their community merged with others. As an elder, it was Aama's obligation to assess Uki's current state of mental health.

After all, Uki was their group's huntress for quite some time now and was responsible for much of their food supply. They needed to know if she could still fulfill her duties.

Rumours were based on some truth, although Uki had her fair share of misfortune, with the near tragic birth of her first child and the subsequent death of her husband. Uki and Aama sat quietly, watching the little baby drink from her mother's breast. Strangely, Uki sensed herself grow stronger with every pull and gave thanks.

Aama's chief concern was always the welfare of the next generation, and today she felt relieved when she saw the look of pure joy on Uki's expression as her child drifted off to sleep.

Although what she didn't see was a young mother holding back her tears as a familiar smile spread across her daughter's tiny face. A smile she saw many times before, on her beloved Asbjorn as he slept.

Aama got up from where she was sitting and approached the two. It wasn't the sound of her movement which drew Uki out of her thoughts. It was the one word she spoke aloud. "Siqiniq." The elder called the child *Siqiniq*, the sun. Uki didn't understand at first, but Aama clarified everything for her.

Tapeesa's name stood for Arctic flower and it was why she called her late daughter the sun because one would not live without the other. No matter how much she disliked the midwife, Uki couldn't begrudge her the name.

Aama helped adjust the sleeping child so Uki could pack up her belongings for the long journey ahead. It would only be a matter of days before their departure, and she still had a lot to do.

Some of her younger kinsmen offered their help with heavier objects, but Uki faced the daunting task of donating Asbjorn's belongings to those in need.

As she went through his clothes and weapons, the

realization dawned on her, she might bequeath something he valued to his murderer. She wanted to throw up. She quickly got her possessions in order, and to her surprise, the family of another hunter who had also fallen on the same day as her beloved gave her the use of a far larger dog sled.

Uki lent her own smaller sled to one of the young men who helped her. With one very important stipulation, he must promise to treat her dogs as his own until their group reached its destination.

Every day with Siqiniq was indeed a blessing, although she still cried herself to sleep at night only to awake each morning with her beautiful baby girl to greet her and give her continued strength. The child truly brought her joy and gave her purpose, but Tapeesa became the burden she would have to bear.

The woman took her duties as midwife, literally, and let them devour her life. She was none the kinder, but she appeared to cherish her time spent with Uki's daughter.

THEY WERE ONLY A COUPLE OF DAYS ON THE TRAIL WHEN the subject of baptism came up again. It wasn't a ritual attended by the entire community. Because of the present circumstances, the elders thought it best to make a celebration of the event for morale sake.

On the day agreed upon, their migration drew to a halt early to set up camp for the large assembly which followed. Uki would have preferred to carry on to their destination since the weather was agreeable of late, but today was exactly eight days since Siqiniq came into the world and the Inuit were nothing if not superstitious.

Their trek, so far, had been slow and steady and quite

uneventful. Most of the remaining hunters involved in the battle were only superficial wounds, while the more seriously injured were being transported via dog sleds.

Uki wanted to interrogate her fellow kinsmen, but resolved to wait until the journey's end. With the miles and miles of endless white terrain still ahead, she had plenty of time to ponder what those questions would be. All afternoon she kept to herself as her kinsmen and women hurried about, making last-minute preparations for the evening's important gathering.

Since the Inuit consider nature their most sacred place, they decided not to erect a tent to house the actual ritual and conduct it outdoors.

She couldn't help but overhear the whispers around camp regarding her child's appearance. Some people thought her light skin might make her unwanted. Uki was appalled to learn the killing of an unwanted child would not be "murder" as long as it was carried out before the naming of the child. If named then killed, the spirits would become angry.

Uki couldn't believe her people condoned these barbaric customs in the past, but when she thought about it, she realized her day-to-day life was based solely on the pursuit of food. Honing her skills and later teaching them to the young. She lived in the periphery of a male dominated world, never having to deal with the inequalities of her gender.

By pure accident, she met Asbjorn, and if it hadn't happened, she would have been content to live her life similar to her friend Alornerk. Or would she?

She would have been sorely mistaken to think things would not have changed if she ceased to be an asset to the group.

Later as she cradled her daughter in their makeshift

tent and fed her, Uki couldn't help but call her faithful dog to her side. Dejected, but thankfully not alone.

With no warning, Tapeesa appeared at her door and in relatively good spirits for a change.

She wanted to escort both mother and daughter to the naming ceremony tonight. As Uki's daughter would be given her *atiq*, soul name, in honour of the little girl who lost her life. She even tried to coerce Uki into letting her carry the child to the rite, saying that, as sanaji, it was her duty.

Deep down, Uki knew the woman had ulterior motives, and this was only a ploy to have all eyes cast upon her as she entered, but Uki squashed the plan. Uki didn't even have to lift a finger because Amka's hackles were instantly up when Tapeesa attempted to lay her hands on the infant.

As they made their way through the camp towards the central bonfire, indeed everyone's eyes were upon them, but for different reasons. For it was common knowledge there was no love lost between the two. The shaman who led the ceremony was brief in duration, although it was overwhelming to know Tapeesa would now govern so much of her daughter's life.

The Inuit believed the essential ingredient of a human being was its name and now Siqiniq would take on the personality, skills and character of the deceased name-giver.

Reincarnation of a sort.

Uki felt terrible about the woman's loss, but no one seemed to take into consideration what she herself lost. Very few kinsmen thus far displayed one ounce of integrity by offering their condolences publicly or privately regarding Asbjorn's death…murder.

As the night wore on, Uki's forbearance reached its limits. She found it necessary to control herself from speaking out and maintained a smile for hours, all to avoid conflict. Until Uki addressed those in attendance with the utmost propriety she was capable of, considering the circumstances.

"My brethren, I would like to thank all of you for your kindness and the faith you placed in me by honouring my daughter, Siqiniq. I would also like to acknowledge our revered shaman for performing tonight's baptism. Thus providing spiritual protection and ensuring the name-soul of our departed daughter has found its way safely back to the world of the living."

Before Uki dragged out her speech any longer, Siqiniq picked the perfect moment to become rather flustered, giving her mother a convenient out. Uki apologized and excused herself from the celebration, voicing her daughter was hungry, before taking her leave.

As she maneuvered through the dark camp on her way back to her tent, Uki is alerted by the sound of breaking twigs as something obviously quite large was making its way through the underbrush skirting their encampment.

Despite the lack of moonlight through the low-lying clouds overhead, Uki could not see well, but her hearing remained unaffected. Immediately, Siqiniq bawled, sensing her mother's agitation, and then she heard a growl, followed by the sound of every dog in the camp's cacophonous barking.

Uki quickly looked around, as she needed to assess her options. If it was indeed a bear, she was defenceless except for the small hunting knife she always carried. Uki felt confident she was at the very least downwind from the animal, but her daughter's cries were almost impossible to muffle.

Suddenly she caught sight of the animal's shape as it cumbersomely stood up on its hind legs and appeared to be sniffing the air. It was a polar bear and an immense one at that.

Uki wanted to run but couldn't risk falling with Siqiniq in her hood. She couldn't yell for help either, because the animal would surely be upon her before any sound even finished leaving her mouth.

Just as full-blown panic was about to consume her, out of nowhere, several hunters came to her rescue, armed with bows and arrows. Although their confrontation was fleeting, they scared the animal off, but not without injuring it first.

Breathing deeply, she tried to calm herself before having words with her fellow hunters. "You saved my life and my daughter's and for that, I am eternally grateful. However, we cannot just allow a wounded animal to walk away, with the possibility of returning later. We need to assemble a hunting party immediately to track the bear and finish what was started. An injured animal is highly unpredictable, and that makes it even more dangerous. I don't have to tell you there are women, children and injured men still in camp, all easy prey for a rogue polar bear."

Uki's petition fell on deaf ears as hunters and kinsmen alike paid her no heed, choosing instead to make their way back to the celebration as if nothing happened. Uki could not believe her brethren's total disregard for the severity of the situation, or did her opinion cease to matter the moment she gave birth?

Disheartened, she apprehensively navigated her way through the darkness back to her tent, but her heart filled with joy upon arrival when she saw her faithful dog.

Amka slept in her tent once again, which allowed her to rest easy, knowing her faithful dog would alert her to anything or anyone venturing too near.

THE FOLLOWING MORNING, UKI WAS UP BEFORE THE SUN'S upper limb even crossed the horizon. She needed to see what size of an animal they were dealing with and to examine the blood trails.

Lo and behold, the polar bear's foot prints confirmed it was indeed a male and a very large "boar" at that. Not to mention all the broken branches and large spots of blood as it retreated through the dense underbrush on its way back to the open ice. One well-placed arrow through the vitals would stop a bear dead, but a hundred poorly placed shots won't kill it.

Armed with more pertinent information, she voiced her concerns to the elders but was yet again declined. In their minds, they believed the group was already spread too thin with their defences, and they thought the evidence showed the animal would likely wander away and die from blood loss.

After a meager breakfast of leftovers, they tore down the camp, reloaded the sleds, and resumed their journey. As the day wore on, Uki found herself once again absorbed in thought, mesmerized by the motion of her large sled as it made its way across a vast sea of white. All the while fixating on the details of the evening past and the hunters who came to her aid.

Was someone watching over her protectively, or were their motives not so pure?

She prayed it was the former, but she couldn't shake her memories of when she was first heavy with child and Asbjorn was called upon to accompany his brethren on many hunting trips.

For in his absence, several of her kinsmen indeed took an unwholesome interest in her alone time.

15

UKI

As the days became weeks, Uki's paranoia flourished. Not only about her fellow kinsmen, there was also evidence a certain polar bear was tracking them. Tapeesa became a permanent fixture, begging to watch over Siqiniq so Uki could have what she claimed was a much needed respite.

It gave her time to get back into shape and start leading hunting parties of her own. The region in which they would eventually make their semi-permanent camp was full of game and sealing was Uki's forte.

The only problem, whenever she returned to camp, prying her daughter away from her midwife was becoming more difficult with each passing day. Uki believed she caught Tapeesa in the act of teaching Siqiniq to address her as 'mother', but when Uki questioned her about it, Tapeesa chuckled and declared all women were her mother.

One evening, while returning from a hunt, a severe storm descended upon the region. It was fast becoming "whiteout" conditions, and Uki couldn't get home soon enough.

As her sled dogs made their usual announcement to the rest of the pack they returned. Uki broke into a cold sweat as the unmistakable roar of a bear answered their call. Even in the reduced visibility, she saw there was no one outside and hopefully all were safe.

She jumped off her sled and unharnessed her dogs. If the bear were to attack, she didn't want them tied down and unable to defend themselves.

Her fellow hunters took her lead and followed suit, except some of their dogs, which were not as well trained, headed off in the direction the bear's last huff came from. The sound of the dogs were also heard by the occupants of the camp and the children awaiting the return of their fathers. No one anticipated what happened next.

Half a dozen small children ran into the storm searching for their parents, followed by scolding mothers and caregivers. They did not know a large wounded bear was roaming between their tents, searching for food and retribution. Uki watched in horror and said a brief prayer of thanks that Siqiniq was too small to venture out on her own.

As the storm whipped up clouds of snow, she lost sight of her fellow kinsmen and women, but when it cleared, everything was obvious. The small pack of sled dogs circled around the back of the rogue bear. Driving it forward straight into the group of women and children unknowingly stepped out into its path.

Time seemed to stand still as everyone involved realized the gravity of the situation. Suddenly, hysterical screaming filled the night air, followed by women and children running in different directions. Uki knew she needed to keep a level head because as soon as the other inhabitants of the tents heard the commotion, they too would come out to investigate. Uki peered at her fellow hunters and motioned for them to dispatch the polar bear pronto. She proceeded to search for the errant children.

Lamentably, two young ones froze in sheer terror and thus became easy prey. Within seconds, the charging bear decapitated one girl and disemboweled the other using its massive paws. The bloody massacre of those they held dear stopped the hunters in their tracks, but they could not afford the hesitation.

Uki started screaming orders to the men and anyone who was in earshot, "The bear must go down, use your bow and arrows!"

Uki prayed abstaining from using spears hopefully resulted in no other casualties. After all, there were women, children and dogs running amuck.

To add to the chaos, the storm chose to increase its fury. Uki ran into frantic parents in search of their children. She understood their dilemma, but had no time to explain the danger and hindrance their very presence was causing.

As she argued with a desperate parent, she heard the growling sound of the gigantic bear, which was too close for comfort. Uki reacted the only way she knew, given her surroundings. She pushed the woman into a nearby tent and demanded she stay put. Regrettably, the woman did not listen and tried to exit the tent. Uki cold-cocked her for her own good.

In search of the scattered children, she came across one rushing towards her in the whiteout. The little boy clung to her legs, making it almost impossible to walk. Uki knelt down so she could piggyback the boy and have her hands free in order to hold a weapon. She carried on in this fashion throughout the camp, calling out sporadically until she was hoarse. Hoping someone heard her voice and know help was near.

Although her actions seemed in vain, Uki did not give up her search. Finally, and unexpectedly, she came upon two children huddled behind a sled accompanied by an older caregiver.

Under normal circumstances, this would have been a terrible idea because the hunters did not unloaded their earlier kill. However, this bear seemed to be interested in moving targets. After leading the four back to safety of a nearby tent, Uki began her search anew. Suddenly several kinsmen, women and even hunters came into view as they charged directly at her from out of the haze. She hesitated for only a split second as she realized they all must be running away from the bear.

Uki reacted by stepping to the side, making way for them to pass and avoiding being ran over herself. She perceived the loud snorting noises before seeing the animal and when it emerged from out of the camouflage of the heavy falling snow, its head was down and its ears were back as it ran blindly past, after its intended quarry. Uki could not believe her luck, but she needed a much larger weapon if she was going to bring this beast down on her own.

Even in the storm, she saw the evidence of blood loss from the bear. Blood stained its fur and several arrows remained embedded in its hide, but the animal moved like a force of nature. Uki's tent was too far away from what she thought was her current position, so she needed to find another's spear to finish the polar bear. All she thought about was making the kill shot successfully and dropping the bear in its tracks. If she had to cut its heart out after to ensure no one else died tonight, so be it.

Luckily, as she followed the animal's trail, she came across a discarded spear. Someone in their terror must have dropped their weapon.

She gripped the well-used weapon in her hands and tested it for balance, and then made haste after the rampaging animal. As Uki ran deftly through the camp, she reassessed the situation and her possibilities.

There was not enough time to circle the animal and get between it and its prey, but she might catch up to it and attack it from behind. This seemed to be her better option if she aimed true and didn't overshoot. She hoped the rest of her hunting party would be as prudent.

It took no time to catch up to the enormous bear. She considered shouting at it to divert its attention away from her fellow kinsmen and women, but decided against it because the animal would see her coming.

As she ran full bore after the polar bear, Uki adjusted her hand position and hefted the large spear above her shoulder and backwards, keeping it parallel with the ground. She aimed for its head, but got a better shot when it reared up, exposing its spine.

Uki instantly turned her body sideways and launched the spear with all her might…this time it stayed down.

16

UKI

As Uki stood there trembling, trying to catch her breath, a small group of her people surrounded her. Everyone tried to touch the great huntress and thank her for her bravery.

However, she wanted to avoid attention and find Siqiniq and her dog before retiring for the night. Unfortunately, as a hunter, she had the unpleasant task of collecting the dead bodies for burial. So few lost their lives, although in Uki's mind, all life, great or small, was important.

Later, when the wind died down, and the storm moved on, the rest of the community ventured out of the safety of their tents to survey the carnage. They soon discovered another child was unaccounted for, and now everyone was looking to Uki for guidance. She truly despised the position people thrust upon her, but she also couldn't fathom the pain the missing child's mother must be experiencing.

As the night skies lightened with the approaching dawn, Uki dug deep into her reserves. There was still so much to do.

She gathered any able-bodied hunters and instructed them to spread out and find the little boy. She took on the unpleasant task of looking after the remains of the two little girls. Anyone left who was not a caregiver, would undertake the chore of butchering yesterday's kill and preparing it for travel.

It didn't take long for the hunters to find the ravaged remains of the boy on the outskirts of the camp. He was not just dismembered. The bear took its time ingesting him.

Uki found it hard to believe the bear's actions, as they were so uncharacteristic. Surely, the earlier wounding caused the animal's disposition?

If the elders only listened to her in the first place and taken the time to send out a party to destroy the animal, then three children would not be dead. Everything about this night hurt her heart. She couldn't wait to get back to her daughter, but the community was counting on her and she wouldn't let the innocents down.

As morning's first light spread across the horizon, fragile eyes could no longer hide from the horror of the night before. The blood of children splashed the snow-covered landscape. Despite her efforts, Uki was unsuccessful in hiding all the bloodshed after removing the body parts.

For the burial, they would wrap what remained of the children's bodies in caribou hides and placed them into above-ground ice graves made of carved blocks to keep the wild animals away. Family members and friends were expected to place treasured items of the deceased upon the graves, followed by five days of mourning.

However, since the group was on a tight schedule, they set aside only the rest of the day for that purpose. Those who were not directly affected by the loss prepared everything for tomorrow's final push north to their winter camp, while the shaman and elders attended to the spiritual needs of the people.

By the time Uki was reunited with her daughter, she wanted to cry and she did, but only in the privacy of her sparse tent. Unfortunately, she still had plenty to accomplish before paying her final respects to the families of the fallen children.

A part of her felt she already did so much. It was an absolutely terrifying task, dealing with the dead and attempting to distance herself from what she witnessed and accomplished, truly the stuff of nightmares to come.

Thankfully, Tapeesa was there for her of late looking after Siqiniq. The elders were indeed correct that her duties as midwife would help the young mother manage her grief. Uki hoped Tapeesa would also be of comfort to the parents who were mourning today, but alas, she had other plans.

As people gathered around the ice graves to honour the dead children, Uki was happy to see Tapeesa was in the thick of things as she flitted from parent to parent. Although it soon became quite clear Tapeesa was up to something, because Uki couldn't shake the feeling that all eyes were on her as she made her way up to the front of the gathering.

Uki planned to give her condolences quietly as Siqiniq slept soundly in her hood, but to her surprise, the community requested her to make an address.

At first, she did not know what to say, and then it came to her. She needed to pay homage to Asbjorn in front of everyone, as well as the other hunters and children who lost their lives on their migration north. She hated being on display, but the alternative of keeping everything inside was not healthy. By speaking to them directly, she would have time to look into the eyes of her fellow kinsmen and women and see the truth.

Uki couldn't have picked a better backdrop as she took her place of honour in front of the crowd and the night skies were alive with the dancing colours of the aurora borealis. She heard crying throughout the crowd as everyone gazed in awe at the spectacle above her. Some believed the lights represented the lit torches of the spirits of the dead, who were there to help guide the feet of the children to the highest heavens. This was only one interpretation of the Northern Lights, others being rather dark.

When everyone quieted down, Uki had the chance to speak.

"It is with a heavy heart I address you all tonight. We as a community have lost many loved ones on this journey. The spirits have seen fit to accompany our children as they cross over to the other side. I would like to pay tribute to the hunters who lost their lives in the service of our people because without them, we would not be here."

As Uki spoke, she couldn't help but look around, hoping to see her kinsmen nodding in agreement, but what she saw was anger on the faces of the mothers who had recently lost their children.

"Yes, I too experienced hostility towards the spirits when my beloved Asbjorn was taken from me, but that was all she said before the crowd's entire demeanour changed.

Several people began pushing their way to the front and voiced who they thought was responsible. "You have offended the spirits by committing a taboo. We blame you, oh great huntress!" one woman spat.

"Our children were slaughtered because of you!" another person screamed.

"Why did you do nothing when that beast was ripping my boy limb from limb?" on and on it went.

Uki was aghast by their accusations and it didn't take long to narrow in on the one person who had gone above and beyond to sow discord amongst her brethren. Tapeesa stood eerily still and smiled back at her from the distance.

Out of nowhere, "Asbjorn was a traitor! What did you expect by taking up with a Norseman? Think you're too high and mighty to bed your own kind?"

As the crowd surged, Uki could no longer tell where any of the yelling was coming from, but she knew she needed to protect her daughter. She quickly adjusted Siqiniq in her hood so she could shield her with her arms and began a shoving match on her way to the outskirts of the gathering.

"Please get out of my way for the sake of my child," she pleaded. It was downright frightening to know so many of her so-called "people" felt this way. An elder's voice rang out and the crowd instantly settled down.

It was someone Uki knew since childhood and although he never approved of her mannish ways, he showed respect where it was due. Especially for the many contributions she made over the years to her adopted people. Uki discerned from the expression on his face he was not at all happy with the herd mentality of the crowd. Some of them had the decency to at least appear embarrassed for their actions when she made direct eye contact.

"My kinsmen and women, how soon you forget all our huntress has done for us. She has risked her life frequently for the well-being of our community. What happened last night is no one's fault, least of all Uki's. She even honoured Tapeesa with the naming of her firstborn. Her future offspring will pay homage to other fallen members of our community."

Uki felt flabbergasted. She could not believe what just come out of his mouth.

Surely the elders could not expect her to give birth again so soon, and with whom?

She knew of arranged marriages, but people arranged them when the woman was much younger and they sought certain alliances. She needed to talk to Aama.

17

UKI

The elder's words seemed to appease the gathering, and Uki made her way back to her own tent unhindered.

After putting Siqiniq down for the night, she tidied up her few remaining belongings so she would be ready bright and early the following morning. Before turning in herself, she felt uneasy. Was she safe amongst her brethren?

She poked her head out of the tent flap and whistled for her dog. At first there was no sign of Amka, which made her even more anxious and just as she was about to call again, he appeared. Uki would feel elated when they reached their winter camp.

First thing she intended to do was return the borrowed larger sled and get hers back, that way her pack would always be near. Unfortunately, she didn't know what to do about Tapeesa. Her midwife was most certainly an instigator in tonight's brouhaha. Who knows what would have transpired if an elder hadn't stepped in? Should she just keep quiet and play along?

After all, she didn't believe Siqiniq was in any direct

danger and hopefully there were enough good people left that gossip hasn't poisoned?

That night, Uki tossed and turned, obsessed with the fact someone believed Asbjorn had been a traitor. If it was the last thing she did, Uki would get revenge on behalf of her man. Siqiniq would never grow up hearing lies about her parents.

She wanted her to be proud of both of her heritages and hopefully they would feel the same about her. What was this talk about committing a taboo?

When morning came, Uki had one cranky child on her hands. She wasn't sure if she had kept the baby up all night by moving around or if the child was merely feeding off her mother's fears.

Uki was thankful to have the help of several young hunters to assist her in the final teardown of her tent and was confident their motives were pure and not tainted by blather. The young men had even offered their help when they saw Uki struggling to adjust Siqiniq after putting the child in her parka. She would have none of it even though she was bone-tired. This was something she needed to do on her own and she had no intentions of adding to the rumours.

Once everything was in order to her liking and her baby girl finally asleep, Uki made a few last-minute adjustments to the heavy load on her sled before heading off on foot to join the rest of her kinsmen and women for their morning meal. She kept her eyes down and her ears peeled.

After breakfast, she returned to collect her borrowed sled and finished harnessing the team. However, whilst preoccupied with trying to calm down the overly excited dogs, Tapeesa unexpectedly showed her face, even sporting a rather large, clearly painted on smile.

Uki could not believe the woman's nerve. Especially after what had transpired the night before. She was hoping to carry Siqiniq along with her on the last day of their migration north and even had the gall to insinuate she was doing the huntress a favour. At first Uki didn't even want to humour her with a response, but then thought better of it. She needed to know her adversaries currently in her life and keep them close.

So it was with great effort she fought to maintain her composure and talked civilly with the midwife. When all she wanted to do was cut the vindictive woman's tongue out of her mouth.

Later, as prearranged, Uki dropped off one very irritable little girl at Tapeesa's campsite and smiled to herself, knowing full well the child's undergarment was rather fetid, before joining up with the masses.

Once the last of the campfires were extinguished, the group started out on the last leg of what has been a rather solemn journey thus far.

Uki couldn't help but gaze upon her so-called kinsmen as they filed by her sled and strangely felt an almost tangible animosity emanating from some of their number. Scolding herself for such mistrustful thoughts, when in actuality only a few were to blame for her misgivings. This would not ruin her day. After all, there wasn't even a cloud in the sky.

Eventually, after hours of travelling across the packed snow and ice, the group made one last stop to allow those unfortunate souls who had been forced to walk to rest and those riding to stretch their legs. Because their destination was close, no hot meals would be prepared, but that didn't bother Uki. She was happy eating dried meat while breastfeeding her baby.

Today, everyone was in high spirits, especially the hunters because they had seen such a wide variety of game along the way. Including telltale signs of a bear, whose tracks crisscrossed the landscape nearest the ice floes.

This was a land of plenty and thankfully they were a people with no aversions to eating polar bear meat or its prey. One thing they didn't see was any evidence of another large grouping of peoples inhabiting the land. This made them all happy to know they wouldn't be competing for food.

However, a few laid claim to having spotted a small "unknown" object in the distant sky that afternoon. In the end, they simply attributed it to the effects of snow blindness, as most of them denied seeing or hearing anything of the sort.

Even though the men and women of their community led a very sheltered existence, they still heard tales of light-skinned explorers, whalers, and traders frequenting their sacred lands from time to time.

These Qallunaat were strange indeed with their noisy animal-less contraptions both on the water and in the air. No one dared to make contact. It was common knowledge between the other Indigenous Peoples no good would come of it since they presumably carried diseases and could anger the spirits.

Try as she might, Uki could not make out the actual size or shape of the flying object in the sky that day, but she had most certainly heard a faint noise accompanying it. Unfortunately, though, she had nothing to base her observations on and no one seemed interested in discussing it further. The matter was closed as far as the group was concerned. Although the more she thought about it, the more curious she became.

After all, it was her fellow kinsmen who first warned her years ago about the appearance of hostile Norsemen crossing into their territory. These so-called giants ravaged the Inuit's land. Searching for ivory and big game, and at the expense of its people.

They had been wrong then, and she had since seen bloodshed, but only at the hands of other Indigenous Peoples. Not the starving ill-prepared easterners. Maybe one day she would be brave enough to head out in search of a new beginning, look for Asbjorn's descendants and hopefully find in them a people who would not judge her daughter by the colour of her skin. But until then, Uki had a child to protect and a family kinship she wasn't about to give up on completely.

About an hour later, everyone headed north again, hoping to set up camp before nightfall. One of their seasoned hunters had scouted out the actual site earlier.

It was unfamiliar territory, since they had never stayed in the same place twice. This made much more sense considering their game had a propensity to move around and so did the ice floes. It was much more convenient to be semi-nomadic, not to mention safer. That night, all members of the group would sleep in the largest tent. The one usually reserved for communal gatherings because tomorrow they would begin the laborious task of building igloos. Unfortunately, this meant families would have to share their living spaces.

In the past, Uki was lucky enough to sleep with the sled dogs. But now that she was a mother, her child's safety would be in question, and she knew damn well Tapeesa would have other plans.

Finally, their lead musher gave a hoot and a holler,

waving his arms exuberantly. Uki looked around, hoping for some shelter in the area, but all she saw was a sheer rock face and the ocean. Upon closer inspection, she was relieved to see the movement of water between several sand bars positioned only a short distance from the beach. Most likely caused by strong winds and the coastal polynyas, open water, they can create.

This had to be the sole reason for her kinsman choosing such an inhospitable place to set up their camp, but alas, being a female, it was not her place to question the powers that be. She checked on the status of her daughter before lending a hand to erect a few of the utility tents.

As assumed, Tapeesa already had ideas abound about just where they would live during the winter months and what the sleeping arrangements would be. For Siqiniq, herself, and her husband, she wanted a medium-sized igloo, with a much smaller one attached to the front side so Uki could come and go as she pleased when not wet nursing.

She really wasn't all that surprised by the woman's cheek, she would probably not bat an eye if something happened to Uki. Possibly an accident on a hunting trip. After all, they happened all the time. If Tapeesa believed Uki could be removed from the big picture, she was mistaken.

Later that evening, the group partook in their first communal meal at the new location. The sheer warmth of that large a number of people in such a big tent, eating, talking, laughing, soon made everyone forget what they had overcome to get there. All except the families of the recently departed, for they had formed a clutch of sorts, all sharing in each other's sorrow and blame laying. Uki wanted to go to them and speak her peace, but what good would it do?

She did not know why they would even condemn her. Out of many hunters, she was the only one. She could not fathom the mindset behind such an accusation, but the more she observed Tapeesa interacting with the group, her suspicions were confirmed. The thought of sleeping under the same roof as that woman made her skin crawl.

Thankfully, she still had time to suss out their future sleeping arrangements because tonight she was part of one extensive family. Uki had not bothered to unpack her sled yet, but she had collected several blankets, including the large white bearskin.

It might have been in poor taste considering what happened only days before, but Uki was not about to let Siqiniq freeze to the ground overnight if the fire should burn out.

That night as she lay under her blanket feeding her daughter, she could hear all the muted sounds of her people...some carrying on whispered conversations in the dark...others coughing, sneezing, laughing, clearing their throats, making love and crying...she couldn't help but care about them.

As sleep began to envelope her and her daughter, Uki could have sworn someone nearby had addressed her as "Nuliajuk", followed by an almost indiscernible utterance, presumably for her ears only. "You had better behave, girl, or you too will meet the same end as the Sea Spirit."

She thought she had only been dreaming, but the unknown man's voice would not leave her head. Uki could not put a face to the voice.

Although with the mere mention of the ancient Goddess of the Sea's name, all her childhood memories came flooding back in an instant and the similarities of their lives were more than prevalent now.

Deep down, she knew the stories the elders had told around the campfire were only there to keep her people respectful of the environment, but all tales were loosely based on some small truth and Uki could only hope hers would have a happier ending.

Nuliajuk: Mother of the Sea Beasts, also known by the Inuit as a Sea Spirit. Legend has it the mother and father of an only child, wanted for their daughter to be married so they could have a son-in-law to contribute to the family's food supply.

Unfortunately, their daughter refused, so her father took her to an island a great distance away, with only her dog for company. She was left there to ponder her decisions. The parents hoped she would change her mind.

In time it was said she fell in love with her dog, had sexual relations with it and gave birth to many babies through this union. The resulting children were all different nationalities: some White, Black, Indian, Asian and so on. These children left the small island to disperse all over the world. After some time had passed, the father returned in his kayak to retrieve his daughter and bring her back to their camp.

On the way back, he again became angry at his daughter for falling in love with her dog and not wanting to marry. In an impulsive act of violence, he shoved her out of the kayak and into the ice cold water below. Before going under, she made a grab for the side of the kayak. Her father took his hunting knife and cut off all his daughter's fingers one by one. She sank to the bottom of the sea. Her amputated fingers became the animals of the sea and herself, the goddess of all under and in the sea.

As one would expect, different versions of this tale have resurfaced around many a campfire, depending on the specific region. Some believe she had been an orphaned girl mistreated by her community.

While others tell a tale of a young girl whose family had no animals to hunt and they were starving. She, too, had refused to marry, thus providing a husband to support her. Her parents loaded up their boat with their few belongings and headed off to find better hunting grounds, leaving her behind. Likely panic-stricken, the poor girl had swum after them and grabbed onto the side of the boat. To which her father responded without thinking, using his axe to chop off her fingers and causing her to slip into the depths of the sea, where she lives today.

This story claims her fingers became the animals of the sea and when provoked, the waters boil with waves, making it impossible to hunt. That is why their people are taught from a very young age to always show the proper respect for all life and, even in death, lest feel the vengeful spirit's wrath.

People still fear Nuliajuk and believe she has the power of life and death over them because she is responsible for their livelihood.

If angered, the only ones who can truly calm her are the shamans, making it safe once again to venture out on the water to hunt and fish.

18

UKI

The view at first light turned out to be much more agreeable than Uki initially surmised and if the weather remained static, their new camp could be up and operable in only a couple of days.

After all, an experienced builder should be able to construct an igloo in as little as one hour, while novices usually took anywhere from three to six hours to do so. Though, some of the injured hunters were the most adept.

Since the community wouldn't need to look for food sources right away, everyone could now focus their energies on the tasks at hand. The center of the camp was pretty much in place because the community had erected both large caribou tents the evening before, along with the cookhouses, leaving only the chore of building homes for the elders and the rest of their people. The group had also transported a large amount of firewood with them on their journey to above the tree line because they expected at some point, they would have to rely on seal blubber fires in soapstone dishes if the kindling along the shoreline became scarce.

Uki was happy to see Tapeesa that morning since she could leave Siqiniq in her care while she and some of her fellow kinsmen surveyed the rest of the camp, leaving markers for future igloos. Nothing of great importance, but at least she was still in the loop for certain decisions.

Although she could not persuade the elders to assign her an igloo of her own. She understood their misgivings, but was not happy with the outcome, as she did not want her new home to be attached to her midwife's family dwelling.

On the bright side, though, as a respected huntress, Uki would have her own separate entrance and Amka could share their space while the rest of the pack slept outside to protect the camp from intruders, both two and four-legged.

The next couple of days were a whirlwind of activity, leaving no time to further dwell on trepidations. As nightfall came and Uki's hands remained idle, she was once again reminded of the community's last memorial gathering and the elder's request for her to name her next born after one of the fallen children. Not to mention only days before someone in her group had the audacity to threaten her life if she should plan on remaining unmarried. She didn't feel fear, but she had concerns about what would be expected of her in the future.

As the winter weather would soon separate their community from the rest of the region, Uki, an expert seal hunter, knew her time would be consumed solely with hunting and taking care of her daughter. Surely, they couldn't expect her to find time for alliances with any eligible bachelors?

She did not like being put into this type of predicament and she knew the harder they pushed, she would reciprocate tenfold. The weather chose to co-operate and gave the group plenty of time to send out search parties.

They needed to know just where to harvest their food sources, because when the inevitable winter storms hit, no one wanted to get caught without an adequate stockpile of food.

There was always the added danger of the winds changing direction out on the sea. Resulting in their highly valued hunters being trapped on an ice floe for weeks at a time, exposed to the elements and possibly succumbing to a white death.

Caribou, like muskoxen, sporadically moved across the tundra, but were found closer to the tree line. During the dead of winter, they would always rely on seals as their prime food source, as they could hunt them on the ice. The dogs were used to sniff out their breathing holes or at the edge of ice floes. Walruses stayed where the strong currents kept the sea ice thin, making it very dangerous to hunt them on the newly formed ice that would bend to their weight and the hunter's.

Everything came with risks, but it was a chance every hunter would take because, if not, famine was not a desirable alternative.

Entire communities risked being wiped out in one season, or at the very least, they would sacrifice their children and elders for the sake of their able-bodied kinsmen and women. Uki knew this as a sad reality for other Indigenous Peoples. But thankful in all the years she called these people her own, life-ending assistance were the only mercy killings she witnessed. Time would tell.

She only hoped the spirits would see fit to grace them with bountiful game and a mild winter.

As a huntress, Uki was always mindful of traditions by adding to her collection of tattoos whenever she made a kill. Honouring the spirit of the dead animal and ensuring future prosperity.

Uki wore her many tattoos with pride, and rightly so. It wasn't until she began the further filing of her teeth she once again became the topic of many a campfire blather. Instead of just making grooves in them as Asbjorn had done, she now began subtly filing her teeth into points, mimicking her carnivorous quarry.

In time, the community's elders and their shaman grew to accept her modifications. Although some of her kinsmen and women found it rather alarming whenever Uki bared her teeth. She was laughing on the inside because her new look worked wonders to deter the advances of any man, taken or not.

Only the young ones dared to spend any time alone with her. They usually honed their hunting skills, and as a bonus, even Tapeesa began keeping their interactions to a bare minimum. A feat rather hard to accomplish since they lived basically in the same extensive structure, but it kept the midwife from making small talk or complaining about something. All Uki was interested in was providing for her people and making sure Siqiniq had a happy childhood.

As the weeks turned into months, the weather inevitably changed, but unfortunately for the worse. The north winds now roared across the open water on their way to the group's camp.

Until this point, the game in the surrounding area was plentiful. Kinsmen and women had grown fat from the abundance of meat, so when the status quo abruptly changed, all felt it. The harsh weather forced hunting parties to spend longer periods of time away from camp, leaving their families sequestered to their igloos.

Children had become more irritable since they could no longer play outside, resulting in shorter fuses on their caregivers. This was really nothing new to the elders. After having spent years of nomadic living, seasons changed. That was the only constant.

Siqiniq was growing like a weed, and with each passing day, she continued to look more and more like her father's people and less like her adopted ones. Uki hated to be away from her daughter, but marvelled upon each return at how much she had developed, both mentally and physically. Some of this she could attribute to her midwife's care, but over time, her concerns grew as she noticed unexplained marks on her daughter's body. When she inquired how Siqiniq obtained the marks, she was made to feel as if it was her fault for being away for so long.

Sadly, there was no one else she could entrust her child's care to, whereas Aama was much too old for the task and her community needed her now more than ever. Even their stores of firewood had dwindled, but thankfully the seal blubber kept well in this hostile environment.

As time passed, Uki and her fellow hunters needed to brainstorm where the animals could be taking cover during these prolonged periods of almost whiteout conditions. After all, they had to be held up somewhere. They couldn't have all left for warmer climes. Weather was always changing.

If they could just wait it out a little longer, it had to get better. Time was not on their side. Every morning, they awoke to the sound of howling winds and blizzard conditions. It was more than clear the well-being of all was quickly becoming at risk.

Everyone in camp had an antagonistic mood, seeming to be at each other's throats…wanting to lay blame on something or someone for their people's turn of bad luck. The inevitable happened much sooner than anyone could have ever predicted when their communal meals became threatened. Egregious talk surfaced.

Uki's fellow kinsmen and women had discussed the mercy killing of the very young and anyone who was of ill health or frail. She would not stand by and watch the breakdown of her community from within. Her daughter's life was at stake.

In the early hours of the following morning, she exited her igloo from her private entrance, taking Siqiniq with her. She was not sure how long she would be away, but she knew she would feel better leaving her daughter in the care of her only true confidante, Aama, in case anything should go awry. Thankfully, she was back using her own dog sled and team, so travel should be much quicker, giving her time to cover more land mass.

As she kissed her child goodbye and expressed her concerns with the elder, Uki cried. "Times of plenty will come again. Please protect my daughter. I think of you as her grandmother and entrust her life to you." More tears fell as she tried to articulate her thoughts.

"This is not your burden alone to bear. Don't be so reckless. I beg of you to wait until the weather changes or at least the sun comes up," Aama implored. But Uki had already decided and would not hear of changing it.

With a heavy heart, she headed out into the almost pitch black of the approaching Arctic dawn. Thankfully, she dressed properly in her caribou parka and pants, not to mention a layer of seal skin and polar bear boots.

She could hardly see because of the continually blowing snow which had barraged their camp daily for more than a month, but this would not deter her. Surprisingly though, the weather cleared as soon as she got several miles away from camp, but she still had trouble with visibility since she needed to keep her face covered because of the extreme cold temperatures.

Uki didn't know where to search, since most of her fellow hunters had already covered a good section of the coast and portions inland.

As luck would have it, after several hours, Amka picked up a scent and started heading for the sea cliffs. A part of Uki thought the dog had gone mad, but the other side of her wanted to see this through until the end. As they neared the steep precipice, it was downright astonishing to see a wide variety of animal tracks in the snow.

Apparently there must be a steep trail somewhere down the embankment, but leading to where?

19

UKI

Uki quickly halted the team. She couldn't have them in their exuberance, tearing down the face of the cliff into the unknown.

As she approached her lead dog, Amka's urgency surprised her to be unharnessed. There was something of interest below. It scared her as her dog disappeared over the edge into thin air, but she still had the ability to hear her companion's barking as she followed behind as fast as she could.

Uki couldn't help but hesitate before peering over the ledge. Praying Amka was still alive and well. Without delay, a huge smile spread across her face as she saw her faithful dog down below, making its way down a well-beaten path disappearing mysteriously into the hillside. If not for the hoof and paw prints in the fresh snow, she would have never guessed there was anything of interest hidden further down.

She pondered returning to camp to enlist the help of her fellow hunters, but another part knew time was of the essence and if the weather changed again, the trail might disappear forever. Uki returned to her sled to arm herself, since she did not know what might take refuge inside the probable cave waiting. As she descended the steep trail with her spear in hand, she couldn't resist pausing to survey her surroundings. The discovery of this refuge was a miracle, hidden from almost all vantage points.

As she got closer to where Amka was standing with his hackles up, Uki couldn't believe the sight before her eyes. From the looks of it, Uki observed part of the hillside had glaciated, forming a large ice cave leading somewhere. She did not know how her dogs found the sanctuary, most likely by pure accident.

Uki knelt to get a better look at the tracks and felt overjoyed to see the telltale hoof prints of a muskox, as its front hooves were much larger than its back. There were even small deer tracks, hare and fox from the looks of it, all strangely cohabitating. Possibly because of the drastic deep freeze or this cave was much older and bigger than she could envision.

Once she stepped out of the direct sunlight while continuing farther into the entrance of the cave, the air grew colder with each step, the ice closing in around her. Uki was able to see her breath but as she made her way down into the earth following the beaten path before her, she smelt what she imagined was dirt, along with animal feces. She wished she had a torch to light her way, albeit the opening was very large. What if she ran into a bear?

For all she knew, this could be a den of some sort. Uki thought she heard muted animal noises coming from the depths of the passage. She sighed in relief since she did not imagine caribou or muskoxen would live alongside a polar bear. Amka heard the noises as well because he was now in hot pursuit of the source. Barking aggressively as he charged headlong down the path.

Uki followed as fast as she dared. The steepness of the path eventually changing for the better, along with the temperature. The ice-covered passage itself spilled into a much larger geothermal labyrinth of caves, complete with stalagmites and pools of water. She stopped dead in her tracks as she stared in utter amazement at the sight before her. Losing track of her dog as he disappeared farther into the elaborate caves. Uki couldn't believe what she was seeing. No one had ever spoken of anything like this before. Was she the first Inuk to have crossed the threshold of this enchanted realm?

She couldn't wait to explore, but first she must find Amka. As she was about to whistle, Uki heard the unmistakable bawl of a young muskox and the sound was getting louder. Down in the depths of the cave, sound seemed to reverberate off the walls. Making it almost impossible to judge exactly where it was coming from.

The echoes filled the cave, leaving Uki wondering how many animals had sought refuge. Amka appeared on the path before her with a very large puppy dog smile on his face, barking happily and looking back in the direction he had just come from. Once a hunter, always a hunter, Uki gripped her spear tightly in her hand and followed suit.

At first, she experienced a sense of claustrophobia as she navigated the dark passageways while tracking the noises, but then suddenly, she became aware of light in the distance. Uki had no idea what the source could be but was thrilled when a large clearing presented itself.

To her surprise, the ceiling above seemed to be made of glass, as if the topside of the glacier had been windswept. Again, it was chilly because of all the humidity, whereas the darker tunnels were much warmer because of their dirt walls. Uki couldn't help but stare wide-eyed at the wonderful sights before her. Nature was truly amazing.

She saw small herds of muskox and deer, and the reflection of many eyes staring back at her, presumably the much smaller Arctic inhabitants. Astonishing to see them living peacefully together whilst waiting for the storm to pass. The more she thought about it, the more she worried her people would slaughter everything in a hurry to replenish the community's stores. Eliminating a potentially sustainable game supply.

Uki knew deep down that the animals needed to feel safe in their refuge if they expected them to continue using it on a year-round basis. While lost in contemplation, she couldn't help but notice the cavern had become markedly darker. Where had the time flown? Uki called Amka to her side and made her way back through the tunnels, on her way topside.

If night was indeed falling, she needed to get the rest of the team safely inside. The closer she got to the cave's mouth, the louder the wind noise became. Despite the absence of nightfall, another fierce storm loomed.

Uki quickened her step as she made her way back up the path to the precipice overhead. Once cresting the rock face, she ran for her sled and the visibly nervous dogs.

As she looked back over her shoulder at the horizon, Uki made out a small amount of light in the distance between the horizon and the vast bank of low-lying storm clouds. Rolling across the ocean ice on their way to the cliff banks. If she thought she had more time, Uki would have staked her sled to the ground, but her current concern was with her dogs' safety.

She hastily collected her overnight supplies from the sled's cargo bed and raced back towards the disappearing path. Thankfully, Amka was there to lead the way as the currently hammering snow-laden winds made it near impossible to traverse the steep path back to the cave safely.

Once inside the opening, Uki led the dogs back down the subterranean path, keeping them behind her, so they wouldn't charge ahead and cause a stampede. Hopefully, the storm would only last the night and they could share this phenomenal sanctuary with its other occupants.

Luckily, she had packed enough dried meat for herself and the dogs to sustain them overnight. Pools of glacier runoff provided an abundance of fresh drinking water, eliminating the need to melt snow with fire. As she huddled with her dogs for warmth, Uki could have sworn the surrounding wild animals were indeed creeping closer, hopefully only out of curiosity.

She soon realized her premonitions were true when she heard the occasional sound of her dogs growling under their breath, subtly warning intruders to keep their distance. Sleep took her and when she awoke afterwards with a start, Uki wasn't even sure if it was morning or night because her light source remained, albeit dim. Uki wanted to get back to camp as soon as possible so she could share the news of this much needed windfall with the rest of her community.

All talks of culling her brethren needed to be stopped. Fortunately for her, she could rest easy knowing Aama was looking after Siqiniq. She hoped her request had not caused a rift between Tapeesa and the elder, but she was prepared to deal with it upon her return. Whatever the case may be.

Finally, realizing she would not be falling back to sleep soon, Uki, as quietly as possible, made her way back up to the entrance of the cave. Alas, she had been right about the storm's intensity. As she peered out toward the sea while gripping the surrounding rocks for stability in the buffeting winds, no horizon was evident. Her world vanished.

Distraught, to say the least, Uki knew it was still much too dangerous to make her way back to camp, but waiting patiently had never been one of her virtues.

Hopefully her sled would be where she had left it. Strong winds had been known to carry heavier objects over great distances. Once she backtracked to where she had left her pack, Uki made a small fire of seal fat to shed more light on her surroundings and fashioned a torch to explore further. For all she knew, the storm might continue raging most of the day, and she wanted to use her time wisely.

The animals chose not to panic as soon as the aroma of smoke began wafting through the tunnels. This could partially be because of the sheer height of the ceilings or the fact they knew it wasn't safe to venture outside. Uki genuinely found comfort, as Amka followed her throughout her adventure.

The labyrinth of caves was mind-boggling and if truth be told, she wasn't sure if she could make it back to where she had started without her faithful dog's help. It was so strange watching the plethora of animals' responses as she passed them in the dim light. There appeared to be no animosity or fear.

She felt a tinge of remorse for wanting to share the knowledge of their haven with her community. Although the thought soon passed. Her people must remain at the top of the food chain if there was to be a future for her daughter.

20

UKI

Uki checked on the weather multiple times throughout the day by going back to the mouth of the cave. Each time, she felt filled with sadness because the storm had not yet dissipated. She was becoming more and more anxious, but resigned herself that returning to camp now would be suicidal.

Once back down below with the rest of the pack, she doled out the remaining meat to her dogs. They would need to keep their strength up to make the long journey home, and she didn't want them chasing down prey in the tunnels. Everyone needed to stay as quiet as possible.

When she decided to go looking for a meal of her own, she chose not to use a snare in case her quarry should not die a quick enough death. Instead, she waited patiently in the dark for something small to venture by and, as luck would have it, a plump hare made a rather fatal mistake. She was quick to dispatch the animal and overjoyed it was indeed something quite palatable.

As she cooked the skinned hare over her small fire, the many animals that shared the cave did not become agitated by the smell of cooking meat in the air. Uki thought several times she saw the shape of a small fox coming closer to investigate.

Now, with nothing but time on her hands, she couldn't help but further ruminate over the fact these caves could most definitely be a blessing to her people. No more living in tents and igloos during the harshest winter months, but that was a discussion for another time. Foremost, she needed to figure out a way to mark the hidden path as soon as the storm lifted. To prevent it from being lost for good.

As she made her way up from the depths of the cave and out into the light again, Uki's excitement heightened at the sight of large patches of blue sky overhead.

She gave a holler in her excitement and was surprised as several deer ran by her on the path, making their way nimbly up the slope on their way to the cliff's edge above. Uki gave thanks because, from the looks of it, all traces of the path had disappeared with the wind.

She and her pack made their way up to the top of the cliff, but what greeted them now was a rather smooth sheet of freshly fallen snow as far as the eye could see. With no sign of her sled. Devastation overwhelmed Uki. How was she going to make her way back to camp? On foot, it would take days, and who knew when another storm might hit? She needed to find the sled immediately.

Amka let out a strange bark, followed by nervous sounds emanating from the rest of the pack. They seemed to be combing the last known spot where the sled had been left. Uki, the ever-growing optimist, knew Amka was an exceptional dog, but no one had ever instructed him to find his own sled before.

"What you smelling, boy? Where's your sled?" Uki tried to sound upbeat as she gave her commands, just as she would have if asking for the dog to find prey. "Go get it! Go find your sled!"

It took a while for the dogs to circle the area, looking for a viable scent. Uki so hoped it was the right one. Suddenly, they were off, running parallel to the cliff's edge. Heading down the coast to where the shore was easier to breach. She ran as fast as she could through the snow, following them. It was not too deep since the earlier winds carried a large percentage of it inland.

In her pursuit, she lost sight of the pack several times due to the undulating coastline. She could still hear their baying from a respectful distance away, at least.

Uki couldn't help but scold herself for not marking the path as intended, since her sled was missing. All rational thought unfortunately left her. She couldn't go back now and risk losing her dogs. Hopefully, they find the sled undamaged, leaving enough time to return to the cliff path to mark it before heading back to camp. Weather permitting.

Deep down, she knew she had a tall order to fill, but there was no alternative. Uki could now taste blood as she ran frantically after the dogs. In her panic, she had been gulping large quantities of frigid air, not bothering to protect herself from the elements by simply breathing through her nose or covering her mouth.

Upon cresting a small rise where the cliffs gave way to the shoreline, Uki stopped to catch her breath and survey the landscape. Bending forward with hands on her knees, joy overcame her as she saw the dogs found something of interest in the snow. Followed by the unmistakable sound of a man yelling as sleds approached from inland. Uki covered her eyes from the glare of the snow while trying to get a better look.

Relief flooded her senses as soon as she recognized her

fellow kinsmen's caribou clothing. They had been out looking for her when she hadn't returned the night before. Or at least that was what she thought.

The half a dozen sleds surrounded her and in all the commotion, her dogs headed back in her direction. She couldn't believe her good luck as she rushed to the closest man and threw her arms around him before he even dismounted from his sled. Uki knew she was talking a mile a minute, but in her enthusiasm, she couldn't wait to share her good news.

"Listen to me. I've found a cavern full of animals. The entrance hides in the face of a sea-cliff not far from here. I can show you. Help me find my sled…" unfortunately that was all she got out.

As she searched the eyes of her fellow kinsmen, it became obvious her brethren must have thought she was half mad from wandering around, lost in the storm, all this time. Albeit, she probably looked a sight with her face caked in ice and mucus. Ranting about some cave where all the Arctic animals were living harmoniously together. The man she embraced untangled himself slowly and now held her at arm's length rather roughly.

"At least your dogs had the brains to stay together in the storm, but why did you unhook them, and where is your sled, woman?" he gruffly barked.

Uki couldn't believe his attitude towards her, as if reprimanding a child. After all, hadn't she risked her life to find food for her people and this was how they treated her?

Not knowing who she was addressing and time being of the utmost importance, Uki made an error in her indignation. "I'm your huntress. Help me find my sled and I'll show you!"

Suddenly, everything changed.

The men's demeanours became atypical. Instead of

showing compassion for their fellow kinswoman, they appeared downright aloof. Uki didn't know how to respond. She thought they were her saviours, but as they guardedly got off their sleds without lowering their face masks, she now knew she had been wrong.

Uki, reluctantly, called Amka to her side while backing away and keeping her eyes on the advancing men. Instantly postures changed. In the blink of an eye, one man withdrew his bow and arrow, taking aim at her dog.

Uki quickly appraised the situation as it now presented itself. Hoping for a connection, she surveyed the circle of men.

"Please, I have a daughter." Against her better judgement, she couldn't hold her tears back any longer. Which in turn caused Amka's hackles to rise.

She wasn't sure who let loose the first arrow as she tried to shield her dog from her kinsmen's unwarranted retaliation. Thankfully, it only grazed its mark. Amka yelped but continued to growl and bare his teeth.

"I beg of you to spare my dog's life. What do you want of me?" she sobbed.

The largest of the men then stepped forward. "See, I was right. She cares more for that damn dog than her people. Tie it up or it dies!" He spat.

The memory of her first night in the communal tent came flooding back to Uki. The voice in the dark that had threatened her. She had to see his face.

"Why are you hiding behind your masks? Show yourselves, brothers!" She smiled, maybe not as confidently as she had hoped.

In unison, all the men slowly removed their masks. They too were all wearing smiles, along with looks of self-satisfaction. Uki was shocked to discover the identities of the men behind the snow masks. Some she recognized immediately as kinsmen who had known her since childhood. While others were young men, she trained to hunt and the remaining few, known only to her in passing.

Oddly, a few looked away as she searched their faces for signs of intent. When her gaze fell upon the men who only recently made themselves known to her, through seemingly kind deeds or the occasional overstepping of boundaries when she was with child. Their eyes did not waver.

Somewhere in this motley crew was most likely the murderer or murderers of her beloved Asbjorn. Uki smiled again, but this time showing her sharpened teeth. She would get to the bottom of this or die trying.

In her pigheadedness, Uki diverted her fellow kinsmen's attention away from herself as she pointed at a mysteriously shaped mound of snow in the distance.

"I think Amka found my sled over there. Could you help me dig it out and I'll show you where the caves are located?" All said with nary a waver in her voice.

At first, no one made a move. Uki was more than well aware she was outnumbered, but continued testing the waters, anyway. She turned and headed towards the shoreline, but the man quickly asserted his dominance by grabbing Uki's arm. He spun her around, shoving a small length of rope in her face and demanded for the last time she tether Amka before taking another step.

Even though their exchange was not a friendly palaver by any means, more memories resurfaced. "Your name is Nukilik, right? Alornerk trained you, didn't he?" If he was indeed the alpha of the group, she needed to develop a rapport with this man. "Your parents named you well. How did they possibly know you would end up being so strong?" She smiled up at him, trying not to show the points of her teeth.

Thankfully, it had the desired effect on the well-built, rather dull-witted man, but it also created a fledgling rivalry between the remaining small group of kinsmen. She saw it in their eyes and, by how they interacted.

Uki could only pray someone would be her champion while the others fought to defile her.

21

UKI

After fashioning a muzzle and lead out of rope for Amka, Uki started out in search of her dogsled and a workable path through the windrows onto the ice floes.

Uki fought to keep her stride slow and steady. Internally, she desired to flee and conceal, but her sole current safeguard was a short-bladed knife. Since she had left her spear back in the cave.

This assortment of men could have only gathered for one reason and if she hoped to make it out alive, she would have to be shrewder than her opponents. As she retraced her pack's steps across the snow and ice, Uki couldn't help but vocalize her inner turmoil. Thankfully, her brethren were out of earshot and not privy to the conversation she shared with her dog.

Although at no time did she actually relax enough to stop looking over her shoulder and was pleased to see her diligence rewarded when her fellow kinsmen's progress became hindered. The much larger and heavier sleds could not traverse the increasingly rocky terrain of the beach.

Compelling them to abandon the sleds and continue on foot.

Uki had to hide her joy when she was close enough to make out the brush bow of her sled sticking out of the snow. It would take nothing to turn it over and harness her dogs, but she needed to check it over first for damages.

As she observed the surrounding shoreline, Uki was pleased to see there was still enough snow coverage for her lighter sled to maneuver on. However, not enough time for her to make a clean getaway.

As she looked out at the horizon, she understood time was not in her favour. The clouds were becoming almost anthracite in colour and the distance between sky and land was lessening at an alarming rate, along with the temperature. Uki found herself torn between showing them the caves and sneaking out once everyone was fast asleep, or slowing down her sled recovery and making a run for it as soon as the impending storm hit.

Both were chancy, since she did not know what their ulterior motives were and if they even planned to keep her alive. The more she thought, the more she concluded they would never see the caves. Uki quickly busied herself with making a show of cleaning her sled off, beginning to inspect every part, but when she asked her fellow kinsmen to help her turn it over, their responses did not surprise her. Evidently opinions changed and the discovery of the cave was not so far-fetched a tale anymore, as they were all interested in seeing it.

"It's getting late and, by the looks of the sky, we're in for another big storm. Does the cave of yours have enough room for all of us to sleep comfortably?" The men followed this with not-so-hidden looks, half smiles, and muted laughter.

"First, help me with my sled, and we'll look for the cave."

"Look for the cave? I thought you knew where it was?" Several men echoed similar responses. "Your sled can wait and you better not have been lying to us!"

Amka was sensing Uki's agitation and began growling at the men as they invaded his mistress' personal space. One man made a threatening gesture toward her dog, something he likely wouldn't have done if the animal had not been tethered. It took all Uki's strength to stand down as Amka fought his restraints to defend himself, but that wasn't good enough for her kinsmen.

"The dog dies!" She heard before Amka was pierced with several arrows. And as she struggled to claw her way through the throng of men to get to her dog's side, large hands reached out and dragged her roughly away.

Uki ultimately panicked and began to hyperventilate while witnessing Amka's blood being spilt all over the snow-covered ground. If someone didn't act quickly to stop the flow, he would surely bleed out.

"I beg of you! Please let me help my dog and then I'll take you to the caves!"

"Beg…that's what you'll be doing later when I've got you on your knees!"

Uki had no idea of who voiced the remark, but knew if she wanted to get out of this alive, the storm's descent couldn't come soon enough.

"I have to see to my dog's wounds. He's lost too much blood. I promise to be quick. My sled appears sound. Just flip it over. I'll do whatever you want! Please, help me!"

This seemed to appease the masses. Most likely due to their awareness Uki was more than capable of defending herself in a fair fight and unless they intended to restrain her while taking their turns. Tonight might not be as much fun as they had envisioned. But it took very little effort for the men to right her small sled.

"No more stalling, woman! Show us the way to the caves before I lose my patience," Nukilik roared.

Without even waiting for a response, he dragged Uki by her parka's hood, back to where his sled was waiting higher on the beach, stopping only long enough to push her into the sled's cargo bed.

Time had tragically run out for both the huntress and her beloved dog. Looking out at the sea, Uki was relieved to see the storm clouds were indeed fast moving and she might have enough time to lead them on a wild goose chase, a subterfuge. Before hopefully escaping into a cover of blowing snow. It took all her strength of will to not lash out at the men who she had once called family. Conveying an illusion of compliance was now her only hope.

"The entrance hides in the cliff bank, facing out to sea. Last night's storm wiped away all traces of the path from above. We're going to have to look for it on the ocean side."

Upon hearing this, her kinsmen became disgruntled. This would mean they would have to venture out on the ice floes in search of the cave's opening. "Where do you expect us to approach the ice floes from? The beach here is much too rocky for our heavy sleds."

"If this is some kind of trap…? You'll be the one that is sorry. I'll skin you like a seal if you're lying to us!" On and on they went until the wind noise drowned out their voices and they had to shout to be heard.

"I will lead you to a safe crossing, but it's farther up the coast, quickly, my brethren!" She almost sounded sincere.

Uki, of course, led them farther away from the caves and could only hope there was a crossing up ahead to satisfy them. As they started out, Uki couldn't help but look back in horror as Amka and the rest of her pack appeared to be waiting patiently for their mistress' return. The only thing on her mind was to call out for them to stay.

At this, Nukilik seemed to laugh under his breath. As if he knew she would never be back to claim them. After about an hour, they could breach the ice floes closest to the shore and double back. Although still some distance away from where her sled was waiting, Uki instructed her kinsmen to stop so she could get her bearings.

After several stops and starts, the men grew weary of her excuses. Uki knew her time was almost up. Hopefully, she could take some of them with her when she transitioned into the spirit world.

WHILE STANDING ON THE ICE WITH HER BACK TO HER fellow kinsmen, Uki gazed at the cliffs above and sobbed as her last thoughts were of her daughter Siqiniq and what her life might be like due solely to the unfortunate colour of her skin.

Upon hearing her lamentations and realizing they had indeed all been duped, her kinsmen slowly turned to each other for guidance. But who would make the first move?

Operating on instinct as opposed to commands, the men dismounted their sleds and quickly surrounded their huntress before attacking her with a volley of punches aimed at the midsection. Uki refrained from pleading for mercy or defending herself with the small knife she carried. After all, it would just give them more cause to cut her in retaliation later.

Finally, having had the chance to inflict some form of internal trauma, the men tore her clothes off, layer by layer. It wasn't until Nukilik ordered the others to hold her and position her over the top rail of his sled that she fully grasped the gravity of her situation. These men all hated her and it became apparent with every savage thrust and every degrading comment as they took turn violating all of her orifices, except for her mouth.

One man made the mistake by trying to ram his fist into her mouth, much the same as one would do when trying to stop a polar bear from attacking. Her teeth were indeed very sharp and once she clamped down on the man's hand, it was like a vice. Forcing him to slug her in the ear repeatedly so she would hopefully loosen her grip.

In time, Uki's skin thankfully became numb from the intense cold as she stood there naked and barefoot on the ice. Struggling to remain lucid even as they continued to ravage her, leaving bite marks and scratches all over her once unblemished white skin.

At first, she wanted to scream at the heavens because she had felt it all. Every callused hand with jagged fingernails as it explored her nether regions, every mouth as they licked and bite her, leaving nowhere unsullied.

"How do you like having a real man inside you?"

"Did you think you were too good for us?"

"Our huntress, try our whore!"

One man had the audacity to untether one of the largest sled dogs and drag it toward where Uki was being restrained. He then smeared her blood on the animal's muzzle in a chaotic display. When the situation didn't unfold as they hoped, a few of them stepped forward, knocking Uki off balance and forcing her into a kneeling position with cold disregard.

The dog fought back and fiercely defended itself, biting and clawing at the men nearby. Then, without warning, the dog turned and bit Uki on the side of her upper leg, causing intense pain.

Uki didn't just scream, she howled like a banshee and then she fought back with every fibre of her being. At first, the men seemed shocked she had any strength left, but they were smart enough to back away and give her room.

One man left the mayhem, only to return with his bow and arrow in hand. As he gawked at her, Uki recognized him as the young hunter who gut shot his quarry many moons ago. Surely he could not still be holding a grudge?

She couldn't remember his name, but the look on his face told her everything she needed to know. One part of her wanted it to be over with quick, but another part wanted to say her peace. Exposed in every way possible except for the blood spatter now covering her shivering body, Uki fought to stay focused and control her speech.

"I truly never meant to disrespect any of you. I know I was born different, but I believe I spent my life trying to do what was right for our people. Meeting Asbjorn and falling in love was the will of the gods. You cannot fault me for that. I have tried to forgive you for murdering him. Please, let me take my daughter and leave."

As Uki spoke her truth, the blustery winds had kicked up a land spout of snow on the nearby beach, making its way out to sea. Again she looked around at her fellow kinsmen, sickened by the blood smears on their faces, hands and pants.

They would not let her leave.

22

"Asbjorn was easy to kill, but unlike him, you'll see it coming," and then he laughed. It was not Nukilik. It was the man who had paid so much attention to her during her pregnancy. Someone with the ability to blend into a crowd, appearing quite ordinary.

Should she even ask him his name or dignify his statement with a reply? The only thing this man deserved was the edge of her blade.

Her hesitation angered the man further. "You weren't worth waiting for, although I would have preferred to have had my way with you when you were ripe with child. Maybe you'd have been tighter," and then he looked around smugly at his fellow kinsmen. "You're going to regret this…" was all he said as Uki charged toward him in defiance.

Clamping her sharpened teeth around his jugular vein, before ripping it from his throat in a large ragged chunk and spitting it onto the ice.

Her actions caught the rest of the men off guard as they rallied to defend their brother. No one wanted to shoot him mistakenly with an arrow while trying to dispatch her.

In the end, they had to resort to hitting Uki in the stomach and the back as opposed to trying to pull her forcefully off of the man's body and causing further injury. By the time the kinsmen separated the huntress from her quarry, their brethren had already bled out on the ice.

The remaining kinsmen advanced upon Uki, forcing her to the edge of the ice floe. Giving in to the frigid water was not an unfavourable way to pass, and quite prophetic considering what Nukilik called her, 'Sea Spirit'.

Hopefully, she too would one day get her revenge. Then everything changed. Uki couldn't contain her elation as she bore witness to the sheer size and brute force of the snow as it arrived suddenly.

She wasn't sure if her kinsmen had even heard her parting words as she stepped backwards off the ice floe and into the icy water. "I curse you all!" she bellowed.

Although she bobbed back up in the water because of her air-filled lungs, causing her to unintentionally reach for the edge of the ice slab.

Out of nowhere, a man's gnarled hand swooped downward, clutching a large hunting knife and severed all of her fingers on one hand, missing her thumb. In her shock, Uki didn't even cry out. Instead she instantly relaxed and dropped beneath the water's surface. She couldn't feel anything. Just sweet relief encapsulating her entire body.

Her pain was gone.

Uki woke up from her dissociative fugue state. The beautiful young girl, who had reached out to her from below the waves, saddened her because she hadn't held her tight enough in her loving embrace. Instead, the spirit had let Uki simply float back up to the surface and face the harsh reality of her current plight. Coughing and gasping for breath, she glanced around and started swimming toward the shoreline.

Fortunately, her rather slow retreat was camouflaged by the storm and the fact her fellow kinsmen were now preoccupied with more dire consequences than the disposal of her body. Deep down, she knew the moment she ventured out of the water, she would most likely freeze to death.

With no time for further indecisiveness, Uki opted to make her way back to the ice floe and the warmth of her clothes. Miraculously, as everything was looking the same from her current vantage point, she thought she had heard men's voices yelling in the distance.

A beacon.

Uki didn't know where she was getting her strength from, but thanked Asbjorn's gods for giving her at least a slight chance to reunite with her beloved daughter.

After what seemed like forever, Uki finally received a reward as she splashed around in the glacial waters between the ice floes. First by climbing onto a floating slab of ice and second by finding the telltale signs of a recent dogsled crossing. Staying close to the ice floe's surface to reduce her exposure to the buffeting winds, she stumbled along in the advanced stages of hypothermia.

Hell bent on not losing the path. With her appendages screaming in pain as they cramped up and froze, she couldn't help but notice her breathing was fast becoming laborious. Finally, she came upon the scattered remnants of her torn clothing and, as she followed them to their end, she was more than grateful some pieces could dress her ice encrusted wounds.

When she did find the rest of her clothes, the aftereffects of being subjected to such drastic temperatures between water and air were more evident as she shivered uncontrollably. Making it almost impossible to dress herself. But thankfully she had always been ambidextrous or losing her fingers on her right hand might have proved fatal.

Once dressed, Uki started back toward the shoreline. The storm itself had diminished, but the air temperature was notably plummeting. She would have to find shelter if she hoped to survive the night.

AFTER SCALING THE WINDROWS, UKI BEGAN LOOKING FOR shelter among the large rocks on the beach, just shy of the wave-cut notches in the cliffs. Anything which would shield her from the incessant wind.

Sadly, the security the caves provided was no longer easily accessible, nor her dog team and sled. Those men would not defile her and get away with it. Uki made a promise to herself there and then. She would avenge the murder of her beloved Asbjorn and protect her daughter's innocence.

To increase her circulation, Uki would alternate between vigorously rubbing her arms and legs, and marching on the spot. However, she became so absorbed in her routine she almost missed the deafening silence once the Arctic winds ceased to blow.

The night air was crisp, to say the least. She felt the frost on her nose hairs but with her blood now pumping throughout her core and appendages, the pain returned with a vengeance. Trying to keep her mind preoccupied, Uki looked up at the clearing night sky, hoping to assess her current location. To her amazement, the beautiful northern lights danced overhead.

The damaged part of her wished the old folklore had been true and if she chanced to whistle at the lights in the sky, the spirits would come down and cut off her head, thus ending her misery. With resolve in her heart, Uki slowly stood again, testing her strength, and began shuffling about. She would not succumb to her misfortune of late.

As the thought crossed her mind, she was positive she heard a dog howling mournfully, not far off in the distance. Could it be Amka? Was he still alive? Was the pack still together, awaiting her return?

Immediately she yelled for her *qimmiq*, dogs, praying her voice would carry the distance needed since it no longer had to compete with the wind. Tears streamed down her cheeks as she received an answer to her call, but sadly, in her weakened state, she couldn't determine how close they were geographically, so she kept calling their names.

Uki wasn't sure how much time had passed before the first dog showed up. It wasn't Amka, but at least she had tracks to follow. Scooping up fresh snow in her good hand, she eagerly melted it in her mouth. Uki was unable and unwilling to succumb to any disparaging inner voices.

"You beautiful dog," she cooed, but when the dog jumped up to greet her in its excitement, Uki got bowled over and struggled to regain her footing. "Show me where Amka is. Where's the sled?"

The dog suddenly lowered its front paws with its back end still in the air, in a sort of "come play with me" stance, barking at her, daring Uki to follow. This brought a huge smile to her face and gave her the strength she needed.

The lights in the sky now worked to her advantage, for she could easily follow the animal's lead. In no time at all, she found herself happily back with her team, but as she looked around, she realized Amka's noble furry face was missing. Uki had to find him.

She needed to know if he indeed passed from this realm or merely crawled instinctively away to hide. She soon answered her questions as she dug her sled out from the recent snowfall. That's when she discovered his motionless body in the frame's shelter. Again she cried, but as soon as she gently put her hand out to stroke his fur, his nose nudged her in response. This made her cry all the harder, and it wasn't until she leaned forward to embrace him she saw the extent of his blood loss. She must get him to the warmth of the caves at once.

Mustering what little inner fortitude she still possessed, Uki lifted the large dog into the cargo bed of the sled and made haste, fastening the remaining dogs into their harnesses.

"Find the cave, my qimmiit," she shouted and with almost no hesitation, they were away. The dogs intuitively breaching the smaller berms leading from the beach up to the cliffs overhead.

She didn't know if they even understood her commands or they were happy to be pulling their burden once again. Finally, making good time across the tops of the cliffs, Uki felt thrilled to see the snow beneath her sled's runners was fresh. It confirmed that her kinsmen were most likely on their way back to camp.

Camp…she needed to get back there as soon as possible, but first she must see to Amka's wounds and then make a plan. After all, she couldn't show up as if nothing had happened. Surely the men would have already made up an elaborate story to cover their asses? Would the community be mourning her demise or happy she was no longer an obstacle for some?

Again, the brightness of the stars overhead combined

with the polar lights in the night sky helped her to navigate. Not to mention the wondrously keen noses of the sled dogs as they came to a halt on top of the exact cliff bank they sought, before circling the area to analyze further the plethora of smells hidden below the snow shrouded path.

The dogs began baying in unison and pulling at the sled as if eager to launch themselves off the precipice and into the void. Uki engaged the claw brake and reined the dogs in. She didn't know how much time Amka had left, but she knew she needed to stake the sled, so as not to repeat her earlier error.

At this point there was no second wind to access and Uki knew deep down she was no longer capable of carrying Amka safely down the treacherous snow-covered path. So she resorted to transferring the dog's body onto a hide in order to drag it the remaining distance.

After accomplishing that, Uki and the team slowly descended the cliff's face and reached the safety of the glacial caves below. As they breached the entrance, she could tell right away the inhabitants were well aware of their arrival by the variety of sounds echoing from deep within, but no signs of aggression were displayed.

Unfortunately, as soon as the terrain changed from ice to dirt, the going became increasingly more difficult. Uki had to halt her advance. A search for more hospitable surroundings would have to wait. The starting of a fire was not even a possibility, because of her present condition.

Uki no longer possessed the dexterity or the energy to undertake either task currently, so she decided to just gather the pack together and share in each other's warmth for the duration of the night.

While lying in the complete darkness of the caves and listening to the muted sounds of animals sleeping nearby, Uki felt lulled and surrendered to her complete exhaustion.

Hours later, she awoke with a start and quickly reached out to make sure Amka was still breathing.

And much to her relief, all of her dogs were indeed rejuvenated after their much-needed rest, although they were ravenous because of the time which had passed with no kind of sustenance.

23

UKI

Uki was happy to see the tunnels were now flooded with dim light. Daybreak was upon them, hopefully bringing an end to the current plague of winter storms.

Looking around, she was also pleased the pools of runoff were conveniently situated close by. Making it much easier for her to clean and dress her own wounds, along with Amka's.

Upon closer inspection, Uki couldn't believe the arrows had pierced none of her dog's vital organs and the blood loss had been mainly because of superficial wounds. Although he would likely have a limp. She herself had not been so lucky, albeit most of the bite marks, both human and dog, needed a thorough cleaning along with a little packing of moss.

However, she discovered one of her attackers had bitten off one of her nipples, with the change in temperature, the wound was now weeping profusely. Not to mention four of her fingers had been severed and would probably need to be cauterized if she hoped to save her hand. Uki ached all over and didn't even want to consider the extent of her internal injuries, cracked ribs, or the genuine possibility one of her kinsmen impregnated her.

She wanted to cry, vent, hurt something or someone in her anger, but what good would it do?

She had to think about what was best for Siqiniq. Revenge would have to wait. After gathering more moss and kindling, Uki could start a small fire and then prepare herself mentally to seal her wounds and dress them as quickly as possible. One part of her wanted to find a piece of leather to bite down on when the pain got too intense, but she screamed at the heavens to find a little inner peace.

She wasn't sure if she passed out or merely fallen asleep because when she came to later, there before her on the ground, was the body of a partially chewed rabbit. Uki had no recollection of what transpired, but she was more than happy to eat what was left for her. She didn't even bother cooking it, just used her knife to separate the hide from the meat.

After she ate her fill, Uki slowly tried to stand so she could drink from the pool, but the moment she tried to get up, she became instantly light-headed and had to sit back down. The more she fixated, the more parched she became.

Taking a deep breath, she got down on all fours and crawled to the closest pool and could finally quench her thirst. However, the moment she changed into a squat position and relaxed to make water, her guttural shriek reverberated off the walls. Again she lost consciousness and when she awoke this time, it was pitch-black.

Feeling vulnerable, she panicked and searched for anything she recognized through touch alone. Thankfully, her dogs had not left her side, as she felt their welcoming tongues licking her outstretched hand in the dark.

Uki again ventured over to the nearby water pools and

cautiously returned to her place amongst the warm bodies of her sleeping pack. When she awoke, she was rather stiff but well rested and feeling somewhat like her old self. Never one to let moss grow under her feet, Uki started a fire and searched for her spear.

She was hungry and raw meat would not suffice. She didn't want to cause bedlam in the caves, but she was looking for a much larger quarry than a rabbit. Both she and her dogs needed strength for their journey ahead.

Uki successfully dispatched a small reindeer calf and proceeded to field dress most of the carcass. Afterward, she hauled over the remaining parts to her dogs and allowed them to gorge themselves.

Once they all ate their fill, she again cleaned her wounds and Amka's, redressing where needed. She then began hauling provisions, enough for a couple of days, up to the top of the cliffs to her sled.

Luckily, the sky was clear and hopefully would stay that way, affording her enough visibility to reach her destination safely before nightfall.

With a heavy heart, she set out on what would be a perilous undertaking after packing her sled and harnessing all the dogs. There was no way of telling how many days she had been absent from her people's winter home. Hopefully a stealthy and well planned machinate would catch the five men who had sexually assaulted her and left her for dead, unsuspecting and unprepared.

The solitude of the sled ride did just that by giving her plenty of time to weigh all of her options. Did she want the rest of the community to know exactly what had happened to her, thus leaving justice in their hands? Should she take her daughter and leave? Would Tapeesa and her cronies even allow this to happen, or would her brethren kill her on sight?

Drawing ever closer to the winter camp, the skies overhead turned dark. Uki couldn't have planned a better homecoming. She smiled as she basked in the energy of the threatening storm, carefully staking her sled and dogs a short distance out. She proceeded on foot once the gathering of the elements shrouded her arrival.

Upon entering the outskirts of the camp, Uki thought she felt an abundance of electricity in the air and chalked it up to the approaching thunderstorm.

As she continued to move stealthily onward, she couldn't help but feel something wasn't right, accompanied by the hairs on the back of her neck standing on end. The camp itself was much too quiet for her liking. Nary a sign of a man or woman. Even the usual sound of sled dogs barking was strangely absent.

Where were her people and what could have justified the sequestering of the community into their respective homes, at such an early hour?

Uki held her breath as she made her way to the adjoining igloos she shared with her midwife's family and crept slowly in through her own entrance. Upon entering, she was aghast. Most of her belongings were missing. Did they believe she was dead and how did they come to know about her demise?

She quickly gathered what little hadn't been taken and wrapped it up in the polar bear blanket before stashing it outside the secondary entrance. She must find Siqiniq at once, or at the very least, Aama.

Uki could still not shake the terrible feeling which was exploding in the pit of her stomach. As she made her way to the large meeting tent, hoping to understand whatever was going on, she was surprised to hear the sound of people's voices raised in a chant of some sort. None of this made any sense.

What kind of gathering would take place outside and in these frigid temperatures?

Searching for the source, she approached the beach and froze in place when she heard the sounds of a woman's dirge and a child's terrified cries. At first, she didn't want to believe it.

Could they be culling members of their community and under whose authority? She had only been away for a few days at most. What had changed to precipitate such grievous actions?

IT HAD BEEN SO EASY. NO ONE HAD BOTHERED TO QUESTION Nukilik or his fellow kinsmen's stories as they expounded the events of their recent search.

Painting a picture of their tireless quest through dangerous snow squalls, only to find Uki's frozen body near the shoreline with no sled in sight. They assumed she most likely got separated from her team in an intense snowstorm and tragically fell victim to hypothermia. Since there were no visible signs of foul play.

After all, it was common knowledge hunters had a tendency to die long before they grew old. So in honouring her, they had given their esteemed huntress a proper burial at sea before attempting to track down her missing dog sled and team. Unfortunately, during their search for the lost team, the men misjudged the severity of a brewing tempest overhead and became disorientated and separated in the total whiteout conditions.

Only to be reunited hours later, less another hunter. They decided it was too risky to continue their search for anyone or anything, fearing they might lose more indispensable kinsmen to a white death.

Upon their return to the winter camp, the remaining men were quick to take advantage of their newfound security and elevated positions as providers because of what had transpired. The blind faith their community now displayed surprised and pleased them. Not to mention the subsequent lack of accountability. Sensing a people in turmoil and in dire need of guidance as food stores and heating fat were becoming scarcer by the day.

Desperate times called for new leadership and if you were not prepared…god help you.

As Uki crept closer to the gathering, she was rendered speechless by the atrocious sights that lay before her. There on the beach was a large semi-circle of her kinsmen and women, facing out towards the ice floes and open sea beyond.

At the water's edge stood several of the community's elder brothers and sisters, along with the youngest of the children, huddling together for warmth. Although the chosen were awaiting the group's presumable judgement, Siqiniq and Aama were not visible standing with them. Seeing was believing.

There was no longer any doubt about the unbearable truth of what had transpired. But where was her daughter, where was Aama, and why had Tapeesa not protected the child she had claimed to love? Was she too late?

Uki had to muster all her strength to not act as she continued to watch in horror. The sporadic torchlights of her kinsmen illuminated the bodies of the dead as they resurfaced from the shallows and the turbulent waters carried them onto the shoreline.

Everything she was now witnessing screamed for her to

assert her position as huntress. She must protect the weak. After all, it was her obligation. Although considering the circumstances and her current state, her daughter's safety took precedence because she would be of no help to anyone if she threw caution to the wind and died in doing so.

Uki needed to get closer to the ritual, if it was what it truly was because, in all her years, she had seen nothing quite like this before. She surreptitiously made her way to the shore, stepping into the water to look directly back at the faces of the submissive masses.

The moment her eyes fell upon the men who had abused her, Uki couldn't help but see red. Not only had they defiled her, they were leading the current proceedings. Instructing their brethren to toss the frail and helpless into the sea and justifying their actions as sacrifices for the greater good of their community.

All she could do was watch and take heed of exactly which participant did what and while doing so, she couldn't help but notice her five remaining attackers.

Only two were not flanked by a wife and children.

24

UKI

One with the shadows, Uki made her way back up the embankment and waited. She could only pray her daughter and her old friend were safe elsewhere. Once those in attendance had appeased whatever blood lust, these deplorable men had needed to quench, everyone filed back to their homes for the night.

Oddly, as they passed, no one was conversing. Somewhere in this pitiful group, someone must have felt remorseful for what they allowed to happen. Uki looked out at the shoreline below and felt thankful to see a single torch burning. She felt compelled to get a better look at the corpses before the wind inevitably snuffed the flame out. Yes, they had chosen the weakest, but surely there was no call for such measures, and then she saw them.

Floating in the knee-deep black water was the undeniable body of her old friend Aama, appearing to be clutching the tiny form of an infant as if trying to protect or comfort it, even in death. Uki instantly charged into the water and tried with all her might to pry the tiny body out of the old woman's grasp, but to no avail. It was Siqiniq.

Uki wanted to howl at the night sky in her sorrow but could not chance being heard. She gently kissed her beloved Siqiniq on the lips, placed a small piece of ice in her mouth, followed by cutting a lock of her child's hair and placing it in her pocket for safekeeping.

All she could do now was push the bodies farther out into the water and hope the tide would take them. Again, she was forced to think with her head and not her heart.

Revenge would only be hers if she chose restraint over acting on her impulses. As she made her way back through the camp to retrieve her belongings, Uki kept rechecking the secret pocket under her parka to ensure the treasured piece of hair had not fallen out and her knife was still conveniently ready.

She knew exactly where the lone kinsmen slept, the inept hunter being her first choice since he was the smaller of the two unattached men.

Uki waited several hours for the storm to reach its crescendo before sneaking slowly into his small igloo. She could tell right away by the rhythmic sound of his breathing he was indeed fast asleep but she needed to wake him to reap her revenge.

Straddling his static form on the ice bed, she leaned forward and sweetly asked him to light his seal fat burner. Uki braced herself for what might follow and was genuinely surprised to discover the body beneath her had not triggered its natural alarm system. By the look in his heavy-lidded eyes when they finally opened, he had no idea who had come for a late-night visit. However, the moment the darkness cleared, recognition struck, and the young man looked terrified and rightly so.

"What are you doing here? How could this be? I saw you drown!" With every utterance, he became paler and less coherent.

Uki quickly removed her knife from its hiding place with her good hand and flashed it before his eyes, then slowly began cutting open the front of his nightshirt.

"So you thought I had died? No one even took the time to look for my body…how unfortunate," she smiled, showing her fastidiously sharpened teeth.

Uki removed the mitten from her disfigured hand and dragged the charred stumps across his cheek, visibly disgusting her once brethren. As she continued to slice the front of his garment down the centre of his supine body, horror filled her as she discovered what was hidden within the man's clothing. He had taken the time to wrap a thread of sinew around one of her severed fingers and wore it as a memento around his neck.

"Where are the rest of my fingers?!" she shrieked and restrained herself, hoping the wind outside had masked the sound.

The man refused to even look her in the eyes, let alone answer her question. Without warning, he shifted his weight. Most likely to catch her off guard and cause her to lose her balance, making it easier for him to toss her onto the floor. Uki may have had an injured hand, but she still had her wits about her and no man had ever beaten her in any wrestling match.

She planned a retribution consisting of great suffering to be inflicted upon all the men who were responsible for her and Amka's assaults, but everything changed when she witnessed the culling of her community's weakest members, including the deaths of Aama and her beloved daughter.

Vengeance would need to equal the crimes committed

and mere torture was not sufficient. They would have to all die, including their families. Uki wanted to annihilate their bloodlines. The remaining five kinsmen's legacies would be erased forever.

Within the blink of an eye, the man tried to upend her once again. This time, they both ended up on the floor, but Uki quickly regained the dominant position and said, "If I had the time, I would force you to experience some of the degradation you thrust upon me."

Slowly, she looked around his meager dwelling, making her intentions quite obvious as she stopped to pick up various objects within reach, items that she could improvise to brutally violate him.

"They made me do it. I honestly meant you no harm!" he sniveled, but Uki would not let him finish. She bent down and tore his throat out with her razor-sharp teeth.

The young hunter's body was like a geyser as great gushes of dark red blood continued to pump from his lacerated jugular vein. She immediately got up and quickly rolled the body onto his bedding to lessen the radius of blood splatter.

One part of her wanted the whole community to know the killing was her handiwork alone. The other part of her needed to shift the blame for the time being, at least.

Uki grabbed the bedding and dragged the hunter's body out of the igloo. She needed to find a location with heavy foot traffic, somewhere which would ensure its discovery at dawn's first light. Once she found the perfect spot, Uki positioned the body so the man would finish bleeding out into the freshly fallen snow. Making for a more horrific kill site at first glance.

Although now looking down at his lifeless form, she could not help but feel unsatisfied. The man's death had been too merciful, too quick. Uki had so much hate bottled up inside, not to mention she had to remain silent as she stoically maimed the corpse further. She needed anyone chancing upon the scene to believe it was as a result of an animal attack.

Before leaving, she glanced around to make sure she had missed no details, then gently reached down and removed the morbid necklace from the dead man's body. Uki couldn't help but feel incomplete, like a shadow of her former self as she retraced her steps to cover them with snow. Only stopping momentarily at the dead man's igloo for one last walk through before retrieving her polar bear blanket from where she had stashed it earlier.

After throwing the colossal bear's hide "cape-like" over her head and shoulders, Uki bent down to collect her few possessions, along with the soiled bedding. Thankfully, nobody in the camp had noticed her presence. The howling winds had seen to that.

But in the end, one person witnessed her departure and his recapitulated version of the night's events, featured, among other things. The sighting of a blood soaked polar bear as it disappeared into the momentous storm. Uki knew deep down it would not end here and as long as she drew breath, the guilty parties would pay and suffer.

UNFORTUNATELY, SHE EXPERIENCED A DELAY IN HER departure as she took longer than expected to backtrack and locate her dog sled and team. Given they were now blanketed in snow, albeit waiting patiently.

The storm itself had continued with a vengeance of its own. Almost fitting, considering what had transpired beneath the heavens that evening. Uki refused to feel any remorse for the small part she played in the overall atrocities committed. She felt comfort knowing she indeed fought back and was confident they would make the return journey to their new home safely.

By the time the massive cliff's presence cut across the widening horizon, Uki drifted off to sleep several times, thankfully still clutching the handlebars. She had always known random chance brought luck about and not by one's actions, but that didn't stop her from giving thanks to the spirit world for her dogsled and team. Without them, she would have perished.

Again, Uki anchored her sled topside before making her way down the steep path to the caves below. She knew this was a dangerous move, should her former kinsmen venture out this way again in search of the sanctuary she had spoken so adamantly of, but right now she needed food and sleep.

The caves were currently alive with the sound of animals milling about as day broke and light penetrated the glacier ceilings above. As Uki and her team traversed the darkened tunnels on their way back to their previous resting spot near the watering holes, she was already making plans for further exploration. They needed haven within the honeycomb of caves. A place she could defend if need be, possibly dirt walls for warmth with good ventilation for a fire pit, but that could all wait. The dogs couldn't.

Owing to time constraints, Uki had to slaughter another calf underground, resulting not so surprising in a ripple effect occurring throughout the caves as the other animals heard its calls of distress and became outwardly anxious. Their future food sources would have to be killed and field dressed away from where they slept. That way, the other inhabitants of the caves would not fear them and return freely whenever shelter was sought.

After eating their fill, the dogs made themselves comfortable and settled in for a nap. Uki cleaned and redress her wounds before retiring. Sitting naked on the side of a nearby water pool, she slowly cleansed herself as best as she could and used pieces of moss to sooth her nether regions and to pack the skin avulsion caused by her nipple being torn off her body by someone's teeth. Not only did Uki experience physical pain, but she also endured mental anguish, being forced to relive her losses almost every hour of every day and night.

No longer did she have anyone dear to console her or share the fundamental need for human contact, no people to champion her. Worst of all, no daughter to cherish as evidence of the love she had once shared with Asbjorn. Her options were now limited since she could not see returning to her former community in any capacity whatsoever. Maybe she could head out in search of a whole new life as more and more "explorers" had become indisputable?

Uki's head was a jumble of thoughts, but the one thing she was certain of was that the "Sea Spirit" had saved her life for a purpose. She would return to finish what she had started as soon as she regained her strength, again using the cover of night and winter's storms as her allies. This way, she should be able to pick them off one at a time.

When sleep finally found her, it was hours later, but at least the cave returned to its earlier peaceful cohabitation. Even some of the smaller carnivores had dared to venture nearer to her campfire in search of scraps.

Thankfully, the closeness of her pack had afforded her the chance to gain some restorative sleep. When she awoke later that day, Uki was much more clear-headed, with a definite plan. She scavenged what little meat was still on the bones of the calf she killed earlier, but because of the ever decreasing light source, she would need a torch if she hoped to navigate the tunnels. There were still a few embers burning in the fire pit and she could fashion a small torch. With her spear in hand and Amka by her side, she headed out.

As Uki and Amka drew closer to the cave's entrance, it became harder for her to keep the torch lit because of the increasing winds. Another storm was on its way, or maybe this was a normal occurrence because of the shape of the cave's mouth as it faced the sea.

Either way, she needed to check on the status of her sled. Breaching the precipice above, there was her small sled, still anchored securely, but she could now plainly see from her vantage point large storm clouds were indeed gathering again. Not a good sign, but at least this would mean no one else should be out travelling in this kind of inclement weather.

Uki's joy was clear as she saw several small groups of animals racing across the terrain, heading towards her or, more likely, the safety of the caves below. Right away, Amka barked incessantly, which caused the small groups to disperse.

At first, Uki felt annoyed by her dog's actions, but then she felt pleased as she saw the resulting stragglers. Uki readied herself for the moment the second last animal cleared the cliff's edge. Dropping her torch, she took aim with her spear, using her left hand for a change, and could at least injure the calf before Amka went in for the kill.

The storm's fury descended upon them with unbelievable speed, forcing Uki and Amka to drag the animal down the cliff's path. Thankfully, Uki managed to retrieve the soiled hide from her sled and used it to help with their burden. She wasn't sure what the animals below would think of all the smells, but at least it should help cover the odour of the downed animal by masking it with human blood.

Once deeper inside the caves, she stopped to catch her breath and listen for the sound of frightened animals. Uki would have preferred to dress their kill outside of her new home, but circumstances being what they were, she would have to postpone that decorum. Again, she was pleased to bring back a bounty of food for the pack. This would do wonders to strengthen the dogs and herself.

Tonight, she again slept soundly.

THE FOLLOWING MORNING A MASS EXODUS OF ANIMALS filing by awoken her. The storm had broken, and it was safe to go outside. Uki was quick to call her dogs together and follow the herds back up to the surface.

There was excitement in the air as their light source brightened to the point of almost blinding sunshine. It was amazing how the animals knew what was going on outside. Then, racing back into the depths of the cave once the animals vacated, she wanted to get a better look at her surroundings so she could implement her plans for their new home.

Although she still had no idea where she could hide her sled. Maybe she'd build a snow house of sorts to protect it from the wind and passersby, but some of this could wait.

After all, the storm had been fierce and there was absolutely no way she had left any trace.

25

UKI

Back at the winter camp, kinsmen and women finally chanced to venture out of their igloos and tents to examine the damages the storm had wreaked. Only to find the remains of one of their hunters.

By the looks of the frozen body, a wild animal had undoubtedly attacked and killed him. One of their own soon corroborated this, as they had indeed seen a polar bear leaving the compound with bloodstains on its fur. You would have thought there was no further need for closure, but the four remaining hunters' unusual actions inadvertently piqued unwanted curiosities.

Some thought it was odd anyone would even second guess the cause of death, let alone fuss over the passing of one incompetent hunter. The actions in question were initiated after Tapeesa mentioned several items were now missing from her adjoining igloo. Not a significant finding, but enough to give the hunter's pause.

Upon closer inspection of their friend's corpse, they found it was short one nipple. Because of the sheer amount of tissue damage, no one could verify whether it had been removed intentionally or simply torn off in a feeding frenzy. And when you considered the man had been found in his bedclothes, one could only surmise a misfortunate encounter with a bear while possibly out relieving himself.

In the end, the midwife's implications only mildly bothered Nukilik and his three remaining accomplices. Although far-fetched, as they talked about it more, they became more convinced Tapeesa had to be wrong. After all, she was only missing a blanket. Uki could not conceivably be alive after spending so much time in the freezing water.

All the men laughed out loud as they unknowingly clasped the severed fingers they had hanging from sinew strings around their necks, except for the man that had kept her nipple in his pocket as a charm.

The Inuit were indeed superstitious people, and it had been easy to convince them the sacrifices of their brethren had been justifiable to appease the evil spirits who they believed were responsible for their current run of bad luck. The sacrifices were intended to strengthen the community by the culling of the weak or non-contributing members.

However, someone intentionally broke the rules by excluding several of the smallest children from the cull in a mysterious and convenient manner. Those whose fathers had taken it upon themselves to brave the elements, and in doing so, risked their lives in search of their defiant huntress. There was a new order in the community. Even the elders feared their dwindling authority. Looming starvation had definitely changed the pecking order.

Finally, now with a turn in the weather for the good, Nukilik could proclaim his ritual had been effective and exert his power even more over his weakened brethren. In his gut he felt confident the huntress' body was still resting at the bottom of the sea. She had taken quite the pounding from himself and his friends. They had all watched her bleed as they beat her to within an inch of her life before taking it in turns and rutting like animals in competition for sperm precedence.

The cutting off her fingers had been a rather poetic ending, as she pitifully reached for help. Nukilik only wished he had the chance to take the fingers on her other hand as well. That was the last they would ever see of her, but it wouldn't hurt to send a party out to the cliffs to prove or disprove her claims of an animal sanctuary.

The woman had been an expert hunter and a beauty until she had filed those teeth of hers. If she had stuck with her own kind, they wouldn't have needed to teach her a lesson.

That evening, Nukilik and his confidants called for a gathering in what used to be the elder's tent and everyone was to attend. No exceptions, since it concerned the very survival of their people. Some thought a celebration was in order to welcome the fairer weather. While others assumed a tribute to all those who had forfeited their lives. They were all wrong.

The men had only wanted to assess who remained and determine their benefit to the community. They neglected to serve any food, and the communal fire wasn't burning as brightly. The cries of the remaining children could be heard periodically. Possibly due to the overall growing anxiety of the crowd in attendance.

Nukilik paid no heed as he hushed his people and then brashly informed them of the new status quo. Yes, food was their number one issue and he would indeed send out a small hunting party comprising his most trusted kinsmen. He then assured them unlike Uki, he would not put their lives in further danger by heading off into the great unknown. For he and his men had already made plans to explore the outer cliff banks since they had spotted various animal tracks in the vicinity on their last outing.

He expressed his regret for not being able to lead the upcoming hunting party, citing his strategizing skills would be of more value to their encampment at present. Fewer people meant everyone must contribute, including possible changes to current living arrangements to make better use of the larger habitats and not waste precious fuel. Nukilik sensed this would not go over well with the general population, but he didn't care. He would take care of his closest friends and relatives.

In the shadows of the large tent, Tapeesa watched and waited. This new order could work to her advantage. After all, the burly hunter had always had eyes for her.

Alas, losing Siqiniq had been upsetting to say the very least, along with the on again, off again demise of her mother, the huntress. Deep down, Tapeesa felt she would never have had a moment's peace if Uki was still alive. Thankfully, she was still young and could have more children.

Be as it may, her current husband was proving to be more of a hindrance than anything else during these trying times. Surely their new leader would be game for a little dalliance, since he did not possess a wife. Although first she would have to make sure her husband was one of the chosen regarding the upcoming hunting expedition.

In the evening, after everyone retired to their respective homes, there was much discussion between husbands and wives. Even older children dared their parent's fury to be heard. Most were just plain scared. So much had transpired, and they had all followed blindly like sheep when they thought their next meal was in danger.

Tomorrow was a new day and, weather permitting, the community's hunters would once again be able to provide for their people. However, because of reassignment of duties within the camp, there was no celebratory sendoff the following morning, as originally thought.

The reorganization of their people's housing had suddenly become a priority, much to the chagrin of its inhabitants. Most thought it foolish to change their living arrangements so late in the season, since spring equinox was just around the corner and they inevitably would be on the move again.

IT TOOK NO TIME AT ALL FOR MOST OF THE REMAINING kinsmen and women to feel subjugated under Nukilik's new order, especially with the passing of yet another day and still no hunting party being dispatched.

They all felt the weight of their current dilemma and knew taking action was the only answer, but who would make the first move?

More bad luck befell the community. With the change in the weather, the bodies of their culled brethren had resurfaced. Who knew just how long it would be before the smell of decomposition attracted scavengers both great and small to the camp?

Unfortunately, their luck would most indeed include polar bears in search of an easy meal, making outdoor activities of any sort more dangerous. Some thought it was a great idea to wait for the animals to arrive and pick them off one by one.

Nukilik had to take action as family members of the deceased united and refused to accept the fact their dearly departed were left to rot on the shores. No more stalling.

The following morning, the hunting party embarked on their journey, leaving the few able-bodied men who remained with the daunting task of disposing of what was left of the dead. This time, most of their kinsmen jumped at the chance to take part in the hunt.

As Tapeesa waved goodbye to her husband, she was happy, although somewhat apprehensive about how unprotected their winter camp had become.

Nukilik, the organizer, assigned his brethren with collecting corpses from the shoreline. Some were tasked with placing the remains into fishing nets and weighting them, while other dragged the nets farther out onto the ice floes for disposal. He might not have dirtied his hands, but at least he kept watch over his people as they toiled, in case their safety should be in question.

He then hurried the men, women and children to finish their relocations within the camp and to board up the now unused structures.

As night fell, everyone made their way to their new dwellings, pausing briefly to gaze off into the direction the hunters had travelled in the morning.

26

UKI

Uki spent her time preparing her new home. Even braving the ice floes below with the help of Amka and her team to kill a ringed seal and transport it back to the cave for butchering. She still ached all over but was getting used to using her right hand even without her four fingers. Also, the extra hide blanket had come in handy and made for wonderful bedding once she had washed it.

Looking around her new dwelling, Uki was content. She had company, food, water and fuel, but she would not sleep easy until revenge was hers. As if to answer her prayers, the weather changed for the worse. Once again, affording Uki the luxury of cover to return to her former people's camp unseen.

She quickly set about packing food for the journey and harnessed the dogs to the sled, lastly throwing the large polar bear blanket into the cargo bed.

As she cut across the virgin snow, she plotted plausible scenarios which might play out and making contingency plans. This time, she would be the aggressor. Looking back, Uki was happy to see the fresh snow was covering her passage, and like a ghost, she could later pass by several outbound sleds belonging to her former kinsmen.

Undetected in the approaching darkness with mere yards separating them. Upon drawing closer to her old camp, Uki quieted the dogs lest risk being discovered. She anchored the sled and unharnessed the team.

One part of her would have preferred a speedy getaway while the other half was more worried about the safety of her dogs, should a large carnivore happen upon them in the dark. Either way, she was lucky they all took commands well and laid down in the snow to await her return. Except for Amka.

Uki called her loyal dog to her side as she threw the large white blanket over her shoulders, making her way stealthily through the snow, travelling downwind from the camp. She was overjoyed to see that because of the impending storm; the inhabitants appeared to be nestled safely in their igloos. Something, though, wasn't right.

Upon entering the encampment, she observed with surprise several of the dwelling's entrances had been covered over, making them inaccessible. Initially, she worried about people being trapped inside, but upon closer inspection, she felt relieved as she didn't hear any sounds from within.

Slowly, making her way from igloo to igloo, Uki stopped to listen for the voices, at first puzzled, then angered, because almost everyone was not where they should be. Uki was surprised when she looked across the camp towards the elder's tent and saw the entrance's large flap blowing in the breeze and no fire burning brightly within. As she continued on her search, she mentally tried to note the exact locations her kinsmen and women now resided in.

She kept listening for the voices of the few men who would always be ingrained in her memory and appear in her nightmares. When she was about to give up, she heard the unmistakable sound of a woman's laughter, followed by Nukilik's gruff voice.

Uki stopped dead in her tracks as a rush of excitement coursed through her, startling Amka and forcing her to grab the dog by the snout to quiet his growls. Slowly making her way to the side of a large igloo, she quickly dropped to her knees next to the structure and listened closely. She had to be sure. The blowing wind made it impossible for her to eavesdrop, so she had to use her spear to make a small hole in the igloo's side to hear more clearly.

The instant she recognized the woman's voice, Uki became enraged. Her former midwife was entertaining the new leader of the community. This she quickly gleaned from only a small part of their conversation. Uki wanted to march right in there and spill their blood, but again she was forced to think with her head and not her heart. She made herself turn away and stop listening to their mindless chatter.

Looking around, she was pleased to see the storm was indeed increasing in strength and whatever she planned for them, would be masked by the sound of the howling north winds. Uki knew she must plan her attack precisely to take down her opponents as fast as possible. Neither one must be allowed to reach help or anyone within earshot.

Again she waited, but this time for sounds of copulation and the moment they became boisterous.

That's when she prompted Amka to bark incessantly outside the entrance to the couple's igloo. Almost on cue, Nukilik in his nakedness burst forth, looking frantically around for the source of the animal's distress.

Uki commanded Amka to take down the man and as her dog tackled its prey, bringing the man to his knees, she dropped her blanket and ran into the fray, armed only with her knife and her sharp teeth. She had left her spear standing upright in the snow nearby since she would not take the chance of harming her dog, should her aim be anything but perfect. Uki was delighted to see the look on the man's face as realization finally set in. He had taken the bait so easily. Being he was still a very formidable opponent, she kept her distance at first.

Long enough for Amka to take some of the fight out of him. Watching almost gleefully as her dog tore pieces of flesh off the now whimpering man's body until she finally had enough and commanded Amka to stand down.

Uki couldn't help but study Nukilik's response as she purposely smiled, showing all her teeth. "Did you really think I would not avenge the deaths of my beloved daughter and my people?"

Unfortunately, all he did was shake his head in denial and sob uncontrollably. How pathetic, she thought. This was not how she had envisioned their last confrontation, imposing no longer as he kneeled before her on the snow. The man had caused her so much pain and for what reason?

"Why"…was all she got out before she herself wept.

Everything happened so fast, Nukilik made a grab for her at the same moment she impulsively thrust her blade forward impaling his outstretched hand, tackling him as he tried to protect himself, savagely ripping his throat out and spilling his life's blood all over the snow. It wasn't until she heard a woman screaming behind her that she unclenched her jaws and loosened her grip on his neck.

Turning around slowly, there was Tapeesa, blubbering and repeating, "I knew you weren't dead!"

Uki stood and faced the woman. "Start running!" was all she said as she turned her back and started walking toward where she left her spear.

The midwife must not have understood what Uki said because she remained immobile, but once the huntress retrieved her spear. Tapeesa was off like a scared rabbit. At this point Amka became anxious, as if wanting to join in on the hunt, but his mistress was still confident in her abilities and quieted him.

With all her rage, Uki threw the spear high into the night sky and, as the weapon became earthbound, it impaled the woman's body through the side of her neck. Stopping her dead in an almost upright position.

The huntress rushed over to Tapeesa's suspended body, hoping she would at least be able to say a few words before the woman's spirit departed this earthly realm.

"I have no regrets whatsoever. My actions were justifiable. They granted you the revered position of Sanaji. Do you have anything to say in your defence?"

Unfortunately, because of the almost vertical direction the spear had travelled before entering the midwife's body, it was impossible for the woman to speak as blood gushed from her agape mouth and the only word Uki heard clearly was *Itialuit*, meaning damn you. Tapeesa's eyes darted back and forth like a trapped animal and she surprisingly tried to claw at Uki with what little strength she could muster, using her only working arm.

A convulsive tremor shook her entire body before taking her last breath. Uki wasn't sure how long she stood there staring into the face of her former midwife. A woman who she had put her trust in to protect her dear Siqiniq. They would all pay. Amka distracted her from her thoughts as his barks became more urgent. Uki turned just in time to see a large polar bear advance upon Nukilik's bloodied body and bat it around, as if making sure it was dead.

She held her breath in anticipation, waiting for the bear to sufficiently mark the body before waving her arms about, trying in earnest to coax the animal over to the dead woman's body. At first, it seemed apprehensive, most likely because it now saw a human and one large dog as potential threats.

Uki's persistent attempts to lure the bear paid off as it charged at her. Thankfully, she and Amka could easily foil the attack, whereas Tapeesa's dead body took the brunt.

Uki only stopped momentarily to look back as the large polar bear tackled the midwife's body. She thought she had heard the distinctive sound of her spear shaft being broken in two by either the animal's sheer weight or its teeth.

Surveying the entire scene laying before her, it was hard to tell what the first onlookers would deliberate. With the snow beginning to fall heavier with each passing hour, and who knew if the predator was indeed solitary? Alas, nothing further could be done. Uki had cast the die and still had a great distance to cover. As she was about to collect her hide blanket before taking her leave, she felt overwhelmed with feelings of unfinished business and felt drawn to the dead man's igloo.

Upon entering the structure, she didn't know what she was looking for. Then it came to her. Where was her amputated finger since it had not been suspended with sinew from around the man's neck? A quick search through the piles of discarded clothing on the floor and what few belongings the man had possessed she did not find her missing digit, but to her disgust, she found what was left of her cleaved nipple.

Nukilik had been treating it in much the same way as you would an animal hide in order to preserve it. As Uki tucked it safely inside her pocket, she couldn't help but laugh at the thought that this man had actually kept her nipple as a good luck charm but her mirth soon faded because she still had three more fingers to retrieve and the subsequent killings would also involve whole families.

Deep down, she knew these despicable men's offspring were not to blame for their father's actions, nor were their wives. She would need to think harder on the subject. When she finally exited the igloo, Uki pilfered one other object, and that was Nukilik's spear. He would no longer need it and once slightly shortened in length, it should serve her well.

Wasting no more precious time by lingering in her previous camp, Uki reunited with her sled and team before setting out under cover of darkness for the cliffs and the safety of her hidden caves. Hoping the return trip would prove uneventful.

27

UKI

THANKFULLY, HER DOGS COULD COVER THE DISTANCE posthaste after a quick stop for sustenance, and although the storm had continued throughout the night, it had not strengthened in intensity.

Because of the amount of blowing snow, drifts had covered her former brethren's sled tracks, making it impossible to know where they had been searching for game. As with every return, Uki was frightened at the thought of discovery. She cautiously made her way down the steep embankment, she felt relieved to see no signs of movement along the path except for animal tracks.

Tonight she had also taken great care in camouflaging her sled after anchoring it by using a makeshift ground blind of dwarf shrubs and then packing it with snow, in case the hunters should still be in the vicinity when the new day dawned. Lying comfortably amongst her team, Uki couldn't help but go over everything that had happened earlier today and contemplate she might not bring herself to kill a child. Finally, sleep took her and with it some resolution to her worries.

The following morning, as per usual, the moment a glimmer of light entered the caves, the mass exodus would begin again. Uki would have liked to have slept in, but that was not possible. Even though their sleeping chamber was now slightly away from the rest of the inhabitants, her dogs craved fresh air. Again, with feelings of foreboding, she followed closely as her team exited the entrance to the caves, keeping her eyes peeled for any sign of trespass.

Thankfully, the day was cloudless and Uki could see for miles in every direction. Her stores were full, leaving her with nothing pressing to accomplish and more time to explore, both inside and out. The only problem presenting itself was her growing paranoia, because if she could see for miles, so could others.

Taking a moment to breathe, Uki quickly vanquished her negative thoughts. She would not spend the rest of her days hiding in a cave or living in fear. On the bright side, she took pleasure in the notion the hunting party she had encountered had returned to camp empty-handed and were now preoccupied with the inescapable carnage and empty stomachs of their fellow kinsmen and women. But enough pointless woolgathering. Only the spirits knew her destiny.

Today was hers and she would make the most of it. Not only was Uki a talented huntress, she enjoyed a challenge and today's preemptive tasks would include scouring the nearby ice floes for any telltale signs of breathing holes.

So with the aid of Amka, she did just that and was more than thrilled to discover an overabundance of them. There was more food here than she could ever use. Keeping herself busy was a good thing, leaving less time to dwell on the fact she would never see her beloved Asbjorn or Siqiniq again. At least not in this world.

Although with every exertion, the physical pain she still felt was evocative of all she had endured, in time the scars would eventually fade but never the memories.

Sadly, even though she kept herself busy throughout her waking hours, nightmares still plagued her. The more she fixated on what had occurred during her supposed rescue, the more she was convinced that the six hunters had not acted alone.

It ate at her to think her once fellow kinsmen had set out on a rescue mission in search of their huntress, only to change their minds along the way. Such darker deeds could not have been dreamed up on the spur of the moment. Just how long had they been planning their revenge for what they perceived as a slight?

Not to mention her esteemed midwife had most likely been plotting her demise or at the very least, inciting discord within the community's members. Through solitude and sweat, Uki could finally think clearer regarding retribution. There would be no death by association of the innocents.

After all, most of her fellow kinsmen and women had treated her with respect and even kindness throughout the years, and a few she even owed her life to. That night she enjoyed a hearty meal of seal and time spent around the campfire, marveling at all the so-called wild animals that had seen their coexistence as something of a normality.

As more ventured forward to steal small scraps and investigate their human. Now to finish planning her course of action on retrieving the three remaining fingers, the bearers of which all had families, and now the camp had turned upside down. It was going to be even more difficult to locate and segregate them. This meant her plans needed to be carried out in one go, unless the opportunity presented itself.

The weather was still on her side since it never remained constant for any length of time, but she would need to be ready the moment that it changed. Uki wasn't about to alter her tactics now. She knew fulfilling her revenge under cover of night and the reduced visibility of blowing snow was her best option, lest her fellow hunters become the wiser and she inadvertently became the hunted.

BACK AT CAMP, TOTAL BEDLAM HAD INDEED ENSUED AT daybreak and the return of the unsuccessful hunting party. Kinsmen and women were greeted with the discovery of their new leader's mauled naked body along with that of one of their brethren's wife's.

Gossip abounded, but it was easy to tell what had transpired prior to the attack since their clothing had been found strewn about the interior of Nukilik's igloo. Thankfully, the scene had been rather white washed by the snowfall, but the horrific details were still more than clear. No one could fathom why they had both been outside naked. Some thought the midwife had been attacked first and their leader had tried to kill the bear with his spear, only to miscalculate his throw and grievously wound the woman.

Unfortunately, there was not a lot to go by, since from the looks of it, several polar bears had been feeding off of the dead throughout the night. Kinsmen and hunters tried in vain to keep Tapeesa's husband away from the bloodbath, but he fought them fiercely in order to get one last look at his wife.

After breaking free from their grasp, he fell to the ground while sobbing hysterically over her remains. At first, his brethren tried kind words to coerce him away from the body as he futilely attempted to gather the pieces, finally resorting to brute force, since nothing could be gained by his actions and his mental stability had come into question.

Nukilik did not have any immediate family to mourn his passing and there was certainly no love lost between himself and his fellow kinsmen of late, so removal of the body had already begun as the community could not risk leaving the bloodied corpses out in the open.

Three of their hunters had died within such a short period was not lost on those with a sullied conscience and mounting suspicions. Then add to their unsuccessful hunt with nary an animal in sight. They had no leader and their winter camp food stores were almost completely gone now. Something had to be done, and quickly.

It had been customary to first seek guidance from the elders, those known to communicate with the spirit world. But, regrettably, since their recently departed leader's forced cull, they were now few, thus resulting in the burden being transferred onto the shoulders of the group's senior hunters to be rectified.

The rest of the day was spent in honouring the dead, buying the unprepared hunters a little more time to figure out just what their next move would be. Fortunately for them, all involved chose the sea as the least labour intensive means of disposal since the skies overhead had seized on a threatening appearance.

As community members gathered on the nearby shore, the dead's nearest and dearest began transporting what was left of their earthly bodies, shrouded in hides, onto the closest ice floes. And once the remaining elders were given the opportunity to say a few words in homage, the bodies were then weighted and gently pushed into their icy cold resting place.

Tapeesa's husband was heard to have mumbled something about her now being at peace with her daughters, although no one dared voice it aloud.

As soon as night had fallen and everyone had taken their leave, a small party of three could be seen by the stars alone, stealing away to Nukilik's igloo to speak freely. Their community needed a leader, and they knew no one was about to listen to anyone until their bellies were full. They concurred with the urgency of one last trip out to the cliffs.

The huntress had to have seen something out there. Deep down, no one had really believed her crazy on that fatal day, only frostbitten. Finally, it was decided only two of them should make the trip since someone would be needed to stay behind to salvage what their dead friend had tried to accomplish and to keep their brethren mollified. No one was giving up on their encampment just yet. They all still had families here and hopefully futures.

Surely their luck would change for the better?

The very next morning, the two hunters that had chosen the shortest straws headed out with overcast skies above. Their plan was to retrace their steps that fateful night and hope they could find the caves the huntress had so adamantly ranted on about. Curiously, no one mentioned her name or even dared speak it out loud, but they did all still carry her severed fingers around their necks. Some had even fantasized about being the one whose seed she had carried into the afterlife.

The men made good time that morning but unfortunately all that changed as the day wore on, forcing them to seek refuge from the now blizzard like conditions. Seeing as there were no large trees, they had to make do by literally digging themselves into a snowbank to provide shelter for their dog sleds.

MERE MILES AWAY, UKI TOO HAD BEEN CAUGHT OUT ON the vast sea of white as the storm hit, but unlike her brethren, she and her team were quite familiar with the terrain.

At first it had only been an inconvenience, but as the hours passed and the conditions changed for the worse, Uki used more caution as she mushed through the now combination of falling and drifting snow. A rather hazardous phenomenon that hampered her visibility and jeopardized her plans for another furtive return to her former camp because she just couldn't see.

Miraculously, her attentiveness was rewarded when she glimpsed a flicker of light off in the distance. High on adrenaline, Uki quickly changed course and set out to find the source of the light, hoping that her prayers had indeed been answered and she had been given the opportunity to catch her former kinsmen off guard. Thankfully, the wind noise once again gave her cover as her enthusiastic dog team made haste towards a small dark shape from which the light had emanated.

As soon as she drew close enough to make out the shape of a small hide tent that had been constructed haphazardly amongst the larger snow drifts, she immediately halted and anchored her dogs. After unharnessing Amka, she approached the tent slowly and was happy to see the oil lamp burning within as it confirmed the silhouettes of only two people. This was not standard practice for a hunting party, but desperate times called for desperate measures.

Once again, Amka could feel his mistress' anxiety and whimpered, which she quickly silenced with a gentle pat on his snout. Moving closer to the side of the tent, Uki knelt and listened carefully to the voices of those within. As the men conversed, it didn't take long to recognize the sources, the sounds of which she hoped to soon silence forever in her head. Uki could not believe her luck.

What were the odds of two of her quarry being out in the middle of nowhere on a night such as this?

Uki quickly tried to calm herself…she must first assess the situation and not act rashly if she intended to keep the upper hand and dispatch them both.

While scrutinizing their camp, her eyes instantly fell on the distinctive shapes of multiple dogs as they crowded together for warmth under a heavy blanket of freshly fallen snow. Thankfully, since all the animals knew each other, there had been no barks of alarm, nothing at all that would bring attention to Uki's arrival.

Stealthily making her way to where the teams were tethered, she greeted the dogs and quickly hushed them and then began unharnessing every one. In their excitement, several of the dogs had barked and jump around playfully, catching the attention of the hunters within the tent. Though it was only one man who opted to venture out in the storm to investigate the cause of the animal's ruckus and the moment that he saw an unknown figure crouching over his dogs, he was quick to loudly voice his displeasure.

The warning gave Uki the exact time she needed to remove her knife from within her hidden pocket and prepare her stance so that she could attack the moment he laid a hand on her. She quickly held her breath in brief spurts to not hyperventilate as she patiently waited for the man to get closer, all the while keeping her back turned to him; finally as he grabbed her shoulder in order to swing her around, she struck.

Clearly he was not expecting a left hook with a knife and the look of fright on his face that followed was almost satiating. As soon as the blade of her hunting knife entered the side of his head, Uki quickly tried to pull it free so that she could stab the man again, but it was stuck.

Apparently it had not entered the ear canal as precisely as hoped and was caught on bone.

28

UKI

As the two fought for their lives in the snow, the other hunter was oblivious to what was going on only feet away. Again Amka was quick to come to his mistress' aid as he grabbed the large man by his pant leg, causing him to stumble.

As the hunter fell flat on his back while still trying to maintain a hold on Uki, the air was knocked out of his lungs and he immediately loosened his crushing grip.

Uki was quick to take the advantage by straddling him and placing her knee on his chest as she forcefully ripped her knife out of his head using both hands and then began stabbing him repeatedly in the face, hoping to at the very least take out an eye. All of a sudden Amka let out a growl of warning but it was too late as the other hunter grabbed her by the hair and dragged her off of the now dead man's body.

"You…how could this be…I saw you drown?" and then he backhanded her across the face with all of his might. Resulting in a complete loss of muscle tone and inevitably, Uki collapsed onto the snow-covered ground as her eyes rolled back into their sockets.

LATER, WHEN UKI FINALLY CAME TO, SHE WAS HORRIFIED TO discover that her clothing had been removed, and she was chilled to the bone. She had no idea of just how long she had been unconscious, her head hurt and the moment that she tried to move, she discovered that her hands had been tied.

Quickly looking around the inside of the hunters' tent for something, anything to free herself with, her focus was unfortunately sidetracked the instant that Amka's anguished cry reverberated through the crisp night air.

Fearing the worst, Uki started to scream and thrash about, hoping to divert the remaining man's attention so that her dog might get away. Thankfully her plan worked because almost immediately the tent's flap flew open, followed by the emergence of the same hunter who had inexplicably come to her and Siqiniq's aid mere months ago when a certain rogue bear had first shown up at camp.

Alas unlike the other hunter who had stared in disbelief as Uki dealt the killing blow, the look on this man's face was one of triumph as he stood over her exposed body. The same look that he had when participating in her brutal violation, days before.

As Uki looked up into the big man's eyes, she truly wished that she alone could wipe that look of self-satisfaction off of his face but sadly she was presently in no condition to do so.

Then adding to his sheer audacity, he laughed as he perused her flesh, "Well, at least I won't have to share you this time."

He didn't bother to remove his parka, simply dropped his pants and flaunted his manhood for her enjoyment or as a scare tactic.

Not getting the rise he surely expected out of Uki, he dropped to his knees in front of her, all the while never losing eye contact and then began positioning himself for what was undoubtedly coming next.

Uki held fast to his gaze, refusing to show weakness of any kind and then she tactfully averted her eyes as if something had gained her attention and the moment that he looked away, she spontaneously kicked out with both of her feet in the hopes of catching him squarely between the legs with the full force of her extension but unfortunately he was faster.

He gripped her ankles tightly with both hands, then repositioned himself, pressing down on her legs with his full weight, causing her discomfort. As she attempted to move, her actions seemed to anger him further. Without warning, he reached and dug his dirty nails into her healing breast wound, causing it to bleed profusely and prompting a pained gasp from her.

Try as she might, Uki could not hold back the tears as they streamed down her cheeks…initially she had absolutely no intentions of begging for her life if things went south. But when he leaned forward and she caught a fleeting glimpse of one of her severed fingers, hanging from a strip of hide around his neck, her will to live returned.

"I'm sorry…I promise to be good" she almost choked saying those words and then looked away submissively with eyes cast down awaiting his response.

Uki knew deep down that the blow she had recently taken to the head had left her in no condition for hand-to-hand combat with this big man but if her hands were freed, there was still a small glimmer of hope.

"Shut your mouth, I hate those teeth, it makes you look ugly! If I untie you and you make so much as a move to strike me, I will strangle and violate your corpse… do you understand?" he spat. Uki simply nodded her head in agreement.

The man slowly repositioned himself, finally releasing her from his weight-force then grabbed her by the waist and flipped her like a rag doll over onto her stomach so that he could remove the bindings from around her wrists. Once that was done, instead of turning her over onto her back again, he kneaded her buttock before circling her with his calloused fingers.

Uki could not help but squirm at this invasion but the more she tried to move away, he simply grasped her by the hips and brought her ass up to meet his groin. Then he began forcibly rubbing himself up against her, catching Uki off-balance at the speed with which she felt him grow firm. He stopped several times as if teasing her before slapping her harshly.

The man was merciless in his violation and every time she cried out in pain, he seemed to take even more pleasure in what he was doing, literally laughing at her distress. It took all of her concentration to look about the room for a weapon, anything sharp that she could kill or wound him with and then, finally, after what seemed like forever, her eyes fell upon a quiver of arrows that were propped up in the corner of the tent and sadly just out of reach.

She needed to think quickly, so arching her back as if in anticipation, she reached between her legs and grabbed onto him. Immediately he stopped what he was doing and brusquely pulled out of her, Uki froze, puzzled by his reaction, she held her breath awaiting his response and then without warning he flipped her over again so that they were face-to-face.

This time he actually smiled before spreading her legs and penetrating her, apparently he now thought that their coupling was consensual. Uki kept an ever watchful eye on the big man above her as he plunged repeatedly into her and she was more than a little surprised to see that he had let his guard down so quickly, actually closing his eyes with every onslaught.

Thankfully this gave her a moment to collect her thoughts for she wasn't about to endure this position for much longer, she needed to get up the nerve to suggest that she sit astride him. Of course under the guise that it would be more pleasurable, when in reality she needed a better vantage point and position to strike. Evidently this man thought with only his little head as he readily agreed... before getting on top of him, she visibly shivered for his benefit and then crossed her arms over her chest and rubbed the palms of her hands up and down the tops of her arms.

When he didn't seem to take the hint, Uki then suggested that they move away from the drafty entrance to the tent and make themselves more comfortable on his caribou bedding before proceeding. Again he appeared more than happy to oblige, standing up and quickly moving to secure the tent's flap, all the while keeping his back to her.

Seizing the opportunity that she had been given, Uki decided to flirt with danger by abruptly repositioning herself at the back of the tent. Then surreptitiously knocking the arrow quiver over with her foot and dragging it into position while haphazardly throwing her scattered clothing into a pile on top of it.

And as luck would have it, the man was too preoccupied with what he assumed was going to happen next that he never even noticed the absence of his quiver. Uki then took one last look around the room before taking his hand and leading him to the exact spot where she wanted him to lie down.

As she gently pushed him down onto the hide bed, she couldn't help but notice that he was looking at her disfigured hand with revulsion as it made contact with his chest. Then all of a sudden he did something quite unexpected, he rose back up on his knees in order to remove his parka before throwing it onto the nearby clothing pile. Although once bare-chested he seemed to look down almost reverently at the severed finger that hung from his neck.

Uki wanted…no, needed to kill him that very instant but first she must continue with her charade. Slowly she pushed him back down onto the bed and then mounted him, the moment her body grasped him; he let out an almost animalistic grunt, again closing his eyes as he thrusted upwards. Uki leaned forward and rubbed his nipples with her good hand and then almost playfully started moving up and down on his member teasingly, as if she was going to spit him out.

Every time she dropped down, she would try to squeeze his manhood with her pelvic floor muscles, like a game. Thankfully his eyes remained closed as she reached ever further trying to unearth the buried quiver, several times she missed but finally her persistence paid off as she found his rhythm, now with a single arrow grasped firmly in hand, she began the game with even more fervour. Every thrust more frenzied than the last as he now held her by the waist and pushed her down forcefully to meet his pelvis; Uki swiftly raised her arms above her head and let out an unearthly howl as she gathered her strength.

Suddenly a smile of satisfaction creased the hunter's face, followed by his eyes opening just in time to see the woman above him lunge forward while driving the arrow's head as deep into his heart as she could.

Fortunately, Uki held fast to the arrow's shaft and tore it right back out of the man's chest in order to strike again but there was no need because the moment that it was removed, the hunter's heart exsanguinated and he was no longer a threat.

Now running on pure adrenaline, the huntress continued to stab the dead man while wailing loudly and venting her anguish on deaf ears. Exhausted, she attempted to gain her footing and in doing so, his now flaccid member slipped out.

Uki was instantly overcome with abhorrence both of herself and the hunter at her feet, knowing that she had allowed this man to violate her yet again. Once standing, she frantically attempted to wipe away his evidence from off the inside of her thighs.

Again acting on impulse, she lashed out at his corpse by grinding the heel of her foot into his groin and when that did not satisfy her repulsion enough, she then bent down and severed his manhood with one swipe of the arrow's razor sharp edge that she still had gripped firmly in her hand.

As Uki slowly returned to an upright position and regained her faculties, she couldn't help but look around the interior of the small tent in awe as she beheld the aftermath of her actions or should I say reactions.

Yes, two men died but rightly so, there was no pity in her heart for the departed, only the families that they had left behind. Dropping the severed member as she looked down at herself and the congealing coating of blood that she now wore, Uki gathered a few of the randomly discarded pieces of clothing from off of the floor and tried to wipe herself clean.

As she vigorously went about her task, Amka's well-being suddenly returned to the forefront of her thoughts… chastising herself, Uki quickly collected her own clothing and hurriedly dressed.

Throwing open the flap of the tent, she called her dog's name and instantly broke into tears as Amka limped towards her from out of the darkness. Upon closer inspection, she could not see any open wounds but surmised that the man must have taken his boots to the animal.

Reaching down, she daintily retrieved the discarded member, not actually wanting to touch it with her own hands and then presented it to her dog, who without hesitation gobbled it down. Exhausted and battle weary, Uki still found strength to seek out the other hunter's body which was now camouflaged by snow, in order to chop off his member as well.

One part of her wanted so badly to leave both bodies at the mercy of the elements, in the hopes that scavengers would feed off of their remains. Whereas, her more ethical side opted for returning them to their community, not that they deserved a dignified burial of any sort but their families had a right to know the reason for their demise.

Uki quickly began the daunting task of re-harnessing the dogs to the men's sleds before depositing their bodies into their respective cargo beds. She then retrieved her severed fingers from around the dead men's necks, stopping only long enough to collect anything of value from their camp before returning to her own sled.

She actually had second thoughts about keeping the

extra dog teams but unfortunately there was no place for them in the caves and her plate was already full. Uki wasn't even sure what she was going to do or say when she finally arrived at her former brethren's encampment but thankfully the long journey ahead would afford her plenty of time with few distractions, so that she could further collect her thoughts and regroup.

Later as their winter camp came into view, Uki immediately slowed her team in order to wrangle the other two sleds before dismounting her own and anchoring it at a safe distance away. She chose to then enter the community in the predawn hours whilst driving one of the hunter's larger sleds with the other one in tow, so that she would have an out if need be.

Uki couldn't help but have mixed feelings about her return and was quite surprised by the sheer number of kinsmen and women who had surfaced so early from their igloos, to greet their returning hunters, only to discover that their huntress had miraculously risen from the dead.

29

UKI

Soon the camp was a bustle of activity and noise as people ran back and forth. Most seemed happy that their huntress had indeed returned, while others were clearly fearful and some even downright hostile, but everything abruptly changed once the sleds revealed their cargo.

Uki struggled in vain to be heard over the lamentations of the gathering crowd. However, a loud taut voice soon rang out through the cacophony, one that she instantly recognized, causing her heart to sink into her stomach.

"My people, let the huntress speak. Surely she would not return to us after killing her own kinsmen?"

The man's blatant threat left Uki literally struck dumb before everyone, catching her so off guard she could not even remember the hunter's name. Although she would never forget his nervous voice or the cruel things he had said while trying to use his sled dog to harm her.

She had no intention of sharing all the sordid details with her former people, but surely someone had to have seen the fingers that these men had worn so proudly around their necks and questioned their motives?

"Brethren, I beg of you to hear me out. I never meant to stay away for so long, but I was in fear for my life. I don't know what you have were told, but the party of hunters sent to find me, violated me, disfigured me and left me for dead," and then she removed her mitten and raised her mutilated hand for all to see.

Most probably never even heard or fully grasped the gravity of her accusations because of the utter chaos that ensued.

"People, people…this woman is clearly troubled and needs our help," he addressed the crowd before confidently walking towards the huntress. He briefly turned his threatening glare away to get a better look at the bloodied corpses of his friends within the sled's baskets.

Uki could now clearly hear people yelling "murderer" as voices continued to rise along with fists; but as soon as the hunter was at arm's length, she again shouted in order to be heard.

"Brothers and sisters, why would you doubt me now? Haven't I always done everything for the betterment of our community…if I am untruthful, then it is your prerogative to judge me?"

The now claustrophobic surge of the crowd subjected Uki to anger, replacing fear and driving her to react purely on impulse. She reached out and grabbed the front of the man's parka, yanking it down to expose the severed finger she prayed would hang from around his neck. Unfortunately, her "laying on of hands" had quickly changed the sizeable crowd's demeanour to one of antagonistic, resulting in Uki countering with the only thing that she still had at her disposal.

Quickly reaching into her pocket, Uki retrieved several sinew cords with her remaining fingers attached, along with a small tanned layer of skin that her nipple had once adorned. Raising her clenched fist into the air so that all could bear witness to the suffering that she had endured, only to be wounded by her former kinsmen and women's observable lack of indignation and the fact that they could so easily turn a blind eye.

Then she felt it…the crushing weight of their new leader's stare as she turned slowly and locked eyes with the man. Confirming once and for all that he would always be superior in the people's eyes, since she was only a woman. Uki had literally nothing left to lose at this point.

Outnumbered and knowing that mere words would not change the inevitable, she bared her teeth and launched herself at the hunter in one last show of defiance. How quickly her former brethren had forgotten what they had all once meant to each other, but sadly, that was another time and place. Nary a soul stood in her defense as the crowd roughly jostled around her and then nothing as blackness descended upon her.

Sometime later, she awoke to find herself again bound and bleeding, but at least this time, she was clothed. Looking around the inside of the large igloo, it didn't take long for Uki to recognize it as the one that Nukilik had been entertaining Tapeesa in only days before. Because her kinsmen or women were obviously in a hurry, they didn't bother to take the time to remove the small pile of discarded clothing from the floor. If she looked closely, she could still see the small hole that she had made with her spear.

Apparently, this igloo had been appropriated by the community's newest leader as well, but where were his family and their belongings?

As the hours slowly passed, Uki tried to untie her bindings manually without success, as someone had unfortunately taken her knife out of its not so hidden pocket. From what she had witnessed earlier, Uki could plainly see that the people's newest leader was not only charismatic, he also possessed the ability to think on his feet, most likely denouncing her as crazy and a threat to their welfare. This hunter was truly an unknown quantity and therefore even more dangerous…what if he connected the other recent deaths to her and, if so, how long would she still be breathing? Suddenly, the sound of raised voices interrupted Uki's inner dialogue, drawing closer and capturing her curiosity and dread.

Listening closely, she could discern the cause of their heated exchange; evidently someone had seen fit to bring the prisoner food. Uki observed cautiously as they entered the igloo and felt surprised to see what, at first glance, appeared to be a child, accompanied by one of the group's novice hunters. It wasn't until the figure finally removed its hood that she recognized the petite woman within.

Regrettably, she knew very little of this woman, only that the current leader had claimed her as his child bride several children ago and, being she was much younger than Uki, the girl had shied away from her presence. The young hunter was someone that she thought she had known well, but try as she might, Uki could not get him to make eye contact. Sadly, he too abandoned her the moment that the new leader's wife asked for privacy.

Total silence ensued as the tiny woman methodically unwrapped the bundle that she had been carrying and set out a meager meal of dried fish…then she did the unexpected. She untied Uki's bonds. Now facing this unanticipated dilemma, Uki found herself oddly forced to reconsider her usual approach and show restraint.

Whereas her natural instincts immediately dictated that she swiftly dispatch the current threat and flee, but unfortunately she knew it was imperative that she found out just what lies this woman's husband had been spreading, if she had any hopes of making a clean break.

"Thank you for your kindness. What is your name?" Uki kept her distance and spoke softly so as not to intimidate the young girl. Regrettably, she had spent the vast majority of her life in the company of fellow hunters and had not bothered to seek the friendship of her own sex, whom she found to be rather shallow.

After what seemed like forever, the woman finally spoke. "My name is Miki and I am not your friend. I only seek the truth."

Uki was actually happy with the young woman's straightforwardness, but this time she made her wait as she devoured the meal in front of her before proceeding with questions. Uki could see by the look in the girl's eyes as they followed her every move that she thought her a savage, but alas, Uki hadn't cleaned up prior to their introduction. Finally, she handed the woman the small piece of hide that had wrapped her meal and made herself comfortable.

"I don't know what your husband has said about me, but let me assure you, I was violated and anything I did was purely in self-defence. I want absolutely nothing more to do with this community or its people, only to leave in peace…" but before Uki could say more, Miki cut her off mid-sentence.

"Peace…you whore. He told me all about what you did with your fellow hunters, breaking our taboos, trying to play one against the other…we trusted you with our men!"

At first Uki was literally aghast by the lies coming out of this woman-child's mouth… "What about my amputated fingers and the fact that your husband and his friends were wearing them around their necks…one even tore off my nipple with his teeth and kept it as a keepsake!"

Then all bets were off as Uki abruptly made a move to stand, followed ineffectually by Miki's attempt to block the entrance to the igloo with her body, thus resulting in the young woman being thrown to the floor.

"You're going to be sorry for that," she screamed petulantly at Uki. "We let you and that traitor man of yours live with us, treated you like brethren and this is how you repay us…you are not a survivor, you are *Tornuaq*!"

Uki felt physically sickened by the animosity that this woman had clearly bottled up inside her and was now spewing forth. Not to mention the fact that she had the impudence to call Uki "evil" after everything that she had been through. Slowly raising her disfigured hand, Uki pushed back the makeshift dressings to expose the ragged stumps, which she then brandished in the young woman's face.

"For the last time, what exactly did your husband say about my fingers?"

The huntress' actions visibly repulsed Miki, causing her to take more than a moment to respond. When she finally responded, it was in an almost hushed voice, as if she believed Uki's vile deeds should not be spoken aloud.

"My husband's name is Kova, and he has fathered two beautiful children. He has never given me reason to doubt him until you became a widow. All the women in camp feared for their men when you once again began leading hunting parties, parties that had a habit of staying away for days, weeks at a time. He told me how you enticed him into doing unspeakable acts with him and the other men, and when they rejected you, you killed one of your own. They felt compelled to put you down…the men carry your fingers as a charm to protect themselves from your wickedness."

Again, Uki experienced shock as she listened to all the falsehoods that these men had told in order to save themselves, "Surely, not everyone of you would be so gullible as to believe such fabrications…?" and then she was cut off again.

"It really doesn't matter because you won't be alive come morning. Hope you enjoyed your last meal?" She actually giggled like a devious child.

But her laugh was quickly extinguished as Uki straddled her body, knocking the wind right out of the tiny girl as she tried to sit up. Staring down into Miki's face, Uki was astonished, to say the least, by the confidence that this woman exuded. At that moment, her throat swelled inexplicably.

Gasping for breath, Uki grabbed Miki by her shoulders and shook her before pulling her into an embrace… followed swiftly and savagely by tearing out the woman's throat with her sharpened teeth.

Suddenly cramps took hold of Uki's stomach and her vision blurred, thus confirming the truth that Miki had indeed poisoned the fish. Uki let go of the woman and forced her fingers down her own throat to induce vomiting and thankfully, it worked. But she still felt terrifyingly unsteady, fearing that some other symptom might follow and she would have no way to defend herself.

Then, without warning, the walls of the igloo closed in on Uki, exacerbating her current condition. She knew that reacting rashly would most likely result in her death, but if the community found her with the bloodied body of such a small and supposedly defenseless woman, they would execute her on sight. Uki tried to stand and was quickly overcome by dizziness, squatting; she placed her head between her legs until the feeling passed. She wished that there had been drinking water with her meal and could only hope that dehydration might be a contributing factor to her continued light-headedness.

Once steady, Uki again began rummaging through what little there was in the way of belongings inside the igloo to find an implement to dig her way out of the structure. And all the while feeding her thirst with pieces of ice or snow that she had gouged out of the surrounding walls with her fingers. Just when all hope was soon to be lost, she luckily chanced upon the remnants of a timeworn jawbone knife that had been left behind in error. Although the tool's blade had not been cared for, it still would enable her to expedite the shaving down of one of the larger blocks of snow by using the large herbivore's jawbone as a scraper.

But first things first, she still needed to choose the right block to begin with. To slide it outward, the block would need to be situated higher in the structure with less force pushing down on it in order to loosen it enough. Uki worked as fast as she could but soon found out that such a frantic pace was almost impossible to maintain, what with the sound of her own heartbeat and exhalations filling her ears and eventually drowning out any warning signs of passersby.

Finally, she could push the large block all the way through the igloo's wall and just in the nick of time, because as she gave the last wholehearted shove, Uki was instantly alerted to the sound of men approaching. There was no need to wait and listen for distinctive voices. After all, what good would it do since Kova, his friends and their wives had obviously repainted her tale multiple times in very large brush strokes?

Forsaking tradition, Uki attempted to not even dignify

Miki's passing with one kind gesture, secretly hoping that the woman's spirit had since departed to the cold upper world where it would join the other guilty parties. Quickly collecting her only means of protection, the rather dull jaw bone knife, Uki held it before her as she crawled cautiously out of the structure, hoping that the drop-off on the other side of the opening would be cushioned somewhat by the recent snowfall.

Uki instantly felt chilled to the bone when a gust of frigid air blasted her, which was expected given her excessive sweating and fever while she struggled to dig herself out. Her face and hair were once again drenched in blood.

Yet, as she surfaced from the opening high on the side of the igloo, she experienced a surge of elation at the sight of the fading light on the horizon, realizing that the forces of nature had not abandoned her just yet. She quickly assumed a somewhat fetal position as she tumbled down the back of the igloo's sloped exterior and was safely on her way back to her dog sled as the men came charging one by one through the entrance.

Uki could clearly hear their heated conversation and shouting of orders as they resurfaced while she made her way through the approaching night, again giving thanks as the wind picked up and the snow swirled about.

30

UKI

Uki stumbled her way across the last leg to her awaiting sled. Unfortunately, her stomach cramps had returned, but thankfully lesser in intensity…she needed sustenance and sleep. Mushing through the approaching storm, she looked back one last time and was happy to see that her former brethren were but a speck in the distance. If they had not been so careless as to leave her unsupervised for so long and had not unharnessed the teams that she had arrived with, they could have easily caught up with her by now.

However, since her own sled was much smaller and lighter, she was now like a single snowflake amongst a sea of white. Their lack of judgement truly perplexed regarding her captivity but in her bones, she knew she needed to remain ever vigilant. Because the hunter would most certainly stop at nothing to avenge the loss of his wife, possibly enlisting the help of credulous kinsmen. Or would he?

Her former people now had fewer hunters with any genuine experience, and the welfare of the community depended upon feeding them. Surely they would not waste precious time searching for her?

Although she was not through with Kova either, not by a long shot, Uki still wanted her fingers back and justice for what he had done. But the more she thought about it, she could not ignore Miki's words or the vindication of her paranoia…Kova was just one participant in the wanton destruction of her life. One loved one at a time.

Until now she had tried in vain to bury any thoughts of her beloved Asbjorn and his cowardly murder or that of her only child and heart's blood Siqiniq, not to mention her dear old friend Aama, who had gone to her death defending Uki's daughter against her own people. They would all pay, but first she needed to gain her strength back…looking around, Uki couldn't help but smile as her dog sled penetrated the storm front and its wall of blowing snow, much like a welcoming tent flap opening upon her return.

Once back within the safety of the caves, Uki could relax, feed herself and her dogs…and blissfully sleep. Hours later when she finally awoke, the interior of the cave was rather poorly lit, thus making it impossible for Uki to distinguish exactly what time of day it was or if the blizzard had even subsided. The moment that she made a move to stand, her dogs surprisingly came to life and enthusiastically began barking and jumping about. It seemed like they had gotten enough sleep.

Uki then quickly donned her parka and grabbed her spear before cautiously leading the team through the darkened tunnels to the surface above. She could hear the wind blowing long before they even reached the entrance to the caves, verifying the storm had not lessened one bit. Thankfully, she had been proactive and taken the time to anchor her sled the night before, since plainly no one was going anywhere.

The dogs, of course, had no aversion to this kind of severe weather and were more than happy to venture out and relieve themselves. Uki felt confident that no one had followed her, but she still stood guard as the dogs frolicked in the freshly fallen snow.

At the first signs of hunger, she and her dogs promptly returned to the depths of the labyrinth in order to feed. Working adeptly, Uki butchered the remaining portion of a large seal that she had stored for safekeeping days before. And in no time at all, a small fire was blazing and the wonderful smell of cooking meat began wafting through the air, attracting anything carnivorous.

Again, Uki was surprised by how quickly the other inhabitants had grown so bold as to approach her fire and steal food, to which she would always oblige with small morsels. After they had all eaten their fill, the huntress fastidiously tidied up the cooking area and rechecked their stores, just to make sure that no other animals had sniffed them out in her absence and either gorged themselves or tainted the meat.

Since the weather outside was currently not fit for man nor beast, Uki addressed her wounds, but this time by thoroughly washing them before repacking the older ones and simply applying seal fat to the new. The sight of her mutilated breast and the jagged puckered edges of her reopened wound enraged her every time she looked down.

A fury was soon burgeoning with the mysterious return of what she thought at first to be hunger pangs, quickly turned into severe stomach cramps. Although she was thankful for small mercies since the dizziness had finally dissipated after consuming her fill of water the night before. Then suddenly Uki had an overwhelming urge to vomit, which made little sense because there was absolutely nothing wrong with the seal meat that she had ingested and surely the tainted fish could not still be to blame. She would need to continue flushing her system with large amounts of water and seal broth just until she felt better.

One benefit of living a solitary existence was that Uki had plenty of time to ponder without distraction…Kova couldn't possibly have known what his wife was up to or did he…was Miki working alone or had the other wives banded together in their mutual hatred…why had it taken so long for someone to check in on the status of their prisoner?

Her mounting feelings of paranoia were justified. One part of her hoped the storm had completely socked in the coastline, thus affording her the luxury of more time and protection from the outside world. While the ugly part was not so kind…had Kova been devastated by the death of his wife, unable to carry out his duties as leader of the winter camp, his people growing weaker by the day?

Unfortunately, no matter what Uki wished for, she too would always be at the mercy of the weather and would never know the outcome until the storm passed.

Miles away, some of her hopes had indeed come to fruition with yet another violent storm, but this time, making its way inland. Forcing what was left of her former brethren to huddle together, sharing body heat, due to the dangerously dwindling seal blubber they used for heating their homes and cooking. Only occasionally catching fish because they feared being lost in the nearly whiteout conditions or attacked by polar bears, so no one dared venture out alone to hunt or gather.

Morale was at an all-time low amongst the remaining kinsmen and women, who had at one time numbered nearly 100 souls. Sadly, their new leader was of little to no help since he refused to take any responsibility and continued to fixate on Uki, adamantly claiming she caused all their woes.

Even Kova expected the community to honour him with a mourning period, and when he finally addressed their concerns, it was merely to placate them once again with empty promises of sending out hunting parties as soon as it was safe to do so. Although unbeknownst to their leader, his people were already taking stock of their situation…regrettably only novice hunters remained and if the weather continued, all would inevitably starve to death.

Some agreed with Kova that an evil spirit possessed the huntress and cursed their people. While others still believed in Uki and felt that the community's current run of bad luck had been merely retribution for the atrocities that were inflicted upon her by their number. Whatever side you chose, one could not ignore the fact that their leader was currently sporting a necklace with four severed fingers and a piece of torn flesh on it…resulting in more questions than answers.

UKI SAFELY WAITED OUT THE DURATION OF THE TEMPEST, enjoying the warmth of the underworld and the protection it provided. She topped off her food stores, and she even discovered edible fungi growing wherever there were manure deposits, although she missed the light of day and would occasionally travel up to the cave's entrance for a respite.

As the days inched by, Uki's stomach issues continued,

along with feelings of nausea. Much needed rest and a steady diet of protein helped Uki's wounds heal quicker than expected, but her breasts continued to ache. While Uki was washing herself next to one of the water catch basins one day, she noticed with surprise that the dim lighting made her breasts appear swollen. She feared infection and was terrified by the implications, as she had done everything she knew to prevent the bite mark from becoming foul.

Later that same day, Uki had an epiphany…everything now made sense. She wasn't dying; she was pregnant. One part of her wanted to throw herself into the sea from the cliffs above, after all, any of her attackers could be the father and she was absolutely in no mind set to look after a baby…one that she never wanted, one that she would never love and one that would always remind her of what she had suffered.

Uki felt nauseated by the whole terrifying situation she had found herself thrown into against her will. Bending forward, she emptied the contents of her stomach onto the floor and, in between the dry retching, she sobbed. If she was going to seek vengeance, then she needed to do it quickly, before her size and mobility became an issue.

As it was now the tail end of winter, the days seemed to become longer and brighter, but storms became harsher and struck without warning. Uki waited with anticipation for her moment to strike.

Kova would not be alive to raise his children once the ice floes melted and, as far as the rest of the community was concerned, anyone that got in her way would die. Thankfully, this year's snowpack was quite thick, so she could nimbly check in on the encampment from time to time without being discovered.

The winter storms, famine, and sacrificial cull had

decimated the community to less than half its number, but somehow they had carried on. Uki usually made such visits at dusk or dawn to avoid being seen. Watching her so-called people always made her blood boil as they went about their daily lives. Surprisingly, the widows and children of the men she had killed seemed happy with their new circumstances.

Then one evening, while watching from the shadows, Uki was taken aback to hear people dismiss her as nothing more than an old wife's tale to retell around the campfire. A "White Witch" that travelled by day as a polar bear and by night, preyed upon the flesh of innocent hunters as they slept in their tents. Good men that had been forced to spend extended periods away from their families, while risking everything to feed their people.

Apparently she came to them under the facade of needing help but the moment that they let her into their tents in order to warm herself by their *qulliq*, seal oil lamps, the beautiful demon before them would simply smile, showing rows of sharp pointed teeth. And like a savage animal, she would rip their throats out and defile their bodies.

Evidently no one had lived to tell the entire tale except for their leader, for he alone had escaped with his life, but not before severing the witch's fingers as she held fast to his parka while he struggled to get away. The same fingers he proudly wore around his neck as a talisman, to keep her evil spirit away and bring continued good luck to his people.

31

UKI

Uki could not believe what she had just heard. Such a bastardization of folklore. Yes, supernatural beings had always accompanied many Inuit myths... tales of evil spirits, demons, shapeshifters. The list went on and on. Except now Kova would be the hero of this tale for generations to come and Uki, the evil succubus. She so wanted to rush the campfire gathering and kill everyone in attendance, but what would that achieve, besides adding to the infamy of this ridiculous "White Witch" fallacy? So be it.

She could live with the moniker, but she could not live with the fact that Kova was still breathing. Exercising patience would be something that she would need to work on, because the few recognizance trips that she had already made back to the band's winter camp had proved unproductive, since the hunter was nowhere in sight. Perhaps its people had finally come to their senses and Kova's short stint as leader had changed, reverting to a more communal governing body. Anyway, you looked at it. The man's future was predestined.

As far as Uki was concerned, he would die by her blade, no matter where or how he currently occupied his time. Later, as she made her way cautiously through the deep snow, on route back to her awaiting sled, Uki couldn't help but think about just how she was going to achieve her goals.

Although catching the hunter off guard and hopefully vulnerable was going to be a rather difficult accomplishment, but paramount to her success, since most hunting parties comprised of at least 5-6 kinsmen. First, she would need to track the hunters and then wait for nightfall; predictably each man should venture outside the safety of their tent to urinate.

Uki had to admit that she had been dreaming about their confrontation and the amount of suffering that she would inflict, but regrettably, she also had to be practical and spill the man's blood the very moment that an opportunity presented itself.

As the fast approaching darkness set in, Uki embarked on her journey back to the safety of the cliffs and was surprised to see the outline of several dog sleds against the distant horizon. The small party in question was most likely on their way back to camp and, as luck would have it, they were completely oblivious to her presence because of the route they were presently travelling Wanting to keep it that way, she quickly veered her sled off in another direction altogether and only when she was secure their paths would not meet, she halted her team and waited.

Uki smiled to herself as the hunting party passed only yards away, none the wiser that their former huntress was now hunting them. And depending on the size of their current haul, she assumed that the party would venture out again in a matter of days and she intended to be ready and waiting.

Once back at her own sanctuary, Uki immediately began packing food and arming herself. After all, she needed to be prepared for anything and everything that her once fellow kinsmen might use in their defense. Adversity chose that very moment to strike, utterly blindsiding Uki with a nearly incapacitating bout of morning sickness.

At first, the nausea and cramps were so great she thought she was in the throes of a miscarriage. A thought that shouldn't have garnered such alarm, since she had not wanted the child in the first place, but something had changed within. Uki instinctively cradled her own stomach as if protecting the unborn child growing within her womb, as she continued to retch and sob…followed shortly by a feeling of wetness between her legs as blood trickled slowly down her inner thighs.

Uki could not believe this turn of events. She wanted retribution, and she wanted it now, but not at the risk of killing her baby. Raising her voice to the heavens, she screamed in anger and in crushing defeat…Kova and his dead accomplices would probably laugh at her now to think that their seed was responsible for the situation she currently found herself in. As Uki's diatribe finally dissipated, her voice became raspy and somewhat inaudible, but she found comfort in the realization that talking aloud had helped to clarify her thoughts.

She knew that her need for violence would never truly go away because everything had changed that inauspicious night when she had plunged into what she thought would be an icy grave, only to be resurrected by a beautiful apparition.

Ultimately, Uki concluded she would simply wait it out and, depending upon the weather, there should still be plenty of time before the bands dispersed and began heading south in search of more abundant game. But sadly, that was not to be as spring came earlier than normal that year and with it, large migrations of both man and beast. And to exacerbate the situation even further, Uki's pregnancy continued to be plagued with unanticipated complications, resulting in even greater care having to be taken this time around…fewer hunting trips and exploration but at least she was safe in the caves and never wanting for any of the necessities of life.

Kova broke camp the instant that it was safe to travel and led his people south of the Arctic Circle to just below the tree line, ever optimistic that one day he would find the huntress and make her pay. His version of her story would carry on, hoping someone would hear it and maybe chance upon her in their travels. He needed her to know that he still possessed her severed fingers and if she wanted them back, all she had to do was come find him.

As the years flew by, tales of the *'White Witch'* and her nemesis continued to thrive, fast becoming legend. Some thought that it was simply a fable to keep wayward hunters in line whenever they were far from home, while others had seen the fingers in the flesh, worn lovingly around the old hunter's neck and knew that there was definitely more to the story.

UKI DID INDEED GIVE BIRTH TO A HEALTHY BABY GIRL. That she named *Shtiya*, meaning my strength, and through the years she proved this to be true repeatedly. The child was much like her mother in appearance with striking bluish-green eyes but with a somewhat darker complexion and she too excelled at all things that had to do with hunting or the husbandry of animals.

They loved each other fiercely and spent most of their time living in or near the safety of the cliff banks and whenever her daughter would inquire about Uki's mutilated fingers; she would always reply it had been because of a hunting accident. But finally when the girl became of age, Uki saw fit to no longer hide the truth and in doing so, gained an ally in seeking vengeance.

A settling of scores that the return of her fingers would only quell and the subsequent death of the last man responsible. The twosome soon began travelling far and wide during the summer months, at first only observing from a safe distance the everyday lives of the various peoples they encountered along the way.

Then, in time, venturing into smaller settlements in order to make inquiries and eventually learn how to assimilate. With the passing of years and the muddying of waters, Uki's objectives proved more difficult to achieve. At one point it actually appeared as if Kova had indeed fallen off the face of the earth but instead of giving up, she continued to hold fast to the idea that someone from her former community was still alive and could enlighten her as to his whereabouts.

Uki wanted revenge but needed closure and in due time she was rewarded for her diligence when they chanced upon a settlement, only to find that Kova's trail was not so cold as first thought. The locals gave them a very unwelcoming reception upon their arrival because of his well-known exploits in the surrounding area, not to mention his tales of the 'White Witch'.

Previously, their periodic interactions with both the Indigenous Peoples and light-skinned explorers were rather wary, with all concerned keeping their respective distances. Uki and Shtiya had grown accustomed to suspicious eyes following them, whispering behind their backs and occasionally, small children even daring to throw pebbles, but this time was different.

Almost immediately, they could sense the hostility in the air as if some dark knowledge had preceded their arrival. Then one night it all came to a head when Uki confronted one of the overly boisterous villagers.

"Woman, yes you…I see how you look at me and my daughter…how have we offended you?"

At first, the middle-aged woman looked terrified when she was singled out amongst a group of her brethren, as they gathered around a communal fire and then suddenly she seemed to grow in strength in the fact that the newcomers were outnumbered by the settlement's inhabitants.

"We know who you are. We've heard all about what you did to those innocent hunters…take your bastard and leave. There is nothing here for you!" and then she looked around at her peers, reaffirming their shared mentality.

Uki had until this very moment covered her mutilated hand from prying eyes and tried to not smile or talk whilst showing her sharpened teeth, but all niceties were no longer applied since these people had let idiocy reign supreme.

"So you actually believe me to be the legendary *White Witch*, then you all know why I'm here?" she said sarcastically and then smiled widely.

Mayhem instantly ensued as the frightened villagers scrambled to distance themselves from Uki and the woman that she had initially addressed. Now forced to shout over the noise of the crowd, Uki advanced upon the woman while keeping Shtiya safely behind her for protection.

"Where is Kova?" she roared.

❋

Legend has it that many of the settlement's inhabitants died horribly that day while attempting to defend the woman that had outed the witch and her spawn.

Although to this day no one could confirm what had really transpired, only that the pair had mysteriously disappeared into the night, leaving a large trail of blood in their wake. A commonality that seemed to run true whenever someone was recounting any of the witch's sightings, whether they were in human or animal form.

Rumour also has it that the villagers in attendance had adamantly laid claim to having been beguiled by the beautiful blue-eyed demon in her bid to find out the location of her fabled missing digits. Albeit a rather pathetic vindication if one was to be found personally responsible for divulging the whereabouts of Kova or his family members.

The tale of the *White Witch* did indeed continue to stand the test of time but, like all things, it too evolved over the years, becoming simply the *'White Death'*.

A rather broad generalization that came into play whenever one of their brethren should meet an untimely demise. Their bodies froze in a state of rigour, displaying a look of sheer terror across their faces for no distinguishable reason, or their throats savagely torn out by a presumably large predator.

The myth's inception might have been the brainchild of one bitter hunter, but its propulsion was thanks in part to Kova's offspring, along with anyone that shared stories around the campfire late at night. Seasons changed and so too did the tales; however, one particularly gruesome element of the age-old story never reached the masses as it pertained to an oath made to an old man on his deathbed.

They ceremoniously handed down each one of the

witch's severed fingers to the males in the hunter's family, considering it a talisman that would provide protection and secure the future prosperity of their people.

Kova demanded each boy, man, or progeny thereof keep carrying the mantle and never cease their search for the White Witch. They would be honour bound to find and kill the demon, dismembering her earthly body.

The parts immediately dispersed to the far reaches of the north, ensuring her spirit remained fractured and unable to return to this realm. The latter part of the story remained unverified as hunters continued to meet their ends in horrible and unexplainable ways.

32

JOEL

Present Day

JOEL WAS SO EXCITED AS HE WAITED FOR HIS CONNECTING flight in Iqaluit, one which would take him north to the expedition's base camp via helicopter.

Thankfully, everything had gone remarkably smooth since leaving Edmonton, Geri had continued to make herself scarce and his wonderful support team of family and friends had eased his mind by promising to check in on Dinnie from time to time. Unless his ex-girlfriend wanted her day in court, his son would stay put for now as he had already filed the papers.

His good mood persevered, right until the moment that he tried to reach out to his son during his last layover, only to discover the cell phone reception was nonexistent or sporadic at best. Joel felt isolated, then quickly scolded himself for relying so heavily on his stupid phone…after all, he was embarking on the adventure of a lifetime, albeit in the High Arctic.

One part of him still kinda wished that he had a travel

companion to talk to, whereas another part was embracing the solitude, since it would soon be a rare commodity. Joel had never experienced the "joys" of living with complete strangers in a camp setting and could only hope that in such close quarters, tolerance, as well as new friendships would ensue.

Staring out the large windows of the newly revamped red airport, Joel couldn't help but be amazed by the vastness of the horizon and the brilliant sea of white that surrounded them. As he transferred into the airport, even the short distance exposed him to the elements and opened his eyes to how frigid the weather was here. He checked the contents of his bags again to verify nothing was missing.

Finally, after several hours of walking the halls of the terminal and perusing their local art collection, Joel's excitement grew upon hearing an announcement overhead that his flight had arrived and he could board shortly.

Taking one last glance around at civilization, he was genuinely relieved to see that at least one other traveller appeared to be going his way and that it was an attractive 'she'. Joel couldn't help but smile to himself as he hurried to catch up with the mystery woman as she approached their gate, then cleared his throat to get her attention, before offering his outstretched hand in introduction.

Startled at first, she spun around and was more than pleasantly surprised by this tall drink of water before her. Unfortunately, Joel's naivety proved his downfall as her strange facial tattoos visibly took him aback before adjusting his line of vision to take in her more than striking bluish-green eyes.

Joel assumed that the woman did not cognitively register his ever so slight hesitation and then became instantly perplexed by her response as she abruptly stepped back and withdrew her hand.

"Well, that's a fine hello. Did you see something that you didn't like?" she coldly snapped. The woman's spur-of-the-moment retort initially surprised Joel, but her lack of filter only added to her allure.

"I'm so sorry…I've never seen anyone with tattoos on their face before, unless you count tattoo shows on TV," and then he waited expectantly for this exotic anomaly before him to at least smile. Plunging onward, "My name is Joel and I'm a Polar Bear Scientist," he stuttered.

Almost immediately, he regretted the rather boastfulness of his introduction and the fact that he could feel his face turning redder by the second. She sensed his awkwardness and again thrust her hand forward in order to formally introduce herself.

"Hi, my name is Isitoq. Happy to make your acquaintance. Glad to know that I won't be the only indigenous person at camp this season, who isn't cleaning toilets" and then she winked.

Joel couldn't believe his good luck, a fellow scientist and a hot one at that. Why had he never envisioned such a combo? "So what is your specialty? Is this your first time… oh right, you just said that you'd been here before…sorry, I tend to be long-winded when I'm nervous…not that you're making me nervous, just happy to meet you…Isitoq, are you from around here?"

Isitoq couldn't help herself, she just had to laugh at how delightfully untainted this man was, although now it was Joel's turn to look hurt but she quickly saved the day by firmly shaking his hand and touching his arm reassuringly in a gesture of intimacy.

She too couldn't believe her good fortune; this adorably nerdish young man was quite the package and the fact that he was the first indigenous scientist to work on this expedition made her unexpectedly proud. As the two enjoyed a prolonged handshake, the sound of an overhead intercom announcing the last call for boarding suddenly jolted them out of their woolgathering.

Isitoq was the first to speak. "Well, we better get a move on. The camp is still hours away and we certainly don't want to be caught out over the ice in bad weather." Joel somewhat reluctantly withdrew his hand from hers and then made a move to help Isitoq with her bags. "Don't touch those. I'm more than capable of hauling my luggage, anyway you're the one who needs a Sherpa."

This time Joel was captivated by her spontaneous laugh and joined in, when he realized the sheer extent of luggage that he had brought along. The helicopter's small flight crew, who quickly began collecting and weighing all the supplies before loading them aboard, promptly joined them.

Once airborne, Joel realized the difficulties associated with trying to carry on a conversation, even with headsets, because of the amount of cabin noise. Although his spirits might have been slightly quashed, they immediately elevated once he refocused and beheld the mesmerizing scenery below.

Regrettably, during this time of year, the total hours one could feasibly enjoy the daylight and be productive, whilst outside tended to be only around four. But on the bright side, polar winter and the occasional solar storm provided the perfect mix for viewing some rather impressive aurora activity.

Joel couldn't help but smile at the fact that his life had taken a most fortunate turn for the better, he was finally where he had always wanted to be and even the total darkness that soon surrounded them, held promises of better things to come.

Pressing his face against the cold glass of the helicopter's cabin, Joel was re-energized when he finally caught sight of the landing pad lights of their final destination below, moments before their skillful pilot touched down.

Isitoq was very familiar with the layout of the compound as she wasted no time guiding Joel through the immense maze of connecting buildings, on their way to the central command center via the cafeteria and social pods. The overall interior design of the place left Joel impressed. Some might even describe it as "futuristic", since all the lighting appeared to be activated by motion sensors.

However, the moment that they stopped moving and stood perfectly still, he noticed a rather faint humming sound, one which he automatically chalked up to the Aeolian tones of the wind. Strangely, though, he felt quite unnerved by the incessant noise at such a late hour, as if it questioned the integrity of the structure.

He hoped when dawn broke and human voices started humming, the sound would mask it and he would forget his apprehensions. Upon entering the hub of the camp, Joel found it surprising that there was an obvious lack of personnel, although it was neither a moon base nor underwater lab from a graphic novel, so there really was no need for all hands on deck. Unsubstantiated misgivings quelled, Joel took a calming breath of recirculated air, which thankfully did not smell of odourant particles, or fumes, before surreptitiously redirecting his attention back towards his captivating travel companion. Then out of nowhere, who should appear but his former professor, one Dr. J. Pettimore.

Possibly bad timing, but if truth be told, Joel could not find fault in the elderly man's very loud entrance. As the intrusion had most likely saved him from repeating history since he had just been entertaining thoughts of starting a new relationship, based solely on the package's wrappings.

"Dr. Pettimore, it's truly wonderful to see you, but you needn't lose sleep on my account. You could've knocked me up in the morning," both men chuckled at the very English phrase and shared the inside joke that it provoked.

"Joel, my lad, no need for formalities. From now on I would like it very much if you would kindly address me as James. After all, we are more than just passing acquaintances but colleagues," and then they shared a manly embrace.

Seeing a familiar face, especially this one, brought genuine joy to Joel since they had known each other throughout his undergraduate and graduate studies at the university. James had indeed worn many hats throughout their relationship, first as a teacher, then progressing slowly to mentor and sounding board…a second father of sorts.

"I see that you've met our Isitoq. She's a genius in dialects and cultural anthropology, most impressive for one so young," and then he smiled rather conspiratorially at his former student.

Joel failed to notice James' smile and lifted eyebrows as he pondered the sheer extent and validity of his new associate's academic pedigrees.

The professor's eyes might have been as perceptive as ever, instantly recognizing the look of puzzlement on the young man's face but his interjection proved not as diplomatic as intended, "One does not simply study the animals of a region, we need to know how they interact with the other inhabitants of their shared ecosystem. In short, she makes our stay here more harmonious when dealing with the natives."

At first, Joel wasn't really sure just how to take Dr. Pettimore's statement. Should he be offended or was he stepping into an already precarious situation between researchers and the local Inuit population?

"What Dr. Pettimore is trying to say is that I'm his go-to girl when working with the locals in finding the exact locations of the animals that we're hoping to study, it just saves a lot of time and money" and then she took a little bow.

Joel couldn't help himself. "So with all these degrees, what's in it for you?"

At first Isitoq seemed more than a little annoyed by his brash comment, then quickly retorted, "Well, I just so happen to be working on a mythology degree and the elders of the surrounding communities have been incredibly gracious and happy to impart their wisdom on me, since Inuit legends tend not to be written."

Awkward silence ensued, with Joel quickly concluding he had better get some shuteye, lest putting his foot in his mouth any further tonight. "I'm so sorry if I offended you. Just curious and, frankly, in awe of your qualifications. Could one of you please show me to the sleeping quarters before I fall asleep on my feet?"

33

JOEL

Dr. Pettimore seemed somewhat disappointed that their reunion would not include a good chinwag tonight, as he visibly tarried before offering to escort his former student.

Isitoq was quick to seize the opportunity, grabbing Joel's arm and briskly leading him out of the social area and down several long, darkened hallways. Joel was grateful for the help and the fact that she appeared to not be holding a grudge, since he would have never found his way unaided.

Upon opening the door to his new accommodations, Joel discovered someone had already delivered his bags and there was no visible sign of a roommate.

Easily reading his facial expressions, Isitoq quickly laid his mind to rest. "If you're wondering about a roommate, you'll be happy to know that you'll be flying solo until the mothers and cubs resurface from their dens. That should give you plenty of time to get acquainted with the other team members, locals and the general lay of the land." That said, she left him to his own devices.

Joel's introduction to camp might have been a tad whirlwind, scarcely giving his fatigued mind time to process everything that he had seen, but he wouldn't have had it any other way. He spent most of his life mapping out his future in every little detail.

Now was the time for spontaneity and letting life's unplanned events dictate the outcome for a change. After all, he had so much to be thankful for, mainly because of having a beautiful, healthy child…the possibilities were mind-boggling. Not bothering to even unpack, Joel brushed his teeth before turning in for the rest of the night.

Tomorrow was the first day of the rest of his life, and he didn't want to miss a thing. However, the excitement of the day kept filling his thoughts, forcing him to count sheep and waking up a few hours later, far from well-rested. He even tried to go back to sleep but quickly realized the futility of staying in bed.

After glancing at his alarm clock, Joel ventured out on his own in search of the cafeteria. He found it, pleasantly surprised that he could retrace last night's steps, partly by following the enticing scent of brewing coffee in the air. His first view was that of total darkness as he gazed out the large bank of windows that encompassed the mess hall.

It would still be many hours before the sun majestically crested the horizon, or at least that was what he had always envisioned. But at least he still could savour a cup or two of coffee in solitude, before being thrust into the tumult of the camp's daily goings on.

Thankfully, both Isitoq and Dr. Pettimore joined Joel at his table, shielding his assimilation into camp life, just moments before the reset of the expedition team descended upon the cafeteria in search of breakfast and a look-see.

"So did you sleep well?" Isitoq was the first to speak,

but before he could even answer her, Dr. Pettimore followed suit.

"You'll be pleased to know, lad, that we've already planned your day…not sure of the origin of the phrase, but you might as well hit the ground running."

This was like music to Joel's ears. He couldn't help but be enthusiastic, what with the caffeine coursing through his veins and the prospect of getting his hands hypothetically or not dirty, right off the bat. Only a skeleton crew had witnessed their arrival last night, but with this morning's now steady influx of team members, the butterflies in his stomach were growing exponentially as more people joined them by pushing smaller tables together with his.

Joel truly hated being the center of attention and had to work hard on maintaining his focus solely on familiar faces, as opposed to the visibly appraising ones that now surrounded them.

"Thank you again for this opportunity to show you what I've learned and I promise you won't be sorry for hiring me" he asserted and then looked expectantly back and forth between his former teacher and Isitoq's face, as if awaiting further instructions.

"Well, today you'll be at this little lady's beck and call. Isitoq is going to need your help in collecting data from one of the northernmost communities. They've been hard to nail down of late, rather antisocial for no apparent reason. Hopefully, they'll change their tune when you two approach them, maybe even warm up to the idea of a friendly palaver with people of colour like yourselves."

It suddenly all became devastatingly clear to Joel as he looked around the large grouping of tables at his relatively "lily white" team members.

Deep down, he had always had some doubts about why they had chosen him in the first place, but he had never considered his ancestry… How could he have been so wrong about Dr. Pettimore's character?

Fortunately for him, Isitoq was an astute observer, and the moment it became all too clear, Joel did not possess a poker face of any kind. She quickly reached for him under the table, hoping her touch would be consoling and he would hold his tongue. Clearly getting into an argument with his boss on day one would most certainly hinder any chances of furthering his fledgling career before it even got off the ground.

"Don't worry, James, Joel and I will have no difficulties in contacting the Arctic Highlanders. They're my people, albeit twice or more removed," and then she smiled like a fox at her employer.

Alas Joel was like a babe in the woods for playing any sort of mind games, after all, he had come from a tiny town with traditional values, kept his nose buried in his books and achieved his goals the old-fashioned way by applying himself.

Geraldine had been the quintessential inner city girl, deceptively setting her superficial sights on him from the get-go; he was young, handsome and working on obtaining his doctorate. Lamentably, only to find out much too late that she lacked the fortitude to stay in the relationship for the long haul, bailing on both himself and their child when a better offer presented itself.

Joel discovered his mentor and confidante probably hired him based on the colour of his skin and not on his academic achievements, crushing him and being nothing but a diversity hire.

"Come on, Joel. The helicopter is warming up as we speak and we've got a lot of miles to cover before nightfall," and again she smiled, but this time to imply understanding.

And when Joel didn't move fast enough for her liking, Isitoq quickly stood and physically poked him in the shoulder with her index finger. "You're not in school anymore. Stop your lollygagging and dress appropriately for the extreme temperatures. We're heading up to the High Arctic today, hoping to make contact with a seemingly elusive band of Indigenous Peoples," and then she wiggled her eyebrows for emphasis.

"Our goal is to prove or disprove the validity of the popular claim that climate change is directly to blame for the decimation of the region's polar bear population by inhibiting their ability to hunt on the ice floes…yada, yada. Plus, it won't hurt to check with the local hunters to see just who is competing for the seal population. After all, less sea ice makes it easier for the whales to get in on the action too."

Isitoq had plenty of ideas of her own, but unfortunately precedence dictated that the company footing the bills, always predetermined the outcome of any study. She wasn't blind.

They clearly had ulterior motives and she could only hope that any attempts at saving the planet and its people would gain them enough worthwhile press to overlook the occasional minor cuts to their profit margins.

Before standing up, Joel glanced around the tables at his so-called teammates for one last time. The expressions on their faces clearly showed not everyone agreed with Isitoq's opinions and her role was more likely that of a buffer than an esteemed colleague.

Now feeling repentant for his hasty statement the night before, Joel sincerely hoped that she was at least furthering her career by the knowledge gleaned on these expeditions. Isitoq too felt the young man's pain and indignation but right now she needed to get him away from these

Qallunaat…he could never change the world until he realized all the obstacles that lay before him.

About an hour later, both Joel and Isitoq got on one of the expedition's helicopters and flew due north. They were fortunate the weather forecast allowed them to have an amazing view of the terrain below, including pockets of open water, once the sun finally emerged.

Neither teammate engaged in much small talk or physical interaction, except to point out objects of interest as they flew over them. And by the time that they actually set down the bird to get a closer look at a rather impressive *Inuksuk*, a vertical mound of rocks that acts as a guide, both needed a bathroom break, leg stretch and a little sustenance.

Isitoq checked with their pilot to confirm the exact location of the Highlander's last sighting and was happy to find out that they would be approaching the vicinity shortly and that it was now imperative that they all keep their eyes peeled for any signs of hunters, dog sleds or makeshift dwellings.

Hearing this, they forwent their mid-day meal and continue searching since daylight was always at a premium during this time of year. Much to their surprise, the team was barely airborne when Isitoq's keen eye, sighted a small group of dog sleds cutting across the ice floes in the distance, now to get their attention without angering the presumed hunters.

It was unanimously decided that they would fly over the group at enough of an altitude so as not to kick up a snowstorm and then land in front of the sleds while giving them a respectful berth. Isitoq was the first to approach the group, as she was the only team member fluent in most of the regional dialects and, hopefully, they would not perceive her small stature as a threat.

Everything went reasonably as planned, right until the very moment that the group of hunters got a closer look at the female interpreter within their midst.

Isitoq had taken her usual precautions by slowly approaching the men, making sure that they had gotten a good look at the traditional women's *akulik*, parka, that she wore over her modern clothing. She even refrained from using any quick movements or hand gestures that might alarm them, but evidently all was for naught as she removed her goggles and lowered her thermal face mask.

Instantly, they could hear shouting from a distance, and they also observed the waving of arms and raised spears. The hunter's reactions were bewildering, to say the least, for those not in the loop. It was as if the Highlanders were frightened or held some sort of deep-seated animosity towards the woman before them. Both onlookers might have feared for her safety, but Joel was the only team member to rush forward to defend Isitoq, but she would have none of it.

She pushed Joel back, much to his amazement when he made a move to stand in front of her, as if shielding the weaker of the sexes from the visibly armed and angry men.

Isitoq was not the type to back down from any affront and she wasn't about to start now, again slowly narrowing the distance between the hunters and herself. She kept her hands visible and palms out. For all involved, it was impossible to make out the true mood of the hunters because their frozen breath had encrusted their bearded faces and their fur-lined parka hoods, making them look more menacing. Then to add to the intensity of the confrontation, Mother Nature chose this moment for the wind to pick up, causing whirling columns of snow to circle about on the surface of the hard packed ice, masking their presumably heated conversation from prying ears and eyes altogether.

Thankfully, their helicopter pilot could restrain Joel long enough so that the situation did not escalate any further, he assured him that this was not the first time that their interpreter had not seen eye to eye with the locals and it would not be the last.

Inuit culture had always been quite respectful of women, but like all male-dominated societies, they had their place and Isitoq was not above helping them make the shift into 21st century thinking, be it kicking and screaming.

34

JOEL

WHILE THE TWO MEN OBSERVED THEIR TEAM MEMBER RANT and rave from a distance, they were taken aback when she abruptly changed direction and walked back towards them, only to realize that someone had offered them an invitation to the hunter's camp for the evening.

At first, the pilot was none too happy to be spending the night in the company of strangers. "What the fuck do you think that you're doing? Why would you agree to such a stupid thing? They could murder us in our sleep. Anyway, it's too dangerous to leave the helicopter out in the open. The weather could change, and then how are we supposed to get back to our base camp?"

"First, I'm not stupid. We have been given the chance of a lifetime. They've kindly offered their hospitality in putting us up for the night and sharing whatever knowledge they can impart. The Arctic Highlanders are one of the oldest communities and I personally can't wait to have an in-depth conversation with their elders. Plus, I checked your gas gauge and we'll be just fine. All we must do is tether down the blades for the night and park into the wind."

Her retort shocked Joel in a good way, but the pilot did not experience the same. The man paced back and forth in righteous indignation with his fists clenched, everyone half expecting him to voice his frustration by screaming, "I'm telling on you!"

Without even waiting for the pilot to calm down, Isitoq returned to the small group of hunters and thanked them for their invitation, then asked them to lead the way. The journey would be a short one as the men were currently on their way back to their camp after a successful hunting trip.

However, because their sleds carried a heavy load of freshly killed seal meat, the trip consequently took more time. But it allowed adequate time for Isitoq and Joel to plan regarding the questioning of their people.

Later, as the Inuit's winter camp came into view, all were awestruck by how it concealed itself right out in the open and approaching from any other angle would have made it nearly impossible to detect because of the snowdrifts.

Isitoq was quick to instruct Joel to get as many pictures as possible from the air, but warned him not to take any on the ground unless the Highlanders agreed beforehand. She was not sure just how much contact this group had previously had with outsiders and did not want to bombard it with the trappings of so-called civilization. Even being allowed to enter their domain had been incredible, and she was not willing to risk breaking their trust.

Before leaving the safety of the cockpit, Joel's curiosity

got the better of him. He just had to know what the whole kerfuffle had been about between Isitoq and the hunters.

Gently taking her aside, "I know that I'm only a junior team member, but I need to know what you were arguing about earlier with those hunters? And if we're going to be spending a night out in the middle of nowhere with these people, I have the right to know."

At first she seemed perturbed because he had the nerve to even ask her to justify her decisions, then after a small breath of exasperation, she began…

"The Inuit are a very superstitious people. They actually believed me to be an evil spirit from a century old myth that supposedly preyed on hunters…now doesn't that sound ridiculous?"

All Joel could do was laugh at the absurdity but still chose not to share her story with their pilot; after all, he really didn't want to add to the animosity that was currently brewing between the two. After helping securely anchor the helicopter for the night in the increasing winds, the threesome cautiously made their way to where the awaiting hunters and their now emptied sleds stood, just shy of the camp's main entrance.

Luckily for Isitoq and her team, they had seen the community's men and women as they flocked to welcome home the hunters and witnessed them busily carrying off their bounty. If not for that, they would have been left at a disadvantage, unable to differentiate between who was who, since everyone wore similar bulky caribou hide clothing. Awkward to say the least, Isitoq was quick to approach the hunters and thank them again for their hospitality, gesturing vigorously for Joel and the pilot to come forward and pay their respects.

Joel could tell instantly that his fellow team mate was very uncomfortable with the status quo and that he most likely had very little to do with the Indigenous Peoples that they encountered during their expeditions except to operate the copter. Joel greeted the members of the High Arctic community with genuine enthusiasm, smiling broadly at each person he encountered.

A general feeling of camaraderie ensued as the excitement level and noise increased, then suddenly the crowd parted to make way for what appeared to be a delegation of elders. Almost immediately, the cacophony died down as one elder shouted to be heard. The gathering crowd physically guided the three team members along a main pathway, bringing them back into what could only be assumed was the center of the camp. Isitoq smiled reassuringly at the men, attempting to keep them calm as a stream of people physically swept them along, leaving their fate uncertain.

The crowd separating and their hosts revealing their intentions soon put an end to their apprehensions. At the end of the day's journey was a large hide tent, where a communal fire was already burning brightly within. As the tent quickly filled up to capacity and the room's temperature increased, the team's need for their extreme weather gear was no longer warranted.

When Isitoq removed her face coverings and toque again, the gathering crowd became noticeably agitated as they backed away from her, expressing their mistrust. Thankfully, the group's hunters swiftly intervened to calm their brethren's anxieties, and the elders came forward to assist in crowd management.

As Joel looked around, he couldn't comprehend the people's reaction to Isitoq's unveiling, sure she had a mix of facial tattoos, which he believed to be purely traditional. Note to self…he had to know more about this legend or myth that struck such fear into the hearts of so many, even after all these years. Hopefully, one of their number would enlighten him at some point.

Everyone watched quietly as one of the women elders stoically approached Isitoq and gently took her face in their hands, pushing back her hair to get a better look at her facial tattoos. The woman smiled and nodded in what could only be approval as she studied the many markings, then she did something rather unexpected, she used her pointer fingers to push back Isitoq's lips, as if looking for something in her mouth, possibly her teeth.

You could almost hear a pin drop as she carried out her odd inspection, and even a cumulative gasp escaped from the crowd as she opened Isitoq's mouth wider. Whatever they were looking for was not to be found because the moment that she pushed her mouth closed again, there was an obvious sigh of relief throughout the tent.

The old woman smiled again at Isitoq and then held her hand, guiding her towards the far end of the makeshift structure where the rest of the elders had already seated themselves. And as she walked away, Joel couldn't help but feel somewhat deserted. Deep down, he wanted to yell after her, but didn't want to cause her embarrassment.

After all, he did not speak or understand their language, and he was pretty sure that their pilot was in the same boat. Time almost seemed to stand still as she got farther and farther away. Much to his relief, Isitoq came to a halt, said something unrecognizable to the elder, turned around and motioned exaggeratedly for them to follow.

From there on out, the night progressed without a hitch. They ate plentifully on seal meat, although Joel would have loved a salad accompaniment. Even their pilot was caught smiling frequently as he seemed to catch the girls' fancies.

There was also entertainment involving crude instruments, such as drums and throat singing, between the younger women. Overall, the evening was most enjoyable. That was until the moment that Joel clumsily attempted to pronounce a word, in their people's native tongue, that he had heard several of the younger children saying repeatedly in a rather sing-song fashion.

"…what does this word mean?"

Immediately, a hush fell over the crowd as all eyes once again fell on his beautiful team member. At first, Isitoq smiled a brittle smile, then stepped forward and looked around the room, searching for her accuser's face.

"The children are calling me a demon; someday I will tell you the story." Then she turned her back away from the crowd and took her seat of honour with the elders again.

Joel wanted to crawl right into a hole at that very moment; he had disgraced Isitoq in front of all these people and saying anything further on the subject would definitely add to both of their humiliations. But it was unfortunately getting late and without her help, he really had no hope of finding his lodgings for the night. Faced with such a quandary, Joel mustered up what little nerve he still possessed in order to address Isitoq.

"Please forgive me for my ignorance. I meant no harm," said with downcast eyes. "It's getting really late. Could I bother you to ask someone to show us to our sleeping quarters?"

Their pilot was quick to join him as they both waited patiently for someone to be elected to carry out the chore. The wait was not long as two young hunters stepped forward and escorted them to one of the larger igloos, where several much older kinsmen and women were already fast asleep. Not exactly the Ritz, but both were warm and comfortable under the thick animal hide blankets that they were provided. Joel really had nothing further to say to his co-worker before turning in, since he already knew that they would never be friends.

Isitoq did not let Joel's misfortunate outburst ruin her evening. It was still relatively early and several of the elders had been more than willing to share their wisdom, as well as a few of the seasoned hunters. Isitoq hoped she would satisfy her hunger for knowledge, as well as her employer's need to place blame.

However, anyone with half a brain and had lived north of 50 degrees already knew even without the benefit of satellite detection, that the ice in these parts could be so thick the polar bear population didn't always know where their next meal would come from.

Call it global warming or climate change, solar activity and greenhouse gasses be damned, the only thing constant about our planet's weather was the fact that it was subject to change.

35

JOEL

As the night wound down, Isitoq was lucky enough to get one of the elderly hunters alone and find out the real reason behind his people's renewed abhorrence for this so-called *'White Witch'* of old.

Evidently it was because of the seasonal joining and migrating of different groups between various hunting regions, simply old stories shared between new friends around the campfires, a resurgence of sorts. Also, it didn't hurt to keep the men heedful of their wives' warnings and the children obedient regarding potential dangers that might befall them.

He himself remembered his great grandfather telling tales late at night around a communal fire, about a well-known hunter by the name of Kova, who had battled the legendary blue-eyed witch and lived. This man, a prominent leader and provider for his people, saved them from starvation when they were cursed by the witch while wintering in the far north.

"And if memory serves me right…I think that the actual location of the tale was somewhere just west of where we are sitting right now. But then again, I'm an old man and sometimes I don't trust my recollections."

"Please go on, *Atata*, father. I too have heard many variations of the myth. I'm just trying to correlate the similarities. Three things cannot be long hidden: the sun, the moon, and the truth."

The old hunter instantly smiled and nodded his head upon hearing Isitoq's recitation of a Buddha quote. Then he drank deeply from his cup and continued.

"Kova's people discovered her as a defenseless baby, left out on an ice floe to die. And considering the fluidity of bonds between adults and children in most, if not all, of the Inuit communities, a kind person took in the foundling. Though they had not recognized it for what it was and had raised her as their own. Only to have her later repay their kindness by decimating their number, one at a time. Story goes that at a surprisingly early-onset, the *tiguaq*, adopted child, could ingratiate herself with her unparalleled aptitude for blood sports. Some might have found this unsettling. After all, it went against her preordained lot in life as a female. However, her new people nurtured instead of quell, resulting in a very adept huntress and highly valued member of their community, but that all changed when she became of age."

Isitoq couldn't hold her tongue any longer. "So they thought she was a witch because she gave the men a run for their money in hunting?"

"No, it wasn't the men at all who first sensed that there was something not quite right with their *nuka*, little sister. The women were, but by then, it was far too late. She had already begun enchanting her fellow kinsmen, making them do unimaginable things…taboo acts of such depravity, that I do not care to repeat. Legend depicts Kova as a hero amongst his people, holding fast and working together with a few of his most trusted friends to eradicate the witch. Although best laid plans quickly went asunder as she slaughtered them using her razor-sharp teeth, teeth that she had been filing daily in their very midst, most likely to prepare for just such an onslaught..."

"Please forgive me for butting in yet again, but I've heard tell that she was exquisite…exotic, some might say. Do you feel that the harboured jealousy of her fellow kinswomen brought any of her infamy on?"

The old hunter paused, as if to consider her question further. "Your statement has some credence, but the fact remains that whole families were indeed torn apart. It is undeniable wives lost their husbands, husbands lost their wives, and children lost their parents. It was even said that she had also conspired with demons to walk as one with the animals. Hunting parties were warned to never lower their guard when overnighting, as they could become victims of her relentless blood lust in any form she chose. Over the years, she became even more devious, making it harder and harder for her once brethren and the Indigenous Peoples of the north to distinguish the exact cause of her victims' deaths, since she sometimes ravaged the bodies of their people beyond recognition. Sadly, fear is something that the Inuit people know, be it in tangible or spirit form."

This time, Isitoq hesitated before speaking. "I truly feel that she was not a witch or demon, just a scapegoat for the sins of others. I know in my mind she did indeed shed blood, but not unprovoked as alleged."

In the end, both hunter and scholar agreed to disagree, since everything was based on hearsay. But the one thing that they could wholeheartedly agree upon was that the fabled huntress' life made excellent fodder for late night stories.

Her myth did eventually evolve into that of the "White Death" since it encompassed so many scenarios. Kova still held fast to his original story, along with the severed fingers that he macabrely cherished.

The same fingers he had claimed to have hacked off of the witch's still breathing body as he and his friends had tried in vain to drown her all those many years ago. Throughout his travels, Kova made it his life's mission to protect his people from corruption in any form. He repeated his tale for all to hear, hoping to coax her out of hiding.

Of course, years passed and over time, it became even harder to distinguish fact from fiction, although Kova's sons and their sons upheld their honour and swore they had embellished nothing. Including the fact that on their revered father's deathbed, they had supposedly all made a sacred vow to never stop looking for the witch and that each man or boy in possession of a severed finger, would pass it on to their male progeny in the hopes of one day finding the witch and putting an end to her reign of terror.

Isitoq could not help but listen in awe to the old hunter's tale, a version much like she had heard many times before except this one excluded a very pertinent detail, that in all the sightings the beautiful woman had always been youthful, as if frozen in time by some kind of mystical power.

Strangely, there were no tales of the so-called witch in her midlife, or golden years for that matter. It was as if she had magically disappeared or simply gone into hiding. Isitoq would not let it rest until she had learned more. She needed to verify just what had happened to this legend and find out who currently possessed her amputated digits.

Looking across the campfire, she noticed her elderly companion had been overjoyed to find a willing ear to bend. But he was struggling to keep his eyes open as the hours passed.

Before turning in for the rest of the night, she chanced to make one last inquiry. "Atata, are any of Kova's children still alive, so that I might speak with them?"

THE FOLLOWING MORNING SHE WAS UP WITH THE proverbial birds and had already finished breakfast long before her teammates had ventured out of the warmth of their igloo, thankfully allowing her to savour the last of her thermos' coffee in the tranquility of dawn.

Now staring somewhat transfixed at the vast horizon before her, Isitoq was pleased to note that the skies overhead were indeed clear as far as the eye could see and that the weather forecast had been spot-on for a change… even the wind on her cheeks did not possess its usual bite. Therefore, this morning's flight back to camp should be smooth sailing unless the weather became fickle, or one of her teammates was still harbouring a grudge because she had dared to make plans without asking them first. She laughed to herself at the prospect of having a yelling match with her somewhat vertically challenged pilot.

Again returning to the meeting tent, Isitoq was happy to see that her colleagues were finally up and seemed to enjoy their morning meal, although in silence, since neither one had evidently attempted to learn a single word of their host's given tongue. Taking a seat beside them, she quickly began filling the men in on the highlights of what she had discovered from her somewhat impromptu discussions with the community's elders and hunters, regarding the resident polar bear population.

Their fortuitous meeting had indeed been successful, as

their research teams would now be welcome in this particularly fertile region as soon as the cubs grew too large for their dens. Upon hearing such wonderful news, Joel's exuberant reaction was contagious, thus adding to the general high spirits of all in attendance, even if languages remained an obstacle.

Once the helicopter was thoroughly warmed up and ready to go, Isitoq bid her heartfelt goodbyes and then started mentally listing anything that would improve this community's life in the High Arctic ...supplies that they could easily transport on their next flight up.

On their flight back to base camp, the skies were indeed remarkably clear and a beautiful azure in colour, giving the team breathtaking views that only a few people ever get to experience. And to add to their excitement, the team witnessed several large male polar bears making their way across what appeared to be an endless expanse of frozen waves, presumably on the hunt for food.

Upon closer inspection whilst buzzing a few of the bears, the team was pleased to see all the bears seemed to be in excellent condition, unlike some of their more southern counterparts. Joel couldn't wait to try his hand at ear tagging the males and collaring of females, since last year's transmitters should be ready to fall off as designed within the next month. Not to mention the identifying of true maternity dens from the data collected, be they constructed in-land or on sea ice.

Technology truly was a wonderful thing. This way the researchers didn't have to risk life and limb in the brutal climates daily, albeit some things still needed to be done the old-fashioned way...hands on. However, in a pinch, aerial surveys still had their place, being way less expensive and time consuming. And Joel, having only just dipped his toe, was quick to grasp the ramifications implied when the words 'weather permitting' accompanied any task.

When you took into consideration just how much needed to be accomplished during any given sporadic lull…no wonder the team was so large and needed local eyes on the ground.

36

JOEL

Entering the camp's airspace hours later, Joel had trouble wrapping his head around just what had become of the day.

As night seemed to consume their part of the celestial hemisphere…these reduced hours of daylight were definitely going to take some getting used to. Now walking into his new surroundings, Joel surprisingly felt more like a team player as opposed to the token Indian guy. Joel swung around, and his heart filled with joy as he felt a firm pat on the back and saw his old professor upon arrival.

However, calling him 'James' would never come naturally to Joel. Maybe he had misconstrued what had happened yesterday morning, possibly made way too much out of nothing and for that, he couldn't help but feel somewhat remorseful, but still thought it wise to hold his tongue.

Later in the evening, while sitting down to partake in the team's communal meal, Joel's fresh approach, along with his somewhat animated retelling of the day's events, resulted in an unexpected mutual camaraderie between all those in attendance. Which went a long way towards the alleviation of the occasional "nigglings" of self-doubt that he experienced regarding the path he had chosen.

Studious discussions ensued throughout the rest of the evening, revolving around the objects of his unfaltering fascination, namely the polar bears. Some people laughed at his youthful exuberance, but not everyone had become jaded from years of isolation and frigid temperatures. A few even dared to share their research goals and inquired as to if he would assist them... Joel was simply over the moon. Just being in that same room with these amazing people, he couldn't help but feel happily removed from his former life in the big city.

That night he slept like a baby, for the first time in a long time. Though thoughts of Geraldine still resurfaced from time to time and always at the most inopportune moments to cast their dark shadow.

But at least their recurrence was becoming fewer and farther between as he held fast to more heartwarming images like that of his son Dinnie and their future reunion. And a certain female associate, who also began curiously occupying his waking thoughts…the uniquely beautiful and brilliant Isitoq.

Joel genuinely thrived in this new environment and his earlier misgivings regarding the motives of those around him went by the wayside and he could continue his relationship with his mentor.

Every morning he awoke with a smile on his face and a "go get 'em" attitude, taking pleasure in almost every aspect of his day-to-day life, no matter how mundane, which not so surprisingly resulted in the making of new friends. Although Isitoq would occasionally scold him for performing duties which she saw as beneath him and would then try to make him cough up the name of the person who was responsible.

Deep down, Joel felt truly fortunate to know she had his back and looked forward to all the time they could spend in each other's company, be it working at base camp or the occasional overnighters at a few of the local settlements. Isitoq was much more than the team's "Girl Friday" and the fact she had taken it upon herself to teach him a smattering of *Inuktitut*, the traditional oral language of the Inuit, warmed his heart even more.

As the days soon turned into weeks, Joel dabbled in a plethora of advanced research projects, ones that unfortunately kept him away from the lovely Isitoq. She humored him graciously whenever he was bursting at the seams to recount his adventures at the end of a busy workday or week.

One evening, as he entered the camp's cafeteria with excitement, hoping to find her sitting in their usual spot, he was taken aback, to say the least, when he found it empty.

Anxiously looking around with chest somewhat fallen, he couldn't help but stop the first person to make eye contact. "Have you seen Isitoq? She's usually here at this time of night."

"I think she is still out on the chopper, apparently several of the local Indigenous groups have been reporting what looks to be the remnants of scavenged food along with bear tracks, just outside of their camp's perimeters. No one has been physically harmed unless you count the occasional stolen fresh kill," and then the man looked around as if to confirm his story. "Hey, has anyone seen Isitoq?"

"I think she borrowed a sled earlier today and was out swapping stories with one of the old ladies," another man chirped in.

"Snowmobile…surely it has a tracking device on it?" Joel countered rather tersely. He didn't know why this news should alarm him. After all, she was a big girl, and this was not her first rodeo.

Just when he was about to go looking for someone to help him track her down, who should appear with rosy red cheeks and looking the picture of good health but Isitoq. It took all his willpower to not rush to her side. Strangely, he could not account for such powerful feelings.

"Where have you been?" he blurted out in an almost accusatory fashion before he could even stop himself.

Almost instantly, her face transformed from a smile to a look of anger. "I don't have to answer to you…and if you had even bothered to ask nicely or paid attention to anything that I've told you thus far, you would know I periodically visit the nearby communities to catch up with the elders." She then turned on her heels and left the room, but not before grabbing a pre-packaged dinner plate to take back to her room.

Joel wanted to run after her but thought it best he gave Isitoq time to cool down. He knew he had acted out of turn but wasn't sure what to say in his defense, looking around the large cafeteria as if for guidance, one of his teammates actually stepped up to the plate and handed him their dessert…, "Go after her, she probably just had a bad day."

Later, standing outside her room, he still hadn't decided on the best opening line in order to break the ice, after all, she was not accountable to him in any way, shape or form…finally throwing caution to the wind, he knocked on the door.

"I know that you're in there…please forgive my stupidity and thoughtlessness…I'm a man, after all…," the moment that the door finally swung open, he quickly presented her with a plate of pie and what he hoped was an endearing puppy dog look on his face.

"You can add Neanderthal to that list as well!" Then she grabbed the plate right out of his hand.

"Can you forgive me? I really don't know why I said that or acted that way. I guess I was scared something had happened to you…and for the record, I pay attention to everything you tell me. May I ask which group you were visiting and how it went?"

"Actually, I got up early and did my visiting before lunch…the ladies were wonderful, as always. I'm learning a lot about ancient medicine and healing…seal fat…they put that shit on everything" and then she laughed. "I spent the rest of the day acting as an interpreter, flying around looking at suspected kill sites or at the very least, the remains of whatever the bears had thieved and then dragged away to eat in privacy…surprised I can even stomach a meal right now. Something has agitated the locals, even though we have accounted for everyone."

"Is this a usual occurrence this far north…the polar bears stealing food from the locals? I would have thought it more prevalent nearer to civilization, where the animals could rely on town dumps and such for their next meal."

"It's only happened at a few camps so far, but the locals can't help but be nervous. After all, an igloo or tent is no match for a rogue polar bear. Not to worry, I carry a gun with me at all times when venturing out by myself, plus the sound of the snowmobile seems to scare them off."

With fork in hand, Isitoq quickly put an end to Joel's current line of questioning and once again opted to take the high road by not holding a grudge, after which they spent the rest of the evening chatting happily and unreservedly in her room.

Whilst saying their "goodnights" in front of her door,

Joel acted on impulse for a change, surprising both Isitoq and himself by unabashedly reaching out and embracing her. Joel refrained from trying to kiss her. He just wanted to let her know she meant something to him and her not resisting…said everything.

Back in his own room, he felt thrilled and worried when he received a call from his son, hoping everything was alright back home.

Quickly he made himself comfortable on the bed and pressed redial, then waited patiently for Auntie Mona to answer his FaceTime request. She answered almost immediately and was more than happy to oblige him by taking the phone into his son's room, even at this late hour. Joel just about broke down into tears as he saw the somewhat shaky image of his sleepy little man rubbing his eyes on the screen before him.

"Dinnie, Daddy loves you…is everything alright? How's school? Are you learning anything fun? I can't wait for you to see where I work. I'm hoping you can come for a visit before I get too busy…would you like that?"

Joel's heart sank as the little boy dragged his fingers across the screen as if trying to touch him. "I miss you, Daddy, when are you coming home?" and then he cried before flailing his arms about to hug the tiny image before him.

Mona came to the rescue as he could hear her saying something about calling daddy back tomorrow after a good night's sleep.

37

JOEL

JOEL DREAMED OF HIS SON TRYING TO BREAK FREE FROM HIS mother's clutches while she and a dark stranger held him back as he sobbed. And as to be expected, the next morning he awoke looking rather worse for wear, not to mention the pounding headache accompanying his lack of sleep.

He knew he would be of no good to anyone, but could not let down his teammates. So he persevered, albeit lethargically. By midday, he was relieved of his duties and went back to his room to catch up on his beauty sleep. Joel was grateful for the reprieve and happy he didn't have to go into great detail as to the cause of his sleep deprivation.

Although he was pretty sure news of his son's phone call had made the rounds. In the end, he took a much needed nap. After all, he didn't want to disrupt his nighttime sleep patterns. After which he spent the rest of the day in his room, twiddling his thumbs before joining the rest of his teammates for their evening meal.

Upon entering the cafeteria, Joel instantly became

intrigued when he overheard bits and pieces of a rather graphic conversation between several of his colleagues.

"You should've seen it; it was like something out of a zombie movie…intestines everywhere…even ate the poor bastard's pecker clean off."

"Remind me to never piss off a hungry bear because that's what it was. Claw marks don't lie…sure hope it was postmortem."

"You know what they say about accidents happening close to home, although I'm surprised no one heard him screaming. The guy's winter camp was within earshot."

"Hate to run into whatever scared it off mid meal… don't think I'll be eating supper tonight."

"I hear ya…I had nightmares for weeks after coming across my first corpsicle."

Joel's first thoughts were of Isitoq's safety as he looked around frantically to ensure she was in attendance. Out of nowhere, he felt a reassuring hand rubbing his back, so he took a moment to exhale before turning to verify the source. Isitoq's face appeared, answering Joel's prayers.

"I knew that you'd be worrying about me as soon as you heard the news." Then she smiled warmly up at Joel before taking his hand and escorting him back to her table. "There's nothing to worry about. The hunter had been foolish in his actions, field dressing his kill without a fellow kinsman to stand lookout, sheer carelessness if you ask me."

And apparently that was that. Once seated, Isitoq casually picked up her utensils and continued to eat her dinner, as if the topic was no longer up for discussion. However, Joel wanted to know more about the tragic events that had transpired and chalking it up to an unfortunate job hazard would not fly.

"So how was your day? As you probably already know,

mine was a wash." Then he stared adoringly into her eyes as he rested his chin on his knuckles, with his elbows planted firmly on the table in front of him.

"Same old, same old. Although, it's going to get very busy real soon. Are you available to return with me to the Highlander's camp to chart den locations? We are still short a few men since the harsh weather this year, but I want to keep the lines of communication open between them and us."

Joel was more than thrilled to be asked but wondered if it was her place to do so or if she was simply doing it at the behest of someone else… "I know what you're thinking and, yes, the higher ups approved it, they thought we worked well together," she said and then winked.

They had just started dessert when Joel's watch alarm went off. "I'm so sorry. I almost forgot I made a Skype date with my son tonight. Yesterday's phone call was a disaster…I figured a larger screen should make him happier…gotta run." And then he got up and kissed the top of her head before running out of the room.

Now sitting in front of his laptop, waiting somewhat patiently for his call to go through, Joel replayed his earlier actions in his head. Isitoq did not take offense or feel he had overstepped his bounds. After all, she was his 'person'.

When the call went through, he could have a more relaxed conversation with his son. He even could move the camera around, showing Dinnie his room and being more animated in describing where he was and what he was doing up north. Just when he thought their visit had gone off without a hitch, Dinnie brought up his mother's new friend Chris. He wasn't calling him dad, but evidently

Geri had been spending a lot of her free time with this man.

"So, do you like him?"

"Not really…he won't even play video games with me and he's always in a hurry when he picks up Mommy. Auntie usually walks me to school now. She says mom's busy but I know she's lying," and then he looked around as if to make sure no one was listening.

This information truly took Joel aback. What had been going on since he left? Whenever his friends had dropped by for a visit, Geri had pretended to be 'Mommy Dearest' for their benefit and had missed any cues to the contrary.

Not wanting to upset his son further, he kept the rest of their chat focused on the wondrous things he had seen so far and the peoples who inhabited the frozen land. He would have to have a talk with Auntie Mona and sort this out sooner rather than later.

Making a big show of yawning and stretching his arms, Joel then brought his face up closer to the laptop's screen and pretended to plant a loud kiss on it, "Goodnight my little man, daddy sure misses you. We both better get our PJ's on. You've got school and I've got work. Have you brushed your teeth yet…if not, run along and tell Auntie I'd like to say goodnight to her. Love you."

As soon as Dinnie left the room, his great aunt's image filled the screen. "I know we don't have long to talk without prying little ears, but could you call me later once he's in bed? I need to know what's happening with Geraldine."

"I can't say I haven't missed you, son. That woman has been shirking her duties, but don't you worry about Dinnie. Your friends have been kind to him, stopping by to take him to movies and the odd visit to your father's place…," then almost mid-sentence she stopped and looked over her shoulder rather comically, followed by the sound of Dinnie giggling.

"Goodnight, you two," he waved at the screen and waited for it to go blank.

Later that night, Auntie Mona called him back, and they had a long talk. Geraldine was not letting any grass grow under her feet this time around. They had set a wedding date, but suddenly stopped discussing moving away. Dinnie's intuitions had indeed been correct.

This Chris person was not stepfather material and, sadly, Geri had not been forthright regarding keeping the family unit together at all costs. As far as Mona was concerned, the girl was acting like a carefree teenager and Dinnie might as well have been her little brother, not her child. And then almost abruptly she ended the conversation with, "When are you coming home?"

"I don't know, but I'm going to look into the possibility of having Dinnie flown up here for a brief visit, at the very least. I've been working hard and I think I've earned some downtime. And since Dinnie's only in kindergarten, missing a few days couldn't possibly hurt…let me get back to you. Thank you for everything, Mona. I love you."

After turning off his phone, Joel laid back on the bed and began planning just what he would say to his superiors. It wasn't like Dinnie was a baby and needed 24 hour care. Surely a couple of days, even a long weekend, would not be out of the question?

However, right now might not be the most opportune time, but as soon as they were running full staff, he couldn't see any reason for objections to his visit request. He'd run it by James in the morning, giving him plenty of time to warm up to the idea.

He couldn't wait to introduce Dinnie to Isitoq, as he knew she and her tattoos would captivate his son, but he needed to take care of other matters first.

38

JOEL

The following morning, the cafeteria was still buzzing with talk of the unfortunate hunter who had lost his life to a bear attack, or so Joel had thought, but it was revealed that fatal incidents had claimed the lives of more than one person within the last few days.

Evidently, these so-called scavengers were getting more brazen daily, although thankfully the newest casualty was nowhere near the last. Thus leading the scientists to believe that several rogue bears were currently on the prowl and that no one should venture out on their own.

Although somewhat aghast by the findings, Joel couldn't help but find himself intrigued. He didn't know what he would do if he found himself face-to-face with an angry bear. Since he had already promised Isitoq that he would accompany her back up to the High Arctic on another fact-finding mission, he would soon distance himself from the situation.

Later whilst enjoying the last few drops of his morning coffee, Joel spotted his old professor from across the room as he was about to leave, quickly standing, he motioned him over to his table so that he might run the idea of a short family visit by the man. At first, James seemed rather flabbergasted by the inquiry. They were short staffed and the safety of their current members, let alone a small rambunctious child, was in question even as they spoke.

Joel reassured him by explaining that this was only a thought and they would not consider it until after the cubs were tagged. His old mentor settled down and they could go back to happily talking business.

Joel was very excited at the prospect of spending several days away and having time to work alongside the Highlanders' dog sled teams to carry out some of their objectives. Although like a woman packing for an upcoming holiday, he really didn't know just what to bring but fortunately his travel companion had done this many times before and happily went behind him critiquing his choices and removing what she thought to be frivolous items from his pack.

Later that evening, he turned in early to distance himself from certain topics of late. As more stories were surfacing regarding the Inuit hunters and their untimely demises. Although Joel possessed a rather active imagination, so not surprisingly, the two random bear attacks became fodder for his dreams, or should I say, his explicit nightmares.

JOEL HAD ABSOLUTELY NO IDEA WHERE HE WAS OR HOW HE had even gotten there, only that he had foolishly ventured outside in the middle of a snowstorm for some unknown reason, dressed only in his pyjama pants and tee.

Looking around to get his bearings, he was all but distracted by the roaring sound of the wind as it filled his ears and an inexplicable feeling of being suffocated. All he could really make out was the dark silhouette of the expedition's base camp far behind him in the distance, along with the presence of a slight greenish glow in the skies overhead.

Trying hard not to panic, Joel spun around to see if he could find any evidence of his earlier tracks and when there were none, he did the only thing he could do. He tucked his head down and began trudging cautiously through the heavy snowfall on his way back to camp. It didn't take him long to realize the current condition of his bare feet, for they were long past the blister stage of frostbite and were now covered in thick black scabs.

Fearing the absolute worst, he ran, but due to the depth of the snow and the numbness in his feet, it was like running through deep water. That's when he heard it, the piercing cry of a frightened child, his child…Dinnie was out there somewhere, and he needed to find him right now. Jumbled thoughts raced through his head. He couldn't remember even tucking the boy in that night…why was he even outside…had he woken up alone and had come looking for comfort?

Pushing everything to the back of his mind, Joel yelled at the top of his lungs, "Dinnie!" repeatedly.

Suddenly, the deafening noise from the Arctic wind came to a halt, and in its place, a low growl filled the air. Poor Joel, he just couldn't wrap his head around what was happening.

He only knew his son was in danger and he had to get to him before whatever was out there did. Continuing to call out the boy's name in earnest, he ran blindly and was rewarded when Dinnie came barrelling into him out of the darkness. Followed soon after by the utterly terrifying appearance of an immense polar bear charging towards them with its head lowered and ears laid back, teeth bared and literally frothing at the mouth.

Joel wanted to stand his ground, but the astonishing speed with which the bear carried out its attack left them no room for miscalculations. Gnashing teeth and great gobs of flying spittle filled his vision as he fought to separate himself and his child from the bear's deadly embrace...only to find himself unexpectedly caught up in a tangled mess of bedding.

Upon waking early the next morning, covered in sweat, Joel could only berate himself for such ridiculous thoughts. After all, he had always loved polar bears, and they were not now or ever killing machines. As Joel walked into the cafeteria, feeling worse for wear, he was overjoyed to see Isitoq already waiting for him at their usual table.

"What the hell happened to you? If I didn't know better, I'd think that you were white," and then she laughed.

"Serves me right for going to bed on a full stomach, after listening to all those gruesome tales…I'm here and at your service." He bowed gallantly.

Thankfully, she didn't ask him too many questions as they ate their breakfast in relative silence and then even offered to help him with his bags as they later climbed into the helicopter's cabin and were off.

It was still rather dark out when they eventually left the compound, affording them little to no view as they headed north. The weather was on their side and they made good time. Thankfully the pilot on this trip was someone new, an older black gentleman with a gift for gab and a quick smile, who kept a running commentary throughout their journey.

So when the skies finally started to lighten, both Isitoq and Joel were feeling somewhat refreshed and ready to start their workday. As they neared the location of the Highlander's camp, Isitoq made sure to keep an eye peeled since she was worried that their current pilot might pass right by without ever seeing it and rightly so. Quickly sliding forward in her seat, she tapped the man on his shoulder and pointed downward as they flew over the wondrously camouflaged settlement. Their pilot apologized for his error and then effortlessly swung the large bird around in order to land in front of the camp's entrance and its gathering inhabitants.

Joel couldn't help but smile as he witnessed the pure joy on all of the people's faces…he couldn't wait to see their response to the gifts that they had brought. As soon as the blades stopped turning, the teammates exited their craft and began unloading a plethora of supplies…everything but the kitchen sink, that's if you raided a Cabela's store.

Isitoq was quick to formally greet the elders and usher them closer, so that they may inspect the bounty that she had painstakingly prepared. Most of the items brought about responses of happiness as they were instantly recognizable and thus held high for all to admire, while others appeared to be a genuine mystery to those in attendance.

Without delay everything was transported into the camp, whether it be pushed, pulled or dragged by whoever was able-bodied enough to do so. The general atmosphere was downright contagious to say the least as both men and women slapped Joel on the back in good-natured fun and smiles once again abound.

He could only imagine that this was the kind of

welcome that a hunter would experience when returning successfully from a hunt. Thankfully, this time their pilot saw fit to join in with the obvious camaraderie displayed, even though he had never met this particular group before, hence adding to the good will and hopefully continued joint efforts between the two peoples.

Today was a day for celebration; no actual work would be performed, except to get reacquainted and then later lay plans for what they hoped to accomplish in the days to follow. And now that they were actually here, Isitoq could not contain her excitement, after all, it had been many years since she had had the opportunity to get behind the handlebars of a dog sled, something that she had done numerous times in her youth.

Isitoq could only hope that the community's hunters would afford her the latitude to realize just that, as opposed to merely taxiing her around like a helpless girl. Joel on the other hand was a little more cerebral and just pleased to be spending quality time in the company of such an ancient culture and its people. Whereas their pilot was simply looking forward to catching up on his reading whilst his teammates traipsed about the High Arctic.

Again they were welcomed with a reception of feasting and song but this time Joel chose to stay close to Isitoq, almost exuding a couple's vibe, and their teammate cheerfully mingled. And as the day quickly turned into night, Joel began finding it harder and harder to keep his eyes open, especially since he could only decipher a few familiar words from the various conversations that were going on around the communal fire.

In the end, Isitoq urged him and their pilot to retire, after all, Joel had a big day ahead of him and he was not as yet accustomed to labouring in such extreme climates. Without much further ado, both men heeded her suggestion by calling it a day and withdrawing to the igloo that Joel had previously shared with several of the group's fellow kinsmen and women, on their last outing.

However, on this trip their pilot had made a new friend, who almost forcibly escorted him into the large dome-like structure so that he could share her bedroll. Joel laughed quietly to himself and was genuinely happy that the rather robust man had blended in so well with the community as a whole, although he must admit that he was slightly jealous and would love to have been sharing his bed with his other teammate, on a cold night such as this. Sleep did finally take him and his dreams were fortunately only pleasant in nature, albeit when rousted in the early hours of the following morning, he was somewhat disheartened when the image that greeted him was that of a traditionally clad Inuit hunter.

Evidently breakfast was ready or at least that was what he had interpreted from their limited exchange of words and hand gestures. Joel himself would have liked to have had a wash-up and the opportunity to brush his teeth before starting his day but unfortunately the man seemed to be in a bit of a hurry to get the show on the road. Although on the bright side, they weren't sending him off with an empty stomach or depriving him of his morning coffee.

Upon entering the main meeting tent, Joel was not at all surprised to see Isitoq once again in the company of the elders and looking quite at home in her current surroundings.

Thankfully it took no time at all for them to make eye contact from across the large space, followed by her motioning him over quite enthusiastically and then patting the seat beside her in welcome. Sadly there was not enough time for the two teammates to compare notes or for Isitoq to pass on the wisdom that she had gleaned from the night before.

Albeit whatever it was, it must have been rather advantageous because she was positively glowing this morning. Soon afterwards, it all became quite clear as they gathered outside in the crisp dawn air and Isitoq was rather ceremoniously handed over the reins to her very own dogsled.

Contrarily, Joel was cordially offered the cargo bed in any sled of his choosing, although strangely his teammate's was not up for the taking. Apparently she had already decided to pack hers full of the supplies that they would need in order to accomplish today's multitude of tasks. Joel didn't mean to pout but he didn't like being treated like a tourist either.

Deep down he could only hope that his teammate would later indulge him by letting him have a go at her sled, even if it was only for a short distance, after all, how hard could it really be?

Subsequently while cutting across an almost virgin landscape of freshly fallen snow, Joel's earlier sullen expression was quickly replaced by an infectious grin as the team ventured forth at a surprisingly fast speed, under nothing but beautiful clear skies.

He would have loved to have said that he could smell the salty ocean air from where they were; however, he soon discovered a less known fact about dog sledding as the animals were evidently trained to relieve themselves without stopping.

The air was indeed a tad malodorous at times, not to mention the wind biting, but once hunkered down in the sled's cradle, wrapped warmly in an extra layer of animal hide, Joel found the whole experience to be utterly exhilarating and soon forgot that he had even been mad at Isitoq.

Using a GPS the team was able to relatively quickly locate the hidden polar bear dens by collating the satellite data retrieved from the female bear's collars. Quite simple when you took into account that if the animal's positioning had remained rather static for months at a time, it was a good bet that they had been hold-up with their new cubs in their maternity dens. Now all they had to do was mark their location, so that they would be easier to spot from the air and to keep track of the families as they emerged…all from the safety of their helicopter.

Thankfully everything went pretty much as planned, due to their thoughtful foresight in plotting their course days before. But, unfortunately, Mother Nature had other plans altogether when it came to the constraints of daylight…there would be no time today for diversions such as Dog Sledding 101.

39

JOEL

LATER ON THEIR WAY BACK TO THE HIGHLANDER'S CAMP, the teammates were extremely lucky to spot a rather large adult ribbon seal, making its way nimbly across an ice floe.

Be it luck or the fact this pinniped's movements are quite distinctive from all other ice seals, since they move one fore flipper at a time as opposed to caterpillar-like. The direction and ambient noise of the blowing winds played a fortuitous role as the rare animal continued on its way, unaware of the group's presence.

Isitoq was the first to stop her sled, and the hunters followed suit. They had a brief discussion and unanimously made time for the teammates to get a closer look at the animal. Joel and Isitoq unobtrusively gathered their camera equipment and approached on foot from downwind; hoping to get some spectacular pictures of the seal's unique markings, totally oblivious to their guide's true intentions.

Albeit the hunters remained some distance away, one hunter had a traditional spear in hand deftly threw his weapon and skewered the 5 foot long seal, right in front of their very eyes.

The spectacle left Joel aghast and rendered him powerless as the wounded animal began flopping about on the ice, spilling copious amounts of its life's blood. He looked from one hunter to the next as they hurriedly approached, hoping one of them would step forward and quicken the poor seal's death. It was the only humane option.

Their clear hesitation baffled Joel, and the sudden interest of the hunters in his teammate then surprised him as they gathered around her for some unknown reason. Followed by Isitoq and the men exchanging heated words, none of which Joel was privy to due to his illiteracy. At first, she backed away from their insistent gestures and then became rather defiant.

That all changed when the group's finest marksman presented her with the handle of his blade.

Without so much as a backward glance, she approached the struggling animal and dispatched it with one well-placed slash. Joel couldn't believe what he just witnessed and refused to come any closer as the hunters gathered around Isitoq, voicing and showing their approval boisterously. When the opportunity presented itself, Joel stepped forward as the men dispersed to have a word with his teammate.

"How could you do it and, more importantly, why did you do that?" Joel tried to remain calm and hide his disappointment in her actions as he spoke quickly under his breath. He didn't want to upset their hosts.

However, Isitoq's first reaction to the scolding was indignation, but then decided that this was not the time or the place to have it out with her teammate.

"Don't you remember me telling you I spent my

formative years in the Arctic? We couldn't exactly go to the corner store for takeout. Don't worry your pretty little head about it, I'm sure the seal will be delicious…" she said while wiping blood from the hunter's blade onto her sleeve.

Isitoq marched off nonchalantly toward the group's anchored sleds, stopping only long enough to yell something back over her shoulder. To which the hunters responded by racing to collect their sleds and loaded the undressed carcass into one of the empty cradles, before the increasing flurry of swirling snow surrounded them.

Thankfully, they retraced their steps back to camp post haste because the impending storm front had gathered at an alarming rate and the skies took on an ugly greenish hue with each passing hour.

WHEN THEY BREACHED THE CAMP'S PERIMETER, THEY WERE relieved to see the helicopter was repositioned and tethered down to withstand the inevitable high winds to come.

Kinsmen and women, along with their pilot, greeted them and helped to unload their supplies, not to mention one rather plump seal.

In the bustling activity that followed, Joel tried in vain to not lose sight of Isitoq's movements as she made her way through the converging crowds of people, stopping periodically to share a few words. Although you know what they say about "best laid schemes of mice and men…" as he was pushed back and caught up in a stream of shifting bodies.

Joel must have looked like a lost soul in need of rescue, for out of nowhere, their pilot reappeared with his new lady friend in tow and suggested that he join them in the main meeting tent. Once inside, he was pleasantly surprised by the wall of heat that hit him smack dab in the face as he transitioned from extreme cold into the overly packed room. He soon struggled again, but this time to get a better vantage point to discover the whereabouts of his missing teammate. Joel hated how they had parted and the fact she had construed his comments to be chauvinistic. He needed to explain his somewhat snippy response to her dispatching the seal.

Once elevated, Isitoq was quite easy to spot from across the large tent as she stood on the elder's slightly raised podium, in a rather masculine stance with legs apart. Joel could see her lips moving as she appeared to be addressing those closest. It wasn't until he realized she was standing over the dead body of the ribbon seal; he pushed his way up to the front of the crowd.

As he drew closer, he watched in wonderment as she was presented with what looked to be an enormous chunk of sea ice. She inserted it into the animal's frozen, rictus mouth with some difficulty. Things got even stranger yet as she showed her expertise with a knife while meticulously parting the animal from its beautiful hide before butchering the meat.

None of this made any sense to Joel. He needed answers but became inconspicious once the voices of those present grew louder in their approval of Isitoq's actions.

During the festivities that evening, Joel could not help but dwell on the magnitude and diversity of tonight's attendees. But unfortunately, he had no one to verify his observations, as he had lost sight of their pilot again. He really needed to talk to Isitoq. So much had happened today, and he was feeling like a spectator in an almost surrealistic backward step in time.

Thankfully, he did not have to look far to find her, as she could be seen once again, deep in conversation with the Highlander elders at the head of the assembly. Just as he was mustering his nerve to approach, Isitoq abruptly moved from her current position and sat stoically, almost knee to knee, with one of the female elders.

She pulled up her sleeve, exposing her hand, and presented it to the woman, who smiled back at her. They were joined by several other women, one of which presented a large hide bag to the elder and a crude bowl of god only knows what. Joel's curiosity got the best of him. He had to know just what they were up to now. Looking around the room, everyone's facial expressions were of happiness, not alarm.

Again inching forward, he got a better look at the contents of the bag as they were removed and handed to the elder for inspection. At first glance, it appeared to be sewing supplies.

That was until the woman started washing Isitoq's hand with the contents of the bowl and drew on it with a piece of charcoal. It dawned on Joel just what the woman was preparing to do, tattoo his teammate. The entire process itself didn't take all that long because the design was relatively small and simple, consisting mostly of dots, lines and the occasional "Y". Isitoq sat like a champ, as they say and when it was all said and done, she held up her hand and looked admiringly at the dorsum before leaning forward and kissing the elder tenderly on both cheeks.

The rest of the night was a continuous whirlwind of activities. It was damn near impossible for Joel to even get close enough to his teammate to share a private word or two. Leaving him once again the observer, an odd predicament to say the least, but sadly because of his lack of knowledge regarding their spoken tongue, he would always remain out of the loop.

Finally resigning himself to another night of shared

sleeping accommodations, he made his way through what was left of the crowd and hesitated before exiting the tent, hoping it would afford Isitoq a final chance to seek him out. Just as the night air took his breath away, so too did his teammate. As she grabbed his hand, kissed him deeply on the mouth and lead him off rather forcibly into the blackness.

At first, Joel wanted to talk and even tried to halt their movement. "Isitoq, where are you taking me? You haven't talked to me all night and now you're interested. If I didn't know any better, I'd think you've been drinking?"

"You can't tell me you don't want this. I've seen how your eyes follow my every move. I know that you're a good man and that I can trust you…now trust me," she dragged him off toward her sleeping quarters.

Nothing more was said between the two of them as they crawled through the passageway into the entrance of the small igloo Isitoq had been assigned.

Upon entering the living area, a horrifying thought paralyzed Joel. His trepidations were easy to read, and she could allay his fears even before he voiced them aloud by assuring him they would not be interrupted. After which they both laughed and quickly took up from where they had left off, feverishly kissing whilst embracing one another in the darkness.

Isitoq was like no other, as she seemed to want to get to the main event straight away. Pushing Joel down onto the hide covered ice bed before yanking off his boots and then peeling off his pants. Joel was not opposed to the idea but preferred to slow the pace, so he could savour their first experience with the accompaniment of a little light. She seemed a tad perturbed by his request, begrudgingly lighting an oil lamp and placed it on the far side of the room.

The inside of the igloo was awash in the lambent glow of the crude lamp but before he would even let her touch him again, he positioned himself comfortably on the side of the bed, naked from the waist down and then slowly removed his parka and threw it off to the side. Joel motioned for her to approach and removed her clothing, one piece at a time, so he could enjoy the view.

Every time she tried to hurry him along and cover her nakedness with her arms, he hushed her and tenderly kissed the nape of her neck, visibly enjoying the trail of goosebumps left behind. That was until they adjusted their positions in the dim light and he became all too aware of the raised scar tissue that literally covered Isitoq's breasts and stomach, telltale signs of past trauma. Joel couldn't help but be shocked by the severity and sheer number of her wounds.

She had surely suffered at the hands of someone, but who?

Unfortunately, his hesitation and the look of pity on his face brought more attention to her previous traumas than words could have ever done. Immediately causing her to see red and briskly grab for her discarded clothes in which to cover her nakedness.

"No…stop…you're beautiful…I'm truly sorry if I embarrassed you. I can only hope the person who did this to you has been punished."

Fury instantly replaced any meekness that might have crossed her face. "Yes, they paid with their lives."

Joel was at first confused because he was not aware the death penalty was even an option in this region. Unless the perpetrator was from another state or she had been forced to kill them in self-defense.

Any way you looked at it, he did not wish to cause her any further anguish by reliving the events. Joel approached her and took her hands in his, stopping to kiss the dorsum of her newly tattooed hand before leading her back to the bed.

He threw back the heavy caribou hide blanket and bent to lift her onto the ice structure. His gentleness went a long way to easing her worries as she did not resist when he picked her up and laid her on the bed.

Joel turned back towards the oil lamp, bent down and extinguished its flame before joining her.

40

As Joel slowly opened his eyes hours later, he felt thrilled to see that the inside of their igloo remained almost pitch-black and that he couldn't see any seams of light between the blocks of ice.

Stretching languidly, he reached out for the beautiful, warm body that lay beside him and was more than pleasantly surprised as he felt her hand on his stomach and then, as she playfully walked her fingers down his body in search of his manhood.

He didn't know exactly what time it was and wasn't about to get out of bed to check his watch, either. Joel could only hope and pray that since Isitoq was the senior member of the team, the hunters would wait for her word to start the day. And thankfully she was on the same page as she did not hesitate to grasp his manhood and stroked it. Joel then countered with trying to postpone the inevitable by pushing her back down onto the bed and parting her legs, so he could see to her needs as well, but she only laughed and straddled his rigid member.

He couldn't help but hold on to her waist as she

slammed herself down onto his member with every thrust and by the time they both reached climax, they were audibly expressing their mutual animalistic pleasure. Joel loved the feeling of being inside of Isitoq…the smell of her on his fingers…the smell of their lovemaking; somehow, it was even more pungent because of the extreme cold temperatures within the igloo.

Thankfully, they were granted a short break, as the early morning weather stayed blustery, and it would have been unsafe to search for more polar bear dens in such reduced visibility.

Both Joel and Isitoq would have loved to have returned to their hide bed to wait out the storm, but unfortunately they did have jobs to do and being ready at a moment's notice should there be a break in the weather, was one of them. No time could be wasted, data needed to be collected and analyzed, maps charted, supplies accounted for, and packs ready.

Plus, they didn't want to infringe on the community and its members. After all, these people had kindly opened up their homes to the team, and the use and knowledge of their hunters…one could not ask for more. As they later enjoyed their breakfast of seal meat and coffee, Joel couldn't help but admire his teammate's new tattoos in the light of day. Hard to believe that such an intricate design could be accomplished by running a thread of sinew beneath the skin that had been soaked in home-made dye using lamp black.

One part of him actually entertained the idea of getting one himself before their adventure ended, but then thought better of it; he really needed to accomplish something noteworthy first, before taking the plunge. As the day wore on and the skies became increasingly darker, all hope of another day out on the sleds was dashed, but at least they could rest on their laurels somewhat since yesterday's progress had been beyond expectations.

Then, by late afternoon, the community took shelter in their dwellings, awaiting the deluge. They distributed rations to everyone, along with enough seal fat to keep the lamps burning. They could only wait and see what tomorrow had in store for them.

Fortunately, the couple got what they had wished for, time alone, without feeling like they had abandoned their teammate because he was just as happy to wait out the bad weather with his friend. However, satellite reception proved to be very unreliable as the previously forecasted precipitation turned into a blizzard and they were left with no updated weather watches or warnings.

Staying in an igloo might have sounded rather romantic to begin with, but because of the isolation and sensory deprivation of having no windows or doors to look out of, all time ceased to exist. Not that anyone was complaining, but when they dug themselves out through a heavy blanket of freshly fallen snow the following morning, they were alarmed to learn that a visiting hunter had mysteriously gone missing.

To be expected, the news weighed heavily on everyone's minds, especially when it concerned the disappearance of an honoured guest. There was even rampant talk of sending out search parties, although unfortunately no one knew just where to begin since all the sleds were accounted for. Surely the man had not taken a stroll in the middle of a blizzard, but what reason could he have had for leaving the safety of his igloo?

Right away, the teammates volunteered the use of their helicopter so that they could help expedite the community's search. But sadly, after they started up their helicopter and radioed home, they received the information that a very large-scale frontal blizzard had also severely affected their own camp and, based on its appearance, their radar detected another storm front.

All research projects were to be postponed indefinitely, and the team was to return to base camp at once…the shit just kept piling up.

While saying their "goodbyes" to the elders, they could hear a lone male voice shouting in the distance, and everyone within earshot immediately came running because of his unmistakable distress. The teammates, of course, pursued in order to see what all the commotion was about and as they neared the gathering crowd, it became more than obvious.

Local kinsmen and visiting hunters engaged in a heated exchange, raising their voices, but thankfully, it had not escalated to physical violence yet. Regrettably, because of the recent snowfall, there was no overwhelming evidence or blood trail to follow, only a man's body or what was left of it…lying supine on a flat patch of frozen earth, surrounded by a very large pool of congealed blood.

Joel couldn't help but survey their surroundings, searching for any sign of what exactly had transpired during the night. Even if the hunter had gone out to relieve himself, why would he have ventured so far in whiteout conditions…something had to have caught his attention, but what? And to add to his query, surely someone had to have heard the man's screams or cries for help, albeit last night's wind had most likely masked the noise?

Standing next to Isitoq, Joel impulsively grabbed her hand and squeezed it; after all, this could have been her body since she had gone outside to do her business during the storm.

"Did you hear anything strange last night…man or animal?"

At first, she looked perplexed by his inquiry. "What do you mean by that?"

"Well, when I turned over in the night and reached for you, your side of the bed was cold…I figured you had gone for a pee…please forgive me, I went back to sleep."

"Why would I go trudging through the snow in the dark? Just to freeze my ass off while taking a leak? If it hadn't snowed last night, I might give you a heads up right now on where not to step," and then she smiled mischievously before giving his hand a squeeze back.

Unfortunately, both Isitoq and Joel were caught unaware of the increasing velocity of the wind, until it was brought to their attention by the urgency in their pilot's voice…"We've got to get going, there is nothing we can do for that poor man."

The team quickly said their farewells yet again and apologized to their hosts, expressing their heartfelt frustration at not being able to lend a hand and their condolences regarding the deceased hunter.

"I cannot thank you enough for everything that you have done for my teammates and I. If current circumstances were different, we would stop at nothing to facilitate your search for the responsible animal…" Isitoq could only hope that her transparent sincerity would indeed garner future collaborations.

"The fact that a guest should meet his demise while taking refuge in our camp was tragic, to say the least. We mourn his passing as if he was one of our own, but only when the weather changes for the better will we be sending out a hunting party to destroy the rogue polar bear. His people will see to the burial as their customs dictate before returning home. After all, there is absolutely no need to disclose the horrific nature of his death and cause further trauma to those dear to him."

The elder leaned in and smiled uncomfortably. "Nothing will hinder the bond that we have formed thus far."

Then, most inopportunely, as they turned to take their leave, their pilot frantically expressed his concerns for the safety of his new ladylove and the fact that too many bears were getting a hankering for human flesh.

"They need to know that this is happening elsewhere," he urged. "They need to be forewarned!"

Upon seeing the pilot's obvious distress, one elder stepped forward and inquired as to the cause. Thankfully, Isitoq was quick to translate what her teammate had said and give some background in order for the elders to make their own judgement call on what would be shared.

All things considered, no one wanted to create hysteria amongst the peoples of the north.

"Not to worry. Your lady friend should be fine as long as everyone goes out in groups of two or more, at least for the time being. Healthy bears rarely attack this close to camps unless the opportunity presents itself, last night's casualty was no one's fault…" Joel voiced this in order to ease their pilot's fears and Isitoq echoed the same sentiment in the people's own tongue for all to hear.

Fortunately, it didn't take long for their helicopter to finish warming up and once she was ready to roll; they were on their way back to camp with a very large and foreboding storm front in their rearview mirror. Strangely, idle chit chat became relatively non-existent throughout their return flight, due in part to the buffeting winds that had aggressively developed and the reduced visibility.

Even their usually talkative pilot was quiet as a church mouse as he fought the helicopter's yoke and foot pedals to keep it on an even keel. Joel himself felt eerily on edge every time the cabin shook or lost altitude and kept looking over at Isitoq to make sure that she was okay, after all, they had been through so much since this morning's gruesome event and the day wasn't even over yet.

"Why are you looking at me that way?" she voiced with wrinkled brows.

"Are you alright? I should have stepped in front of you to block that horrific view…I still can't get the sight of that poor man's body out of my mind. If you need to talk or just need a hug, please let me know?" he implored.

She hesitated to reply, leading Joel to believe that she might not have correctly heard him because of the cabin noise and the distance they were sitting apart. Before he could even attempt to reword his question, she got up and awkwardly moved to the seat beside him, bracing herself against the rocking motion of the helicopter.

Once seated, Isitoq took his hand in hers and squeezed, all the while smiling reassuringly back at him. Joel couldn't help but rotate his wrist to get a better look at her fresh tattoos, and then raised her hand to his lips and planted a gentle kiss on it.

"You don't have to worry about me. I'm made of sterner stuff than you can even imagine. I might have been educated in a big city, but my roots will always be in the north." She stared off into the horizon.

41

SHTIYA

1954

Fighting against a sudden wind speed increase and premature darkening of the skies overhead, the young hunter tried in vain to search the horizon for landmarks as he mushed his dog team headlong into the squall.

He knew it was inadvisable to go out hunting on his own, but because of the ever changing weather patterns of late, his community was badly in need of food. If only he spotted game earlier, he would have assured its demise. After all, the very best trained him, and missing the shot was not an option.

Although, as luck would have it, a glimmer of light in the far distance piqued his curiosity. It was not his people's camp or a welcoming beacon of shelter, but the twinkle caused him to look port side just in time to catch a flash of movement out of the corner of his eye. Whatever it was, it was large, furry, and dark. Maybe a muskox or deer lost its way in the heavy snowfall.

Reining in his team, he followed the animal as best he

could, considering the elements were against him. In no time, he came alongside the exhausted beast and overtook it. Bracing himself against the handlebars of his sled, he slowed the team, hefting his spear and with every ounce of his being hurtled it at the cow. The spirits were on his side that evening as the large animal fought to stay upright before dropping to the ground in a flurry of swirling snow.

Although because of its sheer size, the hunter could not transfer it to his sled until after it was field dressed, and he did not have the luxury of time. Jumping off of his sled, the young man dispatched the wounded muskox cow, moving his sled and dogs closer, so all could share the cover it provided.

As the storm continued to brew, the hunter tried to make the best of a bad situation by erecting a lean-to of sorts, using the large hide blanket from his sled to block the full force of the wind before attempting to get a campfire started. After all, he hadn't wanted to spend the rest of the night out on the tundra with only his dogs for warmth. Unfortunately, it took hours for the wind to calm down enough for him to light a lamp, not to mention a fire.

After he accomplished it, he was too frozen and exhausted to even cook some of the fresh meat he carved off the animal. Huddling together, man and beasts waited out the rest of the storm and the warmth the morning's sunrise would hopefully bring.

The earnest barking of his dogs awakened the hunter during the night, suggesting someone or something had taken him dangerously by surprise. Regaining his composure, the young hunter held his breath as he squinted out of the entrance of his lean-to at the veil of falling snow before him.

At first, he wanted to hush his dogs because he did not want to give his exact location away, but after a while, when no movement was clear, the hunter called out into the darkness.

"Show yourself or I will release my dogs, and then it will be too late. Your only cries will be of pain," he waited angrily for a response.

A large full moon came into view as the clouds overhead parted, but the size of the snowflakes made the visibility somewhat obscured. Moving closer to the entrance, he could just make out the form of what looked to be a small polar bear approaching them, although the animal's gait was all wrong.

The hunter felt tempted to command his sled dogs to attack, fearing the beast might be injured and, therefore, unpredictable. However, he couldn't afford to lose even one dog because of the massive size of his sled's new load. As he glanced around the inside of his lean-to structure for inspiration, he only blamed himself for his current predicament.

One wall comprised his bloodied fresh kill, and whether the bear was healthy, the scent most likely attracted it. Reaching farther back into the structure, the hunter found comfort as his hand touched the shaft of his spear. The only problem was he needed enough space in order to throw the weapon accurately.

Once again, he looked out of the lean-to and the unexpected completely surprised him. The sight before him was not of a polar bear, but a young girl.

"What the hell are you doing out here? I could have killed you. Where is your family…your people?"

The girl said nothing in response, only lifted a trembling arm and pointed toward where he assumed the flickering light he saw earlier originated from.

Leaving his shelter, he placed the spear just outside the entrance so it was within reach if need be and slowly approached the child. Grabbing the girl's small frozen hand, he lead her back to his lean-to, all the while keeping a cautious eye out for the polar bear.

"Stupid girl! You could have been a meal for the polar bear…didn't you see it? It was probably tracking you. Get inside and warm up!"

Oddly, she still never said a word, merely followed his instructions, and it wasn't until she was at the far end of the structure and his bulk was blocking the entrance. He relit his lamp to get a better look at the stranger.

To his pleasant surprise, she was not a child as he first thought, although she was young, mid-teens at most and exceptionally beautiful, with the most unusual blueish-green eyes.

"Poor thing. You look absolutely frozen, give me your hand," and as soon as she begrudgingly presented it to him, the hunter rubbed it vigorously in order to increase the blood flow to her frostbitten digits.

At first she made small whimpering noises as if he was hurting her, which enraged the young man. After all, he was trying to help. The least she could do was be grateful.

Although when she presented her other hand to him, he became captivated as she donned a small smile on her face, almost coquettish. And it wasn't until she drew closer to the hunter's qulliq for warmth, he noticed the intricacy of her facial tattoos, proclaiming she was indeed of age… the hunter was pleased.

However, he was surprised to note she didn't have any skin-stitching on her fingers or hands…what group of people could she possibly be from that did not honour Nuliajuk, the mother of all sea beasts?

Thankfully, he had plenty of time in which to find out and he would enjoy every minute, unless there was someone out looking for her at this very moment.

"What is your name and why are you out in the middle of nowhere by yourself? Did you get lost, separated from your kin…did someone leave you out here?" he said somewhat curtly.

At first, she glanced around as if searching for the right words, which made the hunter assume her hesitancy meant that her tale was most likely unpleasant. "My name is Bola. While I was out hunting with my mother, we got separated during the storm," she said, hiding her face and sobbing.

The young hunter found her story to be rather far-fetched…what community or people sent its womenfolk out to do their bidding? Women huntresses were the stuff of legends and bad ones at that. What kind of name was "Bola?" Who would name their daughter after a weapon?

"I'm not saying you're a liar, but I find your version of tonight's events highly unlikely. Look, the weather is much too unpredictable to go in search of your mother right now and there may or may not be a polar bear roaming around. Stay the night and I'll help you look for her in the morning."

His promise of help seemed to quell the girl's anxieties, but she was still not a wealth of information, so after a short period the hunter decided it might be best to just get some shut-eye and deal with the matter at first light. However, when he made a move to extinguish his lamp, she seemed to panic again, resulting in him having to waste more seal blubber keeping the shelter illuminated.

The hunter barely closed his eyes when he sensed the girl nudge him while trying to squeeze by in the small enclosed space and when he inquired what she was doing. She replied she needed to make water. At first he was going to offer to stand watch to make sure the bear went on its merry way and then had second thoughts. After all, she made it this far unscathed.

Fortunately or not, he stayed awake until she returned and was genuinely surprised by the time which passed. Pretending to be asleep, he attempted to interpret her every move upon reentering the lean-to, but he was taken aback when she snuggled up next to him... he couldn't believe his good luck.

Now, in the comfort of his embrace, she let him blow out the lamp, but he couldn't fall asleep, unlike her. And with every expiratory breath she took during her slumber, he became all the more infuriated. It was quite a while since he knew the pleasures of a woman and even though he did not trust her, he couldn't help but find her incredibly alluring.

Repositioning himself so as not to wake her, the hunter cautiously reached down and under her parka, hesitating briefly before attempting to touch her stomach and made his way farther up to what he assumed would be small breasts.

He planned out every movement, measured every breath, and when he cupped one of her surprisingly firm breasts in his hand, he felt thrilled that she did not resist but turned around to face him. Now laying face-to-face in the dark, the girl reciprocated by reaching her hands under his clothing similarly; starting at his stomach, feeling the tautness of his muscles and then letting her fingers trace his lower obliques before moving slowly upward. The hunter wasn't sure, but at some point, he sensed she was searching for something in particular as her fingers grazed over his chest and explored his neck.

Unfortunately, he realized the error of his ways too late as her fingers wrapped around the sinew necklace his father gifted him with since becoming a man. Her battle cry was almost deafening as she gripped the severed finger and pulled with all of her might while trying desperately to separate herself from the hunter.

At first he was so stunned that he did not react, he couldn't believe what just happened, sure he heard the stories and seen his own family's collection of mummified fingers but never in his wildest dreams did he imagine the witch was still alive and would come searching for him.

Suddenly, the dogs barked and someone threw back his shelter cover, revealing another person standing ready with his own spear in their hand. It wasn't until the intruder spoke he realized it was indeed a woman and that her sole reason for being there was one of revenge.

"Bola, come to me, daughter! Do not sully yourself any further with this progeny of Kova. You found what we seek and by doing so, we are ever closer to avenging the atrocities which befell my mother, your grandmother, Uki." It took all of Shtiya's willpower to not dispatch the young hunter on the spot. "Where are the remaining fingers?!" she bellowed.

Deep down, the hunter knew that no amount of pleading for his life would suffice, but he wasn't about to share the whereabouts of his family members either, in exchange for one final breath. He solemnly followed the women a short distance away from the shelter and then knelt down to prepare for what he assumed would follow.

Strangely, the older woman handed the spear to her daughter and then removed something from her pack. The hunter wasn't sure exactly what it was, but she seemed to struggle with the large object. Turning to face him, she slowly approached, and it wasn't until she got much closer that he understood what was about to happen.

In the blue hour just before sunrise, Shtiya raised her hands above her head to show her quarry the object that would bring about his demise. Gripped in her hands was the partial skeletal remains of an enormous bear's paw with extraordinarily long claws, possibly because the bulk of the paw had most likely atrophied. The woman then screamed something incoherent and truly terrifying to the skies above before swinging downward with her implement and removing a good portion of the young man's face.

At first she did not move so much as a muscle, only stared down at the dying man as his life's blood drained slowly from his body, and even when he fought for breath and tried to form words with his disfigured jaw. Unfortunately for him, the blow did not kill him instantly, but she would not let her daughter end the suffering with his own spear, either.

Shtiya then retrieved her polar bear hide blanket from where she had dropped it earlier, took her daughter by the hand and headed back across the tundra whence they had come.

42

JOEL

Present Day

THEY MADE IT BACK TO BASE CAMP JUST BEFORE THE NEXT barrage of winter storms hit, leaving barely enough time to secure their helicopter properly.

Afterwards, sitting inside the safety of the cafeteria, Joel couldn't help but be awe-inspired by Mother Nature whilst gazing out the immense bank of windows taking up one entire wall.

Clouds became more ominous, not to mention the sheer force of the wind as it literally battered the panes of glass, so much so that one would expect to see them crack or implode at any minute. Joel could only imagine this was what a fish must feel like when someone tapped incessantly on the side of its fishbowl.

As he looked around the large mess hall, he was thankful for the muted chatter of his fellow teammates because the constant high-pitched whistling of the wind as it tried to force its way into every nook and cranny of the structure was unsettling to say the least. Joel felt pleasantly surprised when Isitoq's leg brushed suggestively against his own beneath the cover of their table, but he felt somewhat disheartened when he periodically caught her searching the room for what he assumed to be prying eyes.

Without so much as a backward glance, his beautiful companion abruptly stood as if to leave before leaning in closer and whispering under her breath for him to meet her in her room. Albeit, with strict instructions she leave first and only after a reasonable amount of time had passed, he should follow. Because of Joel's naivety, he read way too much into her directions as opposed to taking it for the clandestine rendezvous it was. He thought she felt embarrassed to be seen dating the new guy.

Isitoq was getting all too familiar with his lack of experience. So when his response was one of indignation, she reached under the table and gave his upper thigh an obvious squeeze before sashaying out of the cafeteria.

Left to his own devices, Joel couldn't help but stare at his watch as the minutes ticked by and when he thought enough time had passed, he quickly got up and walked down the long hallway on the way to her room. Stopping to gather his composure, he took a calming breath outside of her door, but hardly had time to finish the rhythm of his knock before it swung wide.

She grabbed him by the front of his hoodie, pulling him into her room and slamming the door shut in one fell swoop. Once inside, he wasn't at all surprised to see she had dimmed the lights in anticipation of his visit. Although he couldn't help but note the large white animal fur adorning her bed. Taking her lead, they both discarded their clothes every which way and then fell onto the bed, entwined playfully in each other's arms.

As soon as Joel's body contacted the fur, he knew it was real. "Sexy!" he exclaimed as he ran his fingers through the thick, luxurious animal hair beneath his bare skin.

"So you like it, I take?" she said rather seductively, while raising an eyebrow.

"This thing must be worth a fortune. Maybe we should throw a sheet over it?"

She laughed wholeheartedly at his considerate request. "Don't worry, it's been in my family forever. Just try not to cum all over it," and then she winked.

Both of them broke out into peals of laughter, followed by the best sex Joel had ever experienced. If the sounds coming out of Isitoq were any sign, she had enjoyed herself thoroughly as well. Although as they lay there, basking in the afterglow, he couldn't help but wonder if she was on some form of contraceptive and, of course, he did not know just how to broach the subject. His teammate was getting very good at reading his moods and prodded him to just say what was on his mind.

"I have to ask, are you on birth control of any sort? I'm so sorry, but I'm not in the habit of carrying condoms, not that I go around having unprotected sex with strangers. You're the first person who I've had relations with in years, besides the mother of my child."

At first, his ramblings quite entertained Isitoq and then felt sorry for the man. "Don't give it another thought, I'm using a vaginal ring and I too am not in the habit of having sex with just anyone."

This didn't put a damper on the rest of their evening, although they had to come up with a plan on just how to act in front of their co-workers. As it was company policy to not be fucking your teammates, since breakups were nasty in such close quarters.

Both agreed to take a wait and see attitude with no public displays of affection. Since they were going to be in isolation for quite a few more months. Later that night, as they stared at the oversized digital readout on Isitoq's bedside clock. Dismay washed over them as they realized it was morning.

Adding to their to-do list, they promised to be vigilant about waking up in their own beds so as not to attract unwanted attention and to actually get some sleep. Truth be told, both found the idea of sneaking around even more attractive. As the saying goes, "forbidden fruit tastes the sweetest."

After quietly saying their goodbyes, Joel cautiously looked both directions before entering the long tube of hallways leading back to his own room. He realized tiptoeing would be a waste of time because, the very moment he made a move, the motion sensors became activated to light the morning's walk of shame.

Upon entering his own room, he forwent his usual bedtime rituals in order to catch a few extra winks, then stripped off his clothes and crawled in under his blankets. But the moment he grasped his pillow, he could smell Isitoq and couldn't stop the urge to please himself.

Regrettably, what seemed like only minutes later, his alarm rang and he begrudgingly rolled out of bed, heading for the shower.

THE FOLLOWING DAY'S FORECAST HAD BEEN WRONG AND the skies overhead were clear. Now, everyone had to be on deck, and all research projects were put on hold for the time being.

Joel, being an able-bodied young man, helped repair whatever damage was caused by the storm. The camp had several skid steer loaders and such at their disposal, so it wasn't all grunt work, but by the end of the day, he just wanted to eat and go to bed.

Later, while he was having his evening meal and exchanging stories with his teammates, he realized Isitoq was missing. Trying not to panic, he asked about Isitoq's recent whereabouts, and became alarmed when he found out she had once again taken a snowmobile without permission to check on a nearby community.

Apparently, the storm that had set upon their base was relatively widespread and she was worried about the neighbours, as she called them. Upon hearing the news, Joel could not hide his unease and curtly brought up the fact only days before, polar bears had killed two men in this very region. How could they all be so cavalier regarding their teammate's well-being?

"Joel, my lad, don't you fret. Isitoq was born in this region and if anyone is safe out there, it's her. After all, a group of local hunters has already taken care of the situation."

Joel felt a firm hand on his shoulder and was relieved by the voice of his former professor. Although, as he turned back and made eye contact with James, his façade quickly crumbled.

"If you had witnessed the aftermath of that poor hunter's demise, the utter butchery on our last day with the Highlanders, you would understand my fears. The only way that you could tell what direction the corpse was facing was by the position of the poor man's feet," and then his voice trailed off completely.

Sensing Joel's somewhat fragile state, the older man

bent down to whisper into his former student's ear, so his surrounding teammates would be none the wiser. "Let's go for a walk. It's been a while since we talked and by the time we're done, Isitoq should be back from her gallivanting."

He helped to push Joel's chair back and escorted him out of the cafeteria, just in case things should escalate and tears shed. The boy had to work with these people and he wanted Joel on an even footing with his teammates. Not the subject of idle gossip or childish jokes.

As soon as Joel could clear his mind and focus on their conversation, he was back to the level-headed young man he had always been. Although his old prof noticed him looking about frequently, hoping Isitoq would appear.

By the time they were enjoying their third wee dram of Scotch, Joel was recounting how well their flagging had gone and how his teammates had left lasting impressions on the Highlanders, not to mention Isitoq's newest tattoos.

"Are you talking about me?" she said from across the lounge.

She plopped herself rather dramatically down in the empty seat between the two men and directed her next questions at her boss.

"So what's the status on our return trip up north? Those cubs will not wait for us. You've seen the numbers. They're downright impressive. I'm also making significant progress with the elders in documenting their people's folklore."

While awaiting Dr. Pettimore's response, she couldn't help but take in Joel's overall appearance. "Are you alright? You look like you haven't had a lick of sleep?"

A part of her wanted to touch him, but she knew they had already agreed on no PDAs and now was not the time or place.

"Tell you what, I'll walk you to your room and you can

tell me all about your day, but let's stop at the cafeteria first. I'm famished."

"You two run along. We've got plenty of time to plan our next move. That's if our Doppler radar is correct, as well as our prognosticators," and then he waved them off in a good-natured manner.

43

JOEL

Isitoq had no intentions of dragging Joel through the cafeteria. They went directly to his room. After tucking him in, she excused herself so she could grab a takeout meal from the kitchen, one she could bring back to his room and eat at her leisure.

Even though she had only been gone for a short while, the agitated state she found him in upon her return surprised Isitoq. In her absence, his son's aunt had called because the boy had been acting out, exhibiting aggressive behaviour, something so uncharacteristic of Dinnie.

"When I asked Aunt Mona to explain what she meant by aggressive, she said he'd been picking fights and using the F-word. For God's sake, Dinnie is only 5 years old. When I inquired as to his mother's response regarding the situation, she became quiet at first and then said something about her not being around often. She's going to call back tomorrow and let me speak to him."

"You talked about wanting him to come and visit. If James says it's okay, then why don't you? We've still got a lot of cleanup to do around camp before they let us loose up north again. It's going to be a while before those cubs emerge from their dens. Now is the best time because we're gonna be very busy in a month. By then, all the staff should be back and you won't have a room for yourself anymore." She bent down and kissed him on the nose.

Isitoq's exuberance did wonders for Joel's overall mood. Combining it with a good night's sleep should garner a better perspective on the situation at hand.

Dinnie's well-being would always be foremost, and he was more than grateful for the wonderful support system he had in place. Even though Joel was still dog-tired, he couldn't help but reach for Isitoq's hand and pull her down onto the bed beside him.

"Just one kiss before I go to sleep. You know, I was worried sick about you today. Why do you insist on going out all by yourself?"

"If you hadn't noticed, I'm a big girl. And from what I understand, someone has addressed the scavenging problem. Maybe Dinnie would like to learn how to drive a snowmobile?" she laughed before straddling him and kissing him deeply.

When she came up for air, Isitoq pushed him back down on the bed and, in a motherly voice, said, "I'm going back to my room to eat my dinner in peace and you're going to sleep, young man."

When he entered the cafeteria for breakfast, his fellow teammates warmly welcomed him, and he soon found out why. Their pilot had shared their harrowing ordeal with the rest of the camp. Describing the hunter's remains in Technicolor for anyone who would listen and suggesting everyone go easy on the 'pup'.

He wanted to take offense at the remark but decided there were a lot worse things to be called and he appreciated the big brother attitude from a man he liked. After breakfast, Joel checked the bulletin board to find out his designated work detail for the day, while hoping that Isitoq's name would also appear so he could observe her activities.

There, at the bottom of the sheet, in her own handwriting, was a list of nearby winter camps. He wanted to be mad at her but refused to spend the day dwelling on the pursuits of someone that he had absolutely no control over.

Fortunately, Joel's hard work throughout the day paid off, and he kept his mind, body, and spirit occupied for the duration of his shift. It wasn't until he had showered and changed for supper he sought Isitoq out, hoping to make plans for later in the evening.

Again entering the base's large cafeteria, he truly felt embraced by his teammates and his surroundings, the room was warm and smelled of home cooking, and the background music was pleasing to the ear, yet quiet enough so that a person could carry on a conversation without yelling. He lingered while taking in the sights and waved back in acknowledgement to several people as they motioned him over to their tables.

Giving his apologies as his eyes fell upon the object of his affections, for she was sitting in their usual spot. As if awaiting his return. All was right with the world. Slowly making his way across the packed room, he paused at several other tables in order to quickly say "hello" before joining Isitoq. At which point, he tested the waters and positioned himself right next to her. Mere inches away, without so much as a touch. She seemed surprised and figured out his plan. After all, two could play this game.

Halfway through their meal, Joel realized he was on the losing end of the game he himself had set into motion.

"I can't take this any longer. I want you right now. But I'm expecting a call after supper from Dinnie." His cheeks were flushed, making him even more irresistible.

"Well then, you had better get back to your room, and I'll meet you there shortly. I just have to stop at my room for a sec," she said, biting her lower lip.

He looked around the room, half expecting all eyes to be on them. Their attraction was palpable and even though she was a few years older, Isitoq was everything that he hadn't known that he wanted. On his way back to his room, Joel smiled to himself, wondering what she needed to pick up before making their rendezvous…oh well, he'd just have to wait and see.

But as soon as he entered his room, he couldn't believe the disheveled state that he had left it in and began hurriedly tidying up in anticipation of her arrival. While quickly stashing wet towels in the tub and dirty clothes under the bed, a knock came on the door, to which he enthusiastically answered but was a little underwhelmed as he watched Isitoq unhurriedly remove a plethora of candles from inside her backpack.

Joel really wasn't sure what he had expected, lingerie under a fur coat perhaps, but at least she came back.

"Let me just arrange these around the room and then you can turn the lights off. I assure you'll like the end results," as she smiled.

After Isitoq finished, she turned down the bed and stood next to it, motioning for Joel to turn off the lights. The golden glow of candlelight moved Joel as soon as he flipped the switch, and he understood why Isitoq had brought them.

Shedding her clothes, Isitoq stood naked in all her

glory. Her beautiful athletic body was all the more defined by the flickering of the flames and the shadows they cast. Any signs of trauma were now imperceptible.

Joel couldn't help but stare in admiration at the young woman before him, slowly doffing his own clothing as well. He approached Isitoq and covered her body with kisses. Again, she seemed to want to hurry him along, but he would have none of it, as she threw her arms around his neck. He lifted her up so she could wrap her legs around his torso.

Kneeling down on the edge of the bed, he bent forward and loosened his hold on her suspended body in order to lay her down. Crawling backwards, he positioned himself between her legs and pleasured her orally. At first, she attempted to pull him back and reposition his body higher on her, but when she gave in to his manipulations, she reclined and savoured the moment.

"Where did you learn to do that? I have never experienced that in my whole life. You definitely rocked my world." Isitoq laughed as she felt the residual spasms run through her limbs. She rolled over and got onto her knees before presenting her buttocks to Joel and spreading her thighs.

"Isitoq, I hope you know I care about you and even though I'm not ready to proclaim my undying love just yet, I'd like to think you can feel it in my actions." He reached forward and helped her off of her elbows so he could look her in the eyes before gently planting a kiss on her slightly parted reddened lips.

Her need for satisfaction overpowered his gentleness as she began stroking his member and dropped onto the bed into doggy-style position so he could take her from behind.

However, their coupling had to be cut short when his phone rang and reminded him of the upcoming video chat with his son. He texted Mona and informed her to expect his call within a half hour, leaving little time for Isitoq and Joel to properly say their goodnights and leaving no time for a shower.

ONCE AGAIN SURVEYING HIS ROOM FOR ANYTHING WHICH might catch the unwanted curiosity of his son, Joel threw the blankets back over his tousled bedding and sat in the shadow of his laptop, awaiting Dinnie's call.

Ruminating happily on the events of the day as the smell of extinguished wicks hung heavy in the air. When the call came through, Joel felt alarmed to learn both Geri and her new beau had been so focused on their upcoming "happy occasion" they had practically ignored Dinnie in their small world.

In the beginning of their brief conversation, both father and son had kept everything light, the usual fare… how are you…how's school…are you making friends… have you been over to visit grandpa? Then the boy just clammed up, followed by a bout of tears as he professed his loneliness.

Sure Auntie Mona was there for him, but he missed Joel deeply. "Can't I come and visit you? I promise to be good. You said we'd be together once the weather changed."

As Joel watched his son sobbing on the computer screen, his heart broke, but he was relieved to see Mona embrace his son.

"Tell you what, I'm gonna check with my boss to see if you can come for that visit sooner, rather than later… would you like that? It'll have to be a short one and we'll have to bunk together. I'll see if someone can either accompany you or if a stewardess can make sure that you catch all of your adjoining flights on time. Leave it with me. I should know in a couple of days."

Upon hearing his father's ramblings, Dinnie was ecstatic and quickly attempted to dry his eyes and his nose with the sleeve of his shirt, to which Auntie Mona scolded him, but Joel could also see the look of joy on her face as well.

Saying their goodnights was especially sad because of the hopeful look in everyone's eyes. Joel knew this would not solve all of their problems, but it would at least bring some happiness into his child's life.

Now all he had to do was to have the talk again with Dr. Pettimore and convince him and the company to allow a small visitor for a couple of days. Joel knew he would exchange any freedom for that opportunity.

Hopefully, the weather would also be agreeable and maybe they would even have time to take him for a snowmobile ride after all.

All he could do was express his arguments and hope for the best.

44

UKI

Winter of 1958

AGAINST EVERYONE'S WISHES, UKI VENTURED OUT IN THE blustery weather. After all, she had been a hunter all of her life and a little windy weather would not stop her from providing for her girls.

This was Bola's first pregnancy and even though she was in her third trimester and everything had progressed smoothly thus far, Uki still felt Shtiya's presence was better served elsewhere, in the company of her daughter. She couldn't help but feel a little perturbed they would want to coddle her.

There might be snow on the rooftop, but she still fancied herself as a force to be reckoned with, even after all these years. At a moment's notice, their status quo could change, and any of the women could be ripped from this world, with hopefully those left behind prepared for their own journeys ahead.

Life for the three generations of women had its degrees of normalcy, with both of the young girls spending their formative years in and around their cave home and the cliffs surrounding them. Uki had taught Shtiya and later Bola how to defend themselves and even imparted facets of their Inuit heritage.

Although she had to hold her tongue as the girls became more inquisitive with age and the occasional brush with strangers.

Shtiya had been a loving and obedient child but then again, Uki had not left her alone during her adolescence as all thoughts of Kova had to be put on hold in order to make sure she was also fully self-sufficient.

The mere thought of leaving her child unprepared and at the mercy of the North and its inhabitants, should she herself meet an untimely demise whilst exacting retribution, was a selfish act and not something she could live with.

Years passed before Uki decided her daughter was old enough to comprehend just what had happened to her mother at the hands of her so-called brethren. Her daughter's response surprised her. Pre-teen Shtiya felt horrified, then outraged, but she was eager to take up the search to avenge her mother. Even if it involved the killing of her own kin.

The whole idea of belonging to a group of people or even having a father was foreign to the young girl and not something she craved or missed because Uki was her world. It was at this point they left the safety of their home and traversed their part of the continent.

Uki didn't want Shtiya involved in the blood spilling that would inevitably follow, but after many hostile receptions, the young girl grew disenchanted with her supposed people and was up for the task at hand.

Gossip always ran rampant throughout small

communities and after years of chasing one's tail, Uki and her daughter finally chanced upon Kova's trail.

The famed hunter might have busied himself spreading stories about his exploits throughout the land. Only to become rather reclusive in his later years. This didn't stop his offspring or the occasional notoriety seeking hunter from endeavouring to track down the elusive White Witch, and her spawn.

Uki faced even more difficulty in achieving her goals, especially considering the fact Shtiya's eye colour alone attracted unwanted attention. She would have loved to have seen her daughter lead a normal life and meet a good man. Not some unscrupulous drunken explorer who had his friends hold her down while he attempted to deflower the girl for his clique's entertainment. Bola came into existence because of the act, similar to her grandmother.

Shtiya too kept the child as opposed to leaving it out on an ice floe. Uki wished she had been there on the fateful night, but the girl was almost 20 years old, testing her independence. However, she had the pleasure of hunting the young man and his party down at a later date to settle the score. That was Shtiya's first kill and in time she too became very proficient, a gifted huntress who could dispatch with lightning speed or make her quarry suffer depending on her whim. Many men died but never an innocent.

Many years passed as Bola became the center of the women's world and then late one evening, lady luck shone upon Shtiya and her daughter. They had been out on a hunting trip and had decided, on the spur of the moment, to stop by a nearby settlement to trade pelts for supplies and the odd treat.

The infamous Kova had only recently met his demise in a manner most unbefitting. Peacefully in his own bed, surrounded by his loving family. Word also had it that someone had spotted his youngest son hunting in the vicinity and, judging by the looks of it, he had failed to obtain food stores for his people. There was not enough time for the women to return home to alert Uki and, if the sudden drop in temperature was any sign, another storm was fast approaching.

Both of them were seasoned travellers and knew these parts like the back of their hands. After a little conversing with the local merchants, they had a better idea in which direction to look for their quarry. Locating the man, or at least his makeshift camp out in the middle of nowhere, didn't take them all that long, as they could see its flickering lamp light from a great distance away if they had a keen eye.

As the snow continued to fall, Shtiya and Bola made quick work of constructing their camp in order to wait out the storm but grew anxious after only a couple of hours.

Putting their heads together, they made a new plan and then set out on their dog sled with only the bare minimum of animals, so as not to attract any unwanted attention. After anchoring the sled a short distance away from the man's camp, young Bola then continued on foot with her grandmother's blanket for protection from the elements and to help her blend in with her surroundings. Shtiya followed closely behind. She would not subject her daughter to the same fate that had befallen both her and her own mother.

Everything played out pretty much as the women had hoped. They took care of Kova's progeny and brought back one of their mother's severed digits. Neither could feel any remorse for their actions. What people kept a woman's severed fingers hanging from around their necks as trophies?

All they could feel was empathy for their beloved Uki and what she had endured at the hands of Kova and his brethren. Despite not having the chance to taste the young man's blood or feel its warmth washing over her chin.

Upon returning to their makeshift camp, the women opted to pack up and head back to the cliffs. After all, there was now no need to wait until morning light to travel. The snow was still falling, but the moon had fortunately come out and it would be hours before anyone chanced upon the body.

That's if there was anything left to find once the scavengers got wind of it.

After bestowing Uki with the return of her finger and filling her in on the information gleaned from their current outing, the women embraced in a show of support and unity. Although her response was odd, to say the least, as Uki began sobbing loudly while searching their eyes for something. It then became quite clear. She wanted to scold them for endangering themselves as if they were errant children, but settled on hugging them with all of her might instead. Kova was finally dead.

She didn't know how to process the news, but her aim had not changed. She still had three fingers to retrieve and no idea of just who possessed the digits, but with the help of her girls, it would come to pass. Although they were unaware, they found the body sooner rather than later, leading to unwelcome questions from the man's family about his death. No one could link Shtiya or Bola to the death.

After all, they were merely trappers and womenfolk at that. Popular opinion attributed the young hunter's death to a bear attack and discouraged any ill-conceived acts of vengeance by his family. Although, with the recent death of their beloved patriarch and the perceived senseless killing of their youngest male member, Kova's family and closest friends wanted someone to blame.

They soon inundated the area with their masses and a renewed vigilance for anything out of the ordinary. Especially when it pertained to the weaker of the sexes.

LIFE FOR UKI AND HER GIRLS WENT PRETTY MUCH BACK TO normal, with only the younger ones still venturing into the settlements on fact-finding missions, under the usual guise of acquiring supplies.

Over time, Uki and her girls made casual friendships and sometimes even more with a few of the locals and returning traders, but unfortunately, familiarity bred a lack of watchfulness. Uki had left their cave early that morning hoping to collect fresh game from her traps, but unexpectedly, they had all turned up empty. So she decided then to venture out on the frozen water to inspect the nets that she had placed between holes in the ice the day before, something that she usually did 2 or 3 times a day, weather permitting.

Three years had passed since the killing of Kova's youngest son, and today Uki was surprised while engaging in a routine activity of bending over to inspect her fishing nets. Just how long had the group of men been lying in wait behind the shoreline's windrows, watching her toil and waiting for an opportunity to present itself?

Although they had witnessed her approaching from the direction of her trap line and not the entrance to the caves or else, her pregnant granddaughter's life and the life of her unborn child would have been in danger. Not to mention Shtiya's.

Call it old age or the fact the ever blowing winds were

most likely to blame for masking the sound. Uki did not hear the men until it was too late. Gripping her ulu knife in hand, she swung hard, wide and low, hoping to take whoever it was out at the knees.

The first man screamed in pain, clutched his legs, and fell to the ice beside her, quickly turning the immediate area dark red with his blood. However, the remaining half dozen did not experience the same outcome. Uki refrained from screaming and shouting in fury, in order to avoid drawing attention to the situation, since she and her girls were clearly outnumbered.

Holding her knife out before her as evidence of her intent, she backed away from the men now surrounding her in a semicircle. Suddenly, she had a flashback of what had transpired all those years ago, but this time, she did not know any of their faces.

"What do you want of me?" she bellowed, searching for any sign of recognition, intent, or just mindless malevolence.

"We know who you are. You will curse our family no more. Your reign of terror will end here. We only wish our dear father could be here to witness what we are about to do to you," he smiled.

Uki could have tolerated anger and bitterness, but the man's smile was pure evil. She had lived a long life by Inuit standards but spent a large portion of it in a subterranean labyrinth, protecting her children.

Despite having children thrust upon her, she still felt love for them. One part of her toyed with jumping into the water between the ice floes and be done with it, while another part wanted to fight tooth and nail. But would these bastards continue their search for her children, children that might in fact be their very kin?

Standing at the edge of the large ice floe, Uki smiled

back at the men and dangled her foot over the side. Sadly, a quick death was not in her cards as one man hurtled his spear towards her the moment she hesitated. She fell into the icy cold water but was immediately dragged back up onto the ice. The large spear had impaled her just below her belly button, so death would not come as quick as she had originally expected or hoped.

Uki struggled to gain her footing, but found it almost impossible because of the length of the spear's shaft protruding from her middle. Flipping back her head of long wet hair, she scrutinized the cross-section of Inuit manhood before her, all the while trying to convey her contempt for every one of them with her steely gaze.

The pain was like an all-consuming fire in her belly, but she knew she needed to stay focused so she could taunt them into making a mistake.

45
UKI

"I heard Kova is dead. I hope he suffered in the end. What a pathetic excuse for a man and you, his progeny. I enjoyed killing your little brother," she said as another spear pierced her body.

"You know, he begged me to kill him in the end. Some hunter he turned out to be. Certainly not the pride of the family," Uki forced a laugh.

The next man who approached slugged Uki in the face, but she was quick and snapped her jaws closed around the ulnar part of his hand. Digging her sharpened teeth into the soft flesh and gnashing them together.

As she stared into his eyes in defiance, the man reached down with his other hand and grabbed the spear that had impaled her through the middle and forced its shaft downwards. She cried out in pain and let loose of his now mangled hand. Uki dropped to her knees and sobbed in agony, followed by the sound of her own manic laughter.

Again, she did not receive the desired effect as the men gathered around her and hoisted her lower body using the ends of the spears to lift her into a somewhat standing position. It was utterly excruciating, but she held her tongue for as long as she could.

As soon as she realized what their next move was going to be, she started to struggle and bleed in torrents. If only she could get some traction, she might throw herself backwards and possibly impale the person behind her with the spear's head.

Now it was the kinsmen's turn to laugh as they saw the realization in their enemies eyes, followed by several of them gripping the ends of the spears in order to keep her steady while one of their number made short work of cutting the clothing from her lower body. No one attempted to cover her mouth. Most likely, they were all looking forward to hearing her scream and plead for mercy.

Once again, she stood her ground and refused to satisfy their wants. The man who removed her clothes had no choice but to tear the remnants off her body roughly because of the interference caused by the protruding ends of the spears.

Once she was naked from the waist down, the rest of the men gathered around and forcibly spread her legs farther apart, restraining her ankles and wrists so she couldn't kick, grab or scratch any of them. It wasn't until one man bent her forward and instructed his brethren to hold her tight.

"Uki, or should I call you the White Witch? Which would you prefer?" The man's voice was eerily calm, as if he was talking to a frightened child.

She could not see who was doing the talking because of the odd angle they had propped her up. Although she could still swing her head back and forth, since no one wanted to deal with her sharpened teeth.

"Just tell me where the fourth finger is and we promise to make this quick."

Then she felt a callused hand pat her on the ass and when she didn't answer as quickly as he would have liked, the man roughly violated her with his fingers. Sadly, she wasn't able to disguise her pain or stifle her cry, which elicited laughter from most of the men in attendance.

"I'll only ask you one more time. Where is the finger?"

Uki knew where this was going and had no intention of accommodating these men. Her only hope would be to make this quick and hope they would leave and not bring harm to her girls. Raising her head, she looked around to make eye contact with at least a few of the men, hoping visions of her bloodied face would fill their nightmares.

"At least look me in the eye," she voiced to the man behind her. "You're such a coward having your friends hold me down while you make your demands."

Uki then waited for the man to take the bait and when he came around to confront her, she spit squarely in his face. If things would have gone as she had hoped, his rage would have ended her then and there, but the man was a sadist.

After wiping her bloody spittle off of his face, he actually used it to lube his member before violating her from behind. History repeated itself as every man then took their turn, violating her aged and battered body. Even the one she had injured earlier. She knew this because he took extra care at inflicting pain when he violated her with a foreign object of some sort.

And by the time the last few did their dirty work, they soon had to grip the ends of the spears sticking out from her body in order to keep upright. This was owing to the fact that as they thrust into Uki repeatedly, the sheer amount of blood pooling below her had caused a very large slick.

When they finished, the men released the spears and allowed her body to fall onto the crimson ice. Now lying in a prone position, she could sense the kinsmen gathering around her yet again. Each man bent down and got a firm grip on her appendages before spreading them wide.

Uki did not know what was going to happen next and could only pray the spirits would take her. She noticed by glancing out of the corner of her eye what looked to be the blade of an axe as it hung in the air just over one of her outstretched arms.

"We do this in honour of our father," the men yelled in unison as the blades came down, parting her hands and feet from her body in a geyser like spray of dark red blood.

Not all had the strength or skill to amputate Uki's limbs with one blow, resulting in the men having to hack away at the bones and flesh in order to complete the job. When they were done, there were no shouts of victory as the men looked around at the carnage. It was as if they were trying to figure out just what to do next.

One man rose to his feet and began by using his boot to push Uki's torso over onto her back before gripping the shaft of the spear sticking out of her middle with both hands and planting his foot firmly on her stomach so he could remove it.

The same man stepped on her thigh and extracted the second spear from her body, before throwing it off to the side as well. He knelt down beside her head and brushed her hair away from her face. He didn't say a word, just sat there transfixed. Another man in attendance approached with an axe in hand, but for some strange reason, the first man would not let him take her head. Slowly, getting up from his kneeling position, the first man collected Uki's hands and feet, which he placed in a pile. He pulled out his hunting knife and severed all the fingers, one at a time.

Once this was done, he approached every man, but instead of handing them their trophies, he threw the digits at their feet. Keeping the ninth one for himself. Because of the odd number, some received more than one, so they could gift them to their sons when they became of age.

As in the past, the weather had always been there for Uki, and today was no exception for when the men had finished divvying up her fingers. The skies overhead became suddenly angry. The ice floe they were standing on rocked as if their actions had angered the sea. So instead of dismembering the remains further, the men decided upon offering an indignity to their once fellow kinswoman's body, by simply leaving it where it lay.

They returned to their people, pridefully knowing they had done their part in realizing Kova's legacy. They had destroyed the witch and now they had separated whatever spawn she had birthed from the demon's body, hopefully cutting off its influence.

Kova's progeny would continue to honour their father's memory by wearing the severed fingers with pride and sharing his stories of bravery around the campfire. Although people would never speak of today's deeds again.

LATER THAT DAY, WHEN UKI HAD NOT RETURNED TO THE caves, both Shtiya and Bola grew fearful. They knew she was more than capable of looking after herself, but still worried because of her advancing years.

After much fretting, Shtiya convinced her daughter to

stay put while she went out in search of her grandmother. The weather let up and, with the help of one of her sled dogs, she followed Uki's trail from her morning trap line all the way to the shores of her favourite fishing spot.

Looking down from atop the cliffs onto the random ice floes in the distance, a large dark patch of unknown origin seemed to cover a good portion of the floe. As her heart fell into her stomach, Shtiya trembled and then shook her head back and forth.

"No!" she couldn't believe what she was seeing. How much blood would someone have had to spill in order to leave such a stain, even after a heavy snowfall?

Running on rubbery legs, she stumbled down the hillside on her way to the shore and the ice floes beyond. Only to discover her worst fear had come true. Falling to her knees in the massive pool of blood now surrounding her mother's dismembered and defiled body, she screamed until she was hoarse.

At first she didn't want to even touch her, but she delicately brushed the snow cover off of the body so she could get a better look at her wounds. Who would have carried out such a horrendous act and why would they have cut off her hands and feet?

Frantically looking around, she spied a small mound nearby. That's when it all made sense in her mind, because whoever had done this had been after her mother's fingers.

Looking to the skies above, Shtiya bellowed her promise. "I will avenge you, mother. My progeny and their offspring will hunt down every man responsible and retrieve what was taken. We will bask in every drop of blood shed until we make you whole!"

Shtiya opened Uki's parka and placed the severed limbs upon her mother's chest. She gripped the ends of the parka and dragged the corpse to the edge of the ice floe.

Removing her coat, she placed it lovingly around her mother's body before heading back to the caves. Upon entering, she found Bola waiting at the mouth of the main cave and nearly gave her a heart attack as she saw her mother now covered in blood. They did not have the luxury of time in order for Shtiya to go into any great detail what had transpired.

She began shouting as she rifled through their belongings. "Where is your grandmother's finger? I can't perform the ritual without it!"

Poor Bola, she knew something terrible had happened but could not get her mother to stop long enough to explain. She only knew she must harness a small team and follow her wherever the trail may lead.

The two of them located the missing digit and, with Bola tucked safely inside the sled's basket, they made their way in haste across the rolling hillsides to where the ice floes would be easiest to breach. As they drew nearer, even in the poor lighting, Bola could see the large patches of red ice and hyperventilated.

Shtiya saw her daughter's arms flailing and recognized her distress. Halting their sled, and attempted to calm the girl.

"I cannot lie to you. Your grandmother is dead. We have to respect her wishes for a burial at sea. I have prepared her body as best I can, but her spirit will have no rest until she is whole. Please come and say your goodbyes. I don't want any animal feeding off of her remains. Hurry!"

"But who would do such a thing?" It finally dawned on her, "How did they find us?" she cried. "We have to go after them. They've got a head start, but I'm sure that with the help of the dogs, we can track them."

Again Shtiya hugged her daughter fiercely and

promised to tell her everything once they returned to the safety of their cave home. Thankfully, Bola only had to walk a short distance because in her current condition, a waddle was all that she could manage.

Unlike her mother and grandmother, the man responsible had been someone of her choosing, but not someone she intended to spend the rest of her life with. Drawing closer, Bola recognized her own mother's parka and could not hold back her tears any longer, she yearned to hug her grandmother but the best that she could do with the help of her own mother, was to bend down and plant a kiss on the tips of her own fingers and then press them to Uki's forehead.

One part of her wanted to see just what those bastards had done to her beloved grandmother, but looking around, she realized the brevity of their situation. Bola then quickly reached into her own pocket to retrieve the severed finger from its depths. She handed it to her mother, who actually kissed the digit before placing it inside Uki's parka, presumably next to her heart.

"Tavvauvutit, goodbye, beloved mother. You taught us to believe all things have breath, and these spirits or souls continue to exist long after we are gone. That is why you were such a great huntress, because you always paid proper respect to the souls of the spiritual beings that you killed, be it hunting or fishing. Your death was violent, and you were truly undeserving. Therefore, the suffering you so bravely and lamentably endured at the hands of your former kinsmen has already purified your soul. You are now free to choose your next path, and we can only hope you will continue to act as a bond between the worlds of earth and spirit. Safekeeping your children's children."

Shtiya then retrieved a small piece of ice and placed it gently in Uki's mouth, so that she would not be thirsty on her journey and then carefully pushed her body off of the ice floe into a watery grave.

THE FOLLOWING DAY BOLA GAVE BIRTH TO A HEALTHY BABY girl, she named her Pinga, Goddess of the Hunt, and in the years that followed, it proved to be most fitting.

46

JOEL

Present Day

THE FOLLOWING DAY, JOEL WAS LIKE A CHILD ON Christmas morning. He couldn't wait to confront his boss to re-address having Dinnie come for a visit.

After racing down the long hallway en route to the camp's cafeteria, Joel hoped to catch Dr. Pettimore before the rest of their teammates arrived.

Upon entering the room and seeing him enjoying his morning coffee in the tranquility of the predawn hours, Joel experienced a sense of joy. And as luck would have it, they appeared to have the room all to themselves, although he felt a wee bit guilty for disturbing the man's solitude.

"Top of the morning to you, James. Do you mind if I take the empty seat beside you?" His old teacher smiled and then perfunctorily nodded his head in agreement; evidently his thoughts were elsewhere as he somewhat feverishly studied the small pile of newspapers that were spread out on the table before him.

"Not to be a bother, but do you remember me asking

you about the possibility of my son coming for a visit? Now, before you say no, please let me explain." And then Joel went into great detail regarding what had transpired between himself and the mother of his child.

One might say that it was too much information, but he felt the circumstances warranted it.

"Joel, my lad, please calm down. You actually picked the perfect time, as something is definitely afoot overseas, resulting in quite a few of our esteemed colleagues not wanting to venture all that far away from their homes. Some kind of flu bug…although depending on the rag that I read, you'd think that the end of the world was fast approaching. Make your arrangements, but as soon as we are back to full staff, the holiday is over and I expect nothing less than your full concentration to be focused on the job at hand."

Joel couldn't believe the opportune timing of his request but when he tried to get his former teacher to elaborate on just how he was supposed to coordinate such a visit and who would pay for what, the man simply stifled him with a raised hand and told him to get ahold of his secretary, Noelle, back on the mainland.

At first, Joel was a tad surprised by the man's dismissal of his concerns, then quickly chalked it up to his current distraction. Thanking James profusely, he left him to his fact finding mission and then went in search of Isitoq.

He really couldn't wait to share his amazing news with her. Unfortunately, though, once again she had left the compound early that morning on another one of her neighbourly visits, so he would probably have to wait until after dinner.

All day long Joel couldn't help but smile to himself, what with James' assistant turning out to be such a godsend, appropriating the funds from who knows where and then organizing everything at the stroke of a key. He finally set his plan in motion. Now all he had to do was contact Auntie Mona and bring her up to speed. Even the weather was on his side. Not a single storm was currently on a collision course with their location and, to top that off, there were beautiful blue skies in every direction.

Even the day's cleanup detail went off with almost nary a hitch. No one got hurt and the only object damaged by the bulldozer was inanimate…live and learn.

Later that day, Joel quickly put in a call to his son's primary caregiver before leaving his room for dinner and was thrilled when Mona answered on the first ring. Apparently, she had already been contacted by James' secretary extraordinaire and all the arrangements were in the works, all but one. Geraldine still needed to give her consent by signing a "Form of Indemnity" in order for Dinnie to travel by himself and she hadn't been home in days.

Although Joel had at least been proactive by already discussing with the carrier the hiring of an escort to accompany his son on the long flight, in order to make sure that he made all of his connections and didn't get lonely.

During their exchange, Joel was quite surprised because Mona continued to keep a relatively positive spin on their conversation, but it was all for the benefit of a certain brief set of big ears in the room.

"Daddy, Daddy…I'm gonna fly on a plane…I can't wait to see you…Auntie Mona says that polar bears live up there…how many more sleeps?" he screamed exuberantly in the background.

Under the current circumstances, Joel found it very difficult to keep their banter light. After all, what could he do to fix the situation? Was there a paper that he could sign to make things right?

Regrettably, his earlier trepidations had always been centered on Geri running away with Dinnie, never the opposite. Although luckily he still had Anita's ear, and he knew that she and her lawyer friend were in his corner but that call would have to wait until tomorrow.

After saying their "goodnights", an idea suddenly popped into Joel's head. Quickly searching his room for Noelle's phone number, he called his prof's secretary yet again. He couldn't help but feel bad for bothering her, but at least the time difference was only a couple of hours and when she finally picked up, he actually breathed a sigh of relief. The woman could better assess the big picture since she was removed from the situation…if Geri did not show up at the airport, then Mona would escort Dinnie with his Birth Certificate to his gate and then hand him over to his escort.

The news elated Joel, making a mental note to one day thank Noelle properly in person, for all of her help. When Joel quickly glanced over at the clock on his bedside table, he realized with dismay just how much time had actually passed. He had evidently missed dinner, but hopefully not Isitoq…he had so much to tell her.

Exiting his room, he made double quick time to the cafeteria and upon entering was at first saddened, then alarmed to see that she wasn't in their usual spot. And to add to his feelings of unease, why hadn't she tracked him down in his absence?

Thankfully, he could still grab a meal-to-go before heading to her room, on the other side of the compound. He knocked loudly on her door and then painted a big grin on his face while mulling over just what he was going to tell her first.

Suddenly he was taken by surprise as her door swung open and he was greeted not so welcomingly by Isitoq, as she stood there literally blocking the entrance with her body. At first, her downright frigid response shocked him… was he disturbing her?

To say nothing of being more than a little concerned when the overhead lighting harshly illuminated the large ugly bruises on her face and a multitude of abrasions to her hands.

"Oh my God, what happened to you? Who did this? Was it someone from one of those communities that you are always visiting?"

Then, before she even answered, he dropped his food to the floor and immediately wrapped her up in his embrace, but sadly, all he accomplished was eliciting a cry of pain from her.

Joel quickly loosened his grip and then held Isitoq at arm's length, looking inquisitively at her face and the swollen, blackened eyes that could not be ignored.

"No, I was not attacked…I went ass over teakettle on my snowmobile. I stupidly ran into a small pressure ridge that was hidden under the snow and it stopped the sled dead, me, not so much," and then she glanced away, as if embarrassed by the entire ordeal.

"Are you alright? Did you break any bones? Did you have to walk back? Why didn't you call me?" Joel sounded like a mother hen.

"I'm fine, just a little sore. That'll teach me to go out too early, didn't see it coming until it was too late. I guess I even smashed the windshield as I flew over it." This time she smiled weakly before backing away from Joel as if to decrease their level of intimacy.

Ignoring her cues, he gently grasped her elbow and then began leading her back to her bed as if she were an invalid.

"Don't fuss over me…like I said, I'm fine…my pride is

more damaged than my body, please just turn the lights off when you leave," and then she gingerly crawled under the covers and turned her back to him.

Joel couldn't believe what had happened; Isitoq could have been seriously injured and left out on the ice to freeze to death with no one for miles, or worse yet, killed. He was putting an end to this.

If it was the last thing that he did, but now was not the time to discuss the error of her ways…tomorrow cooler heads would prevail. Joel slowly bent down and kissed the top of Isitoq's head before retrieving his dinner and then retiring to his own room for the rest of the evening, although on his way back, he took a detour.

He couldn't help but dwell on the injuries that his ladylove had sustained and, for some strange reason, felt that he needed to see her snowmobile, possibly as ammunition for tomorrow's talk.

Entering the compound's large equipment storage bay, he wasn't at all surprised to see a lone snowmobile hoisted up on a jack, minus its windshield. However, upon closer inspection, he was alarmed to see an excessive amount of blood splattered across the sled's hood, even if facial injuries bled profusely. Not to mention the belly pan and skis showed no signs of damage, other than normal wear and tear. Something just didn't add up.

But then again, what did he know about snowmobiles?

THAT NIGHT POOR JOEL TOSSED AND TURNED WAITING FOR sleep to take him and when it finally did, he dreamed of his beautiful Isitoq crawling across the ice, leaving behind her a large trail of blood and in the distance, a polar bear standing on its hind legs, smelling the air.

Sadly, the objects of his fascination were quickly becoming the stuff of nightmares and Joel didn't know what to do to remedy the situation, besides getting back out on the ice.

Dinnie's arrival couldn't come soon enough, as far as he was concerned. Hopefully, the sharing of experiences with his son would bring about a renewed appreciation for the species and the "Great White North" that it inhabited.

Joel entered the cafeteria the following morning and was thrilled to see that Isitoq was in their usual spot, although she looked a little worse for wear but still lovely as ever. Grabbing a coffee, he quickly took his seat and then slid across the bench in order to be closer. He really wanted to plant a kiss on her lips but wavered before eventually leaning in to do just that. A quick peck, after all. He had barely seen her yesterday, and they had a lot to catch up on. She reciprocated his show of affection, along with a playful squeeze to his upper thigh.

"You won't believe what happened. Actually, I still can't believe it myself. Dinnie will be here in a couple of days and I really hope that you'll help me show him around? I know that he'll have tons of questions that I probably won't know any of the answers to…I was going to ask if we could arrange for him to visit one of our neighbouring communities…that's if you're feeling up to it? After all, you really shouldn't be out all by yourself. Look what happened yesterday…"

"Shit happens and no matter what you think, I'm more than capable of venturing out on my own. Running into that crack could have happened to anyone. Thankfully, it was rather small, so the sled remained undamaged. But I'll have these shiners for at least a week. So you still trust me to take you and your son out for a spin?"

Joel hesitated at first. "Of course I do, but are you sure

that you're okay to drive? That must have been some whack that you took in the face. I couldn't believe all the blood on your sled?"

Now it was her turn to pause as she ruminated over his observations, after all, how did he know about the blood, she actually thought that she had done an alright job of wiping off the front of her snowmobile and what was he doing in the equipment shop…didn't he believe her?

47

JOEL

AGAIN ANOTHER BEAUTIFUL DAY WITH NARY A CLOUD overhead and nothing to show the reoccurrence of inclement weather.

Joel continued to busy himself with cleanup duties around camp and the surrounding compound, while Isitoq nursed her wounds and spent most of the morning chained to her desk. And it wasn't until late afternoon that she finally sought refuge from the doldrums of her clerical obligations and actually went looking for him.

Thankfully, he wasn't all that hard to locate, especially since he was working alone today. Pulling up alongside the large tractor, she began waving frantically at the cab and its occupant, hoping to get the driver's attention.

When Joel looked down, he genuinely felt surprised to see Isitoq perched upon her sled, dressed in her traditional parka and sporty snowmobile helmet. At first, he wanted to give her a piece of his mind; after all, she had just been injured but thought better of it because she was actually wearing protection for a change…baby steps.

Coming to a complete stop, Joel quickly turned off the

noisy antique before hopping down from its cab and approaching his ladylove.

Quickly lifting her visor, she smiled impishly, "So can I convince you to leave work early today and come for a joyride with me…I promise not to drive too fast?"

"Only if you'll let me give it a whirl? After all, I can't have my son thinking that I don't know how to drive one of these things. By the way, where are you taking me?"

"It's a surprise…" and then she patted the seat behind her.

Joel looked around briefly before acting on her invitation, then throwing caution to the wind, he fervently jumped on behind Isitoq and wrapped his arms around her.

His impromptu "bear hug" caused her to let out a cry of pain the moment that he contacted her ribs, which startled him. Slowly she reached back and retrieved one hand at a time before placing them gently in her lap and restarting her machine, then gripping the throttle, she revved the engine loudly in anticipation of their jaunt.

All at once they were cutting across a pristine layer of freshly fallen snow and the compound was fast becoming a mere speck in the distance. Without so much as a warning, she cut the engine.

At first Joel looked anxiously around, assuming that they had had some sort of technical issue and that they might have to walk back, but was more than happily surprised when she offered the driver's seat to him in a flourish of grand gestures. Immediately a big smile crossed his face, and he motioned for her to lift her visor so that they could talk.

"Are you sure that we're far enough away from anything that I could hit?" and then he laughed wholeheartedly before straddling the seat in front of her.

After starting up the snowmobile, Joel slowly went over everything that she had told him and then hit the gas. He quickly adapted to the responsiveness of the enormous machine and began running it smoothly with less jerky accelerations.

Although he had to cut the lesson short because his eyelashes kept freezing together, hampering his visibility at the higher speeds. It was a great day and he couldn't wait to share the experience with Dinnie…fingers crossed that the weather would indeed continue to cooperate.

Hopping off of the snowmobile, Joel quickly turned around and reached out to flip up Isitoq's visor so that he could kiss her but was truly taken aback by the drastic change in colour to her facial injuries, as they were now an even darker, angrier purple. At his more than obvious hesitation, she quickly removed her helmet and then ran her fingers playfully through her long hair before standing and grabbing the front of his jacket.

Thankfully, it didn't take long for him to get with the program as she literally pulled him down to meet her waiting lips, however after a couple of oohs and ouches, they unanimously decided on taking a rain check.

Donning her helmet once again, she took control of the snowmobile and then waited for Joel to make himself comfortable on the 'seat' behind her. Luckily for them, their camp was only a brief ride away because, unexpectedly, the skies had taken on an almost foreboding hue and Joel still needed to retrieve the dozer he had been operating earlier and return it to the equipment bay.

Later, entering the cafeteria, Joel was not so surprised to see that Isitoq was already surrounded by several of their teammates, although she appeared to be taking quite the ribbing for yesterday's snowmobile incident. And as he approached the table, they all uncharacteristically seemed to scatter.

At first Joel wasn't sure just how to interpret their actions but seeing that their behaviour had not ruffled Isitoq's feathers, who was he to take offense?

After enjoying their evening meal together, Joel suggested they return to her room, expecting nothing from her. After all, she had been through so much. Personally, he just wanted to hold her, but, oddly enough, she seemed more randy than ever, although she had one stipulation that there be absolutely no lights tonight, not even a candle.

So as per usual, they both left the cafeteria at different times, agreeing to meet later in her room. However, this time she instructed him to just knock before entering, as the door would be unlocked. At first, her behaviour surprised Joel, but then he recalled their first encounter and how she had felt the need to cover her scars.

He truly hated the fact that something so trivial as a few bumps and bruises could cause her to have an emotional setback. Later, whilst standing nervously outside of her door, he couldn't help but wish that he could have a do-over as he knocked way too loudly on his first attempt…so much for subtlety.

"Isitoq, it's me. Can I come in?" he whispered and then waited, half expecting that he had done that wrong too.

After what seemed like forever, the door slowly swung open, but unfortunately the pitch blackness within proved to be more of a deterrent than desirable mood setter, causing Joel to hang back yet again before cautiously entering the room.

"Take off your clothes," no please or thank you, not even a hint of emotion expressed.

Again, he was perplexed by her proposition this evening. They had seen each other naked frequently, rutted like animals and made love tenderly at others. But through it all, he had never stopped caring for her, warts and all… why was she acting this way?

"Isitoq, we don't have to do anything. If this is your idea of role playing, then I have to tell you I'm just not feeling it. And if you're worried about a few little scars or those shiners on your beautiful face, nothing has changed for me."

"Joel, I need to feel you inside me…please don't make me beg." It was such an odd appeal; he really would have preferred to see her face and the sentiment behind her request before obliging.

After awkwardly shedding his clothes, he reached blindly for Isitoq in the darkness and was ultimately relieved the moment that he felt her hands guide him onto the bed and into her awaiting embrace. Albeit no gentle foreplay followed as she immediately switched positions and began vigorously stroking his manhood into an erection before straddling his supine body and literally riding him.

Joel couldn't say that he didn't receive any pleasure from the experience, but the usual feelings just weren't there: no small talk, kissing, or caressing. And when she had eventually milked him dry, he felt strangely used up, objectified, as if spilling his seed had been her only goal. Rode hard and put away wet, as the saying goes.

Afterwards, Joel quietly untangled himself from Isitoq's slumbering form, searched for his clothing, and then slipped away. Unfortunately or not, it was a bit of a hike back to his side of the compound, affording him plenty of time in which to go over the events of the day in his mind.

Something was definitely amiss, but he hadn't a clue. If only he had turned on the lights and confronted her, seen the look in her eyes for himself. But then again, exposing her nakedness would have most likely destroyed any trust they had built up between them thus far.

Once back in his own room, Joel's eyes were immediately drawn to his bedside clock and the tabulation of just how many hours of sleep were still attainable if he hit the sheets right away. Despite being a creature of habit, he took a shower to figuratively cleanse his mind first. Later while drying off in the bathroom, Joel was relieved to see that he had sustained no telltale signs of their rough play, fortunately Isitoq had not felt the need to mark him but deep down he knew that not all scars were visible to the naked eye.

Despite everything that had happened, the shower did indeed seem to do the trick as he fell asleep almost instantly the moment that his head hit the pillow. Hours might have passed but to Joel it felt like he had just closed his eyes, for he awoke with such a start when his alarm clock blasted out a well-known heavy metal riff.

After getting his bearings, Joel was actually quite surprised by how well rested he felt, but sadly not any closer to sorting out his feelings toward Isitoq, although he knew that when push came to shove, he would give her a second chance. Regardless of what had transpired, Dinnie would arrive shortly and all focus should be on him and rightly so, not another one of his father's romances, gone wrong.

And if worse came to worst, Joel would simply introduce her as his colleague and leave it at that; surely they could be cordial for a couple of days.

THEN EVERYTHING CHANGED AGAIN IN A HEARTBEAT AS JOEL entered the cafeteria later that morning, Isitoq could be seen from across the large room with a radiant smile on her face and coffee cup in hand, conversing happily and awaiting his arrival as if nothing at all was out of the ordinary.

As he approached their usual table, he didn't wince this time when gazing upon her face because the vibrant colours of yesterday's bruises had actually started to dissipate and change, nowhere as alarming but would still need more than a little makeup to conceal.

Joel couldn't help but second guess himself again. Was he so inexperienced, naïve, he had read way too much into Isitoq's rather strange behavior of late?

However, before he could even ponder the subject any further, a heated conversation had broken out at a nearby table.

"What the fuck do you mean by that? Don't shush me…I think that we've got another rogue polar bear on our hands…I'm not going out by myself anymore until that bastard is found and killed!"

"Truthfully, we don't have enough manpower and until this virus thing is under control, no one's coming to relieve us of our duties…" and then both men roughly pushed their chairs away from their table and stormed out of the cafeteria, leaving a plethora of questions on the tips of everyone's tongues.

48

JOEL

The large mess hall drew eerily quiet, then all hell broke loose, everyone speaking and yelling at the same time. A commanding and recognizable voice cut through the cacophony of the crowd.

"People, people…calm down, we really don't know what is happening around the globe…the news says one thing about the origins of this novel virus, while my sources back home say it's merely another flu strain. All I know is that we are safe here and it won't do anyone a lick of good to blow this out of proportion."

Then he looked around the room as if searching for someone or thing and when his eyes finally contacted Joel's, he smiled. "Joel my good man, your son and his company appointed escort will be here tomorrow…let's all wait until they arrive to get the skinny on world affairs, shall we?"

However, before James could open his mouth to quell any further insurrections, the situation was aggravated by someone adding more fuel to the fire.

"Fine, but what about the local bear population and

their increasing appetite for human flesh…another Inuit hunter went missing a few days ago and from what I heard, the bears didn't leave a lot left of him."

Both Joel and Isitoq instantly recognized the almost accusing voice as belonging to that of their former pilot, the not so chatty one. Then echoing trepidations quickly filled the room as the gathering crowd slowly parted, making way for their teammate.

"Isitoq, what's your take on this? After all, you just visited the man's winter camp on the day he went missing…see anything noteworthy…lucky you to have had your minor mishap and made it home in one piece?" And then he just stood there with his arms crossed over his chest, as if daring her to respond.

Isitoq would not be goaded into an argument with her former pilot, turning to the crowd she addressed them as a whole, "I will sort this out as soon as the weather improves and I can safely venture out…I will contact all the surrounding communities, the animal or animals will be hunted down and destroyed."

Thankfully, this seemed to appease the crowd for the time being but before they could even disperse, someone yelled out, "If this virus is so dangerous, why are we allowing strangers to come and visit, after all, they could be infected?"

Luckily, Dr. Pettimore was quick on the draw, not allowing the gathering to disintegrate any further, "My esteemed colleagues, I would never knowingly put any of your lives in danger, the escort travelling with Joel's son is an EMT and if there were any signs of infection or so much as a sniffle, he will not be allowed on site."

As expected, there was a little grumbling amongst those in attendance, but after a short while, everyone seemed mollified and went about their morning rituals. And to think that only hours ago Joel had been so excited about his son's impending visit, now all he could think about were all the things that were out of his control. Isitoq was quick to notice his furrowed brow and grasped his hand and gave it a squeeze.

"There's nothing you can do about their herd mentality. Just focus on your son's visit and making it special. Fingers crossed that the weather will let up and we'll get to take him out on the snowmobiles. We can combine business with pleasure." And then she smiled reassuringly.

"I did not know another hunter had died. Why didn't you tell me?" Now it was Joel's turn to sound accusatory.

"First, I didn't know they had found a body. And I like you only ventured out for a joy ride yesterday...Joel you are making it really hard to love you."

That being said, Joel was flabbergasted...she loved him? Not wanting to spoil the moment, he quickly embraced her and planted a kiss on her lips, much to the surprise of their teammates.

Thankfully, their public display of affection did wonders for the overall mood in the room. Good-natured chiding followed along with pats on the back. And now that the cat was out of the bag, Joel actually felt like a weight had been lifted.

After breakfast, he would go check on the weather forecast so that he could start making plans.

Thankfully, the bad weather that had rolled in the night before was on its way out. Radar images showed no precipitation near the compound. So if he played his cards right, he could get caught up on his chores before Dinnie arrived, leaving himself free to entertain the boy and accompany Isitoq on her errands.

Who was he kidding...it was actually "keep an eye on"

as opposed to merely accompanying her. She might be from these parts, but she was still a girl. The rest of the day literally flew by and it wasn't until supper that Joel went in search of his ladylove.

After supper, Joel, utterly exhausted but happy and eager to discuss the possibility of Dinnie and himself tagging along, went in search of his ladylove. Initially, he was surprised by her absence in the cafeteria, but he received a thankful update that she had been last spotted in the equipment bay.

When he entered the enormous structure, he heard loud cursing coming from the back of the building. He was then pleasantly surprised to see Isitoq wrestling with a large tire tube. Evidently, she had been way ahead of him regarding preparations for his son's visit, and it wasn't until he saw her securing the tube with a rope to the back of her snowmobile that he understood.

How could he have doubted her and, to add to him feeling like a shit, she had also procured another snowmobile.

Joel was absolutely beaming when he approached her, "Thank you so much…Dinnie is going to love you and I couldn't be happier that you found me a sled of my own!"

Then he threw his arms around her and lifted her off of the ground in his exuberance. That night they opted to eat their evening meal in his room because he was expecting another call from his son, just a last-minute recap of tomorrow's hectic schedule, so that he could hopefully ease any jitters that the child might have since this was his first solo excursion.

Joel would have loved to have spent the rest of the night snuggled in Isitoq's arms but there was still so much to do, thankfully she understood and bid him goodnight early but not without an intimate embrace and her playfully cupping his groin in her palm.

Later, looking around his room, Joel quickly began tidying up, separating piles of clothes that needed to be washed and putting fresh sheets on the spare bed. He was so looking forward to their time together, showing him new things and introducing him to different cultures…this would be a holiday to remember. With the last of his laundry in the dryer, Joel turned in for the night.

Tomorrow could not come soon enough. As he lay there in the dark, he reached over to his bedside table and retrieved his phone, then throwing caution to the wind, he texted "thx again, love you" before closing his eyes. He wasn't surprised to see that she hadn't written back right away.

It was late, but he was glad that he had at least put himself out there.

THE NEXT MORNING WAS A WHIRLWIND OF ACTIVITY, AS Dinnie's flight was scheduled to arrive shortly after lunch, affording Joel just enough time to take care of a few unforeseen responsibilities.

The mood around the camp was jovial. Most everyone had expressed wanting to meet his son, some even going so far as offering to take the child with them on their rounds, citing that their fields of expertise were much more interesting. And later, as Joel waited, scanning the skies for any sight of an approaching helicopter, he was overjoyed to be joined by Isitoq.

Upon first glance he couldn't believe just how much of her bruising had disappeared, it was almost impossible to tell that only days before she had been in an accident but upon closer inspection, he could see that she had in fact used a little concealer. Clenching her hand in his own, he leaned forward and cupped her cheek with his free hand before kissing her tenderly.

As he pulled back, he could suddenly hear an approaching aircraft. Dinnie was finally here. Waiting patiently for the bird to land and its occupants to disembark, he kept smiling nervously over at Isitoq, trying to read her expression and hoping deep down that she and his son would bond. The EMT that had been assigned to escort Dinnie was quite young, at least in his appearance, and they had thankfully hit it off from the get-go, so the trip had been more of an adventure as opposed to harrowing experience. His little boy looked genuinely tired, but couldn't stop talking about all that they had seen and done along the way.

Joel couldn't believe how much Dinnie had changed after such a short time away from each other; he actually seemed more grown-up than he remembered. Hugging the boy fiercely, he covered his small cheeks in kisses, which were thankfully accepted. Joel would have been beside himself if the child had suddenly grown too old for shows of affection.

Releasing him from his embrace, he took his hand and led Dinnie over to where Isitoq was now waiting in the wings.

"I'd like you to meet someone. This is Isitoq. She is a wonderful friend of mine and she'd like to take you snowmobiling tomorrow, if you're up to it? Would you like that?"

At first he seemed hesitant, and then a huge smile spread across his mischievous little face. "Can I drive?" he squealed joyfully.

"Oh, my God! You're just like your father. Let's see

who the better driver is?" Isitoq couldn't help but laugh at the child's spontaneous response.

After collecting Dinnie's luggage, Joel dropped it off in his room and quickly unpacked everything that the child would need at bedtime.

He then took his little man on a tour of the compound, introducing him to anyone and everyone that crossed their paths. Returning him to their room, so that his weary traveller could have a much needed a nap before supper.

Joel couldn't help but look lovingly down at his child as he slept, whilst listening to him breathe and taking in every nuance of his facial expressions as he dreamed what he hoped were only happy dreams. Then slipping away into the privacy of his bathroom, Joel quickly called Mona just to let her know Dinnie had indeed arrived safe and sound, he also thanked her again for everything that she had done and assured her he would not let the child out of his sight.

When he opened the door to the bathroom, Joel was surprised to see Isitoq sitting on the side of Dinnie's bed, looking down at him almost affectionately as she brushed back his long bangs from his face. And it wasn't until he had been standing over them for a short while that she actually realized Joel's presence.

At first she seemed rather startled, as if caught in the middle of a daydream. She then leaned forward and planted a kiss on the tips of her own fingers before pressing them gently to the child's exposed forehead.

She then quietly got up and whispered to Joel, "I'll see you two at suppertime," and left the room.

49

JOEL

THAT NIGHT, HE HAD AN EXHAUSTED LITTLE BOY ONCE again on his hands. As Dinnie fast became the center of attention in the cafeteria, and much like his father, he became quite animated whenever retelling any tale.

He was already asleep when Joel returned him to their room and tucked him into bed. One part of Joel really wanted to get back to the cafeteria to hear if there was any fresh news regarding the outside world.

Was there really a deadly virus decimating the world's weaker population, while he was in isolation all these months, and why hadn't his father or Mona mentioned it? Also, was there anything new to report on the rogue polar bear situation of late? Was it indeed safe for him to take his son out joyriding?

So much had evidently happened in such a short time and he was totally oblivious living his best life. And now that Dinnie was here, he made a promise to himself to be more observant. After all, his son's well-being was paramount.

The following morning, he was up with the birds, gleaning whatever information he could from the most recently arrived flight crew and his son's escort, although opinions were polarizing. Some thought that the current state of the world was "end of days" material, while others chalked it up to a bad flu, targeting the very old.

In the end, Joel figured he had better contact his father before sending Dinnie home and get his opinion, or even his good friend Anita, because neither one was likely to sugarcoat the facts.

Back in his room, Joel waited patiently for Dinnie to pick out which clothes he was going to be wearing today. He had never been out snowmobiling before and no one wanted frostbite to claim any of those tiny fingers or toes.

Isitoq showed up just in time to save the day and get them up and out. She had already planned for lunches and snacks for today's outing, along with thermoses of hot liquids. And as they approached their waiting snowmobiles, Joel could see that she had gone one step further by obtaining a large caliber rifle, just in case they should run into any trouble.

After warming up the snowmobiles, Isitoq gave their itinerary to the men in the equipment bay, stowed their supplies in a large ice sled that was attached to the back of his snowmobile and then hopped onto her own. At first Joel was wondering why he would pull all the supplies, but when she patted the back of her seat and waved at Dinnie to get on with her, he understood.

Whilst heading out across what appeared to be a never-ending expanse of snow and ice, Joel soon found himself more than happy to follow as landmarks disappeared and everything blended into each other in shades of white and off-white.

After several hours of travelling, they finally spotted a small community in the distance.

As they approached, a decent-sized group of men and women came out to greet them and quickly ushered the threesome into their main meeting tent for warmth and shared sustenance. Thankfully Dinnie was the friendly sort and even though he could not converse with the locals, the children quickly gathered around him and they played.

Seeing that Isitoq needed to talk to the group's elders, she suggested Joel hook the tire tube up to the back of her sled and see if the children were interested in going for a ride.

At first, he took it as if "let the adults talk" and then decided that it might be fun. They would just stay close to the camp. In no time at all, the children were laughing and screaming with joy and to the untrained ear, a bystander might have even thought them in peril, but the little and not so little ones were all having a wonderful time.

As the day grew long, Isitoq even joined them for a bit of frivolity before heading home. After saying their heartfelt goodbyes to all in attendance, Isitoq placed Dinnie on her snowmobile seat in front of her this time and then rearranged their remaining cargo in the ice sled. It didn't take long to figure out why she had done this, because Dinnie was fast asleep before the community's shelters and cook houses disappeared from their rearview mirrors.

Joel couldn't help but smile to himself as he saw his son sleeping comfortably and protected by Isitoq's body as they headed back to camp at a fast pace.

The day had truly turned out better than he could have ever wished for.

Although when they returned to the compound just before dark, people were spotted running around as if there was a need to batten down the hatches to prepare for some sort of catastrophic event.

There was another storm front on a collision course with their current location, and it was apparently a doozy. Dinnie's grogginess spared him from witnessing all the widespread havoc.

Isitoq even opted to lay the child down in her own room because it was closest, before returning to help park the snowmobiles in the equipment bay for safekeeping and unload the sleds.

Upon returning to her room, she was happy to see that the little boy had apparently not moved a muscle from where she had placed him earlier on the large bear skin blanket. Gently cupping her stomach, she smiled inwardly, hoping that her future daughter would have such peaceful slumber, but then she was torn from her thoughts by the sound of knocking.

She quietly opened the door so as not to wake Dinnie, and then joined Joel in the hallway.

"Do you want to go get some supper from the cafeteria and then we can eat it in my room, or do you want to take him back to yours? Either way works fine. All that fresh air, your little guy is definitely down for the count."

Joel really didn't want to be a bother but if he moved Dinnie right now, he would most likely become irritable upon waking so he decided on the former and let the child sleep, after all, he wouldn't be gone all that long and Isitoq was no longer a stranger to his son.

Rushing through the cafeteria, Joel was again thrilled to find out that Dinnie had made such a lasting impression on his teammates, as most seemed genuinely disappointed that he would not be joining them for supper tonight.

Meanwhile, Isitoq spent her time quietly tidying up and making room for the three of them to comfortably eat their dinner in her somewhat cramped quarters. When she was finished with her preparations, she found herself oddly drawn to the sleeping child and once again sat down on the edge of the bed.

Isitoq couldn't help but wonder what it would be like to have a baby boy. As far as she knew, there had only been female children in her family. Both her grandmother and her mother had mentioned no male offspring whatsoever, not even stillbirths.

Watching Dinnie playing with the other children today had been unexpectedly eye-opening for Isitoq, not that she could find fault in her own upbringing. Her mother had always treated her like she was special, a gift from the spirits, possibly because she had given birth much later in life. Having an older mother did not detract from the wonderful adolescence that she had experienced whilst living up north with the two women that would indelibly shape her life.

Although sadly after the untimely and brutal death of her mother Pinga, her grandmother had almost overnight chosen to send her away to one of the many forced resettlements in the south, to be educated in the white-man's schools. An unforeseen and drastic move that had caused her to hate her grandmother with a passion, but in time, Isitoq understood the reasoning behind the old woman's decision.

Albeit, being left at the mercy of so-called "Social Services", had definitely toughened her up and helped to prepare her for what lay ahead, since neither Inuit nor Qallunaat would claim the young girl as a foster or adopted child. And like her mother before her, she had been named well as Isitoq meant "justice" in her native tongue and like all the women in her family; she would punish the guilty and endeavour to retrieve what was taken all those many years ago.

Someday she hoped to lead a normal life, whatever that was, and return to the cliff sides with her daughter in order to finally lay to rest the missing pieces of her elder, once and for all. That being said, Isitoq's dreams were instantly dashed when Dinnie chanced to roll over in his sleep and expose the remains of a rather gruesome looking severed finger, lying beneath him in the bedding.

Trying not to panic, Isitoq quickly snatched it up and then gently lifted back the covers to make sure that there weren't any more of them scattered about or traces of blood on the sheets. She had been in a bit of a hurry when getting the last one and had not bothered to clean her hands thoroughly enough before placing the digit in its box for safekeeping.

Yes, she had had setbacks in the past but usually of the hand-to-hand combat variety, this was utterly unfathomable to be bested by a 5-year-old, no amount of childhood curiosity or infectious smiles were going to stand in her way.

Whenever she was hunting a quarry, all of her vital signs were controlled, something that her elders had taught her from an early age. Now she could hear herself breathing much too loudly, not to mention her heart had begun literally pounding in her chest.

How could things have gone so horribly wrong?

They had only left the little boy alone for a very short period of time. Had he gotten up to go to the bathroom and, for some unknown reason, snooped…what had caught his attention?

She wanted to shake him awake and sort this out; after all, no one must know of her ulterior motives for being here. Placing the polar bear blanket back over the child, she slowly backed away from the bed and looked around to see if there was anything else out of place. This mishap would not ruin everything she had fought so hard to achieve.

First, she needed to check her hiding spot to ensure she had accounted for all the fingers and then come up with a plan to handle any consequences. Quickly checking the time, she knew the odds were against her. Joel should come through the door any minute now…she had to lock it. Then, entering her bathroom, she dropped to her knees in front of the vanity and nervously swung open the cabinet doors.

At first glance, everything looked perfectly normal, although the toilet paper rolls were no longer stacked neatly to the side. But upon closer inspection, she realized that the corner of her First-Aid box was now visible and no longer hidden behind the rolls. Grabbing the box, she pressed it to her chest and began to visibly shake as actual fear gripped her…how would she silence the boy?

All of a sudden, she could hear knocking on the outer door to her suite. She had to think clearly, nothing rash… quickly opening the box, she was relieved to see that only one digit was missing, which she replaced at once.

Now to find a new hiding place, somewhere the cleaning staff would not discover by chance…looking around desperately, she settled on placing it in the bottom of her dresser, under her sweaters for the time being.

Taking a deep cleansing breath, she yelled out, "Just a minute! I'll be right there," before running back to the bathroom and loudly flushing the toilet, in order to intentionally wake Dinnie with all the commotion. Thankfully, Joel had his hands full with their supper tray, but immediately handed it off to her the moment that he entered the room and saw the very disgruntled look upon his child's face.

"What's wrong, little man? I brought us all supper. They even had chicken fingers, your favourite," he cooed enthusiastically.

"Let's eat this while it's hot," Isitoq said a little too loudly and woodenly.

"Where am I?" he said, looking around the unfamiliar room, still relatively bleary-eyed from having just woken up. Then he began feverishly searching through the bedding as if he had misplaced something of great importance. "Where's my finger? It's mine, I found it!"

"What are you talking about, Dinnie? Did you have a nightmare?"

In good-natured appeasement, Joel began following his son's lead by looking under the covers as well. And when nothing could be unearthed, he simply scuffed up his son's hair and asked him to go wash up before eating.

At first the child had a quizzical look on his face as if he was now second guessing himself, before slowly turning and entering the bathroom rather forlornly.

Isitoq couldn't help but wonder if, after the door closed shut, he would be down on his hands and knees, looking frantically for any evidence of his earlier find. Although she hoped he was perhaps disoriented or maybe even a little afraid that he would get into trouble for going through her belongings. Anyway, that you looked at it. She had the pilfered finger back, and the child did not currently have enough time to rummage through the rest of her belongings.

As soon as the bathroom door opened, Isitoq instantly painted a big smile on her face and pushed back a chair from her small café style table for her guest. "Dinnie, why don't you come and sit right next to me?"

50

JOEL

The rest of the evening went off without a hiccup and in no time at all, little Dinnie was laughing and exuberantly retelling what a wonderful time he had had with the other children while tubing today.

He also expressed his want to return to the community as soon as possible, since he had made so many new friends and he would not take no for an answer. All pleasantries aside, though, there still was a ferocious storm raging that could not be ignored because of the incessant wind noise that eerily made its presence known throughout the evening.

The child stayed unaffected by the almost continuous ebb and flow of Aeolian tones, but his father experienced the opposite, causing Joel to once again fixate on the perception of being trapped inside a leaky space station. Finally, when the little boy had eaten his last chicken finger and devoured a sizeable piece of chocolate cake, sleep took him along with the white noise that his chatter provided. Leaving Isitoq and Joel to say their goodnights rather awkwardly whilst attempting to embrace each other as Joel cradled his son's limp body between them in his arms.

Later, while walking through the compound's long hallways with their sensor activated lighting, Joel couldn't help but wonder just what his son had been talking about…finding a finger…surely he had been having a dream and not a very pleasant one at that. But it wasn't until he had changed the boy into his pajamas and put him to bed that he noticed a peculiar red stain on the back of Dinnie's tee shirt.

Not being one to jump to conclusions, he still couldn't help but notice that the stain looked very much like the imprint of something 3.5-4 inches long and possibly cylindrical. And if he was really grasping at straws, the weight of his son's body has caused the imprint lying on top of an object while sleeping. He knew he was also in need of some shuteye.

After all, how preposterous was it that his son had found a severed finger?

The following morning, while on their way to meet Isitoq for breakfast in the cafeteria, Joel and his son were quickly made aware via overhead speakers that because of the current blizzard conditions, everyone was to remain indoors for the time being.

Fortunately, there was a recreation room at their disposal, so Joel could only hope that Dinnie wouldn't get too bored. After all, the child hadn't travelled such a great distance to only sit inside.

Upon entering the cafeteria, both father and son waved enthusiastically from across the room the moment that they laid eyes on Isitoq and were quick to join her at her table. Once again, Joel was thrilled to discover his ladylove had found activities to keep his son occupied during the lockdown.

She had even set up a few reaching games, such as the high kick and improvised harpoon throwing using a broom handle. But she didn't just stop at that. With the help of a few of their teammates, they could reenact a blanket toss which used to be a big part of every spring's Nugluktaq, whaling celebrations.

In the day's festivities, you really couldn't tell who was having more fun by all the uproarious laughter that could be heard throughout the base. And much to his amazement and delight, Joel couldn't believe that his son had not asked one time to watch TV or play computer games…mission accomplished the old-fashioned way. So not so surprising.

When suppertime finally rolled around, Dinnie lacked his usual vigour as he sat uncharacteristically silent whilst eating his meal and staring rather droopy eyed out the windows.

Later that evening, Isitoq received a pleasant surprise when her phone finally rang and Joel formally invited her to his room. Dinnie was out like a light, and he didn't think that even an earthquake would wake him.

He couldn't help but apologize profusely for not meeting clandestinely in her room because he really didn't want to leave the child alone in such a big compound. Not that anything was apt to happen, but if he awoke in the middle of the night, scared for any reason, Joel wanted to be close by.

She seemed to understand his predicament and was on her way in no time flat, stopping only long enough to knock softly before letting herself in. Upon entering his suite, she seemed pleased to see the door to the second bedroom was already closed to prepare for her visit.

Again, Joel thanked her for everything that she had done today as he carefully led her towards his dimly lit bedroom and the already turned down bed. Isitoq smiled and began shedding her clothes immediately, although she had some misgivings as she had never had sex with someone before while a child slept nearby.

However, she understood the importance of their bond and held her tongue while Joel thrust deeply into her repeatedly. At first the silence was deafening, causing her to focus on every sound their bodies made when their flesh collided, every inhalation or exhale…she would definitely miss him when they parted.

Later, lying in each other's arms, they giggled like school children, as if having gotten away with something underhanded behind the teacher's back. And it wasn't until Isitoq got up to use the bathroom that a damper was put on the rest of their evening.

While sitting on the toilet, she couldn't help but notice a child's tee shirt was presently soaking in the sink and upon closer inspection, she found it was the one Dinnie wore the night before. And low and behold, there was a small bloodstain on the back of it. She wanted to scream. What exactly did this prove?

Thinking quickly, she casually waltzed back into the bedroom, still naked, and then sat cross-legged on the bed before Joel.

"So what do you think caused that nasty stain on Dinnie's shirt? Was he eating some sort of candy before bed…I even tore my bed apart last night looking for it…?" and then she kissed him on the nose and began gathering her discarded clothing.

"Don't worry about it. I'm sure it was just a nightmare and if he was eating candy, I apologize for wrecking your sheets."

Thankfully, he didn't skip a beat in his retort, leading her to believe that her feelings of dubiety had been misplaced. Joel then smiled warmly before reaching for her hand and trying to coax her back into his bed one last time.

Isitoq knew deep down that her problems were not over yet, what if the child suddenly had a heart-to-heart with his father and mentioned the collection of severed fingers she kept in her First Aid box…she needed to think long and hard on what her response should be.

Later that night, as Isitoq slowly disrobed before getting into her own bed, she was instantly alarmed to see evidence of spotting on the gusset of her panties. It had been quite some time since her last period and all signs had pointed to her being pregnant; hopefully, the altercation that she had had with the unfortunate hunter had not harmed the baby.

He had been a fierce opponent and had not given up easily when she had attempted to rip that last disgusting necklace off of his neck while he was presumably unconscious, only to be miraculously resurrected, fighting tooth and nail to regain his talisman.

At one point, she even thought he might get away. It was until she crawled back to her sled and rammed him with the high-powered machine. It was his blood that Joel saw covering the front of her snowmobile, but the blackened eyes and cracked ribs were all his doing.

Isitoq felt it was essential to safeguard the pregnancy. After all, she made her choice, and she was not giving up Joel until he had successfully planted his seed. She gave up so much in order to achieve her goals and honour the women that came before her.

If not, all of those beloved spirits would have died in vain, never to find peace. Every time she looked at her scarred body in the mirror, it was a daily reminder of all the blood that was spilled through the generations.

One part of her felt some remorse for the Indigenous Peoples that she had befriended along her journey. They entrusted her with their treasured stories. Some of which she had published in her papers for all to share, while others were used to simply track down the men that she sought, in order to retrieve the remaining severed fingers.

Truth be told, Isitoq was tired to the bone but elated to complete what she had set out to accomplish. She looked forward to simpler times, where she could raise her child far away from the north and the memories that it possessed. She had worked hard to gain financial backing, such as scholarships, and saved her pennies where she could. Reinventing herself in warmer climes was definitely a possibility once she carried out her last task of returning Uki's fingers to the ocean and her ultimate resting place.

One part of her hoped and prayed that her honoured ancestor once made whole, would take on the characteristics of the fabled "Sea Spirit" and wreak havoc on all that had wronged her and her daughters…Shtiya, Bola, Pinga and last, herself.

The following morning, the skies had once again parted and miraculously there was not a cloud to be seen.

Isitoq was actually surprised when she was awoken by the sound of laughter and knocking on her door. Throwing it open briskly in an act of mischief, she quickly planted a scowl on her face as if she was mad at the intrusion.

"Now, who would come knocking on my door at such an early hour?" she all but growled. Thankfully, father and son could easily see through her charade and broke out in more peals of laughter.

"Isitoq, please come and play with us. They won't let

us leave the camp, but we can always play hide-and-seek. I'll even let you be the seeker," Dinnie's pleading was actually adorable, a chip off the old block.

"Okay, but don't you want to eat breakfast first?" she inquired.

At first he stuck out his lower lip, as if pouting, then looked to his father for guidance. "Do we have to?" he implored.

"Well, I suppose she has a point. It's gonna be freezing out there. Wouldn't you like something warm in your tummy before we race around the complex?"

That being said, she quickly pushed them back out into the hallway and informed Dinnie and Joel that she needed her privacy in order to get dressed before meeting them in the cafeteria for a quick bowl of oatmeal.

They took her directions without argument and in no time; she was on her way to meet them. Isitoq couldn't help but feel light-hearted; maybe everything would work out, although she must remain cautious.

Joel would always be an easy book to read, but his son was most certainly a wild card. After breakfast, the three of them headed outback of the equipment bays, since there would be snow-covered machinery in which to hide behind as opposed to vast expanses of white tundra and ice.

Right away, Dinnie changed his mind and asked if he could be 'it' with Isitoq. That way, they could hunt down his father together. Everyone laughed as she asked Joel if he wanted her to count to 200. He should have more than enough time to hide.

Standing behind the enormous structure of the equipment bay, the twosome yelled out their countdown along with the occasional teasing, loud enough probably for most of the base to hear. And when they had finally reached 50, cutting it short because of the extreme temperatures, they both called out, "Ready or not, here we come!" Isitoq tried to make it as sporting as humanly possible, but Joel wasn't exactly hard to follow. He didn't even bother attempting to walk backwards in his tracks.

"So where do you think your father is hiding? Dinnie, you lead and I'll follow" and then they were off, heading toward the old equipment graveyard.

At first it was a straightforward decision, then suddenly his foot prints disappeared into thin air.

Glancing around for clues, Isitoq was quick to spot brush marks on one of the dozer's tracks, it almost looked like Joel had tried to clean off both of the tracks in order to hide the fact that he had jumped up on the vehicle, thus disturbing the snow cover.

Clever, but not clever enough. Quickly tapping Dinnie on the shoulder, she placed her pointer finger vertically on her lips so that he would know to shush. Then she pointed upwards at the cab of the large piece of equipment.

"Dinnie, this one's got me flummoxed…where do you think your father has disappeared to?" speaking loudly so that Joel would hear.

"Gee, I don't know. Should we give up and tell him he's won?" It took all the boy's effort to keep his composure as he said the words.

Isitoq then slowly approached the boy and mimed as best as she could that she was going to lift him up on top of the tracks so that he could knock on the cab's door. Again, both of them held their laughter until the little boy was in place. This time she played possum so that Joel would be caught unaware when Dinnie exposed his hiding place.

"Joel, this isn't funny. We give up. Please show yourself" at first there was no response but the moment that he swung open the door, Dinnie was there to yell "gotcha."

"No fair!" He roared, but of course all in good-natured fun.

"Our turn! Our turn!" Dinnie actually said this in a rather sing-song fashion as he danced merrily around his father once he was returned to ground level.

51
JOEL

ISITOQ GRABBED DINNIE'S HAND THE MOMENT HIS FATHER'S back was turned, hushed him and headed out for parts unknown.

They were quick to trample a large section of the ground as they ran willy-nilly through the parked vehicles and storage sheds, thus leaving a very difficult trail to follow. And just when Dinnie was about to demand a break and the eagerly anticipated hot chocolate, Isitoq started methodically walking backwards across their tracks in order to hide the true direction that they were now headed.

At this point, she squatted down and lifted the child onto her back and then quietly let him in on her plans, so that his father would think that they had separated. Dinnie might have been young but not much got past him, he was quite impressed by her ingenuity, especially since she was a girl and all. And the moment that they heard Joel call out "Ready or not," they ducked down behind a large camp shack that looked to have been abandoned years ago, due to all of the rust on its exterior and huge icicles hanging precariously from the eaves.

After a while they heard Joel calling out their names, but oddly he seemed to be going in the wrong direction altogether…finally she had the boy all to herself. Reaching out, she grasped his hands one at a time in hers and began rubbing them vigorously in the hopes of warming the boy up.

"If he doesn't find us in another five minutes, I'll call out…after all, we don't want you freezing to death" and then she smiled and nodded, awaiting his response.

At first he seemed to take longer than expected to reply but what came out of his mouth was a surprise, to say the least. "Isitoq, can I ask you something? Why did you take my finger…I just wanted one and you got a whole bunch?"

Now looking into the child's eyes, she could plainly see that this was going to take some finesse. "Dinnie, honey… why did you even want one, they're so yucky and dirty?" Again he appeared to hesitate, looking around as if contemplating his next words.

"It can be our secret…I won't tell anyone…plcceease, just let me have one finger." If this had been an adult, she would have dispatched him immediately but bargaining with a child was completely out of her realm.

"Dinnie, I can't give you one even if I wanted to, because they are not mine to give. They belong to my great, great grandmother. You see, a terrible thing befell her many years ago; some bad men attacked her and cut off all of her fingers. Do you understand what I'm telling you?"

At first he looked puzzled and then finally nodded his head up and down.

"They left her for dead and at the mercy of the elements with no fingers to grip her spear…defenceless. These barbarians made up preposterous stories about my grandmother. They even called her a witch to justify the fact that they adorned themselves with her severed fingers, strung from thin strips of sinew around their necks. Fortunately, she did manage to regain her strength and with the help of her daughters, she was able to retrieve several of the stolen fingers. This angered the men even more and renewed their lust for blood, years passed and not only did the original men not give up the hunt for my grandmother but their descendants joined in. Until one day, a group of them chanced upon an old woman out fishing and they saw fit to finish what had been started all those years ago. Since then, like my beloved mothers before me, I have remained steadfast in my promise to retrieve that which was taken. Although sadly I must now complete the ritual alone and commit my grandmother's fingers to the same ice water grave as her earthly body, so that she can be made whole again. Does any of this make sense to you?"

"I WANT TO GO HOME," HE VOICED BELLIGERENTLY AND then forcibly yanked his hands from out of her grasp.

But it wasn't until Dinnie tried to back away from her altogether that she knew that she had lost him. This was never going to end well and when those two little words finally escaped his lips, "I'm telling," she was forced to take action.

Unfortunately, as she lurched forward to clasp his throat in her more than capable hands, he unexpectedly managed a high-pitched scream before she could attempt to take his breath away for good.

When no one answered the boy's distress call, Isitoq quickly straddled his body and choked the boy through the thickness of his winter parka. If things had happened differently and she was able to get to him from behind, it would have only taken a mere twist of Dinnie's head to break his neck and end his life.

"Why didn't you just keep your mouth shut?" she yelled into his face as she shook him violently and then took the ends of his scarf in her fists.

Suddenly Joel's enraged voice bellowed at her from out of nowhere, she had been caught dead to rights. "What the fuck are you doing to my son? Get your hands off of him!" he screamed before gripping her shoulders and throwing her violently to the ground.

"Stay down, woman!"

Foolishly, she did not heed his warning. Instead, she reached for the small knife that she kept in her boot and then attempted to regain her footing.

Isitoq did however manage to register a clanking sound just before she caught a glimpse of an indistinguishable metal object that was on a collision course with her head but unfortunately she was too late.

Apparently Joel found a strand of transport chains in the snow and was two-handedly swinging them at her with all of his might. This time she did stay down as one of the binders made solid contact, causing her to be thrown backwards.

Staring up at the blue sky overhead, she simply waited for the inevitable to happen but when no further fury rained down on her, she tried to sit upright this time.

Although something was terribly wrong with her equilibrium and the moment that she reached up to feel the side of her head, it all became crystal clear as she discovered that her skull had been terribly fragmented by the blow and that there was now a pool of blood growing exponentially beneath her by the second.

"Why in God's name were you trying to strangle my son?"

After taking in the gravity of her wounds, everything changed and Joel began to cry.

"I'm so sorry for hitting you but you scared me half to death. Stay perfectly still and I'll go get help."

He quickly removed his parka and laid it gently over Isitoq's torso before reaching for Dinnie's hand and dragging the traumatized boy away.

"Joel, I'm pregnant with our child. Please hurry. I don't want to lose her" and then she began to cough up thin streaks of dark red blood.

Joel couldn't believe what had just transpired between Isitoq and Dinnie, and the fact he had actually grievously harmed her. Was she really pregnant with his child and why was he just hearing about it now…overwhelming to say the least, then thankfully his son's trembling voice broke through the chatter in his head.

"Daddy, I want to go home. Don't believe anything she tells you. I did find that finger in her room…a whole bunch of them!" and then he began to sob hysterically and would only be quelled by the embrace of his father.

Joel was perplexed, to put it mildly, after all, what could that stupid finger have to do with anything?

His world was literally falling apart around him and he was wasting valuable time. Isitoq, on the other hand, had begun looking around for something, anything to defend herself with.

Slowly reaching down under Joel's parka, she stretched her fingers with all of her being in the hopes of making contact with the knife that she had dropped earlier in the snow, whilst keeping a watchful eye on father and son.

Regrettably, she found it but the moment she grasped

its hilt and brandished the weapon in the direction of Joel and his son's now turned back, the damage could not be undone.

Usually Joel had been so easy to read, an open book of facial expressions with not a hateful bone in his body but today his eyes remained dilated as he turned to look at her.

Immediately pushing his boy aside, Joel hurtled the short distance that separated them, although for some strange reason he appeared to slightly hesitate mid stride. Reaching up with one of his arms towards the sky as if grasping for something, he then brought it down in an arc, slamming his fist into Isitoq's cheek. Instantly, she let out an audible grunt and an exhalation of breath as Joel drove the large icicle that he had broken off through her eye socket.

Again blood gushed out of her mouth but this time she didn't utter a word. She only reached feebly for him with an outstretched hand.

Joel's tears quickly turned into moans of grief as he realized just what he had done and the finality of his actions. Then bending forward he attempted to cup her head in his hands so that he could beg for forgiveness before her spirit departed, but unfortunately he was too late as her body now hung limp in his arms.

"Why did you fight me up until the end? I loved you!" And then he could feel his son's hand tugging at his sweater's sleeve.

"Daddy, I'm cold…I want to go back to the base," he pleaded, almost as if he was totally oblivious of the dead body before them.

Glancing around, Joel didn't know what to do first or how he would even explain what had happened to his teammates.

After all, everyone had seen them leave the base this morning and head outback of the equipment bays for a game of hide-and-seek…would they even believe him if he told them that he had come upon Isitoq trying to choke the life out of his son?

Grabbing Dinnie up into his arms he raced instinctively back to the main compound in the hopes of finding his old professor and a nonjudgmental ear to bend. Although as soon as his colleagues laid eyes on him and saw his distress, not to mention his lack of a jacket and blood stained pants…everyone bombarded Joel with a multitude of questions, starting with, "Where is Isitoq?"

Thankfully, James made an appearance sooner rather than later and Joel was able to get him alone so that both father and son could give their statements before sending a party out to retrieve the more than alarming remains of the team's interpreter.

Although it took some food in his belly before Dinnie finally opened up and divulged everything, even the part about him snooping through Isitoq's bathroom cabinet and finding her collection of severed fingers.

The little boy turned out to be quite a wealth of information when he shared Isitoq's family's rather disturbing history, although thankfully he chose not to disclose her claim of being pregnant. After all, if anyone suspected that she was with child and Joel was the father, some might jump to the wrong conclusion and assume that he had tried to rid himself of a mistake.

Although once his teammates retrieved her body, gossip did run rampant throughout the complex but thankfully with it, snippets of her past helped to stir the pot. Adding to the theory she might have been responsible for the deaths of several hunters in the region.

All things considered, the company that they worked

for did not want any of this to become public knowledge, so everything was quickly buried along with their teammate's remains…a task that Joel was quick to step up for since he felt that he owed her that, at the very least.

Being that Joel identified mainly with his Cree heritage as opposed to Scottish roots, he chose to dispose of Isitoq's body in a more traditional way, something befitting both their Cree and Inuit cultures. Although sadly no wake could be performed due to the extenuating circumstances.

The following day, he loaded up an old snowmobile sled with her personal belongings, anything that might have meant a lot to her, such as weapons and regalia that had most likely been handed down through her family.

Then he wrapped her body carefully within her heirloom polar bear blanket and placed it on top, along with some kindling and logs. Once that was accomplished, he kissed his son goodbye and left him under the watchful eye of his former teacher, then headed out for parts unknown.

Thankfully, he possessed a GPS so wherever he ended up, he could find his way home and in the end, his destination turned out to be a patch of open water. Unhooking the ice sled from his snowmobile, Joel pushed it the last couple of feet so that it was right on the edge of a large section of drift ice and the ocean beyond.

He yearned to say a prayer on her behalf but found it difficult to find the right words, after all, what could he say?

They had only known each other for a short period of time and everything had ended so abruptly and abysmally.

Before proceeding, he threw back the edge of the hide

blanket for one last look and immediately broke into heart-wrenching sobs.

Isitoq was so beautiful and he had despoiled her, along with the men which came before him. Reaching into his pocket, he retrieved a small cloth package and placed it over her heart, almost lovingly.

He readjusted the blanket and doused everything with a flammable liquid. Once that was accomplished he managed to find his voice and say a small prayer, in the hopes her spirit would find peace in the company of her ancestors. After igniting her makeshift pyre, Joel stood back and watched it burn.

So much had happened in the last few months, he really wasn't sure what the future now held for him. He was like a kid in a candy store when he first arrived, not that the work was any less fascinating but what of his current teammates, he couldn't help but feel their watchful eyes on him.

Maybe only time would tell, was he prepared to return to the mainland with his son, when and if the virus was eradicated or stay here and home school the boy until the world adjusted to its new normal?

One thing he could be thankful for was the fact that Dinnie did not seem to have any lasting repercussions from what he witnessed, his appetite returned to normal and his sleeping patterns were much the same.

Once the fire burned low, Joel took one last look at everything around him, as if committing it to memory, the colour of the sky and sea, the sounds of birds overhead… even the sound of the wind.

Then he donned an extra pair of gloves and pushed the sled to its final resting place, in the dark frigid waters of the Arctic Ocean.

Surprisingly, it took no time at all to completely submerge the sled and its cargo, he only hoped Isitoq would be reunited with her mother and grandmothers on the other side, celebrating the fact their beloved youngest daughter achieved what no one else could.

Joel heard Isitoq talk numerous times of her early childhood, spent happily on the cliffs above some faraway shoreline but unfortunately he did not know its exact location.

So instead, Uki's severed fingers were currently wrapped up in a piece of soft fabric and in the possession of her great, great granddaughter as she made her transition from one realm to the next.

Strangely, no one asked what he did with the body, not even the teammates she had appeared to be quite friendly with and in time, business continued as usual except with a much smaller staff. Joel eventually became quite fluent in both speaking and understanding the traditional oral languages of the locals, thus becoming even more indispensable to the company and its endeavours.

When asked by the peoples of the north what had happened to the blueish-green eyed beauty, his response was always the same: she sadly met 'a white death'.

He continued to mourn for her in his own way and sometimes late at night, he would wonder what their daughter would have been like…fierce like her mother or bookish like her father.

Then one day, he and Dinnie travelled by helicopter to the far reaches of the north along the mountains of the Arctic Cordillera, and found what he presumed to be the cliffs of which she had spoken so highly.

Standing by the water's edge, Joel couldn't help but skip a rock across the surface and think of Isitoq, hoping she finally forgave him and listened for her answer in the wind.

The End

AUTHOR'S NOTE

This has truly been a learning experience, but something I would have never missed for the world. You really know who your friends are when you hand them several hundred pages of your ramblings to read and ask them to be brutally honest. And yes, they still are my friends. I have been dabbling in writing novellas for several years now because, as made evident by this book, I'm way too long-winded to attempt a short story.

The idea behind "A White Death" came to me while in the midst of writing something completely different, it was initially only a spark, but an insistent one at that. I had always wanted to write about the north and its environment because I come from North of 50. I wanted my female characters to be both strong and capable. And for the story to be about something other than a group of beautiful people being picked off, one at a time, whilst partying at a log cabin or ski resort.

I have been enthralled with anything and everything pertaining to the horror genre for as long as I can remember. Could be due to my religious upbringing? I used to bring books home from the school library, that was until my mother happened upon my paperback copy of The Exorcist. Which I had regrettably left several page markers in, since I found the workings of a church exorcism to be quite fascinating and in need of rereading. Fast forward, that book was ordered out of the house with the threat of being burned along with my other questionable literature, Stephen King, and some of my music tastes. God forbid what she would have thought when I eventually discovered Clive Barker and Jack Ketchum.

Anywho, thank you not-so-gentle readers for taking the time to read my tale, I really hope that you enjoyed it and that you felt something for my characters' plights. I will continue to strive to show you sights unseen, make you gasp in horror or at the very least, laugh out load at the gratuitous amount of bloodshed.

ACKNOWLEDGMENTS

Firstly, I would like to give a great big shout-out to both Raymond and Adam at Wicked Ink Publishing. I knew it was meant to be the moment I read your company's name and then, after talking with you, only confirmed what I felt. I was, and still am, ecstatic you dared to take a chance on me and didn't quibble about what might be deemed offensive to good taste and morals. Let's face it, I'm an acquired taste. Not to mention you blew me away with your own writing prowess, turning my humble first attempt at a synopsis into an intriguing glimpse of the atrocities that might await my characters.

Next, I would also like to express my deep gratitude to my friend and mentor, the renowned author, Richard Van Camp, for believing in me. Without you, I would have never been so bold as to call myself a writer. You have been my cheerleader ever since I darkened your doorstep with my collection of novellas and then my first novel, A White Death.

Last but not least, my dear friends and horror aficionados. Maria and Laura, to name a few. Thank you for indulging my flights of fancy by taking time out from your busy lives to read my earlier works, even if the subject matter sometimes left you feeling squeamish. You rock!

ABOUT THE AUTHOR

© *S. N. Short*

S. N. Short loves everything horror and has been obsessed from a very early age, she fondly remembers her and her twin sister sneaking out of bed late at night in order to watch movies and anthologies on their parent's old B&W TV. Then later, bringing home scary books from the school library, that was up until her mother found them and instantly banished them from the house.

She is always looking for a new way to kill off her characters, something that hasn't been written or seen before, and that will genuinely surprise her readers. That being said, she really hopes that you will also enjoy the journey and come to love, hate or maybe even, understand their motives.

instagram.com/sylvialynnshort